THE SEX LIVES OF SIAMESE TWINS

Irvine Welsh is the author of eight previous novels
and four books of shorter fiction. He currently
lives in Chicago.

www.irvinewelsh.net

IRVINE WELSH

The Sex Lives of Siamese Twins

VINTAGE BOOKS
London

1 3 5 7 9 10 8 6 4 2

Vintage
20 Vauxhall Bridge Road,
London SW1V 2SA

Vintage is part of the Penguin Random House group of companies whose
addresses can be found at global.penguinrandomhouse.com.

Copyright © Irvine Welsh 2014

Irvine Welsh has asserted his right to be identified as the author of this
Work in accordance with the Copyright, Designs and Patents Act 1988

First published by Jonathan Cape in 2014

www.vintage-books.co.uk

A CIP catalogue record for this book is
available from the British Library

ISBN 9780099535560

Printed and bound by CPI Group (UK) Ltd, Croydon, CR0 4YY

For Elizabeth (again)

I must create a system or be enslaved by another man's.

William Blake

CONTENTS

Part One
Transplants

1

LEPER COLONY

2-4-6-8, who do we appreciate?

Numbers are the great American obsession. How do we measure up? Our crumbling economy: growth percentage, consumer spending, industrial output, GDP, GNP, the Dow Jones. As a society: homicides, rapes, teen pregnancies, child poverty, illegal immigrants, drug addicts, registered and otherwise. As individuals: height, weight, hips, waist, bust, BMI.

But the number in my head right now is the one that causes most of the problems: 2.

The argument with Miles (6'1", 210 lbs) was trivial, yeah, but containing enough discord to prevent me spending the night at his Midtown (equals ghost town) apartment. The jerk had moaned all evening about his bad back, talking himself out of any action with that crybaby bullshit. As his eyes grew moister, so my pussy became more arid. Not so fucking difficult to comprehend. He actually shushed me during the last few minutes of an episode of *The Big Bang Theory*; like, come on, dude! Also, his chihuahua, Chico, was yelping belligerently and he wouldn't stick him in another room, insisting the bug-eyed little asshole would soon settle down.

Well, fuck that.

He didn't take it well when I opted to split: making like a sulky toddler, all stiff posture and pouting lips. Like, man the fuck up! Some guys are just not cool enough to do anger. Chico, changing his routine by jumping onto my knee, despite me continually lowering him back onto the floor, has a bigger set of balls.

So I'm heading back to South Beach, a couple minutes short of 3:30 a.m. The night had been calm earlier, a hanging moon and a rash of stars providing shards of light which cut through the deep mauve sky. Then, almost as soon as I start up my wheezy 1998 Caddy DeVille, inherited from my mom, I'm aware of the shift in the weather. I'm not concerned as I have Joan Jett's "I Hate Myself for Loving You" rattling out of my speakers, but by the time I get onto the Julia Tuttle Causeway, gusts of wind are shoving at the car head-on. I slow down as sheets of rain batter the windshield, causing me to squint through the rapid swishes of the wipers.

Just as it suddenly eases to a drizzle and the speedometer creeps back to fifty, two men emerge out of the now starless, inky dark, running right down the middle of the almost deserted causeway toward me, waving their arms. The closest one blows hard, hamster-cheeked under the white flood of the overhead highway lights, his crazed eyes bursting into view. At first I think it's some kind of a joke; shit-faced frat boys or crazy druggies playing a fucked-up daredevil game. Then a stark *fuck* hammers into my consciousness as I sense it's some sort of elaborate carjacking, and I tell myself: *don't stop, Lucy, let the pricks move aside*, but they don't, so I brake hard, wrenching the car into a jarring slide. I'm holding onto

4

the wheel, it feels like a titan is trying to tear it from my grasp, then a thump and a rustling sound and I'm watching one of the men tumble over my hood. The car slows to a halt, thrusting me back in my seat as the engine cuts out, killing the CD just as Joan is about to rock the fuck out on the chorus. I'm looking around, trying to make sense of the situation. A driver in the other lane just in front of me isn't able to react so quickly; the second man ricochets off their hood, twisting in the air like a crazy ballerina and caroming along the highway. The car tears ahead, into the night, making no attempt to stop.

Thank the sanctified asshole of Sweet Baby Jesus that there's nobody else behind us.

Carjackers never had balls that size or were as scared. Miraculously, the guy the other car hit, a small, chunky, Latino, staggers to his feet. He's dripping with terror; it seems to override any pain he's in, as he doesn't even look at the fucker who bounced off my car; he's glaring over his shoulder back into the murky night, as he hauls himself away. Then, in the rearview mirror, I see the guy I clipped, a skinny white dude. He's right up on his feet too; blond hair, greased back in lank tendrils as he hobbles quickly like a semi-crippled spider toward the bushes at the median strip dividing the downtown and beach lanes of the highway bridge. Then I see that the Latino guy has double-backed and is limping toward me. He hammers on my window, screaming, — HELP ME!

I'm frozen in my seat, the burning smell of brake pads and rubber in my nostrils, not knowing what the fuck to do. Then a *third* guy comes marching briskly out of the darkness, down the highway toward us. The Latino guy yelps out in pain, perhaps the shock has worn off, hobbling to the back of the car, seeming to crouch down at the passenger rear-side window.

I open the door and step out, my legs shaky on the firm concrete, my stomach empty and hollow. As I do this, there's a cracking sound, and something whistles just past my left ear. I realize, with a strange sense of abstraction, that it's a gunshot. I know this because of the way the third man, forming out of the mottled dark, is pointing at the car, something in his hand. It has to be a gun. He's almost alongside me and everything freezes over as I clearly see the pistol. I feel my eyelids rolling back in a primal plea for mercy as I'm thinking *this is how it ends*, but he walks right past me as if I'm invisible, even though I'm close enough to touch him, to see his glazed little ferret eye in profile, and even catch a whiff of his stale body odor. But he's in dedicated pursuit of his hunkered target. — PLEASE! PLEASE! . . . DON'T . . . begs the Latino croucher, hunched down by the side of my car, eyes shut, head bowed, one palm extended.

The gunman slowly lowers his arm, pointing the weapon at his victim. Some instinct takes over, and I jump up and dropkick the asshole between his shoulder blades. He's a light, raggedy-looking guy and he tumbles face forward toward his would-be target, dropping the pistol as he hits the asphalt. The Latino looks bewildered, then scrambles toward the gun. I get there first and kick it under the Caddy, as the prey looks at me for a second, oval-mouthed, before rising and hobbling off. But I'm right down on top of the gunman, slamming my weight on his back, straddling him, my bare knees skidding

6

roughly and painfully down on the hot surface of the deserted highway, both my hands round the back of his thin, scrawny neck. He's not a big guy (white, around 5'5", 120 lbs), but he doesn't even try to resist, as I'm shouting, — YOU CRAZY ASSHOLE, WHAT THE FUCK DO YA THINK YOU'RE DOIN?

Some broken-voice baby sobs, and between them a plaintive spiel, — You don't understand . . . nobody understands . . . as another car creeps up, then surges past us. I'm feeling that ominous vibe of one more layer of shit falling on me. I glance up and can see the Latino heading toward the bushes of the median strip, in the direction of his fleeing white compadre. The thought grips me, *I'm glad I'm wearing sneakers*, as I was planning on gladiator stilettos to match this short denim skirt and blouse I put on to try to get Miles to think dick and forget spine. Now that this skirt has ridden up, I'm so fucking glad I remembered panties.

Then an excited voice squeals in my ear, — I saw everything, and you are a hero! I phoned this in! I called the cops! I filmed it all on my phone! Evidence!

I glance up to see a small fat chick, eyes almost hidden by long, black bangs, 5'2", maybe 5'3", and about 220 lbs. Like all overweight people you can only speculate on her age, but I'd say late twenties.

— I called it in, she repeats, waving her cell phone. — It's all on here! I was parked over there. She points and I crane my neck in the direction of her car, visible under the overhead lights, on the hard shoulder of the bridge, almost backed into the causeway's barrier of bushes, shrubs, and trees planted between the road and the bay. She looks at the broken, prostrate figure underneath me, my thighs that lock onto him as he shakes under his convulsive sobs. — Is he crying? Are you crying, mister?

— He will be, I snarl, as sirens tear out and a police car screeches to a halt, swathing us in blue light. Then I'm aware of the gross smell of urine rising from the guy beneath me, turning the hot air fetid.

— Oh . . . the fat chick sings mindlessly, wrinkling her nose. It's like old alcoholic piss, where the bum in question has been drinking cheap rot gut for days. But even as the warm wetness rolls over the asphalt and makes contact with my skinned knees, I'm not relinquishing my hold on this whimpering motherfucker. Then a flashlight shines in my face, and an authoritative voice tells me to stand up slowly. I blink and see the fat chick being pulled away by a cop. I try to comply but my body feels locked astride this pissing wretch, and I'm now conscious of the fact that I'm wearing a short skirt, straddling a urinating stranger on a highway, surrounded by cops, as cars zip by. Then some rough hands tug me to my feet, the muffled cries still coming from the sad bag of bones on the deck. A short, butch Latina in a uniform is in my face, her groping mitts under my armpit, pulling me harshly upward. — You have to step away now!

I can't use my hands and arms to steady myself, or rotate or lean my torso forward, and as I stand up I'm stepping on the guy. This is so fucking embarrassing. My friend, Grace Carillo, is a Miami cop, and I'd drop her name but I don't want her or anybody I know to see me like *this*. My constricting tight, short denim skirt has ridden up into a thick, folded belt around my waist, through my action of kicking and straddling this creep. Denim doesn't fall back into place just by standing up, and the fucking cops won't release their grip so I can smooth the butt of my skirt down. — I gotta fix my skirt, I shout.

— You need to step away! the bitch shouts again. My underwear is visible from the back and front and I can see the frozen, waxy faces of the cops in the headlights scrutinizing me as I step off this pants-pissing prick.

I feel like tearing the bitch a new fucking asshole, before I remember Grace's advice that it's always unwise to fuck with a Miami cop. For one thing they are trained to assume that everyone is carrying a firearm. The two other cops, both male, one black, one white, cuff the sobbing gunman and yank him upright, as I finally get to shimmy and smooth the skirt down. The shooter's face is pallid, his wet eyes set on the ground. I realize that he's just a kid, maybe early twenties at the most. What the fuck was going through his head?

— This woman is a hero, I hear the bloated chick shriek in rabid attestation. — She disarmed that guy. She points in accusation at the cuffed kid, who has gone from stone-cold assassin to pitiable wretch, with a big wet stain on his pants. I feel his gross wetness on my scraped knees. — He was shooting at these two men. She points over to the edge of the bridge.

The fleeing cripples are now standing together, contemplating the scene. The Latino guy tries to skulk away, while the white guy has his hand over his eyes, shielding them from the harsh overhead light. Another two cops head over to them. The chunky little chick is still talking breathlessly to the Latina cop. — She took the gun from him and kicked it under the car, one chubby digit indicates. Then she pushes her sweaty bangs out of her eyes, waving her phone in the other hand. — It's all on here!

— What were you doing stopped over there? the black cop asks her, as I catch another male white officer looking over my Cadillac and then back at me, perplexed.

— I felt sick driving, the fat chick says, — I had to pull over. I guess it was something I ate. But I saw everything, and she's playing back the video recording on her phone to the cops. — Another car hit one of those men too, but they didn't even stop!

Even as I feel the drumbeat of my heart pump more than it does after a cardio workout, I'm thinking how this girl's skin, under the police car's pulsing red lamp, matches almost *exactly* that horrible giant pink T-shirt she's wearing with baggy jeans.

— That's right, he just opened up on us. The white guy with the smashed leg has lurched over, flanked by another cop, pain streaked across his crinkly leather face, as he points to the weaselly motherfucker gunman who is being pushed into the back of the squad car. — This lady saved my life!

My hands are shaking and I'm fervently wishing I hadn't run out on Miles. Even a tepid fuck from an immobilized prick with a bad back would've been preferable to getting caught up in this bullshit. Now I'm being guided into the back of another squad car, the officer saying soothing things

in such a strong Latino accent I can hardly ma
get that they are taking the Cadillac and I hear
mumbling something about the keys probably still being
the ignition and that my friend Grace Carillo is an MDPD
officer, working in Hialeah. Our car pulls off, the fat chick
riding shotgun, craning her blubbery neck around, telling me
and the dykey cop, in some folksy Midwest accent, — It's
the bravest thing I ever did see!

I don't feel brave at all, cause I'm shaking and thinking
what the fuck was I doing opening that door? and I kind of
pass out or drift away for a few moments or whatever. And
when I'm aware of where I am, we're turning into the garage
by Miami Beach police station on Washington and 11th. A
TV breaking-news camera crew are here, moving aside as we
go through the barrier, and the dykey Latina cop is saying,
— Those assholes get quicker all the time, but in an obser-
vational way, without resentment. As if on cue, I turn to the
window to see a camera lens sticking in my face. The fat
chick in the pink, her glassy eyes going from me to the
reporter, shouts, almost in accusation, — It's her! It's her!
She's a hero! And my reflection mirrored right back in that
camera is telling me I'm looking pretty fucking bewildered.

I realize that I need to butch the fuck up here, so when
the fat pinko says for the umpteenth time in that simpering,
fey voice, — Gosh, you really are a hero, I'm feeling a little
smile playing on my face and I'm thinking to myself, *yeah,
maybe I am.*

2

MORNING PAGES 1

I'll try anything once, I told Kim. She said she was getting so much out of doing this thing called Morning Pages. You just free-associate anything that comes into your head. Well, for once, plenty happened to me last night! So here goes me!

I had pulled up on the causeway, got out the car into the thick, wet air, had my hands on the metal barrier, looking out, staring over the black, choppy waters of the Biscayne Bay. Then the heavy rain that was beating down just stopped, this somehow synced with the angry horns, ripping through the night, trailed by the screeching of brakes. Then out of the darkness: the cars, the men, and her. Shouting, screaming, then the sharp whistle of what I knew, from my hunting experiences with my father, was a gunshot. I should have gotten right back into the car and taken off, but for some reason, which I still can't explain to myself, let alone those darned persistent police officers, I didn't. Instead, I took several steps closer into the road and started filming on my phone.

I'm not stupid, I told the police officers. Because by the way they looked at me, judging and dismissive, I could tell they weren't taking me seriously. But it was my own fault, I was talking nervously, overexplaining myself out of insecurity and excitement. — It's her, I shouted, and I pointed to the girl, the woman, who had just overpowered the gunman.

Then I showed them the phone. The picture was dark at first as she decked the shooter, but it became clearer as I advanced toward them. She was on top of him, holding him down.

It was obvious that once they'd seen my film, even the police officers were in awe of this Lucy Brennan. She looked the part with her long, chestnut hair, streaked with honey by the Floridan sun. Thick brows sat over big, piercing, almond-shaped eyes and she had a sharply defined, trapezoidal jawline. In contrast to this Amazonian severity was her dainty snub-nose, which gave her a paradoxical cuteness. She wore a short denim skirt, a white blouse, and white ballet-laced sneakers. One of her knees was skinned, probably due to the way she pinned down the gunman with those sculpted, muscular thighs.

They took us all (me in the same car as the heroine, and the perp and his target in another) back to the station in South Beach. Then they separated me from Lucy Brennan. I was escorted into a stark, gray-walled interview room with just a table, several hard chairs, and skull-splitting fluorescent lights. They put on a tape recorder and asked me all sorts of questions. All I got from them was: Where was I going? Where had I been?

Damned if they didn't make me feel like I'd done wrong, just for stopping on the bridge and getting out of my car to take in some air!

What can you say? I told them the dull truth; that I felt bad about the email I'd gotten from my mom, messed up by what had gone on with Jerry, frustrated about my work, guilty about the animals, about using their bones. Just pretty darn shitty about everything. I felt a migraine come on so I just stopped for some air, was all. They listened, then a woman cop, the Latina officer who had first been on the scene, asked me once more, — What happened next, Ms. Sorenson?

— It's on the phone, I told her. I had already forwarded the clip to them.

— We need to hear it in your words too, she explained.

So I went through it again.

Lucy Brennan. She'd told me in the police waiting room that she was a trainer, like a fitness trainer. It made sense; she radiated health, bristling with power and confidence. Her hair, skin, and eyes shone.

And through my fatigue I was burning with excitement, just being around her. Because I felt that somebody like Lucy could help me. But when the police were done with me, giving me a token for my car keys in the downstairs lot (they'd insisted I couldn't drive my own car back here), I looked for her and hung around, but she was gone. I asked a police officer at the desk if I could get in contact with her. He just fixed me a stern look and said, — That is not a good idea.

I felt like a reprimanded child. So when that news-crew guy talked to me outside, in a civil, proper way, I was happy to let them interview me and I forwarded them the clip of my footage.

15

So that's my Morning Pages. I write Kim an email explaining the same thing, but not Mom, as she and Dad worry enough about my being in Miami. After driving home I was exhausted but still exhilarated. So I went to my studio and started sketching. I'm no portrait artist, but I needed to try and capture Lucy's fantastic golden-brown mane and those searing, vigilant eyes. All I can think about is picking up the phone and calling her.

But where in hell do I start?

3

HERO

Couldn't sleep. Didn't even try. As the sun rises I'm stretching out in Flamingo Park, preparing for my early-morning run. I'm not going to let Miles, a Motor Vehicle Accident, some asshole shooting off a gun, or even the entire Miami-Dade Police Department fuck with my routine. So I'm pushing down 11th Street toward Ocean, at an easy 7.5ish mph. Roadworking Latinos hoist fallen palms back upright, supporting them with wooden stays. The rehabilitated trees gratefully swish and wave in the cool breeze.

When I first came down here, a resentful high-school sophomore, I recall Mom's boyfriend, Lieb, explaining to me that palm roots were shallower than those of most trees, so although they were easily blown over in hurricanes and storms, they didn't suffer such great trauma and could survive this. I was missing Boston and made some bratty comment about how, in Miami, even the trees have superficial roots. But I didn't pay much attention to them at the time, my disdain was fixed on the red patch on Lieb's balding dome. Of course, a couple of months later, when it turned out to be an aggressive skin cancer, which he thankfully got removed, I felt bad for my previous disgust.

As I hit Washington, I slow down to a 4 mph jog for a

couple of blocks, opting to take in the mess of tattoo parlors, sports bars, nightclubs, and stores selling tacky beachware. Even this early some drunk groups are still about, looking into closed store windows for future purchases. Shrill girls check out thongs emblazoned with slogans like DON'T BE A PUSSY, EAT ONE, while snickering guys earmark tees with the silhouette of naked pole dancers and the proclamation I SUPPORT SINGLE MOMS. From plush cocktail lounge to tacky sports pub to seedy dive bar, you can find all social levels in SoBe. Only one thing holds it together: a love of pure, unadulterated sleaze. Convertibles cruise past, their blaring sound systems often as expensive as the car, rolling downmarket as obviously nobody on Ocean or Collins is paying attention, no doubt lost in their own narcissistic concerns. A trio of shivering junkies share a cigarette in one doorway. A little farther down, two people of indeterminate sex lie asleep under a pile of unwashed laundry.

Enough of this B.S.; I turn toward Collins and Ocean, the sand and the sea, skipping past a stumbling drunk who mutters something unintelligible. Without this kickstart to my day, I'd be lost. A day without a morning run is a day you fumble through, rather than one you attack.

I rack it up a few notches to around 10 mph, running down the beachside tarmac path as far as South Pointe, picking up more speed on the way back. I'm flying past them all now, my sneakers slapping the ground in light rhythm, my breathing controlled and even. This is how it feels when you know you are with the gods. The rest of them, the shambling mortals, are just losers; so slow, so limited. Tailing off to what feels around an even 7.5 mph, I cross over Ocean, oblivious to the sleepwalking cars, and head down 9th before turning onto Lenox. Up ahead, I see a crowd of people in the street, outside my condo. Like others in the area, our building facade is art deco but ours is unique in being painted lavender and pistachio with an abstract geometric design of ocean-liner stripes and portholes. But why are there guys with cameras, shooting pictures of the outside of the property? I suddenly worry there's a fire or something, then, as I get closer, I realize in mounting panic: *this shit is for me!*

I quickly spin off down 9th Street, heading for the back entrance to my home, but one asshole has clocked me and shouts, — LUCY! ONE MOMENT, PLEASE!

A stampede of paparazzi; a pack of red-faced, morbidly obese wheezers and skinny vampire alcoholics, blinking in the sun, suddenly give an unlikely pursuit. I'm not letting up, though; ripping my keys out and opening the caged metal door to the back stairs, I slip in and slam it shut, just as the snapping pack crush each other up against its mesh. I'm climbing the staircase, ignoring their cacophony.

Inside the apartment, the open back window streams in cool morning air as sweet as creek water, as I try to regulate my breathing. The buzzer is going intermittently, and I eventually break down and answer it, raising the phone to my ear.
— Lucy, *Live!* magazine, we really want to talk to you about an exclusive!

— Not acceptable! Get the fuck away! Stop ringing my buzzer or I'll call the police! I slam the phone down into its wall mounting. A dark instinct makes me go to the cupboard where I keep my .22 air pistol. I bought it last summer when a prowler was hanging around the building. He somehow gained entry and molested a girl who lives downstairs. I didn't know her, although I'd obviously her seen around. I'm not sure exactly what happened, it wasn't reported in the press, but you heard stories from other people in the apartment building. Some say the asshole raped her, others that he just bound her with duct tape and ejaculated on her. Whatever went down, he was one sick fuck.

My "pistol" isn't a proper gun; it just blasts out lead pellets through air pressure. I'm not down with guns. Jails and morgues are full of feeble clowns who thought that carrying a firearm would compel folks to take them seriously. The incident spooked me, though, and I responded positively and started up a well-attended self-defense class for women.

I check my phone; it must have hit the TV news already as there are missed calls and voice and text messages of support from Mom, Dad, my sister Jos (a "wow, well done . . ." in her low, passionless voice), Grace Carillo from the MDPD (who ran the self-defense classes with me), Jon Pallota, the absentee owner of Bodysculpt (the fake gym I work out of), Emilio from Miami Mixed Martial Arts (the real gym I work out of), friends like Masterchef Dominic, and a host of old college buddies, and clients past and present.

This cheers me, and I take a long shower, the cold tap on full blast but never better than tepid against my burning skin. When I get out I peek through the slats of my blinds. The crowd seems to have dispersed, but stragglers could be lurking. The buzzer goes again. I answer it, right in the fucking zone to tear some cocksucker's head off! — YES!!?

But this time it's a woman's voice, the honeyed tones smooth and reassuring. — I'm Thelma Templeton, VH1 programming. I'm not paparazzi and I'm not from a news channel. I don't want a picture or a press interview. I give you my word if you let me in, I'll be the only one who comes up. I want to speak to you about a fitness-slash-lifestyle show.

Fuck, yeah! I immediately buzz her in. Then it hits me that it was possibly all bullshit and I've been played. So I open my door and peer down the the hallway, ready to step back inside and slam it shut, should some asshole appear. After a few moments I hear reassuring heels on the stairs and see a woman emerge onto my floor. There's no sign of her carrying anything, like a camera. She's around forty, dressed in a business suit, with smooth blond highlighted hair and a Botoxed face, unnervingly immobile as she strides forward, a slightly bowlegged gait. I stand my ground, and when she gets close she's suddenly gushing, — Lucy, shaking my hand and stepping into my cramped apartment. — This is cozy, she smiles, sitting, at my invitation, on my loveseat, and accepting my offer of green tea.

This ol' girl's pins are gym-toned; no cellulite or dimpled fat visible, and Thelma begins to outline her proposition. It's a makeover show. I take some overweight, low-self-esteem bloat-bag who hasn't dated this century or whose husband hasn't boned her in years, and get her to lose weight and boost her confidence. Once I've licked her into shape, I hand her over to some fag designer, who will oversee phase two, the makeup and clothes component. — We have a few concepts, but this is the strongest and simplest model. We'd work with you developing the idea, shoot the pilot, and if the numbers stack up, go straight to series, she explains, then going through the spiel in some detail. When she's done she stands up and asks, — Who reps you?

— I'm, uh, still deciding on representation, I lie.

— Don't wait too long. Strike while the iron's hot, she half warns. — There are some good people we work with regularly, I could pass on your contact details to them if you like. There's no pressure, you have to find the person best for you, but I know one woman you really should meet, she's called Valerie Mercando. I think you two would get along like a house on fire!

— Great!

She hands me her card, and I give her one of my totally rad embossed ones that Jon Pallota made for me:

LUCY BRENNAN
HARDASS TRAINING
No Excuses, Just Results — Be The Best You Can Be!
lucypattybrennan@hardass.com

She takes it in a well-manicured hand. — Wow! That is so impressive, you really do have that no-nonsense, hard-edged persona we've been dreaming of. Somebody to shake America right out of its complacency. Somebody even more out there than Jillian Michaels!

— I'd go head-to-head with her anytime, on the treadmill, the pull-up bar, or in the ring, I tell her, feeling my jaw jut out.

— I doubt that will be neccessary, Thelma laughs, — but you never know!

I escort her out the door and down the hall to the front stairs. — Wow, I'm just so stoked that I could have a series!

— Let's not get ahead of ourselves, Thelma pats her hair in place against a nonexistent breeze, as she steps toward the front door. I jump ahead, checking the coast is clear. It seems to be. Thelma's hand grips the edge of the door, as her eyes blink in the sunlight. — A pilot first, then see how the numbers play out, she says cheerfully. — It's all about numbers, and she pulls a pair of sunglasses from her bag and sticks them on, — Bye, Lucy!

— Bye. I hear my voice, low-key, cheerless, as I let the door swing shut, feeling strange layers of both anxiety and excitement. Through the glass door I wave Thelma off, then bound up the stairs, going back to my pot of green tea.

I grew up in a family obsessed with numbers and measurements. Dad, a former PE teacher, punctuated only by some undistinguished service with the Boston Police Department, would take me to Fenway and bombard me with every player's stats. When a poor or decent performance confirmed a hypothesis he'd made based on those figures, he'd lean in to me and say knowingly, "The numbers never lie" or "Don't ever trust man's subjectivity, math comes from God. Watch the stats, pickle, always watch the stats."

With me the numbers that dominated my youth were my standardized test scores (high = expectation) and my GPAs (low = disappointment). The discrepancy between the two made me an enigma to my mom; she could never figure me out. This deficit had to be explained in terms of character. Or lack of. My dad couldn't have cared less about my scores, though he shared with Mom the lack-of-character paradigm. Only, for him, it was explained by my sporting failures.

Home was Weymouth, MA, a town swallowed by the Boston sprawl, and part of the South Shore "Irish Riviera." My younger sister by eighteen months, Jocelyn, was quiet, academic, and hopelessly non-athletic. Dad tried with her, but even he had to concede defeat, so then she pretty much flew under his radar. Instead, he set about training every weakness of sloth and indolence out of me. He made me hate those characteristics in others and fight them tooth and nail in myself. And for that, and that alone, I thank him. Jocelyn, the "sugar" to my "pickle," became my mom's pet project. It's very hard to say who got dealt the worst hand there.

I finish my tea, as a tired yawn rips through me, and get out to my first appointment of the day. It's quiet now, as I check my mailbox. A card from the MDPD, telling me I can pick up the Caddy from their lot. They had to keep it in to examine the damage to the hood.

I walk up to Bodysculpt, one of the two SoBe clubs I work from. Marge Falconetti appears, a CEO's wife who is 5'7" and 285 lbs of puffy slug (don't think tits—waist—ass, just beachball). After some warm-ups, I get her raising a ten-pound kettlebell.

— Full extension, Marge, that's the way, I cajole the ol' girl, and I'm just settling into the day, battling the fatigue, and the strange creeping silence in this place. So ungymlike and even worse than normal today. Marge is actually trying, but all the time glancing at me and then past me in sheer awe. Then, horror of horrors, I follow her bug-eyes to one of the myriad television screens we have positioned around the walls. A local news channel, then, on the next screen, another one, are repeating last night's story, *me* featuring prominently. Lester, one of the other trainers, lets out a loud cheer, leading off some clapping, as I reappear onscreen, blinking and candy-assed-looking.

— They show this again and again, on the half-hour, he grins.

— You're so brave, Marge smiles painfully. I respond with a thin leer to let her know there will be no slacking, as I crane my neck back at the screen.

There I am, kicking the gun-toting weakling into submission. It's a pretty fucking neat front kick, farther up than I thought, the ball of my foot striking him at speed between his shoulder blades. I'm right on his back as the camera moves closer, my ass in my panties where the skirt has ridden up blacked out by digibars. I see myself slam a couple of hooks into his body which I honestly couldn't remember throwing. His passivity looks spooky, as if I'm sitting on a corpse. I hear a voice screaming, — I phoned this in, as the image shuffles, then I'm in midshot and the tarmac darkens with his urine. Then, a more professional shot of me through the glass of the police car.

Jesus, I'm even keeping pace with the two fifteen-year-old conjoined twins from Arkansas. The girls have had a falling-out as one of them wants to go on a date, meaning that the other, the physically weaker one, will literally be dragged along against her will if she disagrees. I'm thinking of how it might have been to be attached to Jocelyn, have to drag her along to my shit, or, worse, be taken to hers. No fucking way.

All America is enthralled by the so-called morality issue, which really is a degenerate's wet dream. Reading between the lines, one chick wants to fuck her boyfriend, the other is giving it the religious shit. Those girls have divided the nation. I caught some of it with Miles last night, before we got fractious when he contracted pussy vertebrae. Guys like him think that the would-be beau of Annabel, one of the twins, is one sick but lucky little fuck. I remember those twin chicks at high school, always getting hit on by guys about threesomes, who then genuinely wondered why they were grossing the girls out. Would any of those morons want to fuck their brothers? It's called, like, empathy, but even that basic emotion is barely part of Miles's makeup. However, some squeaky-clean kid, Stephen Abbot, who makes Justin Bieber look like the bastard love child of Iggy Pop and Amy Winehouse, is pouting at the screen. — I've known the girls awhile and I really like Annabel. It ain't like I'm some pervert. It's just about going to a movie and grabbing a soda and maybe some candy. But some folks jus got dirty minds and there's always some tryin to make it into somethin it ain't.

As Annabel nods, the other twin, Amy, cuts in and says, — That ain't all it is. They kiss a lot and it's gross!

I tear myself away and watch Marge grunt her way through the last set. Then it's time to load her stout carcass onto the treadmill. I flick it onto 3.5 mph, enough to force her to get

with the project, then ramp up to 5 mph, solid trotting speed.
— Go, Marge, I shout as she reluctantly lumbers into her stride.

— Jesus H. Lester (5'11", 185 lbs) is looking to the TV and saying to his client, some nice thirtysomething, *motivated* college professor chick, who strides evenly on the next treadmill. — It's tough on those girls, that's for sure.

What-fucking-ever. Let them debate the philosphical issues; I tweak the groaning Marge up to 6 mph, as I start pondering another number: 33. My birthday last week. The age that most real athletes seize up. That's when you can tell it's a real sport and not a game: are they finished at 34? They say that 35 is officially middle-aged. I *cannot* afford to buy into that. Part of me cheers when every gangbanger or lardass, like the sweating Marge, ends up on a slab before their time. Bullets or burgers, I don't care how they bite, as it sends the stats for those of us who *try* to avoid either soaring to the heavens. Marge busts out with some pathetic protest as I push her up to 7 mph. — But—

— You're good, honey, you're good, I coo.

— Heugh . . . heugh . . . heugh . . .

But I'm at an age when a woman is expected to have certain things: a husband, perhaps a child or two, a home, and plenty of debt. I got the last to the tune of $32,000 in student loans and credit cards. No mortgage, just a thousand bucks rent to make each month on a crappy one-bedroom apartment on the Beach. I look at the row of photographs of us all, the personal trainers: me, Lester, Mona, and Jon Pallota, who opened this place. Jon looks tan, fit, with his wavy hair and easy smile, and how I'll always remember him, but that was before his accident. Life can change so quickly: if you don't grab the fucker it'll slip by you.

— OH . . . OH . . . OH . . . Marge is petrified, her ass swinging like a semi-truck fishtailing back and forth across a three-lane highway.

— Nearly there, honey, and FIVE . . . and FOUR . . . and THREE . . . and TWO . . . and ONE, and the machine slides back to 4 mph, for the cool-down, and Marge is gripping the handles now, splattering the belt with sperm-thick sweat. — Well done, girl!

— Oh . . . oh my God . . .

I slap the red halt button. — Right, climb off and pick up that kettlebell again and gimme a two-handed swing for twenty reps!

Oh, there's that you-just-ritually-slaughtered-my-firstborn expression.

— Go on!

As Marge sweatingly complies, I think about my other significant numbers. Height: 5'7". Weight: 112 lbs. Number of regular clients: 11. Number of clubs attached to: 2. Parents: 2 (divorced). Siblings: 1, female, playing the fucking saint out in India or Africa or some shithole. Yes, Jocelyn works for a nongovernmental organization, trying to save poor people of color in the Third World; possibly compensating for Dad's somewhat unreconstructed stance on the issue of race.

Marge is playing at this! — Bend down at the knees, get that butt low! KEEP THOSE SHOULDERS BACK! DO NOT LET THEM PASS YOUR KNEES! Better! That's it! Good!

When we were kids we moved from Southie to Weymouth. It was a nice big house with high ceilings and a huge yard out back, and Jocelyn and I had our own bedrooms. I always nurtured a sense that Mom and Dad weren't happy though, and as I grew up, they only seemed to demonstrate togetherness through a shared rancor. He had his ongoing moans about the "Dorchester influx" into Weymouth (I got that he meant the blacks, whom he claimed he'd moved us down here to get away from, despite the fact that our last neighborhood was the whitest, most Irish in the city), while Mom would follow up with a trauma-filled nod of endorsement and a comment about "falling house prices."

— That's it, honey, I encourage Marge, — get that butt lower! All the way down!

But let's go back to 33. It's a dirty age for a single woman, and a filthy one for a personal trainer. It goes (mostly) unsaid, although the sneaky, squeaky Mona, eight years my junior, 5'9", blond, 36-24-36, and the *next oldest* female trainer at Bodysculpt, will occasionally, with cloying fake deference, describe me as the "most experienced." Now there's a bitch who takes acid in her saccharin.

— Okay, Marge, gimme an around-the-body pass, left to right . . . good . . . good, try to keep it at the same height, I tell her. This sucks bigtime for a cellulite-caked fatty. — Better . . .

Now that Jon no longer appears, the only person I really get along with here is Lester. I much prefer working out of Miami Mixed Martial Arts, a proper joint on 5th, run by Emilio, an ex-boxer. The clients are serious about their fitness and goals. Bodysculpt, a corporate glass and pine-floored

29

yuppie chain, is more like a freakin daytime nightclub. They even have resident DJs, like the execrable Toby, thankfully absent today, playing "workout" music. It's usually inspid ambient bullshit for lazy, Prozac-stunned, cocktail-guzzling beachballs who think they're in some fucking *spa*. Most of the clients are women; the fat housewifes on my roster work uneasily alongside fashion-shoot, stick-thin models, and professionals who spend most of their time talking into their phones while doing low-speed elliptical shit. The few men in this gym all seem of the type who'd made fairly advanced plans to shoot up their high school, but chickened out late in the game. Decided studying and then practicing law was a better way of hurting their local community. And they were probably correct.

Marge ends her set and I'm showing her how to do a deadlift on a heavier kettlebell. — As you come down, you brace the abdominals, I demonstrate, — and you're squeezing in the glutes and pressing right through the centers of the heels.

A gaping black hole and two shocked eyes stare back at me out of a sweating red furnace.

— Go on!

Marge gets to five and then she starts that white-flag bullshit. — Can I stop now . . . ? the quitter begs.

I draw in a deep breath, my hands on my hips. — Quitters quit! Doers do! Five more, Marge girl. C'mon, honey, you can do it!

— I can't . . .

— Not acceptable! Gimme five more and we'll call it

quits, I demand, as she bends over, sucking in the air. — Find a way!

The bitch looks at me as if I've just shanked her, but complies.

— FOUR!

Those fucking time-wasters don't want change: they want affirmation. You need to shake them up. You have to slap their fat, stupid faces until they squeal.

— THREE!

To tell them you are gonna carve that suit of pudgy indolence from their bodies and make them *human* again. And yes, they are going to *hate* you for it.

— TWO!

And I don't blow smoke up their gross asses; I lay it on the line. I tell them it *is* like being born again, but in slow motion, and where you remember every sweating, grunting, choking, bone-crushing, violent detail. But what you come out with is a body and a mind fit for the purpose of life in this world. Marge strains with the weight . . .

— ONE! AAAANNND REST!

The kettlebell weight spills out of her grip and smacks onto the rubber floor. She bends over, gasping for breath, hands on her knees. I don't like people dropping weights, so I shout, — You're rockin' it, Marge! Gimme five, forcing her to reluctantly half rise to slap my palm, before fastening her hands back on her knees. She looks up, breathing heavily, like a wildebeest that's escaped a lion's clutches *this time*, but only at the expense of having a chunk of its ass ripped off. *You wish, fat bitch!* Yes, I'm detested now, but as the endorphin rush blitzes her she'll start an all-day love affair with me. Then she'll step out into the sun and see those tanned, lean South Beach bodies and think: *I must work harder*.

Yes you fucking must.

As our clients, Marge and Lester's college prof, finish up and wander off to the showers, we take a break to wait for our next appointments. There is an office, but it's primarily used for payroll, and managing the place, and we prefer to hang out by the juice bar, basking in the light spilling in through the slanted glass roof. The best trainers always want to be visible, even if you aren't working out or training somebody.

Lester is sipping a black coffee, while I'm on the green tea. I like Lester, now that he's cooled it on the South Bronx ghetto tales which bored the living shit out of me. He had that New York arrogance when he first arrived, that tiresome assumption that only interesting, edgy, crazy stuff can happen there, but Florida has chilled him out. He's also learned to use the ghetto talk selectively; great for the boxing and self-defense classes, less so for the one-on-ones with the wealthier white clients. Mona comes in and joins us, laying down her William and Kate mag and going to the espresso machine. Lester is animated as Sarah Palin comes on the TV talking about the need for tighter immigration control. — Tighter immigration control? Damn, she need tighter ass control, he snickers.

— Enough sexism already, Les, but I can't help but smile. I shouldn't encourage him, but I do, as it offends Mona, who is back into her magazine. — Imagine living each day like it's a dream, she gasps under her breath.

— Palin, bitch's ass has gone south, Lester explains. — Compare it with '08. Like shit Tina Fey gonna take her off now. She wish. That slovenly butt is what *really* cost her the 2012 GOP nomination. How far hellbound them handfuls gonna be by '16? Les's eyes bulge. — No good ol' boy who can't raise it to jerk off to her is gonna bother to trek his sorry ass down the polling booth to put his cross by her name. Gimme her booty for six months, man, I'd have it as hard and as smooth as two beach pebbles!

Lester always goes on about his list of fantasy clients, and what he could do for them. Bieber would be pumped with iron and steroids till he looked like Stallone. Roseanne Barr would be ruthlessly melted down till she resembled Lara Flynn Boyle. But his observations never impress Mona. — That is so misogynistic, Les, she whines, looking up from her magazine, her tone of voice indicating a disapproval that a face paralyzed from hairline to jaw by botulinum toxin simply cannot express. — I find her a really inspirational figure.

— I'm gonna go split-ticket against the sisterhood here, I cut in, — cause Les is right. Palin's down to lose two million votes through letting her ass flop like that. I figure that for chick politicos each pound gained represents a net loss of a hundred thousand votes. Ten pounds one way or the other puts more than a few swing states into play, I conclude, picking up an apple from the basket and taking a crunch out of it.

— Damn straight, Les says, high-fiving me. — Warning bells for her and Hillary in '16.

— Well, I like what she says, Mona admits sulkily. — She's one very impressive lady.

— She does handle the media pressures well, I smile, looking up at the screen, watching Mona's eyes follow. There I am again. Damn it, that *was* a fucking exceptional front kick!

Then Lester's face scrunches into a deeper smile. — Jon sure gonna be pleased with you becoming our next big media star. Takes him right off their radar. He might even show his face in here again!

— I hope so, I agree. Jon is the owner of Bodysculpt, but since his much publicized accident has no clients and seldom comes in. A shame, as he was one of the best trainers around.

I pull my iPhone out my bag. I have all of my clients' records and programs on here. I key in another sixty-five cal for the small apple. I came of age as a number-cruncher the day I discovered Lifemap TM.

More than a website, a phone application, a calorie tracker, an exercise, weight, and BMI monitor, but all of those things, Lifemap is an indespensible tool. It's better than a recorder of all the food you eat, of everything you pack into that hole, or every exercise you undertake from walking to the local strip mall to running a marathon. It's a way of life, and it's the device which will save America and the world. Lifemap was invented by a software design company and endorsed by former NBA star Russell Coombes (three-time World Champion rings, 1136 career games for Chicago, San Antonio, and Atlanta. Famous for his number of steals per game, 1.97. Retired at thirty-two . . .)

. . . shit.

The main reason my thirty-three years are significant is that here, in fashion-conscious Miami Beach, they set the parameters for my client base. Nobody with any sense wants a personal trainer older than them. Nobody wants one who looks like shit, and other things being equal (which they seldom are, but never mind), the older you get the more like shit you look. Of course there are exceptions; the celebrity or "personality" trainer springs to mind: trendbuckers like the J-Micks, Harpers, Warners, and Parishes of this world. But it usually means that I get fat, unsavable fortysomethings who aspire to look like me, while Mona gets slightly out-of-shape thirtysomethings who want to look like her, and a disturbing roster of Belsen model bitches, taking time off from sitting with their fingers down their throats, waiting for that Condé Nast hotline to ring. But that is about to change!

Not all of them are time-wasters, though. Ubercool gym bunny Annette Cushing strides in with a cheerful expression and a confident sweep for the juice bar. One of Mona's clients, but she's ignoring her, wrinkling her button nose and focusing her black saucer eyes on *me*. — Congratulations, Lucy! That was soooo brave. Whatever possessed you?

— Didn't have time to think, I explain, as I see Mona's mouth hang open; my deeds have obviously passed the self-absorbed bitch by, — just react as I was trained to do.

— That kick, the one the camera picked up . . .

— What's this? Mona asks. Lester points up to the TV; it's back on the loop again. — OH MY GOD! Mona squeals in excitement, and scuttles under the mounted TV set to hear better.

— A simple kickboxing move, it's like a foot jab . . . I tell Annette, extending my leg to demonstrate.

— You didn't say anything . . . Mona bleats in half-assed accusation, then her chin drops as Annette asks me, — I was wondering if I could do some of that stuff with you?

— Sure, I point at our rack of personal cards. — Give me a call. It'll have to be at the Miami Mixed Martial Arts, though. I glance at Mona: hoe had to eat that one up like it was a one-thou-cal slice of Key lime pie!

— Yes, I'm ready to get my hands dirty, Annette smiles, then walks off with an edgy Mona toward the pristine Pilates studio. That bitch paid eight grand (or rather some fucking sugar daddy of hers did) to get that crappy trainer accreditation and equipment.

We can hear the phone's shrill bell ripping out from the small office. Lester springs off the stool and goes to answer it. His eyes, then his head, pop back around the door. — Call for you, Lucy. They all want you now, superstar. And as I advance toward him, he raises his hand for another high five. — A hero and a TV celebrity! Man, that is good for business!

— I know, right? I grin, slapping flesh and heading into the small, ugly room, lit only by one small window. Workstation desks are built in against the walls, on three sides. I pick up the phone, partially buried under some client worksheets on Lester's desk. Another overhead TV silently shows my open-mouthed shock and the fat chick in pink's chubby pointing finger. I pick up the phone. — Hello, Lucy Brennan speaking.

— Hi . . . The voice is soft and hesitant. I feel I've heard

36

it before. — I'm Lena, Lena Sorenson. I was the witness on the bridge last night. I shot it on my phone. Those guys . . . running in the road . . . and you disarmed the gunman? The police station?

It's her! The fat chick! The one who made me a star! — Right . . . okaaaay . . . I look at the screen, but we're gone, displaced by the picture of a young girl, around ten. According to the bar on the bottom of the screen, she's gone missing. Then the conjoined Arkansas twins reappear.

— I got your number from the Internet, the fat chick gasps. — I Googled your name and the web page for the gym came up, with you listed as a personal trainer.

Right, you creepy, stalking loser. — Greaaat . . . how are you?

— I'm good . . . well, maybe not so good, she says in cagey, semiconfessional tones. — I've kinda put on a lot of weight recently, and I really want to get back in shape. Think you could maybe help me?

— That's what I do. When can you come in for a consultation?

— I'm kinda in the neighborhood, well, North Miami Beach. Could I swing by sometime tomorrow morning?

— Sure . . . and I'm looking up to a smaller screen, on the other wall of the office, where we're back, on a different channel. This pink-clad turkey with a strap of reverberating flesh around her neck is gushingly describing me as a hero. — I'll look forward to meeting you under calmer circumstances. How's ten?

— Ten's good . . . she says without conviction.

37

— Okay. Tomorrow we'll get started, I tell her. Ten o'clock sharp.

— Okay . . . an insipid victim voice wavers back down the line.

I hang up and get my stuff together. I say goodbye to Lester at the juice bar. Then I get outside and walk down to the Miami Beach police station on Washington at 11th. I recognize a cop on the desk from last night, a short, fat, black guy, who just looks me over in vague disapproval, before asking me to sign a form, and eventually issuing me with my car keys. I follow his directions downstairs to the lot and find the Cadillac DeVille. I examine the indented collision area, feeling like I'm taking a much loved but dangerous rescue dog from the pound. I get in and start it up, and it turns over first time. I pull out of the dark basement lot, into the bright sunshine, turning onto my street and circling my block to make sure that no photographers are lurking. But the street is quiet, except for some palms swishing in the mild breeze, the light suddenly weak and fading as thunder clouds roll in from the ocean to block the sun. Have they lost interest so quickly? In the apartment, I've no time for any emails, as it's the big one tonight. Michelle Parish is in town, talking about her new exercise and diet plan!

By the time I've gotten ready, wearing white linen slacks and a blue tank top and—sick of the trainer's ponytail—opting for hair pinned back in a classic chignon, the clouds have passed and it's a beautiful Miami Beach evening. It's still hot and balmy as the sun goes down and insects whir dreamily, and I'm wading confidently through that sexy, tropical air back into my car, content the coast is clear. The Caddy's old stereo is broken, but I have my CDs and put on some Cuban hip hop I bought for five bucks from a hustler on Washington. I never usually do that but this kid had the most amazingly cute eyes. Musically, a gamble, but in this case it's paid off, heavy samba rhythms filling the air as a sneakily cool Spanish vocal kicks in. I wish I knew what the fuck they were singing about.

I take the MacArthur over the Biscayne Bay and down to Coral Gables, parking a block from the bookstore and walking there. I hate Miami proper, I'm a SoBe bum, but the Gables is one of the few mainland spots I can tolerate, and it's largely due to this place. Books & Books is a classy store, with a great patio cafe, a corner of which is usually occupied by some cool musicians. I've even picked up a couple of guys and a chick here, on separate occasions.

I'm sitting keying in my day's calorie and exercise data on the Lifemap TM phone app, as the crowd fills up around me. A woman with frizzy dark hair and glasses steps up to the podium, and I can see Michelle Parish, a bit smaller than I imagined, sitting behind her, all frisky and enthusiastic, just like she is on *Shed That Gut!*

The other woman, sharp-faced with alert, keen, birdlike movements, prepares to intro Michelle, but to my shock, her face expands in recognition as she suddenly catches my eye. — I'd just like to say that we have a local hero in the audience tonight, and she points right at me. — The brave lady who disarmed the gunman on the Julia Tuttle!

To avoid shrinking into my seat, I look around with a

forced grin. There's a split-second pause, before the whole room, about a hundred people, bursts into applause, led by Michelle, who's on her feet, clapping with ferocity. Oh. My. God. No. Get out of town!

I'm examining the expectant faces and want to just crawl away. *Fuck that. Take it. Own it.* And I feel my spine stiffen as I nod, with a self-effacing smile; false, yes, but I'm making an effort. And why the fuck not? I stepped up. I saved two innocent men from a fucking psycho. *Just take it.* I stood the fuck up! I came forward!

The applause dies down and the intro continues, then Michelle gets up and does her thing. At around 5'3", 110 lbs, she's a pocket dynamo, telling us about something called Morning Pages. — I don't know if anybody has come across Julia Cameron of *The Artist's Way* fame, and Morning Pages . . . Michelle peers over the top of her glasses, a hottie who doesn't know it, as a forest of hands rise, — . . . good. I swear by them. They are so easy to do. You must write—longhand preferably—three pages, around 750 words, each morning. Stream of consciousness, uncensored stuff; anything that comes into your head. There are no right or wrong ways to do this. This frees up your thoughts for the rest of the day. I'd add one caveat: do not do this with a snack in your hand!

Some laughter, and then we're down to business as Michelle brilliantly disses the South Beach low-carb diet. *This* is *so* what I came to hear, not artsy writing shit. — A diet without an exercise program is like an exercise program without a diet, just another useless fad, Michelle says, focused like a stone-cold killer, those bright eyes burning me. I'm digging the way her head moves to the side on that surprisingly long neck, and her perky little breasts straining against that tight blouse. — People don't get obese by eating the wrong stuff or by living a sedentary lifestyle. They do it through both. The attack on obesity has to be holistic. The fad diet is dead!

Cue big cheers from the audience, many of whom are from the personal-training community. I recognize one needy bitch who works out of Crunch, and a fag from Equinox. But only *one* is getting a quick chat with Michelle afterward. I'm straight up there, and even the most competitive motherfuckers in the training fraternity *stand the fuck down* and let *this hero* be the first to get into Michelle's face. As well as the chat, I'm rewarded with her business card and her personal email address! — Drop me an email, Lucy, we should talk, she smiles, then turns wearily, with an apologetic shrug, to face the demanding crowd.

I'm driving back home, almost in a state of rapture. I press the remote to open the gates. I park in the rear lot and head up to my apartment. The back-stair bulb on the second floor needs to be replaced. It's dark, and I can't see jack. Then a noise, a blast of music and some voices above me. I feel my body tense, but it's only kids from the apartment below heading out. The young DJ guy who lives there nods to me, as his entourage file past. I get into the apartment and head straight for my laptop.

41

4

CONTACT 1

To: lucypattybrennan@hardass.com
From: thelmajtempleton@vh1.com
Subject: TV pilot

Lucy,

Lovely to meet you at your apartment this morning!

As soon as you decide on your representation issue, do let me know, as I'd like to get things rolling on this pilot as fast as possible. In the meantime, I'm enclosing a document outlining some of our ideas for the show, which we'll expand upon more at our meeting, which I've scheduled for tomorrow afternoon. Does that still work for you? I stress that these are only ideas at this point, nothing is written in stone, and your own input will obviously be invaluable. We were looking at the photographs and footage again, and my colleagues here in production all agree: we have a highly photogenic, potential TV star on our hands. We are so looking forward to working with you!

Please don't worry too much about any news crews or paparazzi outside your door. News people, God bless them, are not burdened with great attention spans. They will soon flock to an Ocean Drive hotel once they hear that some *American Idol* contestant got drunk at the bar or brought somebody back to their room. Again, getting good management/PR representation will help you negotiate that intrusion. As I said, I've taken the liberty of passing on your details to Valerie Mercando.

Best wishes,

Thelma

Fuck, yeah!

To: lucypattybrennan@hardass.com
From: valeriemercando@mercandoprinc.com
Subject: Representation

Dear Lucy,

My name is Valerie Mercando, and I run a PR agency here in Miami representing a diverse client base of models, photographers, artists, actors, and reality-television stars. I obtained your contact details from Thelma Templeton, whom I understand you met recently.

At Mercando PR, we understand that the client is the star. With over 40 years of combined experience, Valerie and Juanita Mercando have carved out an innovative reputation as the leading premium client-centered boutique agency in South Florida. If you were to consider becoming one of our clients, let me assure you that you would be well looked after. We feel that your heroism has captured the imagination and hearts of the South Florida community, and further afield.

We would love to be able to work closely with yourself, publishers, and broadcasters, to ensure that the Lucy Brennan brand is represented as strongly as it deserves to be.

As a starting point, we have some firm ideas about a revamping of your website.

I can be contacted on 305-664-6666.

Please let me know if this is of interest to you.

Best wishes,

Valerie Mercando

CEO

Mercando Public Relations Inc

Fuck, yeah! I get straight on the phone to Valerie Mercando. She does not fuck around. I tell her I can't see her tomorrow as I've clients in the morning and a meeting at the channel/production company in the afternoon. So she suggests we meet for an early breakfast.

Oh yeah. Hello, bigtime! I'm inspired, so I get right onto Michelle!

To: michelleparish@lifeparishioners.com
From: lucypattybrennan@hardass.com
Subject: Hey You!

Hey Michelle,

Not only was it a great honor to meet you tonight, but to hear one of the foremost people in my field endorse everything I've been trying to teach for the last fifteen years—well, it kind of blew my mind! What a sense of validation! So I'm shamelessly taking you up on your offer of getting in direct contact with you.

I'd like to start by saying that you are numero uno, top of the pile, exactly where I want to be. I'm not going to give you all this creepy "I'm your biggest fan" stuff—from what I saw tonight you'll have had that up to your eyeballs—but what I will say is that you are a massively inspirational figure in my life.

As you know, Michelle, I too am a personal trainer, a zealous warrior against the plague of obesity which is swamping our nation in blubber. And as you are also aware, I've recently become something of a media celebrity myself, since disarming that gunman on the Julia Tuttle Causeway. I've had a lot of attention as a result of this incident, with a cable-television company anxious to strike up a deal. I was wondering if it would be possible to pick your brains about the benefits and potential pitfalls of media stardom!

Not that I want to disclose too much personal stuff, but I'm a bisexual woman with an active sex life, and I know that this very fact makes me a target of interest for an avaricious media and public. Help! If you're ever in SoBe, look me up!

Best wishes on your continued success,

Lucy Brennan

To: questions@jillianmichaels.com
From: lucypattybrennan@hardass.com
Subject: I Know It's a Long Shot, But . . . .

. . . on the off chance that you do answer emails personally, I'd like to start by saying that you are numero uno, top of the pile, exactly where I want to be. I'm not going to give you all this creepy "I'm your biggest fan" stuff—I suspect you've had your fill of that—but what I will say is that you are a massively inspirational figure in my life.

Jillian, I too am a personal trainer, a zealous warrior against the horrendous plague of obesity which is swamping our nation in blubber. I've recently become a bit of a media celebrity myself, having disarmed a gunman on the Julia Tuttle Causeway, right here in Miami Beach. I've had a lot of media attention as a result, with a cable-television company anxious to strike up a deal. I was wondering if it would be possible to pick your brains about the benefits and potential pitfalls of TV stardom.

Not that I want to self-disclose too much, but I'm a bisexual woman with an active sex life, and I know that this very fact makes me a target of interest for an avaricious media and public. Help! If you're ever in SoBe, look me up!

Best wishes on your continued success,

Lucy Brennan

5

BLUBBER SUITS

I'm up at 7:07 with the sunrise, as I am every morning at this time of the year. It's like a freakin switch. I can't sleep when the sun's up; even if I'm in a darkened, shuttered room without a chink of light, my body *knows*. So I'm into my workout clothes, stretching out, then pounding the sidewalks of South Beach. I see a couple of runners up ahead, a guy and chick, but I'm easily catching those mofos, then leaving their fake asses for dead. I bomb into Flamingo Park, where I stop at the bars to knock off four sets of fifteen pull-ups and chin-ups. I get back to my place on Lenox and shower, then take the Caddy up to Soho Beach House to see Valerie Mercando. We're having a breakfast meeting at the back patio. I get there early as I wanted to see this joint, and I'm highly impressed. This will be the new Brennan hangout!

Valerie Mercando comes in, shielding her eyes against the morning glare, older than I imagined from her highish phone voice. She's dressed in a light blue power suit, radiating a cool which says "I can do sass, but right now I really want to get down to serious business," kind of like a Latina Oprah.

This is my *beeyatch*, of that I'm sure.

At my recommendation, she orders the same breakfast and insists on paying for both, and we get a table outside.

47

Valerie, putting her shades back on, tells me that Thelma sent all the details for the show on to her. — Conceptually, I think it's sound enough, but that is for you to decide. Financewise, I think they've come in a little low . . .

— I've got to confess, I haven't seen any offer.

— Didn't you open the attachments?

— Not yet, I admit, having overlooked them and feeling a bit of an asshole. — You have to appreciate that this is all happening very quickly for me.

— Yes, it must be quite overwhelming. But at this stage I just want to say two crucial things: one, sign nothing . . .

— I hear you.

— . . . and two, do you want me to come along to the meeting this afternoon? I'm happy to do this, and act on your behalf on an interim basis. There's no pressure on you to formally engage me, and if you go for somebody else, I'd happily brief them. Obviously, though, we'd love to work with you.

— Look, I'm convinced. You're a straight shooter, so am I. As far as I'm concerned, you've already earned your 10 percent, I tell her, feeling a thump inside at my use of the term straight shooter, which came from one of Mom and Lieb's management books.

We shake hands and talk nonstop for over an hour. As we start to vibe, so Valerie's tone becomes less businesslike and more open. — Camera crews are always chasing the cops. Be prepared for that kind of intrusion for around two weeks, she says, when I tell her about the media fuckers, — then it'll be like it never happened, unless some other development puts it back in the news.

— It feels like it's kinda over already.

— Don't worry. You have something real to sell. Heroism is an unusual quality these days, we don't see a lot of it. We try and tout our military, then have the Pentagon practically admit it's also a hotbed of rapists and psychos. But individuals who can step up to the plate, they really capture the imagination.

— I agree.

Then she breaks into a little giggle. — Some say we've got a lot to answer for in TV, especially reality television. Let me be frank. She drops her voice. — I came into this game wanting to do quality stuff, but there's just no demand. People are so scared, dumbassed, and pliable, they just switch over if they feel challenged, into a world of useless parasites like Paris or the Kardashians, who have money. They want to either imagine themselves in that circle, or just see them get fucked.

— For sure, I nod. Hell, I like this woman, she doesn't pull punches.

— So we're crying out for a *real* hero. Therefore you'll be getting a lot of attention, and she lets a sly glance sweep over me, — though I don't suppose that will be a problem!

For a second or two I wonder if this dirty bitch is flirting with me, but quickly dismiss the notion. — One of the things about looking fit is that the damaged goods tend to leave you alone, I explain. — But this is South Beach, so you're never too far away from a cocky asshole, or self-absorbed douchebag.

— Well, be aware that people are obsessed with celebrity.

49

If you suddenly find yourself on the psycho radar, call me, she offers. For some reason, that fat little Julia Tuttle Causeway chick with the bangs and grotesque chin strap flashes into my mind.

Sorenson.

Valerie cracks a smile, albeit a slightly uncomfortable one. She's an agent to her fingertips. — Right, she rises, — I'll see you at the channel this afternoon.

— Wow, I'm so looking forward to it.

I walk Valerie outside as the valets get our cars. We shake again on the deal.

From the sublime to the ridiculous: when I get to Bodysculpt, Marge Falconetti is waiting for me, a lost look on her face. With most clients, and mine are almost exclusively women, you try to find the key. Is it sex: wanting to be seen as attractive, to get some fucking pipe laid? Is it their kids: staying alive, fit and active, and becoming a positive role model for them so they can see them grow up, and meet their grandchildren? Is it fear of the Grim Reaper: has the doc said, lose the fucking blubber suit, or else? With those ones you still have to force them toward progress, but at least you have some kind of handle. With Falconetti, though, it is simply wanting her crappy lifestyle maintained. All I have to do is to keep the scheming bitch on this side of type 2 diabetes so that no medical crisis upsets the apple cart. Seeing me three times a week for an hour gives her approval to sit on the couch watching her soaps, throwing potato chips into her mouth. She doesn't want to change, she wants me to validate what she's was doing. At $75 per session, I am perfectly prepared to offer damage limitation, to go through motions and try to keep her flabby ass from uncontrolled expansion.

But there are some delusions that need to be shattered. After all, I'm a fucking professional. — Losing weight will not help you fight type 2 diabetes, Marge. If you're prediabetic, you have to do what the doctor says with your diet.

— I know, but . . . Her mouth turns down.

— You have Vincent, I bring up her beloved pug, — and you wouldn't feed him chocolate, would you?

— No, of course not.

— Why?

— Because it would kill him!

— Yes, but you'd feed it to yourself. What do you think it's doing to you?

Her face looks blankly at me. Why can they not see? Why do I waste my time with bitches that think a good threesome has to involve Ben and Jerry?

— You aren't going to prevent diabetes by exercising three times a week, I tell her. — Speak to Tony about this, and I'm thinking of her chunky husband. — You know that he's overweight. He has to be constantly cajoling you into cooking and eating the wrong things.

— We're Italians . . .

— You got to sack that mentality. You can't be a slave to an outmoded cultural heritage. I've got Irish roots, but you don't see me stuffing myself with beef stew, soda bread, and Guinness. We're *Americans*, goddamnit!

Marge stares back at me, hurt stinging her eyes.

— Those sorts of dynamics have a lot to do with whether

51

or not people change. It's what I always say: if you want to change you have to decide to do it for *you*.

I get the usual bleating crap about being a wife and a mother. The age-old weakness, and one which I despise: a total dependency on a husband, while raising kids as the next generation of porkers, killing them as you constantly declaim your love for them.

Another major problem with trying to help Marge change was that I disliked her as soon as I set eyes on her. It wasn't that wobbling meat packed into black spray-can Lycra, nor was it the ridiculous makeup. No, that Yankees cap, ludicrously perched on her head, was what sealed the deal. Yeah, I'm a transplant, and I've now spent over half my life here, but it's in my Boston DNA to despise them. Particularly a bitch who has probably never set foot in the South Bronx. Thankfully, I'm way too much of a pro to show her my real feelings.

So I put her through an hour of kettlebells, concentrating on those fat-burning quads. How she hates the sight of those bells! But she's doing sets of step-ups, lunges, squats, leg presses, and forty-yard sprints, to keep that cardio up. I'm watching her like a vulture scans the highway for roadkill, all the time punching in her Lifemap TM numbers. When we wrap up, she's oozing like an alcoholic snail as she staggers toward the shower.

Then the revolving door of fat spins again and I now have another slab of blubber to try and sculpt back into human form. That Lena Sorenson chick waddles in. She's managed to find a pair of shapeless gray yoga pants that are too big even for her. In some ways it's a blessing; usually the problem with yoga pants is women wearing them too tight and jacked up, so you can practically see their pussy. For some reason women like Marge, with her Lycra, think squeezing themselves into a smaller size actually *makes* them that size. But Sorenson's garments still send out warning signs: yoga pants have also become the "go to" exercise attire for women who're uncomfortable with their bodies and, worse, not serious about exercising. The pants suck serious enough ass, but Retardville residency is advertised by her old, pinching Eurythmics tee, exhibiting her muffin bloat to its most nauseating effect.

More to the point, it's 10:07. *Lateness fucking noted, loser bitch.* Sorenson's wearing that bewildered cow-in-the-slaughterhouse expression. The fearful gaze falling over the exercise machines, like they were there to physically tear the corpulent flesh from her bones. And that's *exactly* what they are there to do. I greet her with a thin smile. You get to be an expert on how long a fat broad's gonna last. No way this little dipshit will stick it more than a couple of weeks.

As I get out the tape and lead her to the scale, Lena Sorenson, 5'2", 203 lbs, jabbers on nervously. — I've really been feeling for a while that I need to start training . . . Look, I hope you don't mind that I allowed the TV people to use the footage from my phone. I didn't think. I should have cleared it with you first.

Mind? She's made me a fucking star! — It has been rather intrusive, I tell her, not wanting to cede any power by showing gratitude. — The paparazzi were outside my door.

— I'm so sorry—

— Well, these things happen, let's not dwell on it, I smile.

— Are you ready?

— As I'll ever be, Sorenson lamely replies.

I take her through a light session of kettlebells and stretches, which she does reasonably well, keeping decent posture on the squats. As she finishes, I'm letting her rap on with the loser talk. — . . . but you know what they say about life happening while you're making other plans . . .

Sorenson is evidently the type of chick who can talk and talk while saying nothing, and I still can't quite figure her out. Possibly stopped trying after marriage and a kid. Woke up from an extended Prozac daze doing diapers, and a husband who won't touch her, who's away on business and golf, to find herself a misshapen behemoth. *How did that happen? Why am I fat?* You learn to respect cliché and stereotype in my business; they rarely give you a bum steer. But there's no ring on that chubby finger. Enough speculation: I'll find out what makes her tick soon enough. First, there is fat to be melted, and it's time to check out the sort of juice this bitch has in the bullpen.

I'm not a great treadmill fan, I prefer to use high-intensity free-weight routines to build muscle, core strength, while raising the cardio and keeping the fat burning. But the treadmill is useful to boot up the cardiovascular system and give a couch whale some stamina. She climbs on and I start her on 3 mph, a gentle roll. She's still blabbing, now wanting to talk about *the incident*, but sorry, Ms. Sorenson, if you got the gas to gab, you got the gas to go! I move it up to the point where the hoe *shuts the fuck up and sweats*. It's a heavier session than I normally intro anybody of her size and weight with, but somehow I really don't care whether or not she comes back, which I seldom feel with clients. It is my living, after all.

Marge and one of Lester's clients emerge from the shower, heading to the juice bar. I catch Marge shooting a satisfied smile over at my new girl. Somebody almost as lardy as her—at least in the young, white, and rich demographic—is a rarity in Miami Beach. Yet there's the seed of an impression that Sorenson is perhaps different. Yes, that soupy air of depression hangs over her, and there's something of the self-pitying victim about her that annoys the fuck out of me. But I sense that she really wants to get better; a defiant glint in her eye shines through the creeping dread.

After Sorenson leaves, with some reluctance, looking at me as if there's some dramatic disclosure to come, other than "Same time Friday," I burn four hundred cal on the treadmill, then drive home. No snooping press mofos, so it's all good.

I fix myself a lunch of steamed broccoli and spinach, with a peanut-butter-and-banana protein shake (460 cal). My phone vibrates in the pocket of my shorts, the caller ID telling me it's my dad. — Hey! My baby girl! What a chip off the old block!

— Eh, thanks.

— My heart was in my goddamn mouth when I heard. I said to myself: what in hell's name was she thinking of, tackling an armed guy who was firing off rounds? Then I thought, she's a Brennan: it's the way she's made. That was how it had to go down.

I love my dad, even though he sent me here to live with Mom when I wanted to stay in Boston. Of course, loving somebody doesn't mean you can't acknowledge that they can be a real asshole. He's written a series of five police-procedural detective novels, all featuring Matt Flynn, a BPD dick turned PI. Each one has sold more than the previous, and the current has just made the *New York Times* bestseller list. He now does a bullshit feature on "Flynn's Boston" for the *Globe*. As an ex-gym-teacher, he's very driven. I don't know why he worries excessively about his police credentials, or lack of. You only have to take a lardass cop to lunch to nail the procedural shit, the rest is a testimony to his writerly powers of imagination.

Dad's dust jackets claim he was a Boston homicide detective for eight years. They'll be laughing at that one in a few Mick bars in Southie. He served with the BPD, in uniform, for only three years before he was kicked out for "racist behavior," following an incident at a warehouse in Dorchester. Some achievement that: Josef Mengele couldn't get ejected from Boston's finest for that shit. The real reason was that he took a dive to protect a higher-ranking officer. Dad used the payoff dough well: he wrote a crime novel, which wasn't too bad. Since that debut, he's blossomed as the suburbanites' choice; they can sleep easy knowing that his Boston tec protagonist, Matt Flynn, is out there protecting them, tying everything up in neat resolution. Yes, he's metaphorically grown into that airbrushed jacket photo of him, looking like a chunkier, nightclub-bouncer version of Doctor Drew. I suspect Botox, but he fervently denies this.

— Thanks, Dad. It's scary, looking back, but I just reacted.

— You sure did that! I'm so glad I encouraged you with all that kickboxing and tae kwon do. You saved two men's lives, and probably your own.

I know Dad makes a living through crime hyperbole, but the truth in that statement makes me shudder. While I wasn't the target, there's no telling how an asshole with a gun might react once he's spilled blood.

— I'm glad too.

— And I'll tell ya someting else, I'm gonna make you rich, princess! I got contacts in Hollywood now. Been speaking to agents and producers about Matt Flynn screen and TV adaptations.

What to say to that? — Well, um, okay . . . but you might be too late. A TV company has already been in touch about a pilot. In fact I'm just heading to a meeting in a little while. I've got a local talent agency working for me.

— That's my girl. The Brennan get-up-and-go! But watch out for those guys, kiddo. Keep some native Southie cunning back in the locker room. You know what this wiseass Hollywood agent said to me the other day?

— No . . .

— He said, "I see Matt Flynn as being a down-the-line project for the Damons, Afflecks, or Wahlbergs. Like a nest egg for those guys when the gym-rat stuff gets too much like hard work and the middle-aged spread hits and they can finally do that grizzled, lived-in shit."

— Right. I get that.

— No, think it through, honey, and this is what I said to

him: those guys are fuckin *actors*. By the time they're ready to play hard-bitten, fifty-five-year-old BPD homocide detectives, they'll be seventy, and I'll be in an urn on somebody's mantelpiece!

— Dad, this is taking on a morbid turn, like so many of your conversations.

— Well, the clock's ticking. Give me a grandkid, honey; just do the nine months for your old pop. One that can make me proud. Hell, I'll pay for the kid to attend the best schools. You'll never see him. *It*.

Oh my God, I thought I'd get through a phone call without that old theme recurring. — You know what? Have you ever asked yourself why I become more dykish every time you address me directly? Like, since I was about six years old?

— Jesus, honey, don't do this to your old pop. Anyway, lesbians do the motherhood thing, it's all the rage, he contends. Dad knows I'm bi. He doesn't like it, but at least he acknowledges it. Mom almost physically chokes when I mention it. She would send me for extreme ECT if she could. — Why should a woman be denied motherhood on the grounds of sexual orientation?

I'm about to retort that I could find a hundred men to impregnate me, but, disturbingly, the only face that pops into my head is Miles's. — It's on the grounds of choice, of not wanting my body wrecked. Of things like liking sleep, hard breasts, tigh—

— Don't say "tight vaginal walls" for chrissakes. Remember I'm your goddamn father! I don't have the gift of abstraction when it comes to you!

— Sorry, Pop.

— Think it through, pickle. Ticktock. Ticktock. That's the way it is. The human condition, he wheezes, then sings in pain, — the cocksucking, evil, motherfucking, God-awful human condition . . .

I let a brief silence hang, which he fills. — I gotta go now. But I'm in Miami next month hitting the Sunbelt part of the tour. Let's hook up for some food, a good porterhouse for me, and a nice big helping of rabbit food for you. In the meantime, I'm gonna send you the website details for this insemination project. Think about it.

— Jesus . . . Dad . . . as you say, you *are* my father!

— That's parental prerogative, honey, as you'll hopefully soon know when you succumb to the force. Gotta go, angel. Love you!

— Love you, I tell him, with *I think*, reverberating in my head as the line goes dead. That man is beyond real.

My cal count is low today so I fix myself some tofu and couscous (around 450 cal), then do a routine of hand weights. After working up a decent sweat, I take a shower, before settling down in front of the TV. I try not to let it get to me, but it sucks not having cable, if only for the sports channels. The network news channels bug me, even if there's nothing on me or the twins. It's just that missing kid, Carla Riaz. She looks so small, frail, and angelic in that picture. I hope she's okay. There are some evil motherfuckers out there.

I drive up to North Miami Beach. The TV studios are situated in a three-story concrete building. As I go through automatic doors, I instantly sweat under the blast of cold air conditioning as my body recalibrates. I'm feeling gross as a doorman escorts me to a sterile reception area. Valerie is waiting, her own forehead reassuringly beading. We get a black coffee and exchange bland pleasantries. Soon the producer appears, a late-thirties blonde, with the inevitable Botoxed android half-smile, thinly plucked brows, and pass clipped to her tan jacket, which she sports with matching slacks. Hooped earrings hang at her caked face like satellites over a desert planet, and a dangling necklace droops into a pushed-up rack of silicone. She intros herself as Waleena Hinkle. As she leads us through security doors, I catch her sneak a fearful glance at the young receptionist, the fresher meat who will soon replace her in the corporate sandwich. We follow Waleena, along with the string of inanities spilling from her mouth, down a corridor and into a boardroom.

We sit for a spell, with more talk about the weather. It's just getting unbearable, when Thelma ceases her power play and deigns to join us. I know through Lieb's time-management books that if somebody is late for a meeting they are either 1) an incompetent asshole (62 percent), or 2) trying to make some power statement (31 percent), and seldom, if ever, 3) fighting fires at some emergency (7 percent), as Thelma pathetically tries to make out now. B-fucking-S: I've got her number.

After some small talk about the flash flood I've had from press, camera crews, and photographers (thankfully done now, surely), Waleena springs into some sort of animation, flagging up a presentational display on video, explaining to me the concept of the show (I still haven't opened the email

60

attachments). It seems that they've moved on from the simple makeover premise. — We feel that your profile and Miami as a location allow us to be more adventurous, Waleena gushes. — The show is now tentatively entitled *Shape Up or Ship Out*. It will take place on a boat, a cruise liner, which sails from Miami around the Caribbean for the duration of one series. But this luxurious boat will also have two gyms and be a floating torture chamber. As we go around the islands, we ditch various failures at differing ports—Nassau, Kingston, Port of Spain, etc. — all the way back to Miami. — It's essentially *The Biggest Loser* at sea, Waleena explains, — hopefully with a hint of *The Love Boat* thrown in. We'll have a plank-walking ceremony at the end of each show, the plank also being a scale that tips the fattest contestant into a secured area of the sea.

I burst out into loud laughter, unable to contain myself. From their expressionless faces, it's impossible to tell whether it's the Botox masks or if they genuinely consider my glee inappropriate. I decide to test the water further. — It would be great if we could have some sharks in the secured area of sea, chomping away at all that blubber.

More silence as the masks seem to freeze a few more degrees. — We did want to introduce a punitive element, Waleena nods, — and we will have several menacing nautical and pirate themes running throughout the show.

Thelma chips in, — The one we're particularly excited about is "booty call." She twists her collagen-stuffed lips to Waleena, who carries on. — Yes, this is where we open a series of treasure chests we have mounted on the wall, all of

them displaying the near-naked ass of each contestant scheduled for elimination. A guest panel have to guess, first
the owner of the ass, then the weight lost that week by the
individual on the basis of the size of their butt.

— Get the fuck outta here, I declare.

— You don't like it? Waleena whiplashes to Thelma, then
back to me.

— Shit, no! I love it! They need to be confronted with how
gross their asses look, and I glance around the table, lowering
my voice gravely. — But I do hope you realize that I wasn't
being serious about the sharks, and I wait for a reaction.

— Of course . . . Valerie says.

— We knew that, Thelma agrees.

— Only because it would be totally fucking cruel to
subject animals to the toxins in those junk-fed bodies!

They look at each other, and Valerie smiles, while Thelma
laughs, a low wheezing mechanical sound. — That's funny!
You're terrible, Lucy!

We spend the rest of the afternoon looking at homemade
videos from a previous similarly themed show last year, which
never got off the ground. — We couldn't find a suitably
charismatic, local fitness instructor to present, Thelma
informs me in a smug purr. There are literally *thousands* of
fat losers who have sent clips in, begging to be contestants
on the show. Few, if any, demonstrate real signs of aspiring
to change themselves.

Then I'm telling Valerie, Thelma, and Waleena about the
two clubs I work out of, and I mention Jon Pallota, the owner

of Bodysculpt. I explain that Jon was swimming up in Delray Beach and lost a large portion of his genitals after being attacked by a poisoned barracuda, stunned and lurking in the shallow waters. They tried to save what they could when they detached the fish, but his cock had to be more than half amputated and one testicle was lost.

Of course, everybody remembers the incident, and it becomes the cue for a round of familiar jokes. Tales of the genital mutilation of powerful young men resonate easily with middle-aged, middle-management women who have have been splattered against the glass ceiling by the myopic stampeding of that breed, on their relentless corporate ascent. I look around the table at the three Botoxed witches and think, with a chill, that this is quite probably me ten years on. And that's the best-case scenario. And I feel disloyal, as Jon and I . . . well, we tried but we couldn't make shit work. Now he's been engaged in a lawsuit for three years against the company who were found to have dumped the chemicals at sea, detected at very high dosage in the fish's body. The company had already been fined for illegal dumping, but are contesting that the chemicals could have poisoned the fish to the extent that it would have headed into the shallows and attacked a bather.

— Did the fish attack any other people? Waleena asks.
— Like, before your friend?
— I don't think so.
— Tough one. I don't really see any grounds for an individual suing the company here, unless he can find other

people who've been attacked by poisoned fish and they do a class-action lawsuit.

— That seems to be the legal feedback he's gotten, I tell her.

Jon's been understandably depressed since then, and has spent much more time in the SoBe dive bars than at Bodysculpt. But as I'm telling Valerie, Thelma, and Waleena the backstory, I can see them thinking *it would great to get this in the show*. Then Thelma actually says, — Do you think that Jon would—

— No. Not acceptable, I cut her off. — He hates the media. He might let us film in the club, but that's about all, and I swear I can see her Botox face melt under my gaze.

— Of course, Lucy, she purrs, — you know best!

Despite that hiccup, I come out the meeting pretty buzzed and I'm actually enjoying the drive home, which is almost impossible with all the crazies behind the wheels of Miami's automobiles. The devastating combo of Latin Americans, really old white people, and young all-year-round Spring Breakers is not a mix that encourages complacent driving.

I pull up outside my building—still no photographers (both good and worrying)—and get settled back in my apartment. Miles calls, with more of the same hero bullshit, now all conciliatory after us yelling at each other on our last encounter. He's a firefighter I trained to kickbox in a tournament against the police. He was flirty as hell, and I thought I'd seen the last of him, till he found me on hookup. com, a dating-slash-fucking website I used to subscribe to.

We all make mistakes. He tells me he's still off work with his famous back issue. He never had this going on when we first met, and the shit has been getting worse. — I gotta examination by the service's medical board, then a meeting with personnel and their insurance people lined up. You wanna come round tonight? Or I could swing by your way?

— I'm going out, I lie.

— Who with?

— That's my business.

— Some fucking dyke, huh?

— Which part of "my business" don't you get? Don't call me again. I am so over mercy fucking, I tell him, and switch off the phone. That asshole is way beyond real.

I wasn't intending to go out tonight, but I sure as shit am now. Besides, I got plenty to celebrate, thanks to that nosy Sorenson chick and her iPhone! I head into my walk-in closet and slip into a clingy, short, black denim skirt. Then I roll on some nylons and a purple-trimmed garter belt. A lacy black bra pushes my tits up into the world's face, and I pull on a long-sleeved see-through gray silk blouse. A knee-high pair of leather boots with fierce silver buckles finishes the look. Not quite, as it's all about accessorizing, and a silver heart necklace dangles above my cleavage to draw eyes there. A set of spiked silver bracelets gives the look an edge that nicely hints at S&M. A last-minute change of mind, and I decide to put on some simple black cotton panties. The sort that can easily be pushed aside for dick, dildo, fingers or tongue. Some mascara, lipstick the same purple as the garter, and a few strategic dabs of Givenchy, "very irresistible," and I'm out the door and heading to the club on Washington.

From Lenox at 10th, it's an easy walk in the warm, still night air. Then I'm honked at by two separate cars stuffed with grinning Latino pricks, spewing rounds of Spanish inanities over their loud music. That's the worst thing about slutting up, this gauntlet of a six-block walk. I wish I could just fucking teleport into that club. I wonder how many more years I can carry this look off: thank fuck we age slower in Miami Beach than the rest of the world, or at least those of us who remember sunblock and don't have to work outdoors do.

The liquid display on the clock behind the bar tells me it's just a couple of minutes shy of midnight as I get into Club Uranus. On weeknights you're usually assailed by bad commercial EDM, but there's evidently a new DJ and I'm pleasantly surprised by frothy, bubbling Latin beats. Club Uranus has a cramped aisle with a bar and an inset DJ booth opposite, which makes it look like a five-buck-cover-charge dive, until you realize that beyond this it opens out onto a larger dance area, expanding onto a wrecked concrete yard. The club resembles a narrow-necked vase, and many people say they should refurbish, moving bar and booth to the sides of the dance floor, and ending the potentially hazardous bottle-neck at the door. My friend Chef Dominic always rolls his eyes when I suggest this. "That's the appeal of this place, sweetheart, fighting through that tight passage into some kinda heaven!"

As I weave through the chatting throng toward the bar

there's no sign of Dominic or any other faces, but two android carpet-munchers gape at me, quickly turning away as I meet their eyes. It's soooo pathetic to see one chick trying to be butch and the other femme, but the bitches in fact looking indistinguishable. You can *smell* the U-Haul off them, but I guess we all got to start somewhere. Then I pass a shirt-sleeved, marvelously cut black guy, who mouths, — Hot.

I glance at myself in the mirrored pillar without breaking stride, and I know I'm the shit.

The back bar is lined with an assortment of tourists. Most look too sozzled and paunchy to cut it on the dance floor with the beautiful locals, so they amuse themselves by getting loudly drunk. Two heavy-eyed, swaying, German-sounding dudes ask what I want to drink, and I shake my head and wave to Gregory at the bar, who gives me a soda water. I seldom drink alcohol and I *never* touch drugs.

I take the water and press on. A stick-thin coffee-and-cigarettes slut, huge implants straining against her tank top, practically offers herself to me with a desperate smile. I blank the bitch instantly. *Think again, ashtray breath!* As if that isn't bad enough, she has a total grenade in tow. The grenade has haunted, anorexic eyes but a still-beefy ass and short, stumpy thighs that refuse to retract in the face of her starvation diet.

So I turn and I'm face-to-face with this big, square-shouldered guy, and he grins broadly at me. I don't want to go home with anybody though, so before either of us knows much about it, we're across to the rear dance floor, then out the back, round through the yard and into the alley behind by the patio wall. It stinks of the garbage dumped here from other liaisons, and I can hear tin cans and plastic containers crushing under our feet. — Let's fucking do it, I say, and the guy goes to speak but I shut him up with a kiss. I don't want to hear a goddamn thing from his mouth, and I'm guiding him into a stance between the back wall of the club and a big tree, sort of wedging ourselves in between a space which I know, through previous experience, is perfect for fucking. The vibrations from the sound system drill through the wall, reverberating the bones in my back. The playboy's pressing his hard meat against my thigh, saying shit in Spanish. I don't need that cause I'm already Niagara Falls moist, and I reach down and rub at his crotch. — Gimme that shot of beef, I command in his ear, slut-demanding, and as he backs against the trunk of the tree, I enjoy the little glimmer of arousal (or maybe even fear) in his eye before he unzips. I'm wrapping my arms around his neck, crushing my thighs around his hips like a boa constrictor, levering him against the tree. He pulls my panties aside and I'm enclosing his hard prick. Then he gets some traction and he's slamming into my cunt, practically knocking my breath out with every stroke. I'm bucking like a deranged goat, thrusting my ass up to take more of this motherfucker, pushing him back against the tree and he's screwing me into that fucking wall, the 4x4 beat throbbing through in time with his strokes. — C'mon, bring it home, boy, I'm demanding, — I need more, bring it *the fuck* home!

Another flicker of distress in his eyes, but then he starts to go harder at it, pounding like that fucking bass line. Sometimes they just need a little encouragement. The red mists are coming down and I'm turning inside out in ecstasy

68

in this shit-strewn alley. He's spent, you can tell by those tombstone eyes and his shallowed breathing (it's no mistake that it was a man who described the orgasm as a mini-death), but I'm bucking my way to paradise and he will *hold the fucking line* till I'm done. They can *always* give more than they think they've got. Fucking hammer me, you prick-wielding pussy, I won't lie down to you, FUCK ME FUCK ME, I won't lie down to you, FUCK YEAH FUCK YEEEAAAHHH . . .

As he fades and slips out of me, I climb off him, lowering myself onto unsteady legs. In more than a hint of desperation he croaks that his name's Enrique and he wants to buy me a drink. But the dude is just like a piece of gym equipment to me, and we're now in postworkout scenario. I've had my dose of dick and his is already weeping like last night's leftover quesadilla. So I smile and say, — Thanks, that's very kind of you, but you know what? I gotta go. Maybe some other time, enjoying the sad tumble of his face and the sorrow in those brown eyes. No point at all in hanging around a joint like this once you got what you came for. I go back home and check my emails.

6

CONTACT 2

To: lucypattybrennan@hardass.com
From: julie@jillianmichaels.com
Subject: I Know It's a Long Shot, But . . . .

Dear Lucy,

On behalf of Jillian Michaels, I'd like to thank you for your email. Unfortunately, due to the volume of correspondence we receive, it's impossible for Jillian to answer personal inquiries, such as your own.

Thank you for your interest.

Best wishes,

Julie Truscott

To: lucypattybrennan@hardass.com
From: michelleparish@lifeparishioners.com
Subject: So Good To Hear From You!

Dear Lucy,

Nice to hear from you so soon!

It was lovely to meet you at my presentation in Miami, just too bad that there wasn't much time to talk as such tours tend to be whistlestop! Your heroism is really inspiring to lots of people!

I'm so glad my comments about diet books resonated. Let me make it clear I wasn't dismissing low-calorie, or even low-carb diets. They obviously have their place, but only as part of an integrated and balanced program. I'm afraid I have absolutely no tolerance whatsoever for the "quick fix" merchants. On that note, you should really insist to your clients that they do Morning Pages. It does yield quite revolutionary results.

Thank you for your kind words. Yes, it can be rather daunting being thrown into the media spotlight, as I can testify with my own experience on *Shed That Gut!* I find that when you deal with certain people you really have to keep your cards close to your chest. You can usually see exactly where they're coming from. You're a smart cookie, so I'm sure you'll be able to figure them out!

Congratulations again on your success!

All the best,

Michelle Parish

7

VILLAIN

We're practically all transplants in Miami Beach. Natives are thin on the ground in this town. The guys you can tell; they strut proudly in their home city baseball caps and football tees. Just don't expect to actually see them back in Cleveland or Pittsburg anytime soon. Chicks? Well, I'm not above wearing my Red Sox cap on the odd occasion; at least it tells you where I'm from. You see an asshole in a FUCKING YANKEES cap, they're as likely to be from England or France or shit like that.

Lena Sorenson. 5'2", 203 lbs. Should be one-twenty. That means she is carrying an extra eighty-odd pounds of fat. It's on her gut, her ass, her thighs, and, most of all, that ugly strap around her face and chin. Like she's stuck her head into a pink-colored tire.

I have to admit I'm surprised she's back. Welcome to phat beach, *fat beetch*. If only we were at my friend Emilio's spot at the Miami Mixed Martial Arts gym. I'd come on like a ghetto sergeant major and tell the corpulent hoe what she needed to hear: eat less, eat better, and get off your fat little ass. But I doubt she'd be seen dead in Emilio's place; Mexicans are meant to sweat alone in your garden, not side by side with you in a gym. And despite her having the classic low-self-esteem fat-slob's fashion sense, I suspect there's some wealth here. But we're at Bodysculpt; if I speak my mind and a client complains, my tenure will be over, even given the relationship I have with Jon. So it's a lopsided grin, and a cheerful, — Well, we got a little work to get you back in shape, *Mrs.* Sorenson, and I check her reaction to my assumption of her marital status, but her expression stays glazed, — but the good news is you already made the biggest step by walking through that door.

That's what the lardass wants to hear. They want to believe that it's all easy from here on in. That it can literally be done in their sleep. Because heaven forbid that they interrupt sitting in front of the TV, rising only to refrigerator-raid and pack shit into their sneaky, blubbery mouths. They don't wanna get up before ten, eleven. Perish the thought that any diet and exercise regime should impinge on those basic American freedoms. And I'm sorry, Michelle Parish, you hot-assed little visionary, but what they do *not* need is more procrastination by sitting on those blubbery butts writing Morning fucking Pages. — It's not Mrs., it's Mi . . . Lena . . . please, call me Lena.

— Right, I smile. *You GET Lena, THEN I will call you Lena, bitch.* — So let's just get you on this treadmill, Ms. Sorenson . . . sorry, Lena . . . I smile, as she steps on and I set the speed to 5 mph, — . . . a nice even pace . . . there . . . how's that? It quickly racks up to the mark and soon Sorenson is pounding along, sweating like a skulking schoolyard pervert.

— I . . . I . . .

— Too much! Surely not?

I'm met by the face of the fat moaner: the apologist, the self-pitying, poor-me quitter. — It's . . . really . . . fast . . .

I hate those stupid expressions more than anything. The bloated dumbass oil tanker, where you search for light in those eyes; the frightened child looking for Momma's sweet treats to make it all better; the belligerent asshole who wants to kill themself and really doesn't know why they're here. It doesn't matter which of those archetypes show up, I just wanna punch out every time-wasting bum I see wearing one of those goddamn insults to humanity.

As her meaty thighs wobble in those yoga pants, Sorenson's face blooms florid. — I like to give my clients a goal, Lena. One more specific than just weight loss. A half-marathon, 10k, 5k, it don't really matter.

— I . . . I couldn't . . . I just . . . cooo . . . Sorenson's heavy legs clatter on the accelerating rubber belt.

— Don't wanna hear that word, *those* words; couldn't, can't, shouldn't! You have to stand up. You have to come forward!

Sorenson cringes under the violating impact of my words, but she doesn't stop. Her terror-stricken pout tells me she's not exactly full of grace, but she's *doing*. I burn her this way for a solid forty-five minutes, bringing her to reasonable jogging speed, then back to walking, then jogging again. At the end of it she's glowing like a red-hot ember. Sweaty and exhausted as she climbs off the treadmill, Sorenson finds herself unable, for once in her life, to open her fat mouth to take in anything but the sweet air she's forcing into her puny lungs. — You did well today, I signal her to follow me into the office, and

74

she wobbles behind me, still gasping. — But remember that exercise is only one component to this. I'm giving you a diet sheet, and I swipe one from a stack on my desk. Push it into her grasping paw. As Sorenson looks at it, I watch her face subside.

I grab a card from the rack. — Call me if you start to get cravings for shit over the weekend, and trust me, you will.

Sorenson's face tells me she's got them already. — You're really . . . professional and dedicated, she gulps, fear sparking in her eyes.

— I'm serious about you losing weight . . . Lena, so you need to be too. It isn't easy, especially at the start. So phone me if you feel yourself going off the rails. We are fighting an addiction to crappy eating habits as well as poor exercise ones, I explain, thinking of Michelle's wise words. — We are looking at the whole picture. You didn't put this weight on in one day, and it won't come off in one day.

— I know . . . it makes sense.

— Good. It's important we're on the same page here. So, tell me about you. What do you do for a living?

— I'm . . . Sorenson hesitates, — . . . sort of an artist.

Sort of an artist. Everybody in SoBe who isn't *sort of* a model or *sort of* a photographer, is *sort of* an artist. Waitress, I get it. Or maybe a trust-fund parasite, playing at it. — Cool. . . . Where are you from?

— Minnesota. A town called Potters Prairie in Otter County.

Are you fucking kidding me? — Right . . . I'll bet it's a pretty part of the world.

75

— Yes, Sorenson says, and starts talking about Potters Prairie, before going back to the fucking causeway incident, which seems to have scarred that fat bitch more than it has me. — I can't believe how strong you were on the Julia Tuttle. I need some of that strength and determination.

— Yes, but you aren't a vampire and I'm not a blood bank, I snap. I've long recognized I can ride out an occasional contemptuous outburst, as my clients, in common with most of the fat, possess a considerable ability to edit out the uncomfortable. — Inner strength and focus is in all of us. My job is to help bring it out and develop it. To enable you find that explosive part of yourself that you are, for some reason, keeping buried, I tell her, and glance at the clock on the wall, suddenly anxious to get away from this social leech. — Right, I should go.

Sorenson rocks on the balls of her feet, evidently wanting me to hang around. — Oh, yes . . . right. You, um, didn't tell me where you were from?

No dice, fat girl; some of us have lives. — Boston originally. Now if you'll excuse me, I must go, I tell her, throwing my stuff into my bag, — and you really should shower now before you start to cool down too much under the air conditioning, and I head toward the exit, only whiplashing back to chide the crestfallen chubster, — Remember, watch what you eat!

Outside, there's a sweet, cooling ocean breeze, and I go at a brisk trot across Flamingo Park, wanting to put as much distance between myself and that social predator as possible. Then, at the top end of Lenox, I see a grubby fuck with a camera dangling from his neck, hanging around outside my apartment block. What the fuck is this prick doing here? The show is long over! There's always some lone loser trying to work an angle, some fucking intrusive psycho . . .

Slowing down, I walk up quietly behind him. I tap his shoulder. The greasy prick turns around. — Lucy, he shouts, reaching for his camera.

I tear it out of the cocksucker's hand, the band slipping over his head, and hurl it into the road. On impact, a small black piece snaps off it. — FUCK YOU, ASSHOLE!

— My fucking cam— He looks at me in horror, then runs to retrieve the battered device.

As he cradles it in the street, as if it were the child victim of a hit-and-run, I take the opportunity to get in through the front door, a barrage of insults shrieking behind me.

In the apartment, I head straight for the shower. I touched that paparazzi creep's shoulder and could feel the grubbiness from his filthy cum-splattered and nicotine-caked paw on that fucking camera. I'm just drying off when I get a call. — Lucy, it's Lena Sorenson.

Fuck. Like, already, dude? It was evidently a mistake to give this creepy little porker my number. — Yes? I sharply intone.

— I think you should switch on the TV . . . Channel 6.

I comply with the Porky Princess of Potters Prairie (seriously, who the fuck comes from a place called *that*?) and spark the TV into action. The depressed set finally kicks in. I have a better-quality small-screen portable in my bedroom, but the picture is way too tiny. An anchor, whose face is almost as stiff as her lacquered hair and shoulder pads, is recounting the story of Sean McCandless, the wimpy gunman I disarmed. Between the images on the screen and Sorenson's breathless commentary in my ear, the disturbing picture coalesces. My blood increasingly chills as the nippy air blasts from the vents above onto my wet skin. It emerges that McCandless was abused by a pedophile ring when he was a kid in foster homes. Those guys he was pursuing were both sex offenders who lived in a homeless colony under the Tuttle Causeway. I shiver, then start to convulse, holding the towel tight to me. I saved one, possibly two monsters, and sent down this poor kid who was only out for revenge after some sick-fuck priest ripped his baby-boy ass apart.

It gets worse. As Sorenson's warbling commentary fades out, two talking heads appear onscreen, both of them candidates for the forthcoming congressional elections. Ben Thorpe and Joel Quist are the archetypal worst-case Democrat and Republican. Thorpe is a well-meaning but ineffectual, flatulent-mouthed, carpetbagging Ivy League asshole, while Quist is a rabid, fascist, sanctimonious, Bible-bashing prick, schooled in spewing out populist soundbites. It's hard to work out which one I hate the most. They are debating gun control and Thorpe's defending my bravery, while Quist, agreeing, then says, — Though I'd like to ask that young lady, if she knew then what she knows now, would she do the same?

— Oh my God . . . I hear myself say out loud. *What the fuck . . . I didn't know they were pedophiles . . . the guy was shooting a fucking gun!*

— Well, that's an interesting thought, simpers Ms. Botox,

so firmly embedded in Quist's corner that he has to be fucking her, — what would Lucy Brennan, the so-called Julia Tuttle Causeway heroine, think *right now*?

About what?What difference . . . fuck . . .

And I realize that Lena Sorenson's soft voice is still droning on in my ear, though I can't make out what she's saying. I'm just so *fucking livid* at being dragged into all this bullshit. I'm responding with automatic "mmm's" and "yeah's." I can't talk to this *maneuvering* bitch. I need to think, so I put the phone down. I sit watching the other features, these Siamese twins again, and then I rise, drying myself properly and putting on a tee and some shorts.

A few moments later the intercom goes and I'm ready to bawl out this next stalking creep, probably that photographer asshole, but it's Sorenson! Her voice is rendered metallic and scratchy by the device. — I jumped in the car and got here as soon as I could!

I don't even recall agreeing to her coming here, but there's nothing to do but buzz her in.

I open the front door to hear her slowly climbing the stairs. Sorenson, even smaller than I remember, swings into the corridor and waddles toward me. I move into the apartment, leaving the door ajar. She raps the door with her knuckles as she enters, looking around my tiny space in a slightly disparaging way. Then she says, — You're gonna be under siege for a spell. Come over to my house, have some dinner. I feel so responsible, giving them that phone video . . .

She's right, that creep whose camera I busted wasn't a straggler, he was the fucking vanguard. I need to get out of here and I'm fucked if I can think of any reason not to accept. I pull on some gym shoes and we get downstairs. Stepping outside, all I hear are insect clicks exploding around me like gunfire, and shouts. — LUCY! LUCY!

They're all back! And the van for the TV news, fuck knows what channel, is already here! Sorenson did bring serious heat, and those politician assholes have turned it right back up! I want to double back to the apartment, but some bastards have sneaked round and positioned themselves between us and the front door. — Just wait a darn minute . . . Sorenson protests feebly, sounding all schoolmarm under stress, as I see the rancid fuck whose camera I trashed, firing off a Kalashnikov round on a substitute device, with a zoom lens attached. At least there's one asshole who knows not to get too close. — Ignore them, Lucy, Sorenson says, wide-eyed with fear, grabbing my hand, pushing through toward her car. The rest aren't so shy; a buffed, tanned faggot of a reporter sticks his mike in my face and asks me, now that I know the story of McCandless and Ryan Balbosa and Timothy Winter, the two pedophiles, would I do the same thing again?

I know I should shut my fucking mouth and follow the scared, furtive Sorenson to her car. Instead, in my rage at this violation by the preppy asshole, I stand my ground and shoot my mouth off. — Of course I would. Whatever the circumstances, nobody has the right to start shooting people!

— But you did martial arts at a high competitive level, and taught self-defense classes for women, this *sincere* fag lisps. — Are you saying that women have the right to self-defense, but male victims of sexual violence, like Mr. McCandless, do not?

A crumpling of silent thunder in my ears. I'm stunned. I can't manage a retort. As I hear Lena Sorenson's urgent voice in the background, I can only look fearfully and penitently, my face racked with weakness and doubt, as it's beamed into all those American homes.

Then I feel Lena Sorenson's grip on my arm tighten, as she leads me to her car. — Please leave us alone, she says, softly but quite forcefully. I climb inside, but the squalid asshole is still pointing his camera at me, shooting in through the passenger window, glee etched on his fat chops. I turn away. — Goddamnit!

Sorenson starts the engine and pulls off, dispersing the photographers who flutter away, pigeonlike for a few feet, then resume their feeding frenzy. She turns on to Alton, then floors it and we tear north. — It's okay, Lucy, she gurgles, — this story surely can't have much more legs. Her tone falls ruefully. — If only I hadn't given them that stupid video clip!

A text comes in on my phone. Valerie.

I saw the news. Lie low. There will be heat.

No fucking shit, tinker tailor soldier!

I feel my teeth rattling together as we shoot past the green hand of the Holocaust Museum, and I look back to see if we're being pursued. It's hard to tell; a lot of traffic is ripping by both ways. I get control of myself by venting my anger. — You put yourself on the line and save some motherfucker's ass and you get treated like a fucking criminal! What kind of

81

a fucking country is this? Is this America? Is this what we've become? It's a fucking freak show!

Sorenson lets me get it off my chest, gently touching my shoulder as she keeps driving.

— I'm sorry, I say, feeling better, — Just had to get that out.

— I know. Don't worry about it. It must be so stressful.

We drive up to Lena Sorenson's place on 46th. I try to get Valerie but it goes straight to the ol' girl's voicemail. I text her.

You weren't wrong. Give me a call.

Chez Sorenson is a nice, big detached Spanish colonial house with a pool, which is too small for serious swimming, not that I could conceive of the Sorenson cruise ship docking in that particular berth. Terracotta tiles snake through the home, all the walls whitewashed in gallery emulsion. This shows off numerous paintings and sleek but functional furniture.

She has a rack of CDs and most of them are okay, but there are two Tracy Chapman albums in the collection. A bitch got one Chapman album, that fucker with "Fast Car" on it, you gotta see it as a red flag. She got two Chapman albums, that one plus another, then run for the fucking hills! Too late for that now: I slump back into a leather chair and feel myself being lowered into its guts as I look around the room. My first thought is: no wonder Sorenson spends so much time in Starbucks; decoratively speaking, it's a home away from home. The best feature, apart from the kickass 70-inch flatscreen TV, is the huge stone fireplace, with two metal buckets, one full of coal, the other logs, and a group of fire irons, including an ax, presumably to pretend-chop the already splintered logs. Fake-assed bitch. She makes some coffee (which I never drink) and tells me that she has an outbuilding which functions as her sort-of-an-artist's studio. Despite my expressing interest to the point of fascination, she doesn't offer to show me inside.

The kitchen, however, is a state-of-the-art chamber of self-abuse; the cupboards and big Sub-Zero full of what I call antifood: cookies, candy bars, TV dinners, ice cream, chips, and more soda than you have ever seen. Lena has been cooking up a feast of sugar, salt, fat, and carbs. But nobody, bar her, is eating. — Bakery goods. They are my one weakness, she says, cramming a strawberry-filled donut (450 cal easy) into her face.

I decline her offer to reciporocate, going through to her living room and switching on the large flatscreen. Bitch got every cable station known to man; bitch got full Direct TV package. I channel-hop the news programs and my feature is appearing already. I look weak and stupid, my hair severely scraped back and tied up. My heart drops six inches in my chest cavity as it cuts to Quist's smug, mocking face. — The cat seems to have got that young lady's tongue on the issue of the right to self-defense. Guess she's maybe finding out that it ain't as easy as it all seems, and that ordinary Americans might just indeed have the right to seek recourse against those who would do the work of the devil.

— Fucking asshole! I shout at the crinkled, leather-faced old scrotum on the screen.

Sorenson takes the hint and zaps the TV into black death.

83

— It'll blow over, she says in a voice that is meant to be soothing but which bugs the fuck out of me.

I spring up, startling her, and walk around, looking at the art hanging on the walls. Then I move quickly back into the kitchen. Sorenson follows, watching as I pick up a donut from the countertop. — Hmmm . . . I examine it.

— Yes, these are my mother's, Sorenson explains, — and they're so good! She sends me down a box religiously on the first week of every month. I knew you'd want—

I turn and drop the crud into the trash. Sorenson's face burns like I took my hand across the bitch's fat chops.

— You can't—

— It's imperative that you control your calorie intake. Diet is crucial. You're only going to stand still at best if you eat the same amount and type of the so-called food that got you into this mess, I explain, picking up the box and chucking the whole lot into the bin. Sorenson's squirming, standing back and gripping the kitchen countertop, like she's about to faint.

— Right! Lifestyle inventory! I bark, making a stunned, shaky Sorenson go through the cupboards, systematically throwing out all the crap! Her face is on fire. — This is shit. This is how you are killing yourself! Do you *read* those labels?

—Yes . . . she says in a high mewl followed by a half-hearted moan, — . . . I do read them. Sometimes. Most of the time.

I can feel my thin, plucked eyebrows slanting severely at the pathetic lummox.

— I mean, come on, it's just a treat. We all need treats sometimes, she protests.

— Treats? Treats! What does this one say? I drum my finger on the packet of macaroons then thrust it into her face.

— Two hundred and twenty calories . . .

— Two hundred and twenty calories *per fucking serving*. How many servings are there in this container?

I can see the air being squeezed out of her lungs as surely as if I'd just buried a left hook into her liver. — These things are so small, there's nothing in them . . .

— How many servings?

— Four . . .

— How much of this container do you have in one sitting?

Sorenson can't speak. It's like her voice has just left her.

— The whole fucking thing, I'll bet. That is nearly *nine hundred fucking calories*, Lena, two-thirds of what a woman your size should be eating *per fucking day*!

Sure enough, more feeble protest. — But . . . but . . . if you only ate a quarter of that, the serving size would be nothing!

— Exactly! So what is that telling you?

— I . . . I don't know . . .

— Oh, stop it, I snap, fixing my most merciless stare on her. — I've seen that uncomprehending loser look so many times. I shake my head, and let my voice go high, in sarcastic imitation. — It can't be! It isn't fair. I feel my face altering clownishly. — That big question hanging on every leaden bottom lip in America: How did I become a big bovine juggernaut just through sitting on a couch and eating tons of crap? How did *that* happen?

She's staring at me, absolutely seething with rage. She's thinking, "Who is this person? This is my home! I'm not *paying her* to be insulted and abused!" I'm convinced the chunkoid is about to tell me to get out, so I adopt a more gentle tone. — It's telling you that this so-called *food* is nothing more than a *pile of fucking shit*. And that's before I even start on the fine detail of the ingredients; — the corn syrup, additives, preservatives, emulsifiers, sugars, and fucking salts. Trust me, Lena, and I drop it in the trash can with the rest, as Sorenson looks like it's her newborn, which I've just torn out her snatch, — this is the enemy. This is the shit that makes you hate the mirror, the clothes store and the bathroom scale. This is the shit that's wrecking your life and is gonna fucking kill you!

I've shanked that fat whore through her blubber, struck right at her very core with my words. I can see her psychic wounds bleed in front of me. And the worst thing about it from her point of view is that she knows I'm *one hundred percent* correct; that I'm only saying this for her own good. — I know, she feebly begins; — I know what you're saying is right—

I raise my hand. The fat need to find their voice. But *not* the quitter-victim voice. They cannot be permitted to speak, unless they speak like adults. — Don't give me the big fucking "but," I shake my head in scorn. — They always give the big fucking "but," that caveat that makes it all okay, that renders everything acceptable. Let me tell you, sister: the only big fucking butt is the one you're sitting on.

— You can't talk to me like that—

— Yes I can, and I will, I tell her, my hands on my hips, my jaw thrust out. Then I drop my voice. — Because I want to help you get better. I know you don't want to hear what I'm going to say, Lena, I cup my ear, — because that *not wanting to hear*, it's just all part of the disease. You feel your ears physically shutting. There's a tune, a trivial mantra playing in your head, to drown out my words, which are punching into your chest like arrowheads. Am I correct?

— I . . . I . . .

— Well, sister; welcome to the *real* world. You *are* going to hear my words. You *are* going to take cognisance of those words. Perhaps not today, perhaps not even tomorrow, but I will break down your defenses and you *will* listen to what I'm saying. Cause I'm gonna get you the fuck outta your comfort zone!

Sorenson's physically shaking, quailing away from me, barely able to look me in the eye. I put my hand on her shoulder. Then she suddenly turns her head and stares at me, pushing her hair out of her eyes. I give her a big, open, affectionate smile. — Now show me around!

We walk outside into the backyard. I'm still interested in her studio, which sits in front of the small pool. — That's where I work, she explains, adding, — I haven't done much in a while.

— Can we take a look inside?

— No, it's a mess, she says. — I don't like to show people where I work.

— Oh-kay . . . I raise my hands in mock surrender. — But maybe later, once you feel more comfortable. I look to the studio, then back at her. — Because this place is important. This is where you need to be, here, I tell her, then I point inside to the kitchen, — not in there.

Sorenson nods at me, in the failing light. A breeze clatters the swordlike leaves of the big palm against the window, scoring the silence. Because although it's tearing her apart to admit it, she knows it's true, every fucking word.

She offers to drive me home but I insist on getting a cab.
— I can pick one up on Collins.
— It's really no bother.
— No thank you. You've done enough already.
— But that's nothing, that night on the causeway, you don't know how much you've already given me.
— Honey, I ain't even started yet, and I throw my bag over my shoulder and walk out into the night.

Of course, when I get outside I double-back into Sorenson's yard. I'm crouching under the window, looking at her through the blinds. Sorenson is sat at the computer. She's gaping at what looks like pictures of fluffy baby animals and it seems she's crying. Fat loser tears. Well, let her bubble away, but if I see that bitch take that shit out the trash and stuff her face I swear to God I will kick that door in and ram my fingers down her throat till that poison comes up . . .

Fuck . . . my cell makes a soft purr. I click it onto silent. Sorenson's heard nothing. Some emails have come in, one is from Sorenson! I skulk out the yard to look at it.

8

CONTACT 3

To: kimsangyung@gmail.com; lucypattybrennan@hardass.com
From: lenadiannesorenson@thebluegallery.com
Subject: Did You Ever See Anything So Cute?

Kim, Lucy,

This is to cheer you guys up!

Did you ever see anything so cute?

Lena x

The rabid but pitiful bitch has linked me to a website called Cute Overload. It's all puppies, kittens, bear cubs, hamsters, and bunnies. Judging by the posts on it, everyone is a mentally retarded soccer mom, or a mentally retarded soccer mom in waiting.

9

CUTE OVERLOAD

I blink awake into a mango light that paints the room. The digital display on the clock—9:12—jolts me alert. *What the fuck, I never—*

I have a client at 10:30!

— shut the front door . . .

Heat and mass by my side; a storm of awareness that the bed is co-occupied thuds into my chest. My first dread thought: Sorenson! No, surely not. I turn slowly to look at the slumbering chick next to me; that femme who really liked the taste of pussy and getting fucked good. I went out on a cunt hunt last night, and I hate when I break my own rules and bring a chick back. She even has a leg over mine. As I roughly disentangle she blinks into life and groggily gapes at me. Without makeup she looks so young, a college freshman or sophomore type.

Getting stuck with experimenting bitches isn't my preferred modus operandi, but hey-ho, you can't critique a chick who took the plastic you were packing so eagerly. — Good morning, she yawns and stretches.

— And to you. I force a smile. Then it gets uncomfortable. I'm no good at this.

She gets out of bed; tall, lean and hot. I dig that

90

blond-white hair, cut short, but this chick could *never* be a proper butch, not without at least five years and 100,000 calories. She pulls on her clothes. — I gotta go. Classes. Then she smiles at me. — I can't believe I made it with the Causeway Vigilante Chick!

— Yeah, I say. How the fuck can you respond to that?

— See ya.

She gets out, and I wait till I hear the apartment door open and close, then spring up. In the kitchen area she's taken some orange juice out the fridge and slugged it from the bottle without putting it back. Fucking gross: young bitches got no manners.

I'm pissed at myself for sleeping in, I mean, how fucking lame, so I jump in the shower then swiftly dress. I've got time to quickly check my emails. Fuck me, I cringe as I see that one Sorenson sent me last night. And she at least has a friend, though heaven knows what this Kim chick is like.

Fuck her. I've more important correspondence to be getting on with.

To: michelleparish@lifeparishioners.com
From: lucypattybrennan@hardass.com
Subject: So Good To Hear From You!

Michelle,

Can't even begin to tell you how juiced I am about you getting back to me. My life has gotten a shitload weirder since the incident. I have a manager!

And I've a woman from VH1 TV who's signing me up to do this makeover show for fat suburbanites who've let themselves go. It sounds pretty much like what I do now, but only to camera and on a fucking cruise boat! I know, right? The thing is, they've lined up some preening hair, cosmetics, and clothes guy to partner me. My warning bells kind of went off. I don't want them launching the career of the unemployable faggot son of some TV company exec on the back of my heroic actions, right? LOL!

Not all good, though. A fascist prick running for office down here, Quist his name is, has me on his radar. Turns out the gunman was a kid who had been abused by pedophiles and went under the causeway where those perverts live and started shooting them up. Good luck to him, but like, hello, I was meant to know that? It's all getting sick, but not in a good way.

Please advise!

Oh, and representation, have you heard of Valerie Mercando? What's she like?

Oh, FINALLY, and you wouldn't believe that one of my clients now is this self-styled "artist" girl, the one who witnessed the bridge incident. She sought me out. Creepy or what?

Best,

Lucy x

As I hit the send button, I realize that my nails, clicking on the keyboard, are getting too long. I'm scrolling through my inbox and back to Sorenson's weird animal pictures website. Then I think I really should go, but to my delight, a reply comes right back!

To: lucypattybrennan@hardass.com
From: michelleparish@lifeparishioners.com
Subject: So Good To Hear From You!

Lucy,

Great to hear from you again, and delighted that things are working out so well. VH1 is an awesome channel, and they will give you a great profile. Of course, the right collaborators are important, but this is a golden opportunity! Bite their hand off! BUT leave the negotiations to your rep.

Which bring us on to representation. Yes, Valerie Mercando is very good. She'll be able to handle all the VH1 negotiations.

Clients are clients, I don't think it's important where they come from, as long as there is mutual respect and the proper boundaries are observed.

Yes, I heard that politicians were trying to use your case to gain leverage. Don't worry, that will blow over, but I'm sure your PR person will tell you that.

Well done! I'm excited for you!

Best,

Michelle

PS Did you try out Morning Pages?

I'm so buzzed, and get right on to Valerie.

To: valeriemercando@mercandoprinc.com
cc: themlajtempleton@vh1.com
From: lucypattybrennan@hardass.com
Subject: Let's Do It!

Dear Valerie,

After sound advice from my trusted friend and confidante, Michelle Parish, I'm writing to formally confirm that you are indeed the best person to represent me. I'm copying Thelma Templeton of VH1 into this email.

Let's get the ball rolling and kick some serious ass!

Best,

Lucy x

In my postage-stamp kitchen area I mix and down a protein shake. Emerging into the sunshine, I'm ready to bust the chops of any asshole who comes into my space, but the paparazzi seem to have vanished again. Striding across Flamingo Park, I head toward the gym. A couple of guys in their twenties are running and one stops, pulling himself up on the bar by the basketball courts. He does seven pull-ups, struggles on number eight, fails on nine. I get straight on it. — Here's how it's done, I say, knocking out a dozen, finishing the twelfth as strong as when I started the first, then doing the same number of chin-ups, beaten by nothing other than the clock.

— Wow . . . the guy says.

— It's all in the breathing, I tell him. — If you're doing pull-ups, your grip should be slightly wider than your shoulder. For chin-ups, the underhand grip, keep them around shoulder width.

T2 style! Sarah Fucking Connor! Joan Fucking Jett!

When I get to the gym, Marge's already there, and she's stretching out. She's getting the stink-eye from Toby, the fag receptionist, who describes himself as a DJ, because they let him occasionally spin his flouncy, ambient, anti-music, antilife CDs when the joint is empty. When it fills with suburban housewives, he has to cede his place to Coldplay and Maroon 5 mixes, and I've even grown to accept those wrist-slash inducers as a blessed relief to his tepid shit. I swear my ass turns to peat bog at the very sight of that pretentious, bitter queer. His earshot makes me instinctively drop my vowels into Southie caricature. Heavy-muscled and cut in typical South Beach pseudo-homo style, he's blissfully unaware as he pops his steroids and presses his one-fifty that a throwaway jab would bust his faggot nose and have him in counseling for years, spilling bucketloads of pansy tears. — You've been in the news again, he announces, then his head swivels to a mounted screen. — Oh, look. He points at the TV.

Joel Quist is on the screen. He's running for office on every hate-and-fear policy you can think of, and shit-talking every alternative:

Terrorism: killing innocent Americans

Gun control: killing innocent Americans who can't protect themselves

Higher taxes for the super-rich instead of bailouts: killing innocent Americans

Not killing Arabs: killing innocent Americans

Abortion: killing innocent Americans (before they're born)

Gay marriage: sodomizing, then killing, innocent Americans

I'm on his radar and it sucks. Oh shit: now my big oval mouth is gaping and stupefied into the camera, like Marge's when confronted by a treadmill. I signal for her to pick up the bell weights, but I can't keep my eyes off the screen. All I needed to say was, "Of course male victims of sexual violence have the right to self-defense. This is appropriate when they are being attacked. Mr. McCandless wasn't being attacked, he was pursuing two unarmed men, and shooting at them. If he was the victim of a previous crime then we have a criminal justice system that exists to deal with such cases." But that ship, the vessel of reason, has long fucking sailed.

Thorpe appears, and he's making that very point, but in his rambling, pontificating, lecturing, half-assed way. You can tell that everybody hates him. He's slippery and effete. He's a fucking *lawyer*.

Man the fuck up!

— Right Marge, get that fifteen-pound kettlebell and gimme four sets of swing and squat, twelve reps per set!

Quist cuts right in over the protesting Thorpe, who is waved down by the anchor, a guy this time, though he still looks like he wants to take the dribbling snail of this semi-continent old fuck into his tight, priggish mouth. — Well, I am all for the rule of law, as is well known by my voting record on such issues, especially when you compare it to Mr. Thorpe's one of mollycoddling the criminal element in our society . . .

Marge is going through her stuff. — Raise the weights higher and get your butt lower! Swing and squat! And swing and squat!

They cut to Thorpe long enough for a petty pout of a reaction shot and a muffled off-camera plea, then to the anchor who waves him down with the back of his hand, — Please, allow Mr. Quist to finish.

— But sometimes our politicians and bureaucrats in Washington let the people down, Quist rooster-puffs himself up. — Lemme ask this question: How long was young Sean McCandless let down for? Lucy Brennan, albeit unwittingly, came to help those sick perverts, as everybody seems to do. But who was there for poor little Sean McCandless? Who came to help that kid?

I let my eyes swivel to Marge who is gasping as she lifts that kettlebell. — Goo-ood . . .

Back onscreen: a lot of outraged, angst-ridden hand-wringing from Thorpe, who appeals, crybaby style, to the stern anchor, claiming he wasn't given a fair hearing. The host then takes him to task, making him look even more of an asshole. Then they cut, thankfully, to the story of the conjoined twins.

— Could be worse, Toby, dripping schadenfreude, nods at the screen.

A head shot of Annabel, some mousy aspirational chatter of her love for Stephen, then a close-up on intertwined fingers, as she's revealed to be holding his hand. We pull out in long shot to see Amy looking in the opposite direction from Stephen, away from her sister. Rather than going tight on the lovebirds, the freak-show bastards keep her in shot. With her hook nose poking through her long hair, she resembles a scavenger bird perched on Annabel's shoulder. My cell vibrates and it's Valerie. — Hey, you, I shout with enthusiasm, to show that Toby creep that I'm not fazed. I turn to Marge. — Treadmill, twenty minutes, starting at jogging pace, 4 mph, and I'm moving toward the front door and some privacy.

— Hi, Lucy. I just saw the news . . .

— Yes, but surely it'll blow over . . . I say, gesturing at a stalling, gasping Marge to climb the fuck on and get with it, as I step outside into the sun and look up at the azure sky.

— It's got VH1 nervous. You need to *not talk* to the press or TV.

— Okay . . .

— Sorry if I sound a little strung. A singer client's been caught with blow in some Ocean Drive spot. The promoter who has her on at the Gleeson is some kind of born-again asshole who has a weird antidrugs stipulation in the contract and is threatening to pull tomorrow night's gig. Must go . . . oh, one other thing, the Total Gym people sent me a free home gym for you. They've enclosed a note, one of those "no obligation, but if you do like the product and feel inclined to endorse it, we would be grateful," so that's up to you. I'll send it on.

— Wow! That's rad!

— Yes, it's all good. But don't talk to the media, it's all fuel to them, so just let it burn out.

— Cool, I say in cagey affirmation, thinking, just what I need in my life: a Chuck Norris-endorsed piece of crap fitness equipment, which will fall apart as soon as it's taken half my life to assemble and eat up practically all the space in my shoebox apartment.

The line goes dead and I step back into the gym. I raise a lumbering Marge to 5 mph with a slight gradient, and the point of exhaustion. — Almost there! That's what I need! The warrior Marge! And five . . . and four . . . and three . . . and two . . . and one . . . and the machine goes into cool-down mode. — Good work, I exclaim, as she looks at me like the kid who has fallen on her ass and doesn't know whether she's going to laugh or cry. *Fry that hoe's cellulite. Smooth that bitch's dimpled fat.* — Breathe, Marge: in through the nose, out through the mouth.

Jezzo, they still need to be told to do this! What the fuck is *that* saying? But Marge finishes her session and staggers gratefully to the locker room for a shower. On the screens Thorpe and Quist have gone, replaced by the mother of the conjoined twins, talking about the girls, followed by a nause-ating, breathless voice-over, — . . . like any mother, Joyce fears for the future of her girls. But in the case of Amy and Annabel, their future, like their past and present, is inextric-ably bound up with each other.

99

I'm contemplating the grotesqueness of this setup when Sorenson appears, in new gaudy *pink* workout gear. It's the sort of outfit either a retard or a ten-year-old would wear. — All righty! she sings. — I'm fired up and rarin to go!

— Good, I smile, teeth clenching, moving toward the machines, her following me.

How do I shave the beef off this irritating chubster? I get her on the treadmill, putting her through her paces. I'm upping the stakes, giving her more, nudging it to 5 mph, forcing her to pound that rubber track. *Dance, fat little hamster, dance!* — C'mon, Lena Sorenson, c'mon! I shout, as heads turn, my voice booming over Toby's ambient drivel. I push the treadmill up to 6 mph, watching the blaze intensify on Sorenson's face. — We are fired up and rarin to go!

Every time the chunky hoe catches her breath to do what she does best, even more than eat, namely talk, I push her further, or change the activity. She has to get the message: this is *not* a social club.

But Sorenson surprises me with her cojones. She's taking everything I'm throwing at her. Even after the session, she's still sticking around, breathlessly trying to engage with me when my mind is clearly elsewhere. — That . . . is . . . just . . . soooo . . . good . . . I haven't felt this good . . . in ages . . .

It gets so oppressive that I'm even delighted to meet *Mom* for lunch. *Anything*, if it means escaping my own personal Siamese twin. Annabel, I know your pain. Sorenson practically invites herself along, and then has the audacity to look at me like an abused stepchild when I tell her I have things to discuss with *my mother*. My God, I'm even concerned the needy bitch is going to stalk me all the way to the Ocean Drive joint where we've stupidly agreed to meet! I step outside the gym and make my way toward the Atlantic.

If numbers count in my game, then my mom, Jackie Pride (58, 5'8", 130 lbs), through being in real estate, is probably even more subject to their capriciousness. The market has tanked; she sold twelve condos in Miami two years ago, three last year, and so far none this year. Two years ago she ran around in a big Lincoln; its predecessor was the one she bought to replace the Caddy I inherited. It was the era when real-estate guys imitated lawyers and nobody laughed. Now that she's driving a Toyota and staring hard into the demise of another long-term relationship, zero is a troubling statistic.

She's already seated, laptop fired up Sorenson-style (ha!), and rattling into her cell phone. As I approach she looks up, — Hey, pickle, and she gives me an apologetic nod, her shaved-and-penciled brows arching as she snaps her Apple Mac shut. She's wearing a white top, with a checked skirt and pair of shoes, both black and white. She wears glasses on the bridge of her strong Saxon nose (not like my little button Paddy thing, inherited from Dad), and a pair of shades pushed back on her head to keep her still-brown collar-length hair in place. Mom ends her call and scrunches into her plastic chair, which slides a few inches along the sidewalk. — Oh my God . . . she groans. She looks good; the only really noticeable ravage of age is where the jowly flesh around her chin and neck has sagged to a crumpled bag. Mom keeps talking about getting "work done" but being "too busy even for Lasik."

A young blond chick I recognize (I think one of Mona's clients at Bodysculpt) swaggers by, wearing a yellow string bikini bottom and matching yellow T-shirt, with MS. ARROGANT emblazoned on it in big blue letters. SoBe remains a sun-drenched refuge for strutting grotesques and desperate narcissists. Mom's phone goes again. — Lieb, she pleads. — I'll take this, sweetie, then I'll switch the goddamn thing off, I promise.

— Cool, I say, picking up the menu.

— Lieb, sweetkins. . . . Yes. Gotcha. . . . Gotcha. Just keep them entertained. Gulfstream Park or the like, you know the drill. . . . Check. Just keep them believing that it's a rock-solid investment, which, to all intents and purposes it is . . . Yes, I love you . . . Her brows arch further north. — Gotta go now, sweetie, Lucy's here. Ciao. She flicks the iPhone into silence. — Men. The toughest of them seem to need the most hand-holding. It's so weird. I mean, he can take those squeaky assholes to a bar or a strip club. I don't care. She shakes her head. — God, people are just losing their nerve! That investment is solid!

— I'm sure it is.

— But listen to me go on . . . let's get some food, she says, then looks right into my eyes, following the line of my vision. — You were checking out my sagging jowls! Oh, you cruel child!

— No, I lie, — I was just think of how well you look!

Mom lets out a long, deflated sigh. As she speaks, her

eyes, by turns vapid and intense, always seem to be gazing past me into the disenchantments that lie ahead. — I'm thinking of having work done. It's just time. That and money. She shakes her head bitterly as the busboy pours our glasses of iced water.

— Things still bad in your game?

— Let's not even talk about it, she says, as a hovering, Botoxed, failed model approaches and robotically grates out a list of specials.

No, Mom's putting on a positive face as we order, and then she starts regurgitating some self-help book she's devoured (her personal version of Sorenson's cakes) back at me. — Real estate . . . it's such a bitch in South Florida. I need what Debra Wilson—have you read her?

— No. Have you heard of Morning Pages? They're supposed to be great.

— Marianne Robson at Coldwell Banker says that they're essential. I must try them, once I get to make some time for me.

— What about this Debra Wilson thing?

— Well, I need what she calls a "compelling personal project," and Mom's face creases sweetly in a smile. — Of course, my most wonderful project is my beautiful baby girls, she says, as I think: *spare the fuck out of me*, — but those babies have grown up now. Her brow ruefully creases. — I don't suppose you've heard from Jocelyn lately?

— Still in Darfur with the same NGO, last I heard, I tell her, trying to check out, perhaps a little too ostentatiously, a ripped surfer guy who ambles past.

— Still doing good deeds, Mom sings wistfully. — I swear that girl shames us all.

I feel like telling her if she actually got out of Jocelyn's face while she was trying to do shit growing up, she probably wouldn't be hanging out in the crappiest corners of the globe playing Mother Teresa. But Mom has gone back to her own drama. — So I told Lieb that I really need something else in my life.

— You got real estate, I say, unable to resist it. Mom never wants to talk about anything else when the real-estate market is lively. Now that it's dead, it's practically *all* I want to discuss with her. If you aren't put on this Earth to subtly make your mother's life one suffering hell, then what the fuck is the point of human existence?

— I mean, outside of work, she says as the Stepford-bound server chick brings our tofu salads. They are sorry-assed affairs, the lettuce as limp as bad-back Miles's dick, and the smoked tofu tastes like sweaty old gym socks. Mom winces under the first mouthful. Then she gives me a piercing look. — How is your father? I'm ashamed to admit it, but I frequently google him.

— Well, it's natural that you're curious. But if you google him regularly, you'll know more than me.

— C'mon! You were always his favorite, the sporty one.

— Mom, *he* was always his favorite.

— Ain't that the truth! I still can't believe it about him. She shakes her head, that lacquered mop not shifting a inch. — It's almost like being successful with those books was your father's last great act of spite against me.

— C'mon! He'd always talked about being a writer!

104

— Everybody *talks* about being a writer, angel. If every novel conceived on a bar stool made it into print, there would not be one tree left standing on God's green Earth. No, as soon as he left me—

— As I recall, *you* left him. For Lieb.

Mom exhales and rolls her eyes. She explains, in labored tones, as if I'm still a kid, — I *physically* left him, yes, but only because he didn't have the balls to get out first. But he engineered the split. Then, after me supporting the bum for years, through all that inquiry shit with the BPD, he actually got off his fat Irish ass and *wrote*.

— You get *on* your ass to write.

— Exactly, that's why it's the perfect occupation for him, she says, then her mouth turns down as a grim thought insinuates itself. — I suppose there will be a younger woman in tow, some vacuous bimbo—

— Several, I'd wager, I acknowledge as I raise a forkful of tofu to my mouth, hoping it'll taste better than the last. And being immediately disappointed.

Mom's jaw falls as she gapes at me.

— Well, it's the human condition. How *do* you get older? You behave with restraint and dignity, and then life becomes a colossal bore. If you indulge yourself, then it looks sad and pathetic. Pick red or black, cause ain't nobody leavin this casino with a full stack of chips, baby.

— God, Lucy, catch yourself! You sound *so* like him.

— Well, that's a quote from Matt Flynn.

My mother goes through the client database in her head, before coming up with a blank expression.

105

— His Boston gumshoe protagonist, I tell her.

She tuts and lifts another forkload of soggy spinach leaves to her mouth. Poor Mom, such a breadhead, and the very guy she thought would never be able to cut it, made good as soon as she fired his ass. Must be doubly hard when everything is turning to shit for her. And she lives and breathes this motherfucker of a real-estate gig. That woman will do *anything*, within certain parameters she says (and I have to take her word at that), to close a deal. Mom will get out of bed in the middle of the night to pick up groceries for a client. She'll provide them with any sort of services. Yes, and where the line gets drawn there, I'd rather not even speculate. Her long-term partner, Lieb, seems all but cast adrift, lost to the dive bars of SoBe in much the same way my dad once sauced through the maze of Southie watering holes.

Mom's opted for a ginger sauce on her tofu and she forks up some ludicrously gloopy mix, then grimaces and drops it back onto the plate. — Yuck, a ginger sauce which is all flour. Gross! Ocean Drive: always a dining mistake!

We fight our way through our respective messes in a stoical silence. I'm on Lifemap TM, trying to calc the useless calories in this toxic dressing. I go to say something but Mom waves a silencing hand, pointing to the cell she's lifting to her ear. — Sorry, pickle, I gotta take this . . . Lonnie! Yes, it's all good here! Mmmm-hmmm. . . . Yes, some people are really feeling the pinch but we've been very, very lucky. The super-premium market is still, well, I'd be indulging in the stock real-estate bullcrap if I said buoyant, but it's certainly holding up well. And the property you've chosen is an excellent one. . . .

Mmmm-hmmm. . . . Did I mention that you might have Dwyane Wade for a neighbor? A little bird tells me he just looked at a place across the way, you know, the Spanish colonial? Not a patch on your choice though, I'm sure you'll agree . . .

I'm watching her gesticulations, a born saleswoman. How well do I know her? Dad and Mom's split was as complex to fathom as their relationship. I'd always thought that Mom, flirty in the company of men, was the original infidel. It wasn't a big surprise in my teen years when she ran off with Lieb, a Datafax TM salesman. One of Lieb's last big jobs had been to sell the executive time-management system to senior and middle management at the insurance company in Boston where Mom then worked, and subsequently train them in its usage.

But Lieb's salesmanship skills were good; not only did he sell himself to her, but he also packaged the Florida real-estate explosion. — Real estate is the next big thing. I missed out on the dot.com boom because I hesitated, he'd trumpet. — Never again. I'm jumping on this train.

So was Mom.

When they got together, he confided to my mother that Datafax TM was a great system, but that electronic PC and Mac software programs would soon replace it. Before long, people would get used to keeping their diaries on their computers, laptops, and phones. The psychological cord tying them to a paper system would fray and Datafax would become a niche product, with some aging valued customers, but not the essential yuppie business accessory it then was. So real estate would be his, and my mother's, golden future.

After the split, Jocelyn and I stayed in Weymouth with Dad. The reason Mom gave for us not joining her in Miami was to avoid disruption to our schoolwork. Not that I did much of that; all I wanted to do was train and fight. I was fifteen and hated the world. The previous summer I'd fallen out with Mom and Dad, especially Dad, after a shattering incident in the park, Abbie Adams Green, that my family read wrong, and which had estranged us. I was plenty surprised when he supported my decision to quit track and field to take up martial arts. Mom was horrified. — But why, pickle?

Jocelyn said nothing (as usual) other than regard me with her customary look of highbrow disdain.

— I want to kick ass, I said, and I could see a silent pride blaze in my father's eyes.

And I did. I enrolled in tae kwon do classes at a local sports center, graduating to Muay Thai. This was a great liberation for me; I could give vent to all my pent-up energy and aggression. Right from the start it was evident that very few other girls would be fucking with me. I'd look an opponent in the eye, and watch them crumble. I loved the no-holds-barred aspects of the discipline, and I'd hit my rivals with the fucking kitchen sink—elbows, knees, kicks, fists—and I could tussle and dig like a hellcat. I was the local Thai Boxing Association's golden girl, training with demented purpose, and fighting ferociously.

I did well at their junior events, first at state, then national level. I was successful in three Muay Thai classics at my weight class. My best title was my first, when I deposed the reigning champion, an Asian bitch, who could grapple like a pervert priest, but couldn't handle my speed and my knees pummeling into her snatch. Like so many of the others I fought, I saw her running tears, all the time looking beyond them, trying to get another target in my sights.

I won more belts. Studied different fighting disciplines, karate and ju-jitsu mainly. I fought off all my rage, while Jocelyn buried herself in her books. When pushed, she'd refer to the split as "it sucks" but without conviction. Her personal withdrawal was to read, and she'd mentally left the household before anyone—if she was ever really present in it.

In the meantime Dad took me to all my events. He drove miles with me, paid for hotels, driving back in the early morning and heading uncomplainingly into his job—by then he was back doing PE teacher work at a junior high—while I went to school or bed. We grew close, although the park incident, which we never talked about, always hung over us. But I often think that he got absorbed in my early fighting career to avoid dealing with the breakup of his marriage. On the few occasions he did talk about Mom leaving, he seemed hurt and bewildered, like a small boy.

I'd always thought of Dad as having the bark, and Mom the bite. It was two summers later that I learned otherwise. I was remanded to Miami, at Dad's instigation, doing community-college bullshit in order to get onto the university's undergraduate sports science program. Jocelyn went to stay with Dad's sister, Aunt Emer, in New York, and undertook her own prep course, to gain admission to Princeton. I moved south and in with Mom and Lieb. At first it was tough. I missed Dad. I was still learning to drive, while trying to get hooked up with a gym in the local martial arts scene. Through Mom's indifference to them, I learned the significance of Dad's support of my martial arts activities. One afternoon, Mom and I were sitting in the yard of her old rental that looked from SoBe over the Biscayne Bay to Miami proper. We weren't drinking anything stronger than homemade lemonade when she suddenly locked me in her sights and said, — He wanted you down here, but you knew that, right? You know he sleeps with whores?

I turned away and looked out across the bay. Stared at the sunlight bouncing off the slick, blue-black waters. She seemed not to pick up on my discomfort, just carried on dissing him. I shut it out; couldn't take any more of her bitterness against my father. She didn't know how important it was for me to see him in a certain way. If I didn't, it was all for nothing. After a while, she wound down. — I'll say no more on the subject, Lucy, but you don't know the half of it, and that's probably just as well.

It was impossible to get a scholarship for martial arts, so I'd reluctantly switched back to track and field for the purposes of securing a general sports one, with a coaching bias, at Miami University. Some time later, in my freshman year, I decided to head back to Boston to pay Dad a surprise visit. He had long ago moved from Weymouth to a downtown city brownstone apartment, which was way cool. He'd started to have success as a writer, was living a little and seemed much less uptight. Could have done with being more fucking uptight; after opening the door with a flourish, he looked at me and clearly wasn't comfortable. I soon saw why, as this twitchy young junkie chick showed up immediately behind me. Dad claimed that she was helping him research this novel he was planning. It was bullshit. So in that instant I went from believing that my mom had simply abandoned us, to accepting that he had a shitload to do with it.

— Wonderful, Lonnie, just wonderful . . . Okay, I'll keep in touch . . . goodbye . . . Mom hangs up, as a buffed-and-waxed skating fag sweeps down the street. Mom says something catty about the rollers being a "busboy's convertible." I decide lunch is my treat and signal for the check, waving Mom down when she protests. — Thanks, Lucy, she says sheepishly. Mom might be a snobbish breadhead but she's no tightwad. — Listen, picks, I need a little favor.

— Name it, I say recklessly, instantly regretting it.

No going back now though, as we head to get her car, which she's put in the multistory lot. On Collins, Mom suddenly locks my arm. We've strolled past the tourists, shoppers, diners, and drinkers, crossing to the cheapo strip between Collins and Washington, where Lincoln is all scuzzy low-rent electrical and luggage stores. Bums and mentally ill people try to outdo each other for the attentions of the bug-eyed, camera-wielding visitors who've strolled off the beaten track. A guy comes up to us. — I haven't eaten for two days.

— Well done. Stick with it, but build in cardio. I hand him my card.

— He needed money *for food*, Mom ticks.

— Oh . . . I kinda thought he was too well dressed to be a beggar . . . I can get so myopic, I concede, ushering her down the street as the bum studies the card, and growls something incomprehensible. Thankfully, we cross over Washington and we're instantly back in high-end SoBe.

We pick up the car, heading down Alton, Mom driving me across the great divide of Biscayne Bay, from Miami Beach to Miami proper. What the fuck is the new gateway to the Americas but a goddamn illusion? It's a ghost town; those empty stacks of apartments. Nobody wants to be here.

Mom smells my contempt. — It's really picking up down here, she insists.

I roll doubtful eyes. The sidewalks are empty enough to make most mid-rent LA neighborhoods look like rush-hour Manhattan.

We're driving down Bayside, to the forty-story apartment block in which Ben Lieberman has bought a big share, sinking in all their savings, and which Mom is managing. Practically empty, and not one single purchase. The structure, which her squeeze took off the hands of some shady Colombians (there must be another kind in Miami, but I've yet to meet them) when it seemed like a good idea, has four apartments on each of its forty floors. Only two are currently leased—both discounted—on the seventh and twelfth floors, one to a woman who takes clients there from the nearby offices for lunchtime sex, the other given to a local entertainment and cultural journalist on the basis he'll write some fiction in his column about an emergent vibrant downtown scene. They are basically paying rent for the building maintenance and services, not that there seems to be much of those.

112

— It *will* happen, Mom says in breathless optimism, her crazy eyes rising toward the penthouse on the top of this stacked pile of rabbit hutches. — I mean, Bayside is two blocks away, across the street, and the American Airlines arena is practically on the doorstep.

— Yeah, right.

— Lime have opened up a branch next to the new Starbucks on Flagler, she squeals. — There's the new Marlins baseball stadium, and a new museum square planned—

— South Florida will always be about the beaches, Mom, it doesn't need a vibrant downtown. The city won't spend a municipal buck on jack—

— We got the lowest taxes—

— And that's our choice, I cede, — but the cost of that choice is a ghost town in the sun.

Mom's hand tightens white on the wheel. — You will help me out, pickle? she begs, as we leave the car on the empty sidewalk, not even bothering with the building's off-street parking at the rear. She opens the glass-fronted door of the block with one key. — All you need to do is come in once a week, check everything's okay, pick up the mail from the boxes downstairs and dump it back at the office. Only for a month, honey, well, six weeks . . .

— You and Lieb will be on this cruise together for six whole weeks and you barely talk to each other now?

Mom's voice goes so high it almost breaks. — It's a big risk, and both Lieb and I are aware of that, and she takes a deep breath, dropping several octaves. — I guess it really is the last-chance saloon; it could be the end, or maybe a new dawn.

113

Her eyes mist up. — Whatever, we owe ourselves that shot. Also . . . we need to explore real-estate possibilities in the Caribbean, she says defiantly.

— Oh, Mom . . . I hug her, wincing at the scent of the garlic-heavy dressing on her breath. Mine will be the same. I need to pick up some Listerine from CVS.

— Baby, baby, my darling pickle. She pats me on the back, as a *boing* announces the impending presence of the elevator, thankfully breaking our grip. We step inside and feel our legs tingle as it accelerates impressively to the fortieth floor.

The apartments all have two bedrooms and great views out over Miami, parceled off into its blocks and streets, all the way across to the bay. But the design in this show apartment, which Mom calls "neoloft," just totally sucks. I bite my tongue, but a separate galley kitchen, situated off a hallway, is just lame. If it's "loft," it should be open-plan, flowing into the spacious living room, utilizing the light from the floor-to-ceiling windows on two sides. The only thing "loft" about it is the fake exposed brickwork on one wall and the thick steel beam running along the ceiling, held up by three pillars, one at each end, and one in the middle of the room. The only rad thing about that is you could hang a heavy bag there. It has a big stone fireplace, and a polished, dark, hardwood floor. Mom explains that the industrial "neoloft" style was designed to appeal to northern transplants. I'm sure it seemed a good idea at time, and the architect and developer had a lot of fun when they did all that coke together, but down here in the tropics, it feels like an incongruous mess. There will be no rush to buy or rent these places.

Mom fusses, rubbing Canute-style, at some mark on the window with her sleeve. I'm looking out across to Miami Beach and civilization. That's where I'll have my new crib when the money from that TV deal comes in, one of those killer blocks at South Pointe. Kick fucking ass! Succumbing to the burn of excitement, I call Valerie, nodding curtly to Mom in apology, but there's no need—she welcomes the attempt to get straight into her own iPhone.

Valerie picks up in three rings. — Lucy, glad you phoned, she says, her tone making something inside me slide south. I'm braced for what comes next. — Thelma and Waleena at VH1, and there's no other way of putting this, have basically crapped out on us. The heat from Quist has got the channel nervous. They are trying to go with somebody else for *Shape Up or Ship Out*. I wish now we'd signed those fucking contracts, but I never anticipated this . . . I'm doing all I can to get them to reconsider . . . Lucy? Are you there?

— Yes, I tell her curtly. Botoxed fuckers! Those vagina flaps as stiff as rubber doors in a fucking abattoir. I force down my rage. — See what you can do, and keep in touch.

— For sure. Remember, they ain't the only show in town!

— Thanks, I say, clicking off the phone.

Mom's real-estate agent nose can smell a Florida disaster a mile away. — Everything good, pickle?

No. On the contrary, everything is going to fucking shit, but I'm not going to tell her that. — You know, I sing, looking around, — I'm thinking what a great place this would be to work out!

— There's a gym right here, on this floor. Mom points

115

through the wall. — It has some cardio equipment. I don't suppose anybody would mind if you made use of it.

— Well, there's nobody here to mind, I tell her, watching her face fall again as we head next door to check it out. This is an open-plan space (as the apartments should be), containing two pristine treadmills, standing criminally idle. They are both still partially wrapped in polyethylene sheeting, the packing around them discarded. There's also a set of dumbbells on a rack. My head starts to buzz with the possibilities.

— There are plans to get a full set of gym equipment eventually, Mom nods.

— Once you get a few units rented and bring in some revenue, I suppose.

— Yes . . . Mom winces as if I've just kidney-punched her. She hands me the keys, then drops me off back over on the Beach.

In my cramped apartment, I stretch out and lift some hand weights for an hour, then flop onto the small two-seater couch which practically fills this crappy space. The asshole downstairs is pounding out some butt-fucking techno, forcing me to switch on the TV and drown it out with an infomercial for a faddy home gym, like the one they are supposedly going to send me, which, in any case, is just designed to gather dust in a lardass closet.

I'm thinking about that great space Mom has. Some folks have everything and appreciate nothing. I can feel my own new apartment and car slipping away. I look outside. No paparazzi, except that creep whose camera I trashed. It was

116

a mistake to make it personal; now that soiled fuck will never let go. I feel a steady rage burning inside me. I call Thelma at the TV channel and it goes to voicemail. — I know why you're avoiding me. Well, I've dealt with fake assholes before. Fake, frightened assholes. They never stood in my way. They won't this time. Show some fucking balls!

Fuck . . . I shouldn't have done that! I'm floundering, switching off, when a call from Sorenson comes straight up. She tells me she's started getting back into her work and she'd love me to come over and look at her stuff. — I've sooo much energy since I started this program, Lucy. I know that we met under terrible circumstances, but you know, I sometimes feel it was destiny that brought us together!

— Okay, I'm on my way, I hear myself saying. Jeez, when your best offer is a creepy dwarf, you know your social life is on the slide.

— All righty, she sings. — See ya!

Little does this *beetchball* know that I'm not in the mood to be fucked with. I'm going to inventory the contents of her refrigerator and cupboards, and if they ain't up to shape her Scandinavian ass will know the meaning of the word "pain."

With the Cadillac's engine wheezing all the way, by the time I get to Sorenson's I'm in no mood for bullshit. I decline her offer of coffee and tell her to make some green tea from a proferred box of bags I picked up earlier. She grudgingly complies, asking me about my day. I tell her all about the television bullshit. — Media assholes. They have no goddamn balls and no enthusiasm, unless it comes to cheerleading some Bible-belt, needle-dicked fascist!

117

— I hate them all, Lena says, and suddenly tears across the room, picking up a large piece of black curtain material from the dining table, which she starts hanging over the window curtain pole, trying to turn Florida into Illinois or Minnesota. — I don't want them shooting their long lenses in here . . . I know I keep going on about it, but I am just so sorry about that video clip. It's an artist's thing, we have to record, we have to exhibit . . . but I feel so cheap—

— Chill, I tell her sharply, exasperated by her constant fucking apologies. — Look, I'd really like to see what you're working on.

Sorenson's face crinkles in pain. She lets the curtain fall. — I don't feel right about showing people . . . I mean, I—

— Why the fuck call me up and tell me to come see it if you don't want me to? What kinda games are you playing here?

— I do, she flushes, — it's just . . .

— Just what?

— I get nervous!

— I'm not a fucking art critic, Lena, I tell her, rising out of my chair, resting the mug of tea on the polished wood floor. — The only criticism you'll get from me is centered on your lifestyle. I don't have the qualifications or inclination to criticize your *work*. So either show me what you were gonna show me, or don't waste any more of my fucking time. What'll it be?

— Okay . . . she groans, and reluctantly takes me out to the garden. — You must promise not to touch anything, she says, as she opens the studio doors.

— Why would I touch something, Lena? It's your shit.

— I'm sorry . . . I guess I have trust issues.

— I guess you do, I agree, which doesn't cheer her, as we step inside and she clicks on overhead lights which blink awake, exposing the space. Then she goes over to the wall and pulls open a series a series of thick, dark window shades. The sunlight pours in and she switches off the lights.

I was expecting an arty-crafty chick haunt, but this place is more like a dude's workshop. The first thing that hits me are the smells—vaguely sulfurous, catching in my nose—and I find myself rubbing at my watering eyes. The space has two big benches with loads of power tools—saws, drills, and some shit I've never seen before. There are piles of tins of paint, and bottles of chemicals, obviously where the pungent aroma (which Sorenson seems oblivious to) originates. She notes my discomfort and clicks on a powerful exhaust fan. I'm looking at a huge, steel boxlike device. — Is that a kiln?

— No. She points at a smaller contraption in a corner. — That's the kiln over there. This is my incinerator.

— Right, I nod, impressed, now looking at these huge fucking molds, like they are made for the bones of prehistoric animals. It gives me the impression there's more to Sorenson than meets the eye, another side to this silly girly-girl. There are some big sculptures, with bones set in a fiberglass-like resin. On heavy-duty shelving sit glass jars and plastic containers full of animal bones. It's like a Holocaust scene; you can imagine Dr. Josef Mengele's lab being like this. All those little monster men, being constructed from those cleaned rat and bird bones . . . this bitch is fucking psycho! Is this the same person who looks at animals on Cute Overload?

119

— This is where I . . . sort of work . . . she says apologetically.

And there are some standard Miami paintings, all bright colours reflecting the light, but nothing you won't see in any gallery. What really grabs my attention is a tall structure, which looks like a figure, with a sheet draped over it.

— What's under there?

— Oh, it's just a work-in-progress. I don't like showing it at this stage.

— Fair enough, I tell her, again examining her smaller bone sculptures on the benches and shelves.

Sorenson's lip turns down, and she says to me, — I strip the flesh from the bones of animals and birds, and clean them.

I must be looking in some sort of horror as she's moved to explain, — I don't kill them or hurt them, they're all creatures who have perished naturally.

— Right, I say, bending down and looking at a cluster of little figures of lizard-men.

— All the fur and features, skin and tissue and organs go into the incinerator, and she drums with her fingers on the big iron furnace. — I keep the bones, reassembling the ones of different species into my new skeletal structures, modifying them, giving the creatures, say, maybe longer legs. I'll sometimes recast anatomically correct fake bones in my molds. But I much prefer to source the bones of another animal if possible.

— Wow. Where do you get the animals? Like, you don't go into a pet store and ask for half a dozen dead rats? I start

120

thinking of Miles's dog, poor Chico, how his bones seem to be little bigger than many of the ones Lena has here.

— No, of course not, she laughs, then shrugs and says, — Well . . . yes, in a manner of speaking. After they've died of course. I go around and pick up the dead ones. Parrot World is a good place for me. I also get around the zoos. Obviously, I pay for them.

— But why animal bones?

— It gives the composition authenticity. I'd like to think that some part of the spirit of those poor tiny creatures goes into my figures, and she points to her little mutant men and women on the shelves. — I'm thinking, she says wistfully, — you're a kind of sculptor too. I guess I'm your work-in-progress.

For some reason that strikes me as a creepy thing to say. — I'm just glad I'm making progress with something, I spit, suddenly stung again by the weakness of those TV assholes.

— I believe in you, Lucy, Sorenson responds as if reading my mind, and I'm more touched than I should be. — That man was crazy. He'd have just kept on shooting.

— Yes, he would, Lena, I nod in agreement, now shamed by the power I've ceded to her, which compels me to look her in the eye. — You say you believe in me?

— Yes, she says, disconcerted, — of course I do. I thought I'd said—

— Do you *really* believe in me?

— Yes, she repeats, now all excited and brushing her fringe out of those eyes. — Yes, I do!

I stare right into her loser soul. What do I see? A weak,

121

bullied wretch. — Then will you stop fucking around and help me to help you get better?

Sorenson is so taken aback her breath catches as her hand reflexively flies to her chest. — What do you mean? I *am* getting better, she whimpers. — I . . . I think I am . . .

— No. You're a liar.

— What?

— Follow me! And I storm out the workshop, across the yard, and back into the house.

Sorenson is in frantic pursuit. — Wait, Lucy, where are you going?

Ignoring her, I march into the kitchen and pull open the cupboards. Knew it: she's stocked up on shit again. I pull out a box of crappy cereal and open it up. — Sugar. Nothing more, nothing less, I pour it into the garbage can. I shake my head slowly and point to the bathroom. — The scale, Lena. The bathroom scale can be your best friend or your worst enemy!

I move back down the hallway. Some family photos sit on a bookcase. Parents, friends, student types, though no boyfriends or lovers. But you can almost see the space they've recently occupied. There's some of Sorenson, slim, and a closet hottie if you got rid of those black bangs, and that tense, worried face. I'm gripped by a sudden urge, an inspiration that almost shocks me in its violent intensity. — I want you to take off all your clothes. Down to your underwear.

— What? She looks at me, first a nervous smile, which drifts into horror as she can see I'm not joking. — No! Why would you want me to do that?

— That good shit back in there, I point to the workshop,

— this fucking sham in here, I nod to the kitchen. — How do I reconcile the two, Lena? Because it isn't the same person who is producing the fucking *sick* shit in the workshop who is vegging out here. The person in the workshop has fucking balls! I've seen your exhibition stuff, and now I wanna see what *you* are exhibiting every day to the world. And I want *you* to see it too. All your clothes! Take them off!

— No! I don't want to!

— You said you believed in me. You record me and exhibit it to the world, and you won't even do this! You lied, like you've been lying about everything!

— I . . . I'm not . . . I can't . . . she gasps, and fuck me, the whackoid bitch starts convulsing, struggling for breath.

I begin to get worried. — You're okay, I soothe her.

— I'M NOT! I'M NOT OKAY! Sorenson cries out in pain.

I lower my voice. I'm stroking her arm. — No. And that's why you have to do this. You should not be reacting like this.

— I know, and she turns to me with the most pathetic, beaten nod I've seen, her face creased in pain, — it's just that Jerry, he made me—

I freeze: what the fuck . . .? — Okay, I'm sorry. Forget it.

Then she half turns away, but starts to tug off her top. A bra rips into wobbling, white goosebumped flesh. A muffin belly and love handles hang disgustingly over her sweat pants.

— You have to take off *all* your clothes, Lena, I almost whisper.

She pouts for a second, then shrugs, now ludicrously almost like a defiant hooker, faced with the attentions of a kinky, psychotic john. I'm feeling sick. I think something is going to come up but I force it down. My eyes water as

Sorenson pulls down her sweat pants and steps out of them. God, she repulses me. I can barely look at her, my body tense as I grab her fleshy wrist and pull her through to the bathroom, positioning her on the scale.

— The scale, how I hate to stand on that fucking scale, she says, anger giving her face structure and character.

I'm looking at her blazing, hateful eyes and thinking of the park, Abbie Adams Green, the smell of freshly mown grass in my nostrils. It's nothing to do with that. I catch my breath. Get past that shit. *Seize control!* — What does that say?

— Two hun . . . she sobs, — two hund—

— Two hundred and two pounds! I drag her, traumatized and tearful, to the full-length mirror. I snatch an old framed photo from the bookcase, and hold it up to her face. — Who is that?

— Me.

— Who is me?

— Lena . . . Lena Sorenson.

I point at the blobby mess in the mirror. — Who in the name of fucking hell is that?

— Mi-mi-mi-meee . . . Leee-na—

— Lena who?

— Lena Sorenson!

— THAT IS *NOT* LENA SORENSON! I point at the blobby wreckage in the mirror.

— No . . . Sorenson's hand goes to her eye. She's shaking.

I'm feeling stronger now. Drawing power from the righteous mission. — That is some fat, crazy, obnoxious, sweaty monster who has swallowed Lena Sorenson! Lena Sorenson is in there, I poke at her gross, doughy gut and stare into those frightened

124

eyes in the mirror's reflection. I whisper into her ear, — We have to set Lena Sorenson free. You and me.

— Free . . . Sorenson mindlessly parrots.

— Will you help me set Lena Sorenson free?

A pathetic nod.

— I CANNOT HEAR A GODDAMN THING! I bark at her, as she winces and recoils. — How can that gaping mouth be large enough to shovel all that goddamned crud into it, and yet nothing can come out of it? WILL YOU STAND UP?! WILL YOU COME FORWARD?! WILL YOU HELP ME SET LENA SORENSON FREE?!

— Yes—

— I CANNOT HEAR YOU! WHO ARE WE GONNA SET FREE?

— Lena . . . Lena Sorenson—

— SHOUT IT! SHOUT IT IN MY FUCKING FACE! Go on, tell me: who in the name of holy hell are we gonna set free?!

Her eyes crinkle, fists balling at her side, as she erupts in a beautiful wail of righteous anger. — LENA SORENSON!

— WHO!

— LENA SORENSON!

I turn toward the mirror, looking at her blotchy red face, snot running from her nose. — They've locked Lena up—do you see how they did that? Do you see how you let them lock that beautiful woman up? I wave the photograph in her face.

— Yes, yes, I see. She looks at her reflection, now focused in loathing. — How could I have been so stupid?! Oh God, what have I done?

125

— You're angry, I tell her, grabbing her plump shoulder, — and that's where I need you to be. But I don't want the anger turned in, because we call that depression. That's when we start eating shit, packing stuff into our mouths, to reward ourselves when we feel that things in life aren't going our way. I stand behind her, wrapping my arms around her wobbling mass. Whisper into her ear, — We've played that game, and it's a loser's game. No more.

— No. No more. She shakes her head in rage, as I step around to look into her eyes.

— We stand up. We come forward.

— Yes.

— But will you help me to help you? Will you work with me, *really* work with me, to set Lena Sorenson free?

— Yes! Yes. Yes. Yes, I will!

I've got Little Miss SoBe where I want her, a whimpering but defiant mass of wobbly Jell-O, here in my arms. And I feel her letting it all go—the self-hate, the abuse, the anger, the denial, the victimhood, and, very soon, the fat. The embodiment of all that ugly fucked-mind shit. — We're ready, sister, I tell her. — We are ready to start fighting back, and I offer my hand up in a high five, which she at first waveringly, then properly responds to. — Welcome to the Lena Sorenson Escape Committee!

10

CONTACT 4

To: michelleparish@lifeparishoners.com
From: lucypattybrennan@hardass.com
Subject: I Don't Get It

Hi Michelle,

Once again, I'm shamelessly hitting you up for professional advice. I have a client, an artsy chick, who seems to have everything, but she's been eating herself to death. She makes sculptures and figurines out of animal bones, yet she sends me pictures of furry animals from hokey websites! Is this bitch a raving psychopath?

Her family live back up north in Minnesota. It's a part of the world I've never taken to, probably because I had a bad experience with a guy from St. Paul once. Anyway, this chick has no boyfriend and seems to be friendless. Maybe she needs to get laid—don't we all, right?!

Any advice on how to whip this particular self-indulgent lardass into shape?

Best,

Luce x

PS The world-domination project is suspended. I've been getting a lot of heat through all this pedophile stuff. Bizarre shit, right, but the cable company have totally pussied out. I'm smelling fake people, Michelle. I don't do fake.

PPS Morning Pages . . . I dunno if I can roll with that. Each to their own but I don't think it's *pour moi*.

To: lucypattybrennan@hardass.com
From: valeriemercando@mercandoprinc.com
Subject: Please, Calm Down!

Lucy,

Thelma called and said that you left a highly abusive and somewhat threatening message on her voicemail.

Please do not contact her or anyone else at the channel when you are in such an agitated state! You are undermining everything I'm trying to do on your behalf!

I know this is distressing, but there isn't a whole lot more that I can say to you, except that it is absolutely imperative that you don't speak to the media. Leave the communication with the TV people with me—it's what I'm paid to do!

Best,

Valerie

Another fake ass!

128

11

DEMON

Paradise has a smell, and it's sewage. A little rain, the drains go down, and there are very few Paddy dive bars in Southie whose shithouse smells as bad as SoBe after a tropical storm. Unless you wanna paddle through stagnant water you can't even walk across Alton to Taste Bakery to get a healthy breakfast. I'm not down with that, not in sneakers. The sun is pumping out and it will soon evaporate this lake of shit, but it'll take two or three hours.

A text comes in from Grace Carillo, asking me if we're still on for our sparring session later. This arrangement slipped my mind but that's *exactly* what I need. I go back home and fix myself a protein shake (450 cal), and Miles calls. — Lucy . . . how's things going with you, babe?

— I'm good, I say cagily.

— I'm calling to apologize for how I was the other day.

— Accepted. I was a little short too.

— Cool. I hear him clear his throat. — Listen, there's another thing . . .

Here it comes. — Riiight . . .

— . . . and there's no way of saying this without sounding a total asshole.

I'm instantly thinking: in your case, there's no way of

saying *anything* without sounding like that, but I'm biting that caustic tongue. It was a mistake to leave trash talk on Thelma's voicemail. You confront a bitch direct. Now bitch got witnesses. Bitch got evidence. I suck down some air.

— Lucy? You still there?

— Yes . . . it's a very bad connection though, I lie.

— I need you to spot me five hundred bucks. For my rent. I've been put on a leave of absence pending this invalidity insurance investigation, and I'm maxed out on my Visa and MasterCard.

— I can't hear you for all this static . . . I tell him, scraping my nail against the cell's mouthgrid. — What a terrible reception . . .

— I said I need you to spot me—

— You're breaking up, Miles . . . I'm driving . . . let me get back to you . . .

I click off my phone, lowering it to the table, and finish my shake. Then I'm heading over to Bodysculpt and a session with Sorenson. After our shit last night she comes in with a slightly candy-assed stare, but there's determination in her stride. I don't trust the shitty loser scale in her bathroom. I know through experience the tendency of a fat bitch to simply fuck with a scale until it produces the numbers she craves. So I give her the kettlebell routine, and in between I'm hammering her with starbursts, squats, lunges, burpees, and squat thrusts, and a rake of floor ab exercises—straight crunches, vertical leg crunches, bicycles, Russian twist (with medicine ball)—until she's gasping and glowing. Then she's gloved up and even though I show her how to throw a jab,

130

right cross, left hook, right hook, uppercut, she's hitting the bag like a pussy till I shout at her to step it the fuck up. Then I have her back on the other exercises and she's gasping, groaning, and reddening, and I can see Lester's raised eyebrows, so I cool it, and stick her on the elliptical, making her pump those pedals and levers at high speed. Sorenson cannot speak when she steps off the machine, like Neil Armstrong onto the lunar surface; I'm watching her burn like a motherfucker, while gently urging, — Breathe in through your nose, exhale through your mouth!

She's feeling pleased with herself through the pain, and I am too, but when I haul her ass onto a real scale, she's still over 200 lbs at the weigh-in, 200.75 to be fucking precise! — That's so disappointing, she says, then smiles, all back in ass-licking Scandi-Minnesota mode, — but I'm moving in the right direction!

I fucking say when a bitch move! I fucking say when she breathe! — You're not going anywhere, I bark. — Do you really think that two fucking pounds at this stage, with what you've been doing, means jackshit? I lower my voice, as I see Mona's ears prick up. Hovering bitch has an anorexic Condé Nast twig on a mat nearby, doing pussy stretches, purely for eavesdropping purposes. But it's unprofessional to curse out a client, and it won't have gotten past that scheming creepette. That hoe manipulates and undermines. Like Sorenson here. Where did she go for breakfast? Jerry's Deli? Pork chops and fat shit stuffed into her own fucking porky chops? She gotta be told. — I'm less than impressed, Lena. It's all about numbers. I wanted a substantially bigger drop.

— Well, I did too . . .

Bitch still cramming for the big-booty examinations. — Are you following the diet sheet?

A guilty pout; caught with her fucking doughy fist in the cookie jar! — I, I'm trying, I—

— We don't *try*, we *do*! You need to *do*, I tell her, as I catch Mona's devious, glacial features light up an amp or three. Fuck you, Frisbee flaps! I turn back to Sorenson. — Right, I gotta go, and I pick up my bag. As I head out I can feel her abandoned-child eyes tracking me out the door. The sun is bright, and I squint, realizing I've forgotten my Ray-Bans, but I'm not going back in there. I try to stay in the shade all the way down Washington, to the Miami Mixed Martial Arts club on 5th.

The air conditioning blasts you when you walk into the MMMA but it can't displace those satisfying real gym aromas of sweat, liniment, and adrenaline. Thank God for this place, all heavy bags, pull-up bars, and solid weights and cardio equipment, two full-sized boxing rings, and an octagon. Emilio (5'10", 145 lbs) emerges from behind the desk to greet me with a big hug. — Hey, you!

— Hey!

He breaks off and jumps back like a kangaroo in reverse gear. — Lookin good, Lucy B!

— You too, honey, I crack a bleachtray-whitened smile, which I hope mirrors his more professional and costly job. Emilio had a solid boxing record as a pro (24-2-8, 11 KOs). He was a ranked IBF number 8 contender and WBC number 10 at one time. Of his eight losses, three came in his last

trio of fights, with two of them by stoppage. The writing was on the wall; he'd gone from being a hot prospect to a decent scalp for rising, hungry young guns, and (uniquely in the lemminglike world of dude boxing) he had the good sense to read it as such. His nose has been broken a couple of times but it's set well, and his pretty, boyish face is almost unmarked. He always was a boxer rather than a slugger. Now he runs this place and keeps to his fighting welterweight poundage.
— Great to have a *proper* workout today though, I tell him, and he gives me an affirmative nod; Emilio has his own roster of lardasses at some fake joint, in order to pay the bills.

I stretch out for a full twenty minutes. The older you get, the more essential this boring routine becomes. A muscle strain or, worse, a tear, takes longer to get over and being sidelined is not an option. I *need* to work out. Without it I'd go fucking crazy. Especially now. It centers me. I need to do more of this in order to stay cool. Mercando's right: I need to shut the fuck up and keep my head down.

I do a further twenty minutes of jumping jacks, squats, burpees, and some hops, in preference to the jump rope, as that messes up the lactic acids in the arms if you plan on throwing punches later. Then I wrap up my hands and do three rounds of shadowboxing with three-pound hand weights before gloving up and doing four rounds on the heavy bags, mixing up combos—jab, straight right, left hook, jab, double jab, right, right hook, right cross, uppercuts—finding a beautiful rhythm that takes me into another place. As always, sad nemesis faces materialize on the battered leather bag as I strike:

BANG! The fascist shitbag Quist.

BANG! The insipid slimy Thorpe.

BANG! The fucking coward McCandless.

BANG! The filthy creepy pedophile Winter.

BANG! The scheming fake Mona.

BANG! The rubber-lipped faggot Toby.

BANG! The Botox fake ass Thelma.

BANG! The Botox fake ass Valerie.

BANG! THE ASSHOLE IN THE PARK . . . FUCKING CLINT AU—FUCK THAT! FUCK THAT! FUCK THAT! GET PAST THAT SHIT!

BANG! The greedy needy loser Sorenson.

BANG! The greedy needy loser Sorenson.

BANG! Sorenson. BANG! Sorenson. BANG FUCKING SORENSON . . .

I'm panting and drenched in sweat as the rounds fly past. Then I wind down and get in four times ten pull-ups on the bar. I drop to the mat, feeling that burn, that delicious purr inside, and take a long, frosty drink of H_2O. Grace Carillo from the MDPD has come in, and greets me with a croc's smile. Her strut is good, catwalk-arrogant, but her ass belongs to me. After a sleek, pantherlike stretch, she's wrapping her hands and I'm gloving up again, mouthguard in and headgear on, as we climb through the ropes with Emilio. I wear a Title protective sports bra with reinforced chest guards, which is fine for sparring, though I note Grace is clad in the heavy armour: the full female training chest protector. She looks real badass, with that dusky skin set off against the black headguard, titguard, gloves, no-foul-groin and abdomen protector, and the shin-high boots. Way too much for sparring though: I smell gun-shy.

Emilio sets the bell and Grace and I touch gloves and commence our tight dance. With those long rangy arms, she's a tough, awkward motherfucker; there is a solid left jab to get past. Let that bitch control the distance and she'll torture and frustrate you all day. I'm looking at the beads of moisture spotting on her face between the lines of the headgear, my thoughts drifting to her pussy and how sweaty it would be, but how sweet it would taste . . .

BANG!

Motherfucker! I see stars as a solid straight right pushes through my guard, snapping me back into the here and now. *Que perra se determina . . . bitch got game . . .* I can't have this, and I shake my head and move forward, determined to get inside this fucker. I have to take another, but I snap it off, cause I'm where I want to be, and I let go with a vicious hook to the body, Micky Ward style. *Sweet spot*, I purr to myself, watching the wind squeeze from her accordioning frame. — Sorry, sugar, I say as she winces and sucks in air, still folded like a razor.

— Easy, ladies, Emilio warns, as Grace shakily gets upright, and we're back at it again.

It's now a technical show, as the sting has gone out of Grace's jab. When Emilio earnestly calls time we end on a sweaty embrace and I'm digging her musky scent as it mingles with her perfume.

We hit the showers and Grace strips off unselfconsciously. Oh, man, the body on that chick. — You really got me good

135

there, she smiles, rubbing that taut, sleek torso as she steps into a cubicle. If she didn't have a boyfriend, I swear to God I would try and tap, tap, tap me that MDPD ass until it pooped nuggets of gold! I'm berthed in the adjoining trap, touching myself, thinking of how I could just step next door with my terry cloth and soap up that pussy . . .

In my mind I make that short step and Grace's big lips are on mine and I'm sliding my hands around her ass and we're grinding our crotches together and then I'm hunkering down onto my knees to feast on that sweet bounty . . . no bitch tastes finer than one with a fusion of Latin and African American blood coursing through her veins . . . — Ohhhh . . .

— You okay, Lucy? Grace's head snaps around the corner of my stall.

— The water got kinda cold all of a sudden, I say, stepping back in terror.

— It can do that, she smiles, stepping out, big yellow beach towel like a candy wrapper around that sweet block of milk chocolate.

I'm too mortified to say anything so I get myself dried off and pull on my clothes.

Sometimes Grace and I grab a drink or a sandwich, but she's back on call, so I'm on a solitary walk up to Lincoln. It's hot now, the Bank of America clock is saying 80 but it feels more like 90, and I'm heading down the street, browsing in store windows, and to kill time I go into Books & Books. I start looking at the art books, which I generally never do, and I realize why I'm acting this way when I see the spine:

LENA SORENSON: FUTURE HUMAN

I pick it up and leaf through the pages. There are numerous plates of the little bird-boned monster men with their reptile-green translucent skins I saw Sorenson trying to assemble in her workshop. I'm scanning around shiftily as I read, worried the stalking loser will come in, catch me red-handed, and identify me as being *like her*. So I take the book up to the cashier and pay the ludicrously expensive price of $48. I feel both relieved and exploited as the sales clerk slips it into a brown bag. It makes me wonder what Sorenson or the photographer and/or author team of Mathew Goldberg and Julius Carnoby get paid for this?

Retracing my steps, I continue down Washington. On 14th I'm arrested by the presence of a man with greasy blond, sun-bleached hair, his skin tanned under a coat of grime, clad in the middle-aged Miami sex offender's uniform of grubby Hawaiian shirt and stained beige shorts. I can't quite believe it: it's Winter. Timothy Winter. The fucking pedophile, the short-eyes whose miserable ass I was stupid enough to save! He's with a balding obese guy with a grimy layer of sweat on his pustular face. This guy wears a buttoned vest and nothing else on top; a brown gut swells down to an underpants waistband with *David Beckham* embroidered on it. Although this fucking tramp must be in his forties, his pants hang hip-hop style below his gross ass. It's Winter who revolts me most, though; his sneer of entitlement as he tries to bum cigarettes from smokers standing outside one of the Irish themed pubs. He doesn't even recognize me when our eyes meet! A doorman, sitting on a stool outside, tracks him and Fatboy Gross down the street.

I follow him, watching as Winter, egged on by his blubbery sidekick, panhandles some change from a group of vacationing girls who look grossed out, as well they might. I want to punch that monster's smug face in. But it's Washington and it's broad daylight and this asshole has caused me enough grief as it is. Flight takes over from fight: exit stage fuck.

I go home and lay the art book out on my small coffee table, flipping through some of the plates. What is it with all this sci-fi and monsters stuff? I'm betting Sorenson was the love-starved chunky goth chick who hung around with the fucked-up losers and nerds, the type who attend those science-fiction and comic-book conventions. It all makes sense. I can smell her pathetic cosseting of those twitching semi-autistic weirdos, as I turn every page to let myself pause over the nauseating notes. Something makes me check my cell; I knew it, a couple of bland messages from Sorenson. I am *so* going to hunt this bitch down.

I change and drive up to her house, parking around the corner. Creeping into the backyard, bending down behind the big hibiscus bushes, I look into the living room. Sorenson is stuffing her face from a bag full of cookies. I know the brand and there are 250 calories per cookie, and ten to a package. She's about halfway through that poison and on course to self-mutilate further by finishing the fucking lot. She disgusts me; she's worse than any pathetic junkie or alcoholic, no better, really, than those sniveling predatory pedophiles who can't keep their cruddy hands off children.

The weak fuckers; how they always wear that same stupid, hapless expression. Looking for help. Well, I'll help you, you motherfuckers! I'll help every last one of you fucking pricks by drowning you like kittens! Cute fucking carnage!

I gaze through that window with hatred at the time- and energy-wasting beached whale washed up on the sofa, gaping mindlessly at her cable television. I pull my cell out my jeans pocket and hit her digits. — Lena. It's Lucy. What are you doing?

— Hey, Lucy. Sorenson pulls her bulk into an upright position. — I'm just watching TV.

— Are you eating shit? DO NOT LIE TO ME, LENA! I WILL KNOW IF YOU ARE LYING TO ME!

Sorenson shuffles a little bit, looking around, as if I'm in the room. I move back, further into shadow. Then she springs off the couch. — No . . . I'm just going to do some work . . . she cries, bustling into another room, causing me to lose visual contact. Now I can see her coming out through the back patio door, heading out toward her studio, looking nervously around again as she waddles through the falling darkness.

— I'll probably pop by in about twenty minutes or so.

— Oh . . . oh . . . oh . . . okay . . .

She turns and runs back into the kitchen. I steal forward, watching her through the big window, as her cookies go straight into the garbage. *I've just saved that fat fucking fool two hours of running on the treadmill.*

I stealthily tiptoe out the yard and down the street to the Caddy. Victory. Of sorts. I drive home and watch some of *The Biggest Loser* repeats and immediately fall into a fantasy about a three-way with Jillian and Bob Harper. Jillian has me on the treadmill, she's shouting at me, but I can tell that she's hot for the femme fake tears I'm shedding in order to lure her into my web. I'm storming along at 15 mph and Jillian ups the speed, and I spin off, into Bob's tattooed arms and I'm sobbing into his naked chest which smells of sweaty-man talc. I feel Jillian's hand in my hair, tearing my scalp, saying "you suck" and pushing my head south towards Bob's crotch. I look up and catch that manic gleam in his eye as I pull his dick out of his sweat pants. I'm sucking on it, taking it to the back of my throat as Jillian lets go my hair and joins me on her knees, alongside me, and is pushing my face away to get her share of Bob's cock. I'm ceding it to her hungry mouth but only in order to position myself behind her and get her into a ju-jitsu choke, and as her eyes bulge under his cruel thrusts, Bob starts to look a bit like Miles and I realize that Jillian is really Mona. *Not Mona and Miles, Bob and Jillian, Bob and Jillian* . . . My phone is on vibrate and I push it down the front of my panties. As I'm thinking about Bob and Jillian, it goes off, and I know it's Sorenson . . . that's it, you needy bitch, keep ringing . . .

. . . ooohhhh . . . shout louder, Jillian . . . tell me I'm a lazy bitch . . . slap me, Jillian . . . Bob, Jillian hurt me . . . kiss it better, Bob, kiss the fucker better . . . ooohh . . .

OOOOHHH . . . AAAAGGGHH!!

Holy moly . . . that was a goddamn tea party . . .

I'm fucking wet and breathless after that explosion as I pull the dripping phone out of my panties. It stops vibrating in my hand. The caller ID flashes up: LENA S. I get my breath, watching Jillian onscreen, bawling out one tub of lard, cutting to Bob shaking his head in that disappointed-but-caring parental way, the *exact* look Dad excelled in when I came up short in track and field or, later, in martial arts. Then I get back to Sorenson. — Lena, something came up. I'm not going to make it over.

— Oh . . . oh . . . oh . . .

— See you *mañana* at the gym, bright and oily!

— Oh . . . okay, I thought we could have—

— Till tomorrow. I click off the phone, then immediately call my dad, and tell him about the gun-shy TV mother-fuckers.

— Tough shit, pickle. I guess the moral of the story is: never trust the media. It's one big conspiracy by old WASP money—

— Fabulous segue into "you," Dad. What took you so long?

— Whaddaya mean? Can't I offer some support to my daughter—

— I've read all your shit, Dad. This is the plot of the second Matt Flynn book, *A State of Nature*. The one where Matt befriends the TV presenter in New England who's being sexually blackmailed by her own bosses at the corporation—

— Wow . . . you *do* read the books!

— Of course I do. I take an interest. You're my father. And I'm you're daughter. So reciprocate!

— Cut me a break, picks, your old pop is still reeling after the *Globe*'s review of *The Doomsday Scenario*. And I quote: "Try as he might, Tom Brennan will never be Dennis

Lehane. Which wouldn't be a big problem if being Tom Brennan was anything to write home about. Here's the news: it most certainly isn't. Matt Flynn is every corny, clichéd wish-fulfillment stereotype straight from the late-middle-aged Irish American male's fantasy list, as he hauls his wheezing bulk onto a bar stool and mops down some Guinness with his beef stew . . ." and this from my fucking hometown paper! The asshole that wrote it, Steve French, would never have the integrity to tell his dwindling band of readers that he's been papering his shithouse with publishers' rejection slips for fucking years! I oughta remind him that one Bostonian is a millionaire on the *New York Times* bestseller list, and the other is a prick clinging on to his miserable hack job—

— Enough already! I'm sorry to hear about the review. It might not mean anything to you, but I called you for support cause my life is going to shit!

I push the red button, then power off the cell.

Thankfully, as I switch on the local news, the tide does seem to be turning. There's no mention of me, for the first time in days! The most interesting feature is about the Wilks twins. About the organs they share and the ones they don't, and whether they can or cannot be separated. But now both twins have filed lawsuits against the other. Annabel Wilks has said that her sister, Amy, is preventing her from going on a date with her boyfriend Stephen. Amy has countered, claiming that her rights are infringed if Annabel drags her somewhere she doesn't want to go. Her lawyer is making a case for coercion. Their mother appears on the screen. — I don't wanna see them fight. They need to be together. Maybe we ought to have considered the operation to separate them when they were babies. Joyce Wilks's eyes grow big as she inhales on a cigarette. — But I believe it was God's will they came out together like they did.

I feel a little shaky and lie on the couch. My blood sugar must be low. I pick up the Sorenson book.

12

FUTURE HUMAN
—INTRODUCTION

"A science-fiction comic-book illustrator who gate-crashed the art world" was one critic's unflattering description of young American artist Lena Sorenson. Despite the derisive nature of that statement, it's true to say that Sorenson's futuristic, dystopian view of humanity greatly informs her perspective.

Lena Sorenson's mission, as expounded by her in her most successful exhibit of sculpture, *Future Human*, is to examine "what human beings, should they still be on this planet, will look like, and how they will behave, in several million years' time."

Sorenson, somewhat uniquely, had huge initial success as a freshman student at Chicago's renowned Art Institute. Her first exhibition, *Void*, the series of dystopian futuristic paintings, was exhibited at her own co-run Blue gallery in the city's West Loop, before being curated by Melanie Clement at her GoTolt gallery in New York City, after several pieces were purchased by influential collectors. The exhibition then went on to London, eventually touring the world to great acclaim. The major piece in the exhibit, also entitled *Void*, acquired by influential New York-based collector Jason Mitford, owed a debt to biblical-inspired English painter John Martin (1789–1854), whose huge canvases were set against panoramic and often apocalyptic backgrounds. Sorenson had reputedly seen Martin's work on a visit to

London's Tate Britain. Rather than look to Martin's biblical, creationist past, Sorenson, an avowed atheist, used the Englishman's scale and form to produce futuristic, dystopian landscapes. *The Fall of New Babylon* (2006), for example, is based on Martin's *The Fall of Babylon*. New Babylon is Los Angeles as viewed from Hollywood Hills.

Zero (2007) derives from Martin's *The Destruction of Pompeii and Herculaneum* (1821); Sorenson depicts a crumbling New York City. It's Ground Zero 9/11 reconstructed as the whole of mid and lower Manhattan Island. She confessed that as a teenager in Potters Prairie, MN, she was haunted by television images of the World Trade Center collapsing. *The End Trinity* (2007) is strongly based on Martin's *Last Judgment* triptych, with the end of the Earth and resurrection forecast.

Her smooth painted surfaces also recall the accomplished hyperrealistic offerings of illustrators, whose works are almost never seen in major galleries, and the likes of Dali, who himself was often denigrated as repetitive and populist by critics.

Yet if the critics dismissed Sorenson as a one-trick pony, this view had to be revised when she produced a satirical painting that garnered much political controversy. In *You're Lost Little Boy* (2008), a predatory Abe Lincoln cradles a clearly sexually aroused Minnie Mouse in his lap, as a tearful Mickey, head poking out from the side of Abe's chair, looks helplessly on. Sorenson's Lincoln appears to have slightly oriental features, and some have speculated that the piece could be a reference to America's changing (and increasingly subordinate) relationship with China, particularly with America's capitalist class's continuing investment there at the expense of developing the domestic economy. Sorenson steadfastly refuses to comment on this, trotting out the standard line, which artists love but makes the rest of us want to tear our hair out: "When an artist explains their art, it's no longer art. I am not a critic."

Some saw Sorenson's work as derivative of the earlier Young British Artists (YBAs), and coterminous with the type of shock tactics deployed in the UK by this group. Although she personally declared herself to be "unmoved" by the YBAs' work and processes, this seems somewhat disingenuous, as she was collected and championed by Manhattan socialite Mitford, in much the same way the YBAs had enjoyed the patronage of Charles Saatchi a decade earlier.

Though Sorenson's paintings would enthrall collectors, critics remained unimpressed, and the artist herself declared that she herself was dissatisfied with results, expressing a wish to move into sculpture. *Future Human* (2009) was the result. The sculptures of the evolved humans, adapting to the environment of a toxic Earth by scuttling like rats or feeding like flies on garbage mounds, moved collectors even more than the paintings. Sorenson's figures have been influenced by the bronze sculptures of Germaine Richier, particularly *Man of the Night,* the batlike Alien/Predator precursor of her effigies. This sculpture is on exhibit in Sorenson's alma mater, the Art Institute of Chicago. Like many of Sorenson's sculptures and paintings, the *Man* also has a prominent phallus. Her male figures are always strongly endowed to suggest a sexual potency and perhaps even high reproductive fertility, yet, paradoxically, there are many illustrations of dead babies. Thus we assume that Sorenson's humans are like rabbits; they must breed prolifically in order to ensure the future of the species. It is like medieval times, and the opposite of where we are at now, in that it is accepted that we are breeding and consuming toward our own extinction.

The critical establishment remains largely hostile, and in their exasperated, often ungracious and even vitriolic comments, one senses a genuine incomprehension of exactly why Sorenson has achieved such prominence. The phantom frustration in the words of Max Steinbloom is never far from the surface of their reactions: "Lena Sorenson should be in Hollywood making models for the big studios in their next productions of *Aliens* or *Predators*. Whatever else she is, she clearly is not an artist. She uses the gimmick of animal bones. That's all it is."

While Sorenson's work has often been decried by art critics ("speculative, of its nature fantastical, and thus bearing no relation to the human experience of today, other than serving as a rather trite warning about the stock ecological threats to the planet"), her series of sculptures of futuristic man, using the bones of small mammals and reptiles fused together in molds and resins, have nonetheless proved popular collectors' items. One of the pieces, *Plaything* (2009), where a mother cradles a dead or dying infant, while a male figure, presumably the father, looks on in bemused concern, garnered almost unprecedented attention and was purchased by a private collector for a reputed $14 million.

Lena Sorenson has now relocated to Miami, where she stated her appreciation of the work of Hong Kong-born Englishman Mark Handforth, who was the first Miami-based artist to exhibit at MOCA in 1996. It was his work that was said to have encouraged Sorenson to make her models and sculptures on a larger scale. "Small models lend a work no human perspective. The power of art like Mark Handforth's comes as much from scale as from concept. That was a valuable lesson for me." This indicates her desire to work on those larger, life-sized future humans.

13

CONTACT 5

To: lucypattybrennan@hardass.com
From: michelleparish@parishoner.com
Subject: My program is not about "whipping self-indulgent lardasses into shape"!

Lucy,

I don't want you to get the wrong idea here, because I really appreciate your zeal in the battle against obesity. But I think you must have a little more empathy with your clients!

These are people who have somehow lost their way in life, and have grown depressed and demotivated and then sought refuge in comfort food in order to give them a short-term spike.

They didn't get that way overnight, and it is often a long and painful road back to health for them. Yes, you need to be firm, but you need to look at the history, the needs and big life events for each client, including this artist lady. Remember, respect and love are the cornerstones of success!

I appreciate that programs have to be tailored toward individual needs, but I really do strongly recommend that you adopt the device of Morning Pages for this client. If you can get her to write 750 words every morning, then these might be able to form the basis of a discussion—though I stress that this has

to come from her, as they are her property. This woman is hurting psychologically. If you get to the source of that pain, then you're pushing at an open door.
Morning Pages can be an invaluable tool in helping you do that. Try it! Nothing
ventured, nothing gained!

I'm sorry to hear that you've been having problems. The media can be both
fickle and cruel.

Best,

Michelle

14

LUMMUS PARK

It's "unseasonably hot" today, as those assholes on the weather channel keep trumpeting. It said 92 on my cell-phone weather app, and I believe it. Thankfully, there's a cool breeze coming off the ocean. I'm running backward slowly down the track in Lummus Park, barking encourage-ment at the waddling Sorenson, who pants, groans, and sweats. — Go on, Lena! No room for quitters!

— Yes . . .

I burst into an impromptu chant. — Sack that bullshit, we ain't gon-na fucking quit! C'mon, Lena!

— Sack . . . that . . . bull . . . shhh . . . Sorenson pathetic-ally gasps, her dull, unfocused cow eyes indicating a soul vacationing in limbo.

What's the story, Morning Pages?

I start to get that song, the one about Nelson Mandela, into my head. *For ten years a prisoner of obese-i-tee . . . it make her so blind that she cannot see . . .* — Free-ee-hee-hee Len-na Saw-ren-son . . . sing it in your heart, baby, I roar at the side of her head, — I know why the caged bird sings!

Sorenson just trudges along in confusion. I'm trotting along-side her, almost in reverse; by God she's fucking slow, but at least she's doing it. — We ain't gon-na . . . darn well . . . quit . . .

It's the food. Eating. That's her main problem. We're just wasting our fucking time unless I can get her brain rewired to stop swallowing goddamn excrement. But there is hope. It's about educating their taste buds, weaning them off that constant diet of sugar, salt, corn syrup, and chemicals they've been subjected to since childhood, usually by their lazy, tightwad, dumbassed mothers.

We finish up and the bitch is gushing like a Southie hydrant in a heatwave. Once she recovers I take her for a salad at my favorite spot on Washington. Juice & Java is a small, brightly lit cafe, with cream walls and a pink-tiled floor. We sit in the high chairs in the large windows, as the light streams in. The clientele are generally, with the exception of Sorenson, in magnificent shape. It's very rare to come in here and see somebody who isn't fuckable. Sorenson's pores discharge bullets of sweat due to the air conditioning. Gross.

I peruse the menu: these salads are so flavorful and filling, the traditional lardass rabbit-food defense can't hold up. — This is the shit you should be eating, and I start taking pictures of the menu on my iPhone, instantly emailing them to her. — Those food groups. No excuses!

I order a grilled tofu salad; Lena follows suit. — That's 380 cal, plenty of protein, fiber, low but complex carbs and the fats present are good ones, I explain. — With a twelve-ounce glass of water they will fill *anybody* up for four hours!

Then Sorenson's telling me about growing up in Potters Prairie, Otter County, Minnesota. It's all fresh, piney woods, adorable trash-raiding black bears, and Momma's apple pie. (Double helpings with loads of cream, no doubt.) The last I buy, the rest . . . sorry, Lena, you just ain't cutting it, you chunky Scandinavian depressive, you. When did the Pop-Tarts start to get swallowed like M&M's? What happened? I await the disclosure; the stepdad's creepy touch, the dysfunctional alco mom, or the psycho kid's bullying mob. Fuck them. But no. Sorenson ain't moving from *The Little House on the Potters Prairie* script, and with a reasonably wealthy papa thrown in, just to suck any sting out of that rustic poverty.

The food arrives, and as she starts shoveling it away, Sorenson's evidently impressed. — This is soooo good, she bleats, as a couple of skinny uberbitches give the oblivious blimp a disgusted once-over.

— Glad you like.

Then Sorenson moves on to Chicago, and her time spent at the Art Insitute. — It was my town, my place, my time; that was where I met Jerry . . .

Nee-naw . . . warning bells . . .

I'm all fucking ears now. We've been building up to this. Since I first heard that name mentioned by the bathroom scale. I let her tell the story of her and this "Jerry" character. It seems Sorenson left Minnesota for art college in Chicago, met this guy, got fucked properly for the first time, and partied like hell. The big problem, although she can't quite bring herself to say it, was that he just happened to be a total asshole. This became more apparent when Sorenson and lover-boy Jerry went to Miami, him freeloading into an art scene that embraced Lena because of her talent.

— I had an acclaimed exhibition in Chicago, then New York—

— Can I say something here? I cut in. Sorenson looks at me, as if I'm about to violate her pussy, then her ass, with a vibrating, jumbo-sized dildo. But yet her eyes are telling me *she fucking wants it.* — 'Sounds to me like you let your own considerable talent go to waste in order to support this gutless leech who couldn't get arrested if he tried to exhibit himself outside the gates of a junior high, I tell her. Somehow, when I think of this Jerry asshole, I get an image of that chicken-hearted pedophile fuck Winter, whom the pussy McCandless ought to have wasted. And that bastard in the park, from high school, the one I should have fucking laid to waste like the sick little insect he was. THE PARK THE PARK THE FUCKING PARK.

— But—

I raise a hand, and shake my head in the negative. — Hear me out. Maybe I'm outta line here, but I saw this book on you, up at that Books & Books store on Lincoln. You have talent, Lena. You're fucking famous, for chrissakes!

Now *she* is shaking her head, her timid eyes nervously flitting under those bangs. Like a fucking retarded thirteen-year-old. — No. It was just a time when that thing was vogue. I was lucky. I had a lot of criticism from people in the art wor—

— From jealous, talentless fucks, who've never made a fucking dime from their shit! And you sold a little sculpture of bird bones and fiberglass that made you eight million big ones! *Of course* you had critics! *I'm* your fucking critic, you lucky bitch, and I punch her on the arm. — And that fact doesn't make *you* a bad artist, it makes *me* one jealous mother-fucker! Own your talent, Lena. Not facing up to your own unique and special gifts is what's killing you. Junk food is just the device: your own personal little weapon of self-destruction. It could as easily be drugs or booze, and she nods grimly in agreement. — This Jerry character, he never had a book about his work, did he?

— No, she says, a little smile playing across her lips. It transforms her: she looks so fucking cute.

— But I'll bet he preened around like a pompous asshole, thinking he was some sick shit. Right?

Lena smiles, shaking her head, then, as if worried about appearing disloyal by badmouthing this prick, says, — But Jerry has real talent as a photographer—

— Fuck that noise! I know jack about that stuff, but even I get that photography isn't art! It's just fucking around with light. Good photographers are like pigeons here in Miami Beach, I tell her, picking a piece of nut out from between my teeth.

Sorenson gives a collusive smile, before doubt slams home, almost jackknifing her. — I know how it looks . . . but you don't understand, she begs, then sniffs, raising a napkin to her moist eyes, — Jerry wasn't just bad . . . there was more to him than that. There was more to *us* than that!

— I'm sure there was, but that's gone now, Lena, I'm whispering urgently. — It's the outcome you gotta think about. Him, playing you for a fool, then probably going off and fucking some model bitch . . . I can see the truth in that one as Sorenson takes a sharp inhalation of breath, — . . . and you, mutilating yourself, cause that's what it is Lena—self-mutilation with sugar and fat!

A defiant pout, as Sorenson sweeps back her bangs. — Have you ever been in love, Lucy?

What the fuck has that got to do with anything?

— Yeah, I have. And yeah, sometimes it sucks, sometimes it ends bad, I tell her, and I'm thinking of Jon Pallota. We had something, but were both a little too fiery to make it work on a day-to-day basis. I always thought that maybe we'd get back together sometime, but that was before the big fish came along to fuck up his dick and his head. — But it never has *any chance* of working out if you don't love yourself, and go into a relationship looking for the other person to affirm your fucking existence!

— Jerry gave me so much!

— And took plenty, I'll wager. I meet those sad green eyes. — Lena, it's obvious his art stuff sucked serious ass, and nobody gave a flying fuck. I don't need your coy shrugs to tell me what happened next—seen that shit a million times before. This Jerry creep undermined you, didn't he, Lena?

— He could be so fucking cruel, she spits, back to riding her anger.

— While spending your money, I'm betting, I tell her, as the two bony-assed uberbitches settle up and leave. One shoots a nakedly hateful glance at Sorenson, catches me catching her, and we exchange flashbulb screwed-up controlling smiles. Fucking bitch.

Sorenson is sitting in a livid silence, tapping a fork against the table. I swear if this Jerry creep walked in here right now, she'd gouge his fucking eyes out of his head.

— He watched you bloat up with the cookies as

consolation, while he drank, snorted, and popped his way through *your* money, made through *your* work.

— Yes, he did! I hate him! I fucking hate him!

A couple at a nearby table look over at us, and Sorenson, *my Lena*, faces them down with a glare. God, I'm so proud of her! They grow up so fast!

But I gotta keep this *bee-yatch* on the boil. I bend into her reddened profile. — And as you blimped up, he hooked up with a younger, slimmer chick. You sought even more solace with your nose in the donut bag. Am I right on the money, or am I bustin that piggy bank with a fucking claw hammer?

— Yes, she says, turning to me despondently. — How come you understand all this?

I take a deep breath. For a second I feel like I'm going to say shit I shouldn't. Like how I know this psycho Jerry creep, how we all do, and that with generic pricks only the name ever changes. But no: keep it client–customer. — I see a lot of clients; it's an archetypal story. Too much investment in the supposedly ideal guy, the supposedly perfect children, or totally high-flying career, and not enough in Y-O-U, I point at her. — Then the big love comes and goes, and with it your sense of affirmation. So that prick left you a worthless couch potato, too depressed to paint and sculpt, to use the God-given talent you have. Transplanted down here, his idea, on your money, I'm betting again, while he played the big shot, then fucked off?

A slow but empathetic nod. — He's in New York. Brooklyn, I believe. Living with some rich . . . some wealthy woman who owns a gallery, and Sorenson is struggling to keep her breathing even.

I reach over and grab her hand and give it a squeeze. — I'm proud of you, Lena.

Her eyes are filling and she grips the table edge. — What do you mean? I'm a goddamn clown! I've been a fool!

— Yes, but show me a person on planet Earth who ain't, and I'll show you a liar or a dead asshole, or, worse, somebody who might as well be. At least you're getting to the root of the problem. You're facing up to things about yourself that it's easier to repress. To keep buried, I tell her, as the hunky Italian approaches with the check. — To bury under layers of fat.

— The art world can be cruel if you aren't producing, she moans. — I thought I had friends there. I guess I was wrong. Jerry was always the gregarious one. I was just a loner.

— No. He built a psychological prison around you, and handed you the key. Then he said "jail yourself." And you did that, because he and other assholes in your life undermined your own sense of self-worth to the point where you thought that's all you deserved. I've seen that shit sooo many times.

Sorenson's silently stewing in her own sweat.

— Listen, I want to try something out. Have you ever heard of Morning Pages? Julia Cameron?

— Yes . . . Sorenson says warily, my friend Kim said I should try it. I gave it a try, but I dunno, I don't think it was for me . . .

— Might be worth giving it another shot, I tell her, and she looks blank as we settle up and head down to the beach, walking, at my instigation, along the sand. We're talking about

157

the concept of writing those pages, how they are designed for artists and creative people.

— That's what Kim said . . . I will try it again, and stick with it.

— Cool, I nod, but the reason I've brought her down here is to see how Miami Beach flesh should look, how *she* should look. I'm checking out some fuckable young frat boys, all waxed, bronzed bodies, throwing a Frisbee to each other, trying to impress the giggling girls sprawled out on sunloungers. Then we fall upon a volleyball game featuring these fabulously surgically enhanced Brazilian chicks who commandeer this section of the beach. Lena is still gassing away, looking ahead, miserably, into space. We take a stroll down the sand, heading south, looking at the glistening domes of skin stuffed with silicone, and the sleazebag trawlers gawping at them, the more shameless snapping pics.

— Now we start again, I tell Lena.

— What?

— C'mon, I urge her, breaking into a trot. She hesitates for a bit, then starts to follow.

We cut off, heading down 5th toward the Biscayne Bay. Lena is slow, so slow, but steady. We pass West Street, the skyscrapers easing away, and on Alton a blaze of heat hits my back as a low, slanted sun falls mercilessly on us, stretching our shadows out in front of us like beanstalks. Sorenson's now starting to sweat like a truck-stop hooker waiting on her crank connection. — I don't think—

— You don't need to think! Just do! Come on! Compete!

We turn back toward the ocean, calling it a halt in Flamingo

Park, as Sorenson struggles to get her breath back through her elation. — I feel . . . so . . . good . . .

— Deeply, in through the nose, hold it . . . hold it . . . and out through the mouth . . .

Once she recovers, we head to Starbucks on Washington, where I order two green teas. Sorenson glances enviously at a neighbor's mocha, which would have decimated her entire food allowance for the day. She tells me that she usually has a blueberry scone (400 cal) or a couple of oatmeal cookies (430 cal) as blueberries and oatmeal are good for you. And that's not counting the fucking coffee . . .

— Oatmeal was meant to be eaten as oatmeal, blueberries as fresh fruit. They were not intended to provide flavoring to a filthy chunk of flour, dough, and sugar. A woman your size can easily eat half of her daily calorie allowance in one visit to Starbucks.

— But . . . I go twice a day.

— There you go. I also go twice a day. And I only drink green tea. Calories: zero. Antioxidants: high.

A copy of *Heat* has been discarded on our table. The twins have now become full-fledged celebrities. To get to that point from being a news story seems to take about two days. The Valerie Mercandos of this world don't let the saw grass spread under their manicured feet. The headline:

AMY: I'D LET ANNABEL SLEEP WITH STEPHEN

Further below, a picture of Stephen, displaying a miffed pout. The caption:

Stephen: "This has all gotten too much."

Lena's warbling voice in my ear. — I feel so sorry for those girls.

— Yeah, it's tough shit, I tell her, then I hear myself saying, — How would you like to go out tonight?

Sorenson looks sheepishly at me. — I haven't had a night out in ages.

— All the more reason. Pick me up at nine-thirty.

So we depart the coffee shop as the sun goes down. Sorenson leaves with a decided spring in her step. When I get home, via Whole Foods, I grill myself some high-omega wild salmon with brown rice, as my cal count is a bit low today. I give it an hour to go down, then do a workout on my hand weights and wall bar. I really wish I had a heavy gym bag here as I feel like pummeling off some aggression, but there's no room in this fucking shoebox.

Sorenson calls about nine (I said nine-thirty). I buzz her up, concealing the *Future Human* book in my bedroom closet. She looks a total fucking grenade; it's certain I'm getting no action tonight double-teaming with that little dweeb. Even the things a normal chubby chick can do to minimize the damage a greedy mouth inflicts seems to be beyond her. Her clothes are way too small, from a previous life; a skirt that cuts her in half, letting her doughy muffin flesh spill over its band, and a tan blouse that clings to her like a second skin. Through superhuman effort of will I remain silent, but

160

as we head down to Washington, she gets the "who dat retard" look from the gangbanger doorman at the velvet rope outside Club Uranus. I even worry that we're going to be denied entry. Fortunately, he knows my face, and looks from me to Lena, then back to me, his expression a mix of contempt and compassion.

Thank fuck it's dark inside. The DJ has dropped that catchy tune "Disco Holocaust" by the Vinyl Solution. We find a nice corner, away from the pulsing light. A waitress appears and we order some drinks; vodka and diet tonic for us both. (Around 120 cal, at a rough estimate.) A few faces nod at me, but they don't stop to engage in conversation above the loud, pumping track, where the diva vocalist asks and answers: *Did six million really dance, yes they did!* One chunky straight bitch, adorned in the saturation-bombing Washington Avenue tattoos people get when they are having their cocaine year out, or exiting from a volatile long-term relationship, looks in open-mouthed contemplation from me to Sorenson. The Liposuction Fuck, a chisel-faced blonde who's had more work done than the City of Miami Port, arches a superior brow and toys with her white wine and a half-her-age Eurotrash suitor. Two almost-dead anorexic chicks known to go on the elliptical three hours a day, and who have been banned from at least four SoBe health clubs as they keep working to (and often past) their point of collapse, briefly interrupt their suicide pact to gape in gaunt, undisguised horror at my companion. Yes, I'm with a fat chick and if you're obese in Miami Beach you might as well be in the advanced stages of leprosy, and be crumbling over the dance floor. I've committed a major faux pas by bringing a whale to a nightclub. I deserve to be ostracized, and if I wasn't me I'd be the party leading the fucking charge.

Lena looks around, wondering, like just about everyone else in the place, exactly what she's doing here. — I never really liked going out to clubs. I never liked loud noise. And that song is pretty darned tasteless.

— It has a good beat and the artists are just young kids; all that war shit is nothing to them. I just come out to stop myself vegging. But there's another South Florida which isn't all parties and hedonism. Sports. The beach, I say, nodding over toward a sculpted blond hunk, simpering at the bar with a Latino partner. If it's who I think it is, I don't recall him being a fag back in the day. — I think that guy went to the University of Miami at the same time as me.

— I hear the University of Miami is a really good school, Lena nods.

— Don't kid a kidder, girl, I say in those sage, world-weary tones that disconcertingly remind me of my father. — When Sly Stallone and Farrah Fawcett are your best-known alumni you know that a degree there is worth less than a Twinkies wrapper. And to think there was a time when I was *proud* to go to a place of learning where the campus bookstore displayed only rows of sports clothing, mainly for the Miami Hurricanes, and you had to ask for the textbooks, which were crushed into an understocked corner upstairs. Now I feel like an asshole and I wish I'd gone to a *school* instead.

162

— But that's what you wanted to do, that sports science stuff.

— Yeah, it was.

— It's important to do what we want. Heck, I wish I'd been more athletic. I never got into it.

— I always was. My dad was sports crazy. He wanted boys, so my sister and I were on every team—basketball, soccer, softball, tennis—then she went bookish but I stayed sports crazy. I did track and field, karate, kickboxing, you name it.

— That must've been tough, Sorenson suggests, — exhausting, I mean.

— No. It gave me discipline and strength, I tell her coldly. Fucking fat troll. What right does that loser have to try and psychoanalyze *me*? — So what else do you do in your spare time?

— Well, I read a lot, and I watch movies.

— Yeah, I go to that joint on Lincoln sometimes. The last film I saw there was *Green Lantern*. Only got dragged along cause my friend thought Ryan Reynolds was hunky, I explain, feeling a bad taste rise in my mouth at the use of the term "friend," as I was there with Mona.

— I prefer the Miami Beach Cinemateque. You ever been there?

— No . . .

— It's an arthouse cinema. They show really interesting stuff there. We have to go!

— Eh . . . yeah . . . okay, sure, I struggle. But I'm fucked if I'm watching some subtitled Bosnian or Iranian or Scottish

163

shit, full of weirdly dressed, out-of-shape people. Lena's already fucking guzzled her drink and wants another. — No, I declare. — You know how many cal—

— But I *need* one. She fingers the charm around her blobby neck. Like anybody would want to draw attention to *that* with jewelry.

— Of course . . . I hear my voice going that crappy, simpering, passive-aggressive way that Mom's does, and I hate myself, then Sorenson, for it. I must be getting to that time of life where you recognize the worst aspects of your parents in your own behavior.

Sorenson stands up and signals the waitress over, who looks at me in mild embarrassment, as if to say: "What the fuck are you doing with *that*?"

But we reorder, and as the drinks arrive, I turn to Sorenson. — I don't like drinking a lot and I'm antidrugs. I like to be in control. To keep discipline. Drugs fuck with that.

— I hear you, she says. — I guess I went through a phase of partying a little too hard and it didn't do me any good. She raises the tall vodka glass to her mouth. — It messed with my work.

I'm nodding in agreement. — It'll do that all right. Your parents, do they drink? I put the cold glass to my lips, feeling it satisfactorily numb them.

— Very little. And they don't know what drugs are. Well, that's not true. My mom's medicine cabinet is full of all sorts of prescription stuff for anxiety, depression, and fatigue. I often think if she cut them all out, though, the net result would be the same.

It's obvious that the Sorenson parents have done the damage. But as I sip on my drink, I feel my head start to burn in that horrible *out-of-control* way. I'm not used to alcohol and I hate being drunk. I look around at the faces, slackened and buckled with drink, lust, and desperation. The scene here always disintegrates at a certain hour. A gross old bulldyke I once gave an enema to, as part of general health package (we all go down blind alleys), and who is now a hopeless lush, clicks ludicrously long fingernails around an overfull martini glass. It's as pathetic as trying to grab a cheap toy with a rigged claw at those fairground games. Fearful of spillage, she concedes defeat and lowers crinkled parchment lips to the rim of the glass, sucking on it like it was pussy. A chick wearing sweat pants, a white tank top, expensive jewelry, and orange fake tan, struts in. The Liposuction Fuck—we've never been properly back on speaking terms since a confused encounter on a boat party last year—gives me an "I know" glance. We make strange alliances, but this is Miami Beach and Eurotrash need to be kept in their place. Worse, I feel the jolt of attraction, like a hand grabbing and twisting at my intestine, and a tiny metronome of dread now pulsing within me. Wanting Sorenson to fuck off, but also strangely glad that she's here, though in the shadows, out of range of the throbbing lights.

Then my friend, Masterchef Dominic Rizzo is coming over, his grin expanding in recognition as he zigzags through the crowd. I haven't see him in, like, *months*. — Dominic!

— Scalp me, sugarpie, scalp me, Dominic theatrically begs, arms and palms flying from his torso.

— Where have you been? I've been calling, texting, dropping emails . . . Bruce told me about the split.

— A verboten word, sweetcakes. I'm moving on. Got him out, capital O-U-T, of my system. You wouldn't believe the holes I've been in, both psychologically *and* physically. But I'm so *done* fucking and drinking that man right out of my hair. I'm coming round to Bodysculpt next week. His eyes plead as he thrusts a slight paunch at me. — Make me look a fairy prince again?

— Diet first. What have you been eating? Sampling your own recipes?

— Oh, honey, the damage has *all* been done by the demon drink. I forgot the particular bottle of wine in my cellar, within which I had secreted the answers to the riddles of life and love!

— When you find out, let me know, a lit-up Sorenson interjects.

— Oh, I'm *totally* the wrong person to ask, Dominic says, not introducing himself to her, but turning brightly back to me. — But here I am, fifteen days sober and with a crush on my sponsor that fucking chokes me. An architect. It never works with me and nine-to-five types, though.

— I know, right, I concede the point. — Well, now that you're thinking of *you* again, and not you-know-who, I say to him, but with a pointed glance at Sorenson, — it should all be straightforward.

— You know, Brennan, Dominic looks at me in fatigued indebtedness, — I wish you were the son your father always wanted. We'd be in Canada now, with a license.

166

— Closest I've ever come to a marriage proposal, but it'll do.

Dominic arches his back, placing his hands on his hips. — What about that hunky firefighter?

I note Sorenson taking an interest, shifting weight from one fat buttock to the other. — You gotta be shitting me. I know that you fags think you're the ultimate narcissists, but this is one straight fuck who would give you a run for your money!

— Well, I'm moving on, honey, physically as well as metaphorically. Dominic kisses my cheek. — Too bushy and not cocky enough in here, and he turns to Lena, with an awkward, reluctant nod of acknowledgment as he departs. Some would call it rude and superficial, but looking as out-of-shape as Sorenson really *is* a crime against the esthetic order in South Beach, perhaps the last bastion of sanity in a fucked-up world.

But the alcohol has gone to my head. I find myself touching Lena's arm; so swollen, but her skin is still young and taut. She's got about two years to lose that weight before she has to move into the realm of plastic surgery, and get big water-wings of skin removed. If she loses it right now it'll snap back to where it should be. I smile at her and run my finger down her arm, eliciting quite a fetching giggle. — The difference between being a healthy 140-pound woman and an obese 200-pound one is big. But the difference between being an obese 200-pound and a morbidly obese 300-pound one is small. Do you want to have ankles like loaves of bread? I shake my head in Lena's face.

— Can we not talk about—

— No. We can't *not* talk about it. Because those giant women didn't talk about it. They got fat, got depressed, depowered, addicted to sugar and comfort-eating to spike their mood up, and went into free fall. They will always be mutants. Even if they lose weight they will carry obscene scars where they've had folds of skin removed, or have to fill that empty parcel of skin with megamuscle, like the older fatties you see on *The Biggest Loser*. Not you. You can still look normal again. You're young. You've got good skin.

— Oh, thank you! But you've got great skin!

I suddenly realize that I wanna work that flesh. Her armor facinates me! It slips out. — Tell me about your first kiss, Lena.

— What? Through her drunk buzz, the pseudobohemian affectations retreat and that hokey small-town schoolmarm persona edges to the surface. I want to find the MTV-schooled artist. That's the Sorenson I need.

No going back now. I spell it out. — Tell. Me. About. Your. First. Kiss, and I fix a big grin, — Lena!

Sorenson looks defiantly at me. — No! Then she chortles again. — I mean, you first.

Suddenly my ears are fucking ringing. I can't hear a fucking thing. First fucking kiss . . .

— Lucy, are you okay?

— Just not used to alcohol.

— There was I thinking that you were spooked about telling me about your first kiss!

I suck down some breath. I have to think past him, past that prick, that fucking Clint asshole, to the harmless Warren.

— Okay, no biggie. There was this kid called Warren Andover. He had huge rabbit teeth, you know, buck teeth, so it was a pretty unfortunate given name. But every time I saw him I got so wet. All I thought about was those white teeth scraping on my clit.

Her hand goes to her mouth. — God, Lucy, Sorenson semiblushes, — you remind me of my friend Amanda from college!

Did she go to art school or fucking convent school? But I look up to notice I'm getting the lazy eye from a chick at the bar; short straight brunette cut in a great wedge, slender figure, but with a bust in that purple top, and, as I recall from a previous checkout, an ass inside those yellow tight pants. She sees Sorenson, and looks pointedly away. Now that ship has probably sailed as she's doubtlessly marked me as a chubby-chaser. So I turn to Sorenson. — You keep in touch with your college buddies?

— Oh yes, though obviously I don't see them so much, being here . . . Sorenson starts waffling on. The way she curls into that couch, like a big fat stuffed cat, but a cat nonetheless, confirms the fat suit hasn't always been there. Muscle memory generally offers clues. — Kim is working in a gallery, Amanda moved back east and she's engaged to this really cool guy who's a stockbroker. It sounds kinda crass and boring, but . . .

I wanna see those blue veins push their way back to the surface of the skin on your breasts. I wanna watch that skin sear and scorch under my touch like it was meant to, before you turned it into cookie dough. I wanna turn it back.

— . . . so many of those guys were more Jerry's

169

friends—you see that when you split. You really do know who your friends are in those circumstances . . .

But first I want to strap you onto my bed, you fat little bitch, with the rubber sheet down and tickle you till you piss yourself. Don't want her drying out on me. Dehydrated is no good.

— Let's get some water, I suggest.

— Okay . . .

Leaner Lena Leaner Lena.

Leaner Leaner Leaner Lena.

Shit, that vodka's making me crazy. She's a client. *Cool it.* I rein myself in, and kick back into the couch, taking in the growing madness around us. The worst moment is when Sorenson wants to dance. I don't think I'm *that* drunk, but we take to the floor, her in a creaky, self-conscious nursing-home waltz. I feel all eyes on us and I want to get the fuck out of here before that bitch wrecks my entire social life and leaves me the laughing stock of the Beach.

At my suggestion, we exit and go back to her place. When we get there, I cajole her into letting me see more of her stuff in the workshop. This time it's uncovered—a full-sized skeletal creature. It has all the bones wired together—legs, arms, spine, and ribs—the only replacements, Sorenson explains, are the molded plastic hip and skull, which are a slightly different color and texture.

— It's a work-in-progress, Lena says. — But I don't know if it's me anymore. The bones, the animals. Jerry used to say— She catches herself and puts her hand to her mouth.

170

I prompt, — The prick said what? The talentless fuck who undermined you said what?

— He used to say that it was too morbid. That I was making myself depressed. That I needed to work on brighter, more uplifting stuff. That I didn't have the *personality* to do dark.

— Tells you all you need to know, doesn't it? I stand close to her, grab her hand, and whisper in her ear, — Finish it. And tomorrow, you start on those Morning Pages. They will help. Because something is blocking you, it's like there's a giant cork up your ass . . . and I start to laugh uncontrollably at her expression. — I said "cork" . . . and now Lena's laughing too, doubled over, and I see her, see how repulsive and how fucking beautiful she is.

15

CONTACT 6

To: michelleparish@lifeparishoners.com
From: lucypattybrennan@hardass.com
Subject: You Got It, Girlfriend!

. . . and how! Just saw you on TV! You're the best, Michelle! If I say "bitch got game," I hope you take it the right way!

Got my own bee-aych on Morning Pages! See how it goes. As you say, nothing ventured, right?!

L x

16

ART WALK

The crowds sashay by on Lincoln. The locals showing off;
strutting, posing, skateboarding. The tourists with their
relaxed strides, oozing money. In the doorways, the odd
skulking bum or hustler watching proceedings, often under
the not-so-discreet supervision of a chunky cop.

I'm still thinking about Sorenson's studio. How it's so
different to her bland house. It was fabulous chaos. Not
mindless, alcoholic dissolution: it just oozed sweat, industry,
and focus. It showed me the inside of a head that knew that
stone-cold, abstract planning, while essential, could only ever
get you so far. That you needed to get your hands dirty to
achieve anything in life. The workshop told me that Sorenson
once knew that. She had to relearn that lesson. She had to
get down and fucking dirty. Well, I will fuck that bitch. I will
fuck her shit right up!

So, lunch with Miles, at the World Resource Cafe. I'm
paying, so Miles, bleary-eyed, looking more soft-boiled than
of late, is gorging on a steak sandwich and fries (800–900 cal).
Like, double-carbing, dude: a no-no. Triple, if you count the
Peroni (180) he's drinking. Going into the *four figures* for
lunch in *South fucking Beach*? How gross is he? Pilot to
navigator! Please assist!

— Lemme get this straight, Miles is asking, chomping on his food, — all I gotta do for five hundred bucks is bang some fat loser?

— You got it.

He shakes his head, lowers his sandwich to take another quick suck on his beer. Screws up his eyes as he sets the bottle down on the table. — So why am I smelling dirty Bostonian rats here, Brennan? What's in it for you?

— I want her to lose weight. She's depressed, she eats too much. Why? Cause some asshole she was in love with ditched her. I want you to fuck her good, get her some perspective back. A good pussy-pounding will make her feel much more worthy than a thousand pep talks from me. You do have a certain expertise in that area, I lie flirtatiously, in order to hook the sucker.

— Well, I guess you did come to the right place, for sure, he grins, then his brow furrows. — Exactly how fat is this chick?

— One hundred and eighty-two, I tell him, taking a little license, cheating with the numbers like Sorenson does. But it's for the greater good.

— I can suck it up, he has another slug on his beer, — and take one for the team. I once balled this fat chick in Vegas when I was loaded. Larry and Joe and I had a bet. After a Floyd Mayweather fight.

— How delightful for you both, I smile, signaling for the check.

— When do I . . . you know?

— No advances, this is a strict C.O.D. job.

Miles goes to protest, then shrugs it down. Asks me if I've had my hair done, tells me it makes me look like Blake Lively from *Gossip Girl*. I don't know who the fuck that is.

— I've never seen that show.

— You should. You would dig it the most.

— Righto, I say, knowing that I will now never watch that show, *ever*.

So I meet Lena Sorenson at my place and she's driving us over the Julia Tuttle, where it all started. I thought I'd feel queasy as we passed the spot, but there's nothing, indeed the only stomach-churning aspect is Lena's big haunted eyes, fishing for a reaction. I ignore her, turning away to look out over the bridge onto the bay. These are only places, they can't spook you. After the incident in the park back in Weymouth, I would walk to the same spot, alone, at night, and feel nothing. It's the people who make them scary, one specifically, and that's who I was waiting on. But he never fucking showed.

Now we're heading for the Design District and Art Walk. I've only been on this once before, with, as it happens, Miles, who ended up shitfaced on the free beer the galleries provide, leering at all the pussy, trying to interest me in getting some chick involved in a threesome. He is so gross when he's drunk. In fact, strike that, he's gross all the fucking time.

It's a hot night, and the ocean breeze seems to have died down. My legs suddenly feel very tired, and it's a struggle to walk through the dense, close air. To my surprise, Sorenson, although sweating like a prize sow, is striding on ahead, very excited. All because she dipped under two hundred pounds on her crappy scale. That's no fucking progress at all, she should be in double-digit weight loss every week, with what I'm giving her. But she's a fucking time-wasting trash disposal!

We get off the crowded street into a gallery's (air conditioning—yeah!) that sells art books, and one of them features more plates of Lena's stuff, her weird monster men and women. I know it's nerdy, but I kinda like her shit. — This is so good, I tell her, — you should never give up on that stuff.

— I don't know if you mean it, or you're just saying it to be kind, but it really is exactly what I need to hear right now. Thank you.

— Lena, I don't do kind. I do straight. Brutal fucking honesty is what I do.

— I think you sometimes sell yourself a little short.

I shrug, trying not to let her see that I'm lit up inside. Praise is always weakness, it's the staple diet of the quitter. The strong woman doesn't need that shit. The strong woman just *knows*.

A cool-looking skinny bitch dressed in a black blouse, Medusa-like hair extensions coming out from under a black hat with a big feathery trim, is checking out Lena. She leaves her lisping flock of culture vultures, and comes across to engage her. — It's you . . . isn't it?

— Andrea, Lena smiles. — So good to see you!

— I scarcely recognised you.

— I've put on a little weight, Lena concedes.

— It suits you, darling, the bitch says, flashing the hangman's smile. — You working on anything?

— Well, trying.

— Very good. Anyway, she grimaces at me and I mirror

the expression, — look, this has been so gooood, but I really must fly. Dinner reservations. Call me!

I track her fake ass to its company, and watch them pushing off into the throngs outside. — Who the fuck was that asshole?

— Oh, an old friend. I always thought that she and Jerry . . .

Jesus, she needs to learn to pick her friends. Any fucking friends. Never known a bitch so isolated. The encounter has certainly left Sorenson deflated, and as she drops me off at my place, she can't even be enticed to come in for a protein shake. In her absence I try and settle on the couch in front of the TV, then there's a knock on the door. It's the DJ kid from downstairs, and he's holding up a big FedEx package almost as tall as him. — This came for you, he says.

I take it in and open it up—the gratis Total Gym they sent to the agency. So I set it up and try it out. After real gym equipment it seems flimsy, but it's actually well made, with cable-system technology. Holding on to the handles attached to the cables, I lie down and start to work my chest. After a few sets I move on to other exercises: some kickbacks for my triceps and seated rows to work my back. I can work every body part and I like the position variations I can do: leg raises for my abs and bicep curls. On a chest-press machine my arms are in one position. I can replicate this movement on the Total Gym with the cables, but I do have some variance. I've been working out for over fifteen years, and there's possibly too much flexibility in the Total Gym for a novice. Even with instruction, somebody like

Marge or Sorenson could hurt themselves on this if their form wasn't right. I think a more controlled machine would be more effective and safer for the likes of them. And as with all machines, although there's some cardiovascular benefit, it won't replace sweat work on the treadmill, elliptical, or even just walking outside. It's the kind of machine that would suit somebody like Lena Sorenson, *but* only in a controlled environment.

That is the key: Sorenson's environment must be *controlled*.

I should go to bed, but can't settle after my workout, so without being conscious of what I'm doing, I'm showering, getting done up, and heading out into the early morning, following a familiar path.

I'm back in the Club Uranus, looking for that chick who gave me the eye when I was stuck with Sorenson last night. It's a dirty, edgier crowd at this time, most of them now ready to strike out at their prey. I've packed an eight-inch dick, not too veiny, and a pair of fur-trimmed handcuffs. I'm in a party dress and femmed up to the max. Some butch is gonna get the shock of her life when I whip this on her. I wanna make some faux hardass bitch cry like a baby.

It doesn't take me long to find my girl. She's at the bar, like she's never moved since I saw her here last night, giving it that tomboyish Hilary Swank *Boys Don't Cry* mischievous fourteen-year-old urchin look, the one a lot of bet-hedging butches favor. A butch in yellow pants? Bitch's kidding no mofo. I sidle up to her. — Hey.

— Hey . . . she says. — Where's your friend? The chunky chick?

I go all pretend bashful, and even bite into my knuckle.
— Oh, I guess that was a little experiment.

— I like experiments.

We know where this is going—straight out and down the street to the Blenheim on Collins. It takes no time to check in, the sly clerk giving us the unofficial hourly rate. He hands us the key and we climb the staircase. The waft of piss from the old carpet tickles our nostrils as we enter the room. Carpets are always gross in the tropics, but carpets in a roach motel designed for the regular spillage of every conceivable body fluid? Forget it. There's a creaky-looking bed, two battered nightstands, an old wall clock stuck at 9:15, where a second hand tries to rise, like a spider in a bathtub, clicking pathetically as it falls back to its original position.

The yellow walls have a golden nicotine stain, and gummy blinds which don't shut properly. A cursory look in the bathroom reveals a deeply stained toilet bowl and sink, with a cracked mirror, and a shower tray I'd be utterly loath to step in, sheathed with a plastic curtain festooned with a rash of black-and-blue spores. But we're not here for the fucking decor. I move against Swank Boy, and as we exchange heavy, slobbering kisses, I let her feel the bulge of my plastic against her own. A vented aluminum box under the window rumbles into life then immediately shuts itself off with a dramatic clatter. Her big green eyes widen. — You packin heat? I want—

I reach up and pull back her hair. It's short but there's just enough to get purchase. — Ow . . . she goes, as my grip's stronger, and I'm wrapping my other arm around her neck, twisting behind her as I tighten her in a lock.

— Ow . . . this isn't cool . . . She's half struggling, surprised by my strength.

I'm whispering in Swank Boy's ear, as her writhing in my grip gets weaker, — You're a very naughty boy and you're gonna get spanked, I whisper, stepping back toward the bed, dragging her with me. I twist quickly, getting her locked face down on the gross comforter as I grope in my bag for the cuffs.

— No! I don't take it, Swank Boy protests. — I don't do femme shit, I just give it—

— Don't take what?

— Cock . . .

I let the cuffs drop by her side. They are superfluous. — I think that's B.S., Yellow Pants. You're teasing me, girlfriend!

— No, it's true, she squeals. — I never—

— Bullshit! I think you want my cock inside you!

— No. She gives a throaty croak, struggling more, as I tighten my grip.

— Don't fucking try and break my grip, Judy Garland, I hiss in her ear, but it's all performance now, — I could snap your fucking skinny girl-bitch neck like a twig!

— But I—oh my God—this is *so not* what I—

Her stage-protests fall on deaf ears as I wrestle her yellow pants down, and she's acually helping me, while still ludicrously half protesting, — I didn't sign up for this, as my dick is out, shoving against her ass and my pubic bone. I pull her panties aside I'm pushing into her glistening pussy with it.

Her body is as tense as live electrical cable, but that pussy is hungry, slowly eating up those inches. — Oh my God . . . I don't doooo this!!

— If there are two bitches in a bedroom, *I'm* the psycho one. Every fucking time!

Then I thrust deep into her, forcing a gasp. — Oh . . .

I'm pounding the bitch for all she's worth, while chamfering the edges of my clit with the dildo base.

— Take it easy, for fuck's sake! You're hurting me—

— Shut the fuck up; no pain, no fucking gain, I taunt, thrusting, scraping the base of the dildo hard back onto my pubic bone, in long, performative, hip-whipping strokes. In what seems like no time at all, we both cum like storm troopers.

The postcoital rest is perfunctory, and I quickly get off her and dress, as she sits in shock on the bed, knees pulled under her chin, in a dissonant state—oscillating between rape victim and somebody who's had the best sex of her life. — Thanks, sweetie.

— Eh . . . yeah, right. Thanks, she manages. She'll be working through that ID crisis for years. Then she looks up and says, with a half-smile, — Dressing up and coming on like a fucking Olsen twin . . . You are one mean, twisted bitch!

— Believe it, I acknowledge with a wink, walking out the door.

CONTACT 7

To: lucypattybrennan@hardass.com
From: michelleparish@lifeparishioners.com
Subject: You Got It, Girlfriend!

Why, thank you!

You'll find that Morning Pages will be a massive help with this difficult client of yours!

Michelle x

To: michelleparish@lifeparishioners.com
From: lucypattybrennan@hardass.com
Subject: Success

Michelle,

I'm on it, honey! I hope the Morning Pages will help me find out where the blockage is. Then get rid of it so that all the bloated shit comes out as it should and doesn't back up, swelling her out like Jabba the Hut!

Superstar 'Chell! I love ya!

Best,

Luce x

LENA'S MORNING PAGES 2

Lucy has given me these Morning Pages to write, like the ones Kim told me to try. Don't think, she says, just write. Well, okay. But I didn't. Now I'm in agony, my butt stinging from some kind of bug bite, and she's coming over. So I had better write, even though it isn't morning, it's evening, and I can barely sit down. So what happened today?

Times are times, and dates aren't business appointments. But there are defined limits. When Miles asked me to go for a coffee, I hesistated. I knew he had some kind of history with Lucy, but they certainly weren't an item. I met him in the gym, and I was feeling good about myself cause I'd worked like crazy and weighed in at 197 pounds! It was the first time for so long I've been under the 200 mark! I was delighted, and I told Lucy that I wouldn't get into that state again. But she still wasn't happy, fixing me in that supergrump gaze of hers.

Then Miles came over and started chatting. He was a dark-haired, square-jawed, gym rat of a man, with a pearly smile. There was something sleek and strong yet functional about him, like a marble kitchen counter that could speak. (I wonder if Miami just attracts the intellectually challenged and the vacuous, or whether the baking sun and the toned flesh on show short-circuits the brain, thus inducing all this simple-mindedness?) He asked if I wanted to go for a coffee.

I was kind of flattered by the attention; in fact, at first I thought, "Oh, snap." But with Lucy being so uptight, I reckoned I should clear it with her first. I went over to her, looking back at Miles, who was sat at the juice bar, talking to Toby, who works on the desk. I told Lucy that he'd asked me out. She didn't seem jealous or angry, quite the reverse. "You should go. He's a harmless hunk, as dumb as a sack of rocks. It could be fun," and she winked at me in such a lascivious manner!

I told her it was only a stupid coffee!

So Miles and I went outside—Lucy reminding me to stick to green tea as we left. It was lush, warm, and fragrant, a diffuse golden light bouncing off the art deco buildings. We headed to the Starbucks on Alton. Miles was friendly; charming even, in a limited kind of way. He seemed so small-town, I imagined him coming from somewhere like Potters Prairie, and was almost disappointed when he told me that he was a native of Baltimore.

"I liked <u>The Wire</u>—that was a great show."

"Nothing like Baltimore," he retorted, seeming irritated, and picking up the pace down the street. "Every city has its dark side, but they should also be showing the good side of a town. TV assholes are just irresponsible!"

I was keeping up with him. "But I think any artist only has the responsiblity to be true to themselves, to tell the story that makes sense to them—"

"Now <u>The Sopranos</u>—that was a show," Miles cut in, opening the cafe door and moving toward the counter. There was no line. "What you gonna have?" Without waiting for my response he turned to the barista. "I want a skinny latte with soy."

I <u>really</u> wanted one of those blueberry muffins with the frosted sugar on top and a cappuccino. But I'd worked so hard, so I stuck to water and espresso shots. No doubt Miles would report back to Lucy, and I could feel her diet sheet (so hard to adhere to) weighing heavy in my shoulder bag.

We talked for a long time, mainly about (his) exercise and diet regimes and work. "People kind of get a certain view of firefighters from shows like Rescue Me. We aren't those empty, macho guys, well, not all of us," He smiled in a kind of contrived boyish way.

"I'm sure," I said, a little embarrassed for this guy.

"So where are you from?"

"Minnesota."

"You guys had Little House on the Prairie and Coach, but a lot of failures after that; like Get a Life and Happy Town never really took off."

"Sounds like you watch a lot of TV."

"Only premium shows. I don't just stay home and gape at shit." He was almost offended. "Life's too short, right?"

It was Miles who suggested we got something stronger. I was doubtful as the sky had darkened and it looked like the clouds were going to rupture.

I didn't want to stay out, but was even less inclined to go home alone. I guess that says how my life is. It made me realize that I didn't know what I was doing: in Starbucks, in Miami, even.

We went a couple of blocks north to this place on 14th called the Club Deuce. We got inside just as thunder rumbled in the dense air and yellow whipcrack lightning lacerated the dark, bruised sky. Everybody in the place seemed to know Miles. We sat on stools in a corner at the back of a long, snaking island bar. I stuck to vodka and soda, Miles opted for rum and Coke. As we heard the rain drum on the sidewalks, and watched soaked drinkers jump gratefully into the bar, we carried on chatting. The drink was going down nicely, warming and soothing, and the relaxed bonhomie of the bar was a nice contrast to the wild, lashing rain outside. We got another round. The mood changed as Miles looked me in the eye, his lips creased in a smile.
— You know, you are one pretty hot lady. I was watching you working out with Lucy.

He'd turned up the heat and I didn't like it. I tried to deflect the subject to Lucy, but I was aware of him edging closer as he told me there was nothing between them. His aftershave assailed my nostrils through the cigarette smoke. There was something on the solitary plasma behind the bar about the conjoined twins, the Wilks sisters from Arkansas. "I guess what I'm saying—" Miles dropped his voice as his eyes hooded — "is that I think it would be great to make love."

When I told him I wasn't like that, he misunderstood me, his eyebrows sloping upward. "You dig chicks?"

I told him I didn't just sleep with people I'd barely met. He shrugged and said he guessed his problem was that he tended "to work on that side of things at South Beach speed." He let his face crumple into a smile, then raised his hands to yank on imaginary reins. "Slow down, cowboy!"

I wanted to tell the Mileses and Lucys of this world that I don't do casual sex, not because I'm a prude, but because I simply have to like or at least be excited by somebody before I sleep with them. And I certainly won't do it a second time unless I'm fond of them. "It's just the way I'm made," I told him. "Casual sex always seems to me like glorified masturbation with a narcissist who needs an audience."

I was hoping that would put him in his place, but it didn't even seem to register. "You know, I respect that, but, and I gotta be honest here, I think you're a hot girl and I really want to get to know you better."

A pulse banged in my temples; one of those migraines I'm prone to; it came on like a flash flood. The pain is often so intense it produces burning, excruciating images behind my retinas. I really needed to be lying on my couch in the darkness, or distracting myself; on the Internet looking at cute animals, doing my emails, or even mixing resin in my workshop. I didn't want to be in the raucous bar with this guy anymore.

As the jukebox got louder, I could feel myself growing less present. Miles's eyes seemed to sink back into the shadow of his deep, dark sockets. I could barely see them, but I could still hear his voice, soft yet insistent, ". . . and I don't play messed-up games," his baleful face telegraphing the painfully sincere response I was supposed to give him.

"Right . . ."

Then he said, ". . . because honesty is the coolest currency you can bring into any relationship."

That was exactly the sort of thing that Jerry would say. I almost felt like laughing, anything to forget this banging pain in my jawbone, which spiked through the depression I was sliding into. Too much alcohol. As Miles shouted up another round, I kept thinking of Jerry, the way he'd encourage me to drink, then get me to take all my clothes off and stand still, by the entry to our bathroom. Then turn round. And again. And Lucy. Making me go through the same damn thing.

I should have spoken out. And I did, when I felt Miles's tongue in my ear.

"No," I shouted, causing a few people to turn around. I pushed him away, sprung to my feet, and rushed outside, heading onto Collins and hailing a cab. I don't know if he came after me and shouted my name: LENA, WAIT, or if it was just something I imagined through all the tumbling chaos inside my head.

The cab driver, Latino, a cross dangling from his mirror and statuettes of Jesus and the Virgin Mary on either side of his dash, smiled at me in something resembling pity. I remained silent as the cab sliced through the flooded streets.

When I got back home I couldn't stop thinking about Jerry. The good times; when he and I were untouchable. I started crying. I emailed Mom and then stayed online to order a chorizo thin-crust pizza and a whole Key lime pie. The

migraine pressure abated as I ......ed ......
Overload and the food was delive.......
minutes later. I settled on the couch.......
on: a film where Al Pacino was a Holly.......
movie director, concealing from the worl.......
the leading starlet, whom he discovered, is ....
a computer-generated program. I looked at the
pizza, its oils staining the cardboard box, those
red slices of chorizo vividly clashing with the
molten cheese they sat embedded in. Then I
focused on the pie in the plastic container,
anticipating that wonderful rush of blade-sharp
citrus tang in every bite. But first the pizza. One
slice of each, then into the refrigerator with the
rest. A treat that would last all week.

Pacino's character was using the computer-
generated starlet to get back with his ex-wife,
who is played by that lovely actress Catherine
Keener. She who has never, ever been, and never,
ever will be, a single pound overweight in her
life.

Then the end credits came up, tearing me out of
my trance. I looked at the empty packaging on
the floor in front of me. All the food was gone.
The burning clench of fear inside my chest, as
tears ran down my face. I calculated the calories
and wailed in my pain.

impulse was to go to the bathroom and
force myself to puke it all up. Instead I headed to
my studio to try and work through it, like Lucy
suggested. I was outside fiddling frantically with
the key in the lock, desperately trying to take
myself into another place where I could forget
about what I'd just done, when there was a
horrible stinging pain in my buttock, like some
kind of bug had bitten me!

I hobbled back inside in agony, and lay face down on the couch, deluged in my tears of despair. My cell started to vibrate: it was Lucy. I told her what had happened (the bite, not the food) and she said she would come right over. I forced myself up and hid the empty boxes under my bed as I knew she'd go through every cupboard. I had to do those Morning Pages, which actually made me feel better. Then I switched on the treadmill I'd set up in the living room, and even though my backside was still stinging, I started to walk.

19

ASS ASSASSIN

I rose early and bundled the Total Gym into the back of the car. Morning was the MMMA and some kickboxing with two stressed-out bulldyke parole officers whose patch includes Little Haiti. *Sacré bleu!* Then lunch at Whole Paycheck, a spinach wheat lasagne nestling on a bed of more spinach; no more than five hundred cal struck up on the iPhone's Lifemap app. Then off to the erroneously named Bodysculpt to meet with Lena Sorenson.

Sorenson weighed in at 197.5. And yes, it was on the official scale. But it's still far too slow. The way she squealed with delight that she was under two hundred just irritated the fuck out of me. I decided that I was going to cardio her ass and burn shit off her. I started her on the elliptical, and doing a 4 x 15-minute workout, increasing the resistance level from 8 to 10 to 12 to 14. Then as Miles ambles in, flashing that easy smile which initially passes off as cool, until you realize the guy is just, well, a little dim, I switch Sorenson onto a treadmill, set at 6 mph.

After some stretching, Miles climbs on the machine next to hers. Sorenson turned as he greeted her with a nod and a grin. He made some cheesy remark I couldn't catch. Sorenson responded with a tentative smile, but she wasn't a happy camper. Not only was I working her at increased gradient, I commanded her to go flat out every fourth minute, for one solid minute. — I'm trying to boot up your metabolism.

She responded with the recalcitrant sulk of the fat loser. It cuts no ice. *You do as I say, for I am the higher power, I am the bod god and you will submit before me . . .* For the last five minutes, I ramped it up to ten, asking her to go flat out for the last two. As she gasped toward the end of the session, I pointed to the calorie counter. — Seven hundred and twenty-two! *That's* what I need from you. *That's* what you have to bring me!

She shakily returned my offered up high five and repaired, sweating and gasping, to the juice bar for a carrot-and-broccoli concoction. Then Miles, towel slung around his shoulders, sauntered across to her, and I heard him say, — You seemed to be putting a lot in today.

And then my nice little old Jewish lady, Sophia Rosenbaum, arrived. Sophia has recently lost her husband. It's taken her a long time to come out and start doing things. So I gave her a mild workout on the cycle to protect a knee already pulped to floating shards of bone and slivers of cartilage by the ravages of time. I listened to her tales of children and grandchildren in faraway places, all the time spying on Miles and Sorenson.

And yes, after vanishing for her shower, Lena comes over all candy-assed, to get my approval to leave with Miles, who is waiting by the door, himself showered, wet hair combed back, teeth hanging out to dry. Approve? If only the dumbass little fuck knew that I'd just set her up to have the shit banged out of her! I get back to Sophia as they sneak off out the club.

After putting Sophia through her paces and having an iced tea with her, I picked up the keys for Mom and Lieb's downtown rabbit hutch, then headed over there. From the top floor I looked out and down. On one side I could see Interstate 95 with cars streaming along it, but the sidewalks were empty. Yes, you can work out here, and in total privacy, so I went back downstairs and hauled the Total Gym out the trunk of the Caddy and into the elevator, setting it up in Mom's apartment. Then I went to the gym next door, realizing that the treadmills are on a set of wheels you can lower by use of a foot pedal. I pushed one of them through to the apartment. Not cool, but hey-ho, I was only borrowing it. Looking up at the steel beam overhead, I did a little pole dance, stripper-style, on one of the support pillars, which is scaffolding width, locking my legs around it, supporting my own weight easily as I hung upside down, letting the blood rush to my head. Trying to imagine the likes of Sorensen doing that! I then had a decent workout, while watching the sky change behind all the deserted apartment blocks around me.

By early evening I got to the MMMA, and a session in the ring, practicing combos on the pads with Emilio. If Bodysculpt is a pristine nightclub, then the MMMA is a sweat factory. At the bank of machines, the sound of strained grunts over the crash of metal-on-metal evoke a shithouse for the chronically constipated, housed in some shabby rail-road goods yard. This is intensified by the fuck-you-in-the-ass blare of the boxing rounds signal with its authoritative green-amber-red glow sequence. Across the other side of the hangar, groups of boxers pummel their bags in combos barked out by the instructor, above the pounding insistence of urban hip hop.

Emilio and I have a bond; both warriors, yes, and both almost but not quite good enough. Whatever anybody says, there are winners and there are the rest. Second is as good as last. I hit my wall back in 2007 at the Marriott Orlando World Center, when I lost my last chance to become a World Muay Thai Champion. I'd made the semifinal in Cedar Rapids, Iowa, the previous year, but ran across an unyielding bull of a chick, whom I can't bring myself to name, but who looked like Marvin Hagler in a leotard, with faster, heavier hands and feet. I met her again the next year. I'd trained like a mofo and I was at my peak for the rematch. Once again, I fought gamely, but that animal dyke majored in the hurt business and kicked like a fucking mule. It's not good for the soul to dwell on two bad defeats, so all I'll say is that I realized I was never going to get past that bitch, who was almost four years younger than me. Competitive career over.

Emilio gets it. There's a great shot of him on the canvas after being knocked out for the first time. It's obviously not on display here, but I've seen it, and I can relate. It's that what-the-fuck-just-happened expression; not so much fear, but that slow, sad dawning of the recognition that you've just run into your own limitations, as his executioner strutted above him. But I love Emilio's balls; he'd opted for a warrior pro strike pad rather than full shield, which meant he had to be quick to protect himself from the combos he shouted at me to execute. His nostrils flared, with his face set in blazing concentration, as I unleashed a series of blows and kicks at him.

When we wound up, I had my first session with Annette Cushing, who impressively maintained her composure as she entered the cavernous building. Most Bodysculpt clients would never have made it through those doors. I took her over to one of the heavy bags, and showed her how to wrap her hands. Then we had a good fifteen-minute warm-up, before I demonstrated the basic fighting stance and steps. I had her shadowboxing in the mirror with me for ten. Then I showed her the range of blows and kicks on the bags, working her up to high intensity, only stopping to refine her technique. We finished with some abdominal conditioning exercises and stretching out. Annette was drained, the sweat bursting from her. And also as high as a crack whore with a winning lotto ticket in her purse. — I've never had a workout like that before, Lucy. It's the whole package!

Music to my ears, as I knew Mona, with her femme-girl Pilates, would be livid. So all good. We arranged another appointment before Grace Carillo came in and we trained together on the weights and bar.

Showering afterward, I tried not to think of Grace's pussy (shaved, I imagined, with the shocking-pink interior spread open, contrasting nicely with the ebony skin), then went for a juice with Emilio before heading off.

So I get back home, there are no photographers or journos in sight, and I try to get into *The Biggest Loser* repeats (sometimes Bob and Jillian have the patience of saints) but kept wondering about Miles and if he's fucking Sorenson.

I get the vibrator out, hellbent on pussy satiation but, frustratingly, I'm too distracted to get into it. Even for *Terminator 2*, perennially in my DVD player, which is the finest film ever fucking made, and one of the best feminist movies of all time. Forget the shrivel-dicked steroid monster; Linda Hamilton is the epitome of demented, badass cool. That anorexic fake-assed bitch who replaced Hamilton in the Connor role for the TV series: no fucking way, man. Those puny limbs never hauled that body up on an overhead bar. Notice how the pull-ups and chin-ups are never done in long shot. Give us a fucking break, broadcasters!

Instead I make some calls, gabbing on the phone with Chef Dominic, then send a few emails, mainly to clients. But all I can think about is Miles and Lena. Eventually, curiosity gets the better of me and I jump in the Caddy and head north toward Sorenson's. When I get there the air is hot and close and darkness is starting to fall. I bang on the door. Again. Once more. She isn't home!

I wait outside in the Cadillac, trying to imagine what their sex would be like. Miles is strictly a ground-and-pound man, without a sensual bone in his robot body. It's difficult to see what, if anything, a chubster like Sorenson would bring to the carnal table. I just hope he's hammering her into some kind of ecstasy.

I take a drive, playing the Joan Jett version of "Roadrunner" full fucking blast, singing out loud. I find myself going through Little Haiti, always surprised by the English pub right in the middle of this district; watching small groups of fat ex-pat British men, who all look like chubby packet sausages in a convenience store, marching purposefully into the bar.

It's around eleven by the time I get back to Sorenson's. Her car is in her driveway. I park up in the Publix lot, and move toward her gate. Crouching down, I can see her through her window. She had to have been at Miles's place. But Sorenson doesn't have that freshly fucked look. She seems unsettled, springing outside, then back in again, as I flit behind the hibiscus bush. Her constant toing and froing between the house and her studio, for no particular reason, is starting to annoy the fuck out of me. I sneak back to the Caddy and take out the .22 air pistol from the trunk, scanning the quiet street with stealth. It's always deserted around here, but I am aware that this still constitutes a risk.

I lurk behind a large, flowering bush at the back of the house. Then Sorenson emerges into the yard again, setting off a trip light, making me jump back behind the cover of the hibiscus. Something cracks under my feet, but Sorenson doesn't seem to hear as she struggles with the lock on her studio door in semidarkness under the weak autosensor movement spotlight. I have the gun trained on her swollen ass, presenting an almost unmissible target in those Lycra shorts. — Darn it, she says to herself as I squeeze the trigger and hear a pffft of air, followed by an, — Owww . . . what the . . . oh my God . . . oh . . . oh . . . oh . . . and see Sorenson, mouth open, rubbing her ass, and looking around bemused and in pain.

As she hobbles back toward the house, wincing and massaging her butt, I step back and out onto the street, heading through the open gate and around the corner to my car. I get my phone and hit Sorenson's digits.

— Lena S? Luce, my voice squashed out ghetto-high and sassy. — What the fuck goes, girlfriend?

— Oh, Lucy, I'm not good! My ass has just been stung! I don't know what happened!

— Stung? Like by a bug?

— I think so, but I feel like I've been stabbed, it's so sore!

— Where about? I mean, where did this bug sting you? Silence. Then, — I told you, in my butt.

— Wow . . . I fight back a fucking deluge of mirth, — I'm sorry, I thought when you said your ass had just been stung, you were meaning generally, rather than literally. I'm heading up your way. I'll come by in about a half hour.

When I head back to Lena's, her face is still wincing in pain, as I follow her wobbling ass inside. — My backside is so sore . . .

— Too bad . . . I sympathise, as we go into the living room. — The problem with this climate is we're full of invasive species. I doubt the bug that got you is indigenous. I saw a program on PSB last night about pythons, how they battle with alligators out in Glades—I halt in total shock as I see a treadmill, set up in front of the TV. Impressed doesn't cover it! — Well done!

— Figured I could burn calories while I watched HBO and Showtime.

Bitch being fucking specific to rub her cable shit in my face, knowing I'm stuck on network.

— Did you do those Morning Pages?

200

— Yes . . . she says, and points to six sheets of paper on her desk in the office.

— Good. I pick them up.

— I have to confess, I just did them, I kind of forgot about it this morning.

I throw the papers down on the desk.

— But I found them useful!

— Why do you think they're called *Morning* Papers? Huh? Huh! Cause you do them in the fucking morning! These are no good, I snap.

— Don't shout at me! I've had a bad day!

I take it down a notch, cause I need to inspect that ass. — Okay, Lena, I'm sorry, I soften. — Now let me see this wound . . . and I soon have her lying on the couch, me hunkered over her, her pants around her ankles and her panties still on, but pulled up into her ass cleft to expose those large, white, goosebumped buttocks. Sorenson must be the whitest chick in southern Florida. *I gone branded me that bitch's fat, lilywhite ass!* — That is a sore one, I tell her as I dab the wound with antiseptic. It's already yellowing and smudging blue-black around the shot's red tear. — Invasive species . . . I'd put money on it.

Fuck, yeah, I could spread those wobbly globes till I see the pubic hair from her pussy curl around those panties and . . . no, keep it professional. — I'm just gonna clean this up . . . I hear my voice low and throaty.

— Hmmm . . . Sorenson mumbles into the cushion.

After cleaning the injury and administering a Band-Aid, I get up. — All done.

We then sit side by side on the couch, watching her killer 70-inch plasma, Sorenson trying to keep her weight off the damaged buttock. The Siamese twins are back; there's an information-based program on their disorder. It shows historical photographs of previous sufferers of the condition. The stiff-assed fag actor's commentary: — Conjoined twins are classified by the point at which their bodies are joined. Amy and Annabel Wilks are the third most common type of conjoined twins, omphalopagus twins, comprising around 15 percent of cases. Their two bodies are fused at the lower chest. The hearts are separate but they partially share a liver, digestive system, and some other organs.

— Sharing a pussy? Sack that fucking shit!

— Those poor girls, Lena moans. — I doubt they'll be sharing a vagina, but they will share certain nerve endings. So to all intents and purposes that means if this Stephen character is having sex with one of them, then he's technically having sex with both. It's sick. It's rape!

— What?

— It's against her consent. Amy.

— Fuck that noise! You gotta be kidding!

— Well, it is!

— I see it differently. So you're saying it's okay that poor Annabel can't get fucked, by the boy she loves, cause her frigid bitch of a sister, Amy, that fucking *attachment*, won't take one for the team?

— That's disgusting, Lucy. What kind of a feminist are you?

— One that gets laid occasionally. You seem to be the

other variety, I suggest, watching a red flush rise up Sorenson's cheeks. — So, I've been dying to ask, how did it go with Miles from the gym?

— Good . . . Sorenson looks at me, picking at her nails.

— Gimme all the gory details. Did you jump his mutha-fuckin bones?

— Stop it.

— C'mon! Jesus, Lena! Did you guys fuck?

— That's none of your business!

— That's a "no" then?

— You can be such a bucket-mouthed sorority girl some-times, Lucy, she pouts, then she rises and climbs on that treadmill. It's only set at 4 mph, but at least she went without my prompting.

— Go, Lena!

And I'm trying to see past the fat, that horrible, disfiguring fat. What do I see? Those starey eyes and tight mouth in that pallid face, a crescent of moles on one side of it, like a constellation; only the tense, spooked aspect prevents it from being beautiful. That frizzy, collar-length hair, forever being swept out her eyes and tucked behind her ears.

After her "workout" we go into her studio. Again, the smell of resin and chemicals makes my eyes water. I blink them clear and I see a pile of plastic bones which she's made in her molds, sitting on the workbench. She has the skeleton of the big alien man now hung like a puppet on a series of wires, connected to a beam on the ceiling. It looks expressive and macabre. — This is really coming on.

— I know, but there's still something not quite right, she

says, picking up a camera and taking more photos of it, to complement the ones she has, taken at different angles, all pinned to a series of boards. Then she picks up a skull from the bench. Holds it up to the light, then against the alien man's fiberglass one.

— That isn't a *human* skull? I ask.

— No. It's a gorilla's. He died recently, at a zoo in Atlanta. It cost me a lot of money to source it. Unfortunately, it won't do. She smiles at me and just for a second I'm beset with a terrible unease, then she puts the skull back, and the feeling goes.

20

FUTURE HUMAN—THE PROCESS

As an artist Lena Sorenson is vague on her process, describing it as "differing from project to project." But it is clear that she makes extensive sketches of her landscapes, and then draws her characters into it. It's also known that Sorenson has started to use software previsualization tools, constructing sets and then dropping the figures into these spaces and manipulating their stances and relationships with each other. "I wanted to get a sense that although the image was part of a shifting scene, it would have the same static feel of permanence a sketch would. And these tools help me get exactly the correct spatial relationships between my figures."

Sorenson, who has studied taxidermy, then assembles the skeletal structure of the creatures. Usually, with smaller pieces, this is done with the preserved bones of tinier birds and mammals. Sorenson creates a "new" creature by mixing the skeletal parts of old ones to form the frame, combining bone parts of arms, legs, and spinal columns. With larger compositions, bigger bones (particularly the skull and pelvis, which help define the look and posture and therefore the expressions and movement of this "new" creature) are more problematic. These are usually created from scratch, through the construction of molds. Sorenson then wires the bones together in sections. The next stage is to put "flesh" on these bones. Sorenson has been secretive about how this is done, but it probably involves the use of some synthetic claylike material, which is sculpted around the bones to form the figure, before the entire structure is placed into a huge box and moldings are made of the form. Sorenson then removes the "flesh" from the bone structures and places them into the premade molds and pours a resin inside, which sets around them.

This produces a figurine, or, increasingly, a full-scale figure, with greeny-brown exterior "skin." The molded resin is translucent enough just to make the bones suspended inside it visible. Sorenson claims that she has been subliminally influenced by the chunks of fruit embedded in her mother's Jell-O. She then applies a model-maker's craft to add details; for example, she often puts real human hair spines onto the body.

21

CONTACT 8

To: lucypattybrennan@hardass.com
From: michelleparish@lifeparishioners.com
Subject: Success

All I can say is that my mantra has always been whatever it takes. I don't accept failure. Ever. Succeed by any means necessary.

How are the Morning Pages working out?

Michelle

To: michelleparish@lifeparishioners.com
From: lucypattybrennan@hardass.com
Subject: Success

Thank you. I desperately hoped, but ultimately knew, that was what you would say. Now I'm more convinced than ever that I'm right. You are truly an inspirational visionary, Michelle!

Luce x

To: lucypattybrennan@hardass.com
From: michelleparish@lifeparishioners.com
Subject: Success

Wow, such praise! Thank you! I try!

M x

PS The Morning Pages?

To: michelleparish@lifeparishioners.com
From: lucypattybrennan@hardass.com
Subject: Success

I tried and am still trying with the Morning Pages. You have motivated clients, Michelle, but this bitch, well, frankly she lacks respect. I gave her slovenly ass Morning Pages to write. Of course, she didn't do them but just hastily cobbled some shit together that evening when I went to see her, cause some bug bit her fat booty.

I told her the pages were no good and I didn't want to see them. Mentioned that they are called Morning Pages cause you do them in the MORNING! Duh!

L x

22

A CONTROLLED
ENVIRONMENT

There are a few of them back outside, at the front, just standing around, or sitting in parked cars. Usually at least two, sometimes more. Why do they do it? What the fuck do they want? There are a hundred minor celebs, on any given day, making fools of themselves at parties in South Beach. Yet every time they forget about me, Quist and Thorpe resume their onscreen toxic double act. Valerie isn't returning my calls; other than the ocassional *Keep your head down* text, and checking I've received the Total Gym freebie, the bitch has blown me away.

Morning fucking Pages? Like you can *write* your way outta shit? Fuck that noise, we gotta talk reality.

Sorenson's stats just ain't cutting it. We're almost two weeks into the program and she's lost eight pounds. At this rate it'll take FUCKING YEARS I DO NOT HAVE to sort out that time-wasting loser. The more she calls and the more I see her, the worse my life seems to get. It riles me that that fucking nutcase got me into this mess. If the candy-assed tubster hadn't fucking filmed me on her phone and given it to those TV pricks, I'd never have had this level of celebrity and the subsequent witch hunt thrust upon me. And now she's still fucking with me!

Drastic action is called for.

I'll get nothing out of the Porky Pride of Potters Prairie, so I call up Miles. — So what went down? Or should I say, who? Did that firefighter's hose see any action?

A cagey silence is followed by a half-assed confession. — I couldn't do that Lena chick. I reckon she still has it bad about her ex. We've all had our hearts broken, Lucy. You dunno people's backstory. You can't take advantage of somebody in that situation. She's a nice girl.

Useless prick. Fuck him. — Okay. You tried. You failed. My fault—the task was so obviously beyond you.

— Lucy—

I shut him off. Another pussy who would indulge the weak. Why? Because he's one of them. A six-pack and a nice set of pecs don't change that.

So fuck him. You want shit done you gotta fucking do it yourself. You can't rely on any of them. They're all in it for themselves. They will fuck you over for any crappy two-bit personal gain. So you gotta be strong. You gotta crush all those motherfuckers under your heel, cause make no mistake, they are looking to do the same to you, just as soon as you show any fucking signs of weakness.

I get round to Sorenson's. Despite the wary climb into the Caddy, she's animated. — Where are we going today? The gym? Lummus Park? Or Flamingo Park?

— We're gonna mix it up a little, I tell her, as we head over the MacArthur toward downtown Miami. — It's a surprise.

— I like surprises!

So we're going up in the elevator to floor twenty in Mom's

apartment block. When we get out, I tell Sorenson we're running up the steps to the penthouse at floor forty. A piteous complaint erupts: — Why can't we use the StairMaster in the gym?

— No, we gotta mix it up. This time we climb real stairs. All the way to the top. But there's a reward waiting in my mom's apartment: some wholesome nutritious food, plus one of those peanut-butter-and-dark-chocolate protein shakes you love so much.

The greed-glint ignites in Sorenson's eyes, blitzing away the withered Scandinavian synapses that have probably cursed her family for generations. I can practically see her taste buds dance in that voracious cavern of a mouth.

And we're off . . .

— C'mon, Lena; hup, two, three, four, I rap out, pointing up the stairs, leaving Sorenson gasping in my wake. After a few flights, the panting grows fainter. Soon I realize I've left the fucking blimp behind.

I'm ascending in a backward march, then stopping at a bend, watching that bloated, red-faced, gasping slug struggle around another landing. — C'mon! You can do it!

By floor thirty-two, Sorenson's scarlet face looks up at me. The face of a spoiled, fat child. — Oh . . . oh . . . oh . . .

— C'mon, Lena Sorenson! You can do this!

— I'll try—

— Don't *try*: do! Triers are criers. Winners don't fucking try, winners do! To try is to prepare to fail! Do! DO! DO! Did you do your Morning Pages this morning?

— I never . . . I meant to but—

— NO GOOD! NO FUCKING GOOD! DO! C'MON! DO! DO! DO!

Floor thirty-six, and the fucking disobedient loser Sorenson has slowed down to a crawl. Those weak, stumpy legs struggle to find the pneumatic power to lever this gross pile of blubber up to the next set of concrete. — Oh my God—

— Take your hands *off* the friggin banister! I shout. — C'mon, Lena baby, c'mon, show them who Lena Sorenson is! Is she a big, fat, lardyassed victim?

Sorenson's face looks mournfully up at me. — Please . . . she begs.

I step down and grip her shoulders heavily. I feel flesh. I should *not* be feeling loose, flabby flesh on *shoulders*. I dig my nails into that horrible blubber. — IS SHE A BIG, FAT LARDYASSED VICTIM?! SAY NO! SAY. FUCKING. NO, LENA!

— NO! Sorenson's defiant, miserable scream echoes round the stair in the ghost building, and she's digging deep, galvanizing, pushing at her wobbly frame.

— THAT'S MY GIRL! THAT'S MY BEAUTIFUL GIRL! LENA SORENSON IS A HOT PIECE OF ASS WHO TURNS HEADS IN EVERY FUCKING BAR ON OCEAN DRIVE!

— YES!

And we're off again, and she's puffing and grunting, fighting every step, her metabolism cranked up to the extent she'll be burning fat for hours. — Fat-burnin machine, Lena S!

— Fat . . . bur . . . nin . . . ma-sheeen . . .

212

By the last few flights of stairs she's crawling. Sorenson literally finishes on her knees. — C'mon, Lena! Get up!

She does, and I take her inside, to the unfurnished apartment. All it has are Mom's treadmill, the Total Gym, a chair, and the inflatable mattress and comforter I brought over yesterday, which Lena gratefully slumps onto.

And in the kitchen, my supplies, as I start chopping up some banana. — Relax. Stretch those legs out, I shout through at her, as I put the fruit into the blender, with low-fat yogurt, peanut butter, chocolate protein powder, soy milk, and ice. I pulp it, adding a little touch of my own special ingredient.

As I take the shake through into the living room, Sorenson's still panting on the mattress, raised up on her elbows, her legs sprawled across the hardwood floor. She's struggling to force the air into her lungs. But the greed impulse overrides everything, and as I wave the milkshake at her, a chubby fist reaches out and fastens around it. She pokes the protruding straw into that weeping tomato face and if she sucks on everything like she does that fucking straw, well, sorry, Miles, but you sure missed the goddamn boat.

Her shake goes down, but Lena doesn't get off the floor. Instead her eyes hood and she stretches out and drifts off in a daze. The Rohypnol has done its work, although, with her exhaustion, it was pushing at an open door.

Around twenty minutes later, I'm shaking her awake, pushing a tepid black coffee in front of her. — Wakey, wakey!

— What . . .?

— You blacked out. Sip this . . . Her thin lips purse around the rim of the mug, sucking in some cold coffee.

213

The caffeine takes almost instant effect. — Did I coll-apse . . .? I feel so pooped . . . what . . .?

As I stand up, she sees that one of her wrists is snared by the fur-lined handcuff onto a fifteen-foot length of heavy chain with welded links, the other end of which is fastened by another set of cuffs onto one of the support pillars.

Sorenson shakes the bracelet. — What *is* this? Did I pass out? she asks, as her eyes focus on me. — What's going on? Lucy?

She's rubbing at her chubby wrist, looking at me in disbe-lief as I explain the new rules of the game to her. — This is where you will live for the next month, at least. How much longer after that is completely up to you.

— But . . . but . . .

— The only butt I'm interested in is that lardy one you're sitting on. You are going to hate me for this, but it's become manifestly clear to me that I *cannot* do my job and get you to lose weight unless I can control your environment.

Sorenson looks dumbly at me, then at the cuff, shaking it again. She laughs as if this is all a big college prank. — But you can't keep me here for a month! It's crazy!

I look her in the eye. — There is nothing crazier than trying to kill yourself with food. As Einstein said, the defin-ition of insanity is doing the same thing over and over again and expecting different results. No more. This is drastic, yes, but it's also essential.

She knows I'm not joking now. — But . . . you can't chain me up like an animal. She stands up, shaky on her feet at first, then thrashes at the bracelet on her wrist, the chain rattling across the floor. — This is *ridiculous*! I'm *paying* you!

— You're paying me to succeed, and I'm gonna do just that!

— Let me go! You're fired!

— You don't make decisions anymore, Lena. You *cannot* make adult decisions.

— Who do you think you—

— Your so-called decisions are the impulses of a fat, greedy, spoiled fucking child. I'm shaking my head like a puppy coming out of the ocean. — You lied to me. Lied about what you were eating. I gave you a fucking diet sheet and you told me you were following it and you fucking lied!

Sorenson's looking around the room, then back to me, in utter confusion. — But I tried, I—

— Until you become a real adult, a proper woman, I'm gonna make all the decisions for you, on your behalf. Because your bad decisions are negatively impacting on my life! Giving that video clip of me to the TV people: bad decision! Stuffing your face with shit when I'm trying to get you to lose weight: bad fucking decision!

She steps forward, yanked back by the chain. — But you can't do this to me! You're fucking . . . you're kidnapping me! YOU'RE HOLDING ME HERE AGAINST MY WILL!

— WHAT FUCKING WILL?! YOU HAVE NONE! IF YOU DID YOU WOULDN'T BE IN THIS GODDAMN MESS! I take a step toward her, screaming back into her fat face, watching her shrink away. — I know it's drastic, but you've reached and breached the limits of my patience. Up here I can control your cals in and cals out. I want you to

215

lose an average of ten pounds per week, which will see you ship out here in a month. Those lights, I point to two small lamps I've set up in opposite corners of the room, — are on timers. They come on at six, when it gets dark, and they go off at ten, when you will sleep. I will come by every day, sometimes more than once a day, and make sure you get three calorie-controlled meals, with all the nutrients you need. Those buckets, I nod at the big plastic receptacles full of water and disinfectant, — are for your piss and shit. They will be emptied at the end of every day, or in the morning. I have your phone; most of the time I'll leave it in the kitchen on silent, though I'll monitor it for any emergency calls.

Sorenson paces over to the window, testing the limits of her chain. But her eyes keep swiveling back to me. — Please, Lucy, you can't—

— Can, will, have. I pull her keys out of my bag. — I'll also be swinging by your house regularly to pick up any mail, and check on the place. But this is your new home, so get used to it. I look around the room. — You'll be here some time, so there are certain hygiene issues we have to resolve. In order that you keep clean and don't develop killer cystitis, I'm going to bring up a kiddie paddling pool, which I'll let you bathe in every couple of days.

— This is . . . I don't . . . how . . . Sorenson gasps.

I ignore her bleatings, heading over to the thermostat on the wall. — The temperature will be set at 70 degrees. You should be comfortable in a strapless sports bra and panties, and your gross shorts, if you so wish, and I point to a plastic bag full of these items.

— I can't stay here . . . you can't do this!

— As I've said, how long you stay here is up to you. And these, I point at the treadmill and the Total Gym, — are your escape tools. There will be no hand weights or resistance bands or even medicine balls. They're all you're going to get, so I suggest you make good use of them. And, I smile tightly at her, throwing down a notepad and stubby pencil, — you *will* do Morning Pages!

I slip my bag over my shoulder.

— But . . . you're crazy! YOU'RE FUCKING CRAZY! People will be asking where I am!

— Who precisely? I ask, holding up her cell phone. — Your family? Your friends in the art world? Kim? Jerry? There's a horrible moment as I watch a slice of her perish inside. It weakens me, and I can hear my tone softening. — You come up with the goods, and you'll be outta here in no time, and I move back into the kitchen, switching her cell to vibrate, and leaving it on the counter.

— Wait . . . Lucy, please, wait . . . you can't leave me here on my own! Her voice starts to rise in a whispering plea, before breaking into a drawn-out shriek. — WAAAIIITTT!!!! LOOO-CEEE!!!!

I'm disinclined to listen to this; I'm outta there, slamming shut the living-room door, then the apartment's heavier one, double-locking it, muffling Sorenson's cries to a vague background sound. Then I'm into the elevator and down to the lobby, checking the mailboxes to ensure that no callers or investors are coming round to make purchase or rental inquiries. Satisfied that fat girl really is on her own, I drive

217

back over to South Beach. As I get into heavy traffic on the MacArthur, Miles calls. — I've been thinking about our little arrangement. I'm happy to try again.

— Null and void. You failed to deliver.

— If this is about *Heat*—

Prick talking NBA at a time like this; I'm thinking of LeBron, Dwyane, and Bosh. — Fuck Heat, Celtics rule!

Miles goes silent for a beat, then says, — Cool. The thing is, I actually liked Lena. I'd kinda like to hang out with her. As a buddy thing. She's a pretty interesting lady.

Not a good idea, but if I tell him that, he'll be all over her and that certainly would not do. — Do what the fuck you like!

— Heyyy! Do I detect a hint of jealousy here? After all, if you shaved some beef off of that chick, she would be pretty damn hot!

— In your fucking dreams! Jesus! Could you possibly be any more trivial and inconsequential as a human being?

— I know Lena stays in MB somewhere. What's her address?

— She's my client. I certainly can't give her private address out to you. There's such a thing as client confidentiality, I wince at my own prissy, defensive tone.

— No sweat, Miami Beach isn't a big pond. I'm over there all the time. Now that she's on my radar I'm sure I'll see her around.

— What a treat for you both, I click off my cell.

I get home, park up, take a shower, then settle and read more about the glory days of Lena Sorenson in *Future Human*.

23

FUTURE HUMAN—CRITICAL VERSUS COMMERCIAL RESPONSES TO LENA SORENSON'S WORK

Few artists have been denounced so virulently by the critical art establishment as Lena Sorenson, yet very few have enjoyed such commercial success. It's strange that this mannered, almost old-fashioned, waiflike young woman from the Midwest can arouse such vitriol. For her part, Sorenson's long-term reluctance to talk about herself and her work remains an endearing feature of this enigmatic artist.

Yet the attraction of Sorenson's art, in the face of much critical disdain, is not difficult to understand. Lena Sorenson gets her evolved/ devolved characters to do the very things that make us human. They are not just scavenging on garbage heaps and tearing each other apart, but sharing, celebrating, and, in particular, nurturing children. *The Post-Nuclear Family*, purchased by the McCormick Foundation for the Art Institute, is one of modern art's most tender and emotional compositions. Sorenson's art resonates with Western youth as it appeals to a generation devoid of hope for anything other than a dystopian future, which, for most, will be inferior to the life enjoyed by past generations.

It therefore seems highly disingenuous to deride Lena Sorenson as a "glorified comic-book illustrator." Her work speaks to youth, and their concerns for the future (or lack of) in a consumer capitalist epoch now unable to extend credit for its citizens to continue their relentless shopping and breeding program, and which, now basically exposed as a scam for the megarich, has run out of rabbits to pull from the hat.

Andy Warhol once memorably remarked that he didn't read his reviews, he weighed them. As long as art critics keep devoting column inches to telling us how poor an artist Lena Sorenson is, it seems certain that she will continue to laugh all the way to the bank. However, many more open-minded critics, when they see what Sorenson is representing, invariably, though often unwittingly, fall upon the discovery of her particular genius.

24

CONTACT 9

To: michelleparish@lifeparishoners.com
From: lucypattybrennan@hardass.com
Subject: Success!

Magical Michelle,

The annoying thing about this client: bitch got talent. Big talent. So I'm stopping at NOTHING to make her get control of her goddamned weight. You are right: sometimes you just have to show a fat bitch who's boss.

Luce x

PS Morning Pages WILL be done!

25

HEAT

Looking out at the world through green-tinted Ray-Bans: they make Miami less vivid, oppressive, and hallucinogenic. Throat dry and rough due to some tropical spore shit floating around that has been laying low the Rust Belt transplants. Breakfast at Taste, a concoction called "only for the fittest," then dragging the cart round Whole Paycheck. Two model chicks argue passionately about supplements. One guy scrutinizes another's denim-clad ass. A beachball cop grabs some bakery goods, big smile on his face. Don't the police department have fucking rules about obesity?

Sorenson: wonder what sort of night that fat liar had? Shopping for two is a fucking drag. I load up on: protein powder, berries, oatmeal, low-fat yogurt, tofu, salmon, nuts, seeds, avocados, spinach, romaine, tomatoes, bananas, mango, apples, broccoli, cabbage, fat-free feta cheese. At the checkout, as I'm being fucking fleeced, I eyeball a copy of *Heat* on the rack and I'm flabbergasted to see that *Miles* is at the bottom left-hand corner! I pick it up and *oh my God*, there I am!

INSATIABLE HEROINE LUCY'S LESBIAN LOVE
TRIANGLES SADDEN EX-LOVER MILES

Hunky firefighter Miles Aborgast, 28, is heartbroken about his recent split from beleaguered Lucy Brennan, the "Miami Causeway Heroine," who disarmed a crazed gunman with her bare hands. And he cites not only her newfound fame, but her fondness for same-sex encounters for coming between them. "She's a pretty insatiable lady—not that I was complaining at first. I knew she was dominating and liked to swing both ways, so I can't say I was sad when she introduced other women into the equation, especially as we both dug hot girls. Afterward, though, I felt like just another toy in one of her games. Lucy's problem is that she's incapable of love."

That was what the bastard meant by *Heat*—the fucking magazine, not the basketball team! I turn the poisonous rag around and put it back in the rack. The checkout girl shoots me a nauseating vacant but predatory "don't I know you?" glare, and I'm trying not to react. I look across to the parking lot outside. She rings up my stuff and bags it and I pay the fucker and get out and into the Cadillac, my heartbeat pounding like I've just stepped off the treadmill.

My hands are clammy on the wheel, all the way over the MacArthur. I'm both anxious and excited to see how Sorenson's coped. I park up and remove her provisions. I also have the kiddie pool, ready to be inflated. The building is still eerily deserted. Surely *somebody* (other than the Potters Prairie Penthouse Princess) must be staying here? I take the elevator up and quietly open the apartment door and creep down the hallway. No sounds from the living room. I resist the temptation to immediately check on her, instead going to the kitchen and picking up her phone, where I left it on the countertop. Zero calls, and the six emails are either spam or from the loser websites she subscribes to.

I switch on the kettle, then I start to blow up the pool. As it expands, a cartoon bear with a gross sex-offender smile, which reminds me of Winter, starts to take shape. He's standing on a beach with a spade in one paw and a bucket in the other. I hear a sudden shuffling and rattling coming from the living room. — Hello! Lucy! Is that you! You have to let me go! I've barely slept! This has gone too far, Lucy! You've made your point! YOU HAVE TO LET ME GO!

— Good morning, I smile, stepping into the room to greet her, laying the kiddie pool out on the hardwood floor alongside the mattress, where she sits cross-legged, the comforter draped around her shoulders. I note that she hasn't changed into a new set of panties and sports bra. — Morning Pages done? I look down at the blank notebook. — Obviously not. Not a great start, is it?

— LET ME GO! she suddenly screams at me, then looks to the floor and starts ludicrously pounding it with one blobby fist. — HELP! HELP!

I leave her to it, watching her contorted face throb redder. Then she breaks down, convulsing in heavy sobs as tears run down her burning cheeks.

224

— Scream all you like. The entire building's unoccupied, I inform her, cupping my hands to my mouth and shouting in mimicry, — MY NAME IS LENA! I EAT TOO MUCH SHIT!

Sorenson lifts her half-bowed head up, her face soaked with tears. — Why is this happening to me? she whispers to nobody. — I've done nothing wrong!

— Can the self-pity, it doesn't do a fucking thing for me.

— But what have I done? What have I done to you-hoo—

— I don't speak pig. I don't speak victim. You, too, should stop using such languages, I tell her and she looks up at me like a molested child. I feel myself take a deep breath. — See this as an opportunity. Here. I hand her the new diet sheet and meal plan.

She takes it in her fat greasy paw and sets it on the floor in front of her.

— I'm making you an oatmeal and blueberry breakfast, with flaxseed and a touch of honey. Three hundred cal, and full of complex carbs and antioxidants. All washed down with some green tea.

I take her piss bucket—there's no shit in the other one—and empty the contents down the toilet and refill it. Then I prepare the oatmeal. I'm serving it in a plastic bowl with a plastic spoon. I bring it in with some tepid tea, served in a polystyrene cup, so Sorenson can't use it as a weapon, if she ever got the balls to try and do so.

— This is twisted . . . it's humiliating . . .

— You're talking yourself out of breakfast, I tell her, holding the bowl away from her.

— Okay! Okay! I step into her range and she eagerly grasps it, greedily attacking her food with the spoon.

— Slowly. This has to last you. Savor each mouthful. Chew. Don't just stuff it down.

But Sorenson doesn't listen, and cleans the bowl out quickly. — I'm still hungry, she moans.

— Fill up on water, I tell her, thrusting a liter bottle of Volvic in her face. — Right, let's get you on that treadmill. Two hundred and fifty cal are getting shipped.

— I'm not getting on that! I barely slept! You are fucking crazy!

— And you are *fucking heading* for type 2 diabetes! Do you know what happens when you get type 2 diabetes?

A spark of fear in her eyes.

— If you think I'm gonna back down on this plan, you dunno shit about how I roll. The quicker you lose the weight, the quicker you get the fuck outta here. C'mon!

She heaves herself up, dragging her chain, pouting at me, before slowly hauling her chubby ass onto the machine. The chain dangles by her side. — It's awkward, this chain, she lifts her wrist, — it's so heavy . . .

— What am I gonna tell ya? Find a way. Work around it! You'll just have to work the Total Gym a little more on the left side, in order to compensate.

Sorenson looks at me like a hormonal teenager told to tidy her room. But she's starting the treadmill up at 3 mph then ramping it gradually to a steady 6 mph. — Take your hands off the machine! I do not want you holding it! Move your arms strongly as you run!

She complies, showing me that the bitch can fucking do it without me shouting at her, so why the need for the drama? I leave her and go to the kitchen to fix her tofu and spinach salad lunch. When I return, I get her on the Total Gym for a demonstration session. I prefer free weights for balance and core strength, but, as unlikely as it seems, Sorenson might get the balls to use them as a weapon against me or try to hurl one through a window to attract help. We start a routine, which I break up by getting her to step off the machine to do sets of jumping jacks, starbursts, lunges, burpees, and abdominal exercises. I get more moans about the chain, but she struggles through them.

When we've finished, she settles down quietly on the mat, holding her knees, staring off into space, and breathing heavily. I fill the kiddie pool with tepid water, disquieted by the image of the mincing, predatory bear looking up at me. I'd think twice before getting in that pool. Crazy that it's designed for kids. Still, it's Sorenson's problem, and I leave her the light meal for her lunch. — This is all you'll get till five-thirty when I come back at dinnertime. Eat it now if you want, but be prepared for a long wait.

She looks up at me with those haunted eyes. — You can't—

— Not acceptable, I shake my head. — I don't hear that word, I glare at her, cupping my ear. — Don't ever use that loser word in connection with me. I *can*. I *will*. I *have*. And now, I'm fucking *off*, I tell her, shouting back as I head for the door, — WORK!

— WAAAIITTT!!!

— And wash! I point to the pool, before I split, getting

out of that joint, driving back over the MacArthur Causeway, away from mundane Miami and back to the *real world* of SoBe.

South Beach is a marvel, as impressive and unique in its own way as the French Quarter in New Orleans. I'm delighted that, bar a few notable casualities, the art deco district escaped the bulldozers. Sometimes, though, as I park in the multi-story lot, I have to concede that Lincoln is somewhat short of its Rodeo Drive aspiration, and Ocean is often more like Cancún at Spring Break than the French Riviera.

It's the time of the year when the place loads up with beery frat boys slumming it. Two of them sit in the sun, an upturned hat laid out, displaying a sign: ROAD TRIP—NEED MONEY FOR BEER AND STRIPPERS, but they look too well scrubbed, with those sharp, entitled Vince Vaughn eyes, to succeed as panhandlers.

I swing onto Washington Avenue, the real main street in MB, with its clubs, sports bars, and fast-food joints. In the winter months, it fills up with wandering bums, who roll into town on Greyhounds and Trailways, fleeing the northern chills. Next to every ATM and every branch of Walgreens and CVS, you'll find some drifter has set up in the mooching business.

I'm outside the Starbucks on Washington at 12th, thinking about a green tea, when my blood runs cold as a bleary-eyed, rubber-mouthed jerk, sweating in a Hawaiian shirt, lurches out a doorway, standing square in front of me. *Winter.* — Gotta cigarette?

I instinctively look away.

— Hey! I'm talkin t'ya. I said, gotta cigarette?

I should deck the asshole, but instead I turn and walk into the Starbucks. Once again that prick doesn't even recognize me as the person who saved his fucking life! Why couldn't I have stood back and let that fag altar boy McCandless put a bullet into his sick brain?

I can feel myself shaking with rage. Yet I'm aware of being not quite present in the moment, as if gripped by a fever. I order a green tea, barely noticing the customary look of betrayal on the barista's face for declining their poisonous coffee. Then I move over to the window and sit watching the unspeakably abhorrent creep, Winter, through the glass, hassling people. A couple of tourists stop, an earnest college kid handing over what looks like a five-dollar bill. Winter pockets it with a cold grin and heads off. A sudden scalding pain in my hand: I've been crushing the cup and the tea has burned me. I leave it pooling on the window-ledge table, and follow the pedophile bastard, my mitt tingling painfully in the heat.

Winter crosses the street and heads down 12th, in the direction of the bay. His shorts are stained at the back, like he's sat in something, but otherwise he doesn't look like he's been living on the streets. He moves purposefully, walking with a slightly twisted gait. I'm tracking him as he heads right to Alton, stopping only to make an unwelcome comment at a passing young girl, who heads on without breaking her stride. Winter then turns north on Alton, and stops outside the liquor store. He comes out with a fifth of some horrible shit, a terse smile on his face, and carries on toward Lincoln. I check the time. I need to be at Bodysculpt.

I'm only about five minutes late, but Marge Falconetti is already there, waiting helplessly to be told what to do. Like warm the fuck up, bitch! I get her into her routine and she's actually doing reasonably well, and she's lost a few pounds. — We're going in the right direction again, I tell her.

This scrap of affirmation is like meat to a starving dog. — Yes, I think so, I feel good . . .

— But all that means is that we have to work harder.

Her face falls cause she knows what's coming next. I glance at her short frame. Bitch was bred to squat. — Gimme ten squats, then ten burpees, I sing.

Of course, she hates them. — Why do I always have to do those?

I crisply slap her blubbery thigh, encased like sausage meat in the ludicrously stretched black spandex. — These are your quads. They are the biggest muscles in your body. We build these up, they burn fat like nobody's business. We use these, I grope her thigh, — to burn off this, I take a handful of her blubbery gut. She looks sadly at me, then I watch that pampered lummox suffer for a solid hour.

As Marge staggers off breathlessly to hose down her sweating bulk, I hit the juice bar and join Mona in an acai berry protein shake. She has a distracted air, and a flinty glare lights the eyes in her frosted face.

— You look a little rough, honey, I delight in telling her. — Late one last night?

— Oh my God, Mona's facial muscles try to twitch into some animation, but you can't inject that much toxin and expect a wide range of expressions.

— The things we do for love, I smile, as my next client, Sophia, my sweet old widow with the bad knees, comes in. I gently put her through her paces, using the low-impact elliptical for cardio. I like listening to her talk about her late husband; I dunno if men were genuinely better back then, or if I just meet the assholes. — You obviously loved him very much, I observe, as she spills another anecdote while slowly grinding out the cals.

— I still do. I always will. I know he's gone, but the love I have for him will never die.

— You're lucky, I mean, to have known that kind of love . . . I look to the machine, — . . . and five . . . four . . . three . . . two . . . one.

— Oh, I know that, she says, getting her breath and taking my hand, and stepping off the elliptical.

— Don't try and replace him with sugary snacks and junk food. He'd want you to be the best you that you can be.

— I know . . . She breaks down in tears. — I just miss him so much . . .

I put my arm around her. She smells of talc and perfume from another age. — We're going to get the weight off you. Take the pressure off those bad knees. Make it easier for you to get out more. Eli would want that, wouldn't he?

— Yes, he would. She looks up at me, her eyes strong under the lens of fear. — You really are such a wonderful, kind girl.

— We've got to be here for each other, I whisper gently, letting her go and stroking her arm, — it's all there is.

Then I'm back along to the Lincoln lot to pick up the car,

and inching down the causeway in heavy traffic into down-town Miami.

At the not-so-ivory tower, I bring Sorenson a grilled chicken salad dinner from Whole Paycheck. Factoring in vegetables and the sweet potato, it comes to a roughish 425 cal on Lifemap, not that I get much in the way of fucking gratitude for my efforts. — I'm sick, Lucy, you really have to let me go!

— If you do thirty minutes, Lena, three-zero, that'll be 1,500 cal burned off today.

— No! I can't! I said I was sick!

— It's only your body recalibrating. It's like cold turkey. Fight through that shit! Speaking of shit . . . well done. I pick up the bucket.

Gross bitch has practically shat her weight in dirty chest-nuts. I've been putting flaxseed in her food and with all the water I'm making her drink, it's already starting to pay off. I take the foul, toxic mess to the toilet and flush it away. Soon those stools will be long, smooth, and unbroken, not like she's shat out the Thing from the *Fantastic Four*. And she's used the pool and changed her clothes. I pick up the discarded items to take to the wash.

When I return, Sorenson is still pleading. — I need a Coke, or a Sprite! Just one! My head . . .

God, she disgusts me! Lying on that mattress, comforter swaddling her fat frame, like an obese refugee. Loo-zir! — The treadmill. I pat the machine.

— I can't!

— Uh, uh, uh . . . what the fuck have I told you about the unpardonable rudeness of the "c" word?

She pulls the comforter closer to her, looking at me with those beseeching eyes. — No . . . please . . . let me go! Please, Lucy . . . this has gone beyond a joke! I'll do what you want! I'll follow the fucking program! The point has been made! Just let me go!

I walk toward her, sinking down on my knees in front of her. I point to the treadmill. — If you do as I ask, it means a fifteen hundred debit on your daily calories account. That's half a pound of fat. There, I run my finger under her chin, — and here, I poke her gut, causing her to shrink away.

— I can't . . . she moans in a small voice, — I never slept properly, I'm so tired.

— As I said, that's just your body recalibrating. I spring up. — C'mon, I try to tug her to her feet, — let's go!

— But I can't!

— Losers find excuses, winners find ways, and I take a deep breath and haul the useless little sack of shit upright and push her onto the treadmill, her chain rattling behind her as she steps on. — Find a way! I stuff my phone into the iPod dock and set it on Joan Jett's "Love Is Pain," singing along as I set her controls to 4 mph.

— Okay . . . okay . . . Sorenson reluctantly hits her jogging stride.

I stand back to watch that fat little hamster work her ass to freedom. But you know what? That isn't enough. I spring forward and push at the controls. 5 mph.

— Okay! Okay!

Bitch gotta sweat or bitch gotta bruise. Up to 6 mph, a mild run.

— AGGHHH! The loser sow shoots off the mill like a grotesque comic-strip character, chain yanking at her arm, her fat ass wedged in between the machine and the wall. Her petulant face twists up at me. — Oh my God . . . this is a nightmare . . .

— The nightmare is one of your own making. I point at her, the contempt and derision coming from deep within me, as Joan sings about love being pain and not being ashamed. — I'm trying to save your bloated ass! Now get back on that track, you fucking ungrateful, time-wasting bitch!

Sorenson fearfully complies, pulling herself to her feet and stepping on.

She gets the message. This time she's running strongly. — Better! Put those fuckin dimes in the jukebox!

I make her shave off another four hundred cal, to hit the fifteen hundred goal, before letting her eat her food as a reward. — Slow the fuck down when you eat. Watch every spoonful. Focus on the food. Chew it!

The nervous eyes under those bangs, going from me to what's on the end of her spoon. A passive fucking victim. No balls, no fight. To let somebody do this to them. That asshole guy she went out with; the way she just let that prick fuck with her. You gotta fight them. You gotta hurt them. You can't just fucking well lie down and take it. — Okay, Lena, you've done well. If you keep this up, I'm going to bring you a book tomorrow. Then, at the end of the week, I'm suddenly thinking of my portable, — you might get a TV.

Sorenson's face is still crunched in misery. — Please, Lucy. The point has been made. I'll come here every day. Just don't make me spend another night here. I *need* to sleep in my own bed. I *really, really need* to get on with my work, she begs, her eyes red-rimmed. — Don't leave me here for another night!

Those urging eyes. Her work is so important . . . but the bitch is playing me. I'm not gonna be manipulated, this won't work if I'm manipulated. — Toughen the fuck up, Lena, and *do your Morning Pages*, because if I come back here tomorrow and find none, there will *no breakfast*. Get that? *No fucking breakfast* without Morning Pages!

And I head outside, double-locking the door, as her cries belt out:

— LUUUCCCEEE!!!! NO!!!! HELP!!!!

But there's still nobody around, and as I summon the elevator and hear it clicking up the floors, I'm thinking: *yes, this building must be a spooky place to spend the night.*

I key the ignition on the Caddy, as a call from Mona comes in on my cell.

— Have you seen the news?

— No.

— Oh. Don't shoot the messenger, she says coyly, and I know it's not good. As much as I loathe that bitch I have to concede that she has a real nose for scenting blood in the water.

Mona recounts the grim story, but no way can her voice remain as neutral as that botulinum-paralyzed face, and irrepressible glee sparkles her tone. I get home, and there's nobody at the rear entrance to the building, and, thank God, a free parking space. In my apartment, the plastic cunt's gloating is confirmed on a local TV channel. The missing ten-year-old, Carla Riaz, has been found dead, in the home of her neighbor, one Ryan Balbosa.

In the swarthy mug shot I'm gaping at, I see the second man I saved that night on the Julia Tuttle. I can't take my eyes off the screen, even when Balbosa's face is replaced by a carousel of other sex offenders. The blood in my veins is like ice; the monster I saved did that to a child. *That* would have been the scum to execute, *that* one.

Chef Dominic calls, but I don't pick up. I listen to an extended voicemail about a party. I can't do that.

Mona calls again; I don't pick up. Another voicemail, offering another party. No way.

Instead, I look through the plates in Sorenson's book, at those monster men and women, scrambling through the debris of ruined cities. Then I leave the apartment and get into the car. The gates open and I pull into the alley. Two paparazzi snap at me, one of them, the bastard with the wrecked camera, shouting, but I look ahead and edge slowly onto the street. When I get there, I floor the gas pedal. The Caddy burns rubber (or as much as it can) and tears toward Alton sounding like a broken hairdryer. I take a long route to Lena's place, over the MacArthur, through downtown, midtown, and back over the Julia Tuttle, paranoid that those bastards are tailing me.

But the coast seems clear as I park in the Publix lot and walk around to Sorenson's house. Picking up the mail, I dispose of those ubiquitous fucking fliers advertising club nights and food deliveries. There's a package among all the junk. I deliberate on whether or not to open it. No, it's Lena's.

That's crossing the line. I also decide against having a closer look at Lena's studio. I dump the rest of the shit in the trash and take the package home with me, again parking a couple of blocks from my building, then head over to Whole Paycheck.

As I come outside with my groceries, crossing the parking lot and passing the bus stop, a contaminated-looking guy shuffles obsequiously toward me. I'm relieved when I realize he's not paparazzi, just a bum. — Excuse me, miss, I wonder if you could help me? I need to get to Mount Sinai hosp—

— Bored already. I wave an upturned palm at him, jumping across Alton as the pedestrian signal comes on. When I get back to my apartment the street outside is full of press. I can't get into my own fucking home! I double-back to the Caddy and drive up to Lena's place where I make some food, and try to watch her cable. But I can't settle. I keep thinking about that kid, and that animal Balbosa. What the fuck have I done?

I go onto Lena's computer. It isn't even password- or security-protected, and opens up straight onto the page of her email account.

26

CONTACT 10

To: lenadiannesorenson@thebluegallery.com
From: mollyrennesorenson@gmail.com
Subject: Did You Get The Caramel Creams?

Lena,

Please get back to me. I know you have a busy-busy, chop-chop life in Miami, but we like to hear from our girl!

Lynsey Hall is rumored to be having a baby . . . I know.

The caramel creams are your favorites. Hope you enjoy! Let me know if they came, UPS have been kind of weird lately.

Dad sends his love.

Love

Mom xxxxx

Good golly Miss Molly Sorenson. What a freakin loser! It puts me in mind to check my own emails on my iPad.

To: lucypattybrennan@hardass.com
From: michelleparish@lifeparishioners.com
Subject: Success!

I don't know if I'd quite put it like that, but you need to be determined and not be swayed from your course of action! Tough love rules! And so do Morning Pages!

Best of luck with your difficult client.

M x

To: michelleparish@lifeparishoners.com
From: lucypattybrennan@hardass.com
Subject: Have I Been Too Forthright In My Sexuality?

Michelle,

You are so right about the media turning on people. I worry that I've been too candid about my bi (veering strongly toward chicks) sexuality, and you're right, I should have taken the "it's none of your fucking business" approach that you and Jillian Michaels both so successfully deploy. I mean, look how the bastards turned on poor Jackie Warner!

Yes, you're correct to exercise discretion. In the public eye it's difficult to come out and say what you mean, with a hostile media so ready to demonize a strong, independent gay woman. Nonetheless, I think it would be great if you gave it the "bi and proud" thing. I think a lot of women in America would be empowered by that.

Love, respect, and sisterhood,

Luce xxx

PS I'm going round to see my artist bitch who better have written her Morning Pages! Cause I'm off to read those suckers RIGHT NOW!

27

LENA'S MORNING PAGES 3

A bright morning, with red skies fusing into azure. I arrive at the penthouse hutch to find Sorenson scribbling into the notepad on her lap. She rips out a sheaf of papers and thrusts them at me. — Thank you, I tell her. Her eyes are darkened and she looks like shit. And the bucket is full of it. Better.

— I need some breakfast, she grumbles. — Didn't you bring any food?

I ignore her, take the papers, and head into the narrow galley kitchen. I place them on the countertop, sit at the stool, and start to read:

I awoke lying prone in a perfect, stifling darkness, not aware of where I was. I struggled for air; there was a sort of cover over me. Raising myself onto my knees, I crawled forward, bumping my head on something, then my stomach lurched, and I felt like I was going to be sick. I tried to push the smothering weight from my shoulders and back, but then my hand snagged, a wrenching grip on my wrist being followed by a clanking sound. My awareness of where I was flooded back in a sick torrent, like it's done the last two mornings. As I struggled more, I felt the sharp cutting edge of metal dig into my wrist. I'm shackled. But my other hand is free. I pushed the harsh, scratchy comforter from my face and blinked into a room faintly illuminated by distant lights spilling in through big windows. I tried my morning yell, "Hello," but my throat was raw and sore. I felt like I'd swallowed a tennis ball.

There was a gut-wrenching sensation as I picked up the bottle of water awkwardly with my left hand, struggling to hunker up with that right wrist still cuffed onto the heavy-duty chain, about twelve to fifteen feet long, attached to a support pillar by identical cuffs. I glugged at the water, emptying half the bottle, and got to my feet. I pulled at the chain with both hands, like a tug-of-war competitor; it holds fast at every link of tempered steel. I worked my way down it toward the pillar, like a reverse abseiler, yanking as hard as I could, levering my entire weight on the chain. It was still absolutely futile.

Guess what. It's like, called a restraint, dumbass, to stop you from getting to food and eating yourself to death. That's why it's strong. It has to *restrain*.

242

I went to the window, again testing the meager limits of my freedom. The room is still bare, except for the home-gym apparatus, a treadmill, and an inflatable mattress, pillow, and comforter, two buckets of water, some rolls of toilet paper, and a blue-and-white plastic cooler. There's also a child's plastic pool with a really cute illustration of a coyly smiling bear, where I wash. They are all within my semicircle of freedom, which radiates from the point of this support pole, one of three that buttress the overhead steel beam. I can get to one window; it faces another high-rise opposite, which seems as deserted as this one.

I look out the window, at the block opposite. Then I look down, thinking of those stairs we climbed. There are no drops on the glass, yet a shining, deserted sidewalk tells me it's been raining. Then I go to the cooler, and get a drink from a bottle of water. With being stuck in the dry air conditioning all day I have to continuously drink water to avoid dehydration. I force myself up in the night to drink and urinate. It's drink and pee, drink and pee. My "bathroom" trips are awful: struggling to maintain an unsupported squat over a plastic bucket.

The washing in that pool is a cumbersome undertaking. I turn the strapless sports bra round to undo the hook (it can't be good to have your breasts squashed so tightly to you) and remove my panties, climb in and squat down, relieved nobody is witness to this infantilizing humiliation. I wash myself as best I can with one free hand, then dry off and sit with the soothing comforter draped over my shoulder.

I think of myself as a prisoner in solitary confinement, but my new circumstances seem way beyond analogy. No clock bar a cerulean sky, which fades in a darkening sweep as the sun drops behind the neighboring towers, or the shifting volume of toylike cars going back and forward on the Interstate 95 below. The lamplight clicking on, for a few hours, before switching itself off and shrouding me back into night. I shout out regularly, but my voice, isolated in the air, sounds strange. Sometimes I'm beset with euphoria. Talking to myself. Laughing loudly. Wondering if I'm going mad.

There's no "wondering" about it. Eating yourself to death? Yes, that's going mad.

My first night here was the worst. A storm grew in potency, whistling and sizzling around the building. As the last of the planes flew over Miami, I imagined them being blown off course, and their *irresistible and unstoppable collision with this tower, ready to crush or incinerate me. Me linked to the pillar and chain, dangling by my arm from the crumbling wreckage of the building. My mind played a grim and terrifying mix of the possible scenarios of my death on a loop, overwhelming me, making me cry and scream until I blacked out. But then the wind awakened me repeatedly throughout the night, smashing up against the building in enormous bursts, so hard I fancied I could feel the structure moving around me. I pulled the comforter over my head and sobbed.*

The storm faded out a couple of hours before dawn. Then something else woke me: the implacable silence. The irrefutable evidence that I was a prisoner, alone in this high-rise. I sat up, and, for want of anything else to do, went to the treadmill.

— I'M HUNGRY! Sorenson shouts through. — Can I *please* have some breakfast?!

I blank out the fat sounds and continue to read.

And, through my sleepless exhaustion, I've done this every day, my feet scrunched into my sneakers, mangling my toes. They have started to blister and bleed. Yesterday I looked and saw black-red blood had caked into one white sock. It makes me glad of the kiddie pool. I tried the home gym; now the muscles of my upper back and shoulders are bound in tense, searing knots.

Today, I've already eaten my meager allowance of tasteless food, and have to wait till Lucy comes to replenish it. As the day wears on I'm lying on this feeble mattress in my sweat, delirious in a reverie both ecstatic and tortured, fantasizing about cheeseburgers, buckets of Kentucky Fried Chicken, nachos, pizzas, chocolate-chip cookies, and, more than anything, about ice cream and Key lime pie. I drink the last of my water.

I don't know how long it is till I hear the dread sound of that key in the lock. Sure enough, Lucy appears, a surly set to her mouth, yet that unhinged gleam in her eye that scares the shit out of me.

Good! But everything fucking scares the shit out of you!

As I've done since this nightmare started, I try to reason with her. But she does that walking-across-the-room thing, like a college professor in a lecture hall full of students, then suddenly making spooky eye contact with me. "We're going to flush that garbage out of your system," she announces, that bewitching, austere, almost abstract rhythm of her movement, and the Mephistophelean gleam in her eyes silencing me. "Not only is Coca-Cola shit, it makes you want to consume more shit. People who drink diet carbonated drinks are still, on average, ten pounds heavier than those who don't."

And with that perfunctory sermon, she puts out my oatmeal and blueberry, and once again leaves me.

Jesus! Check that bitch! What a pretentious fucking asshole! What the fuck is a "Mephisthelean gleam"?

I devour my breakfast, then wash myself as best as I can in the tepid water of the kiddie pool. After a while I take a number two, struggling to crouch over the bucket, convinced I'm defecating on the floor, or will topple it, or even get my butt stuck in it, grotesquely tragicomic. When I'm done I wipe myself, and push the bucket as far to the outer limits of my chain as possible, but making sure I can still retrieve it. It's not far away enough: it's horrible being around my own foul, sour excrement, and I constantly gag.

I'm so tired, and I move back onto the cheap inflated mattress with its fitted sheet and abrasive white comforter. If only I could sleep on it. Every time I drift off and turn in the night, my wrist pulls on this chain, yanking me back into fractured consciousness. Instead, I watch the light decline in a trancy fug. There are no blinds on the

247

windows, and the lights from the neighboring buildings cast a sickly orange glow into the room, throwing up all sorts of horrible shadows. In the reflection of the glass I study my face, remorselessly cataloging its defects. My imagination is running riot and I can't even paint or sketch! Instead my only companion is constant fear, sometimes overwhelming. I'm so scared of this impoverishing silence, broken only by the odd roar of an airplane, or I imagine I hear the elevator outside, faintly sweeping upward on its ghostly journey. When I start to shout, it's either nothing or only Lucy. The day is already measured by her visits. The anticipation, then the dread, as I worry what psycho stuff might be going through her sick mind, yet I fear her visit being over, and being plunged back into this terrifying solitude.

When I half shut my eyes, I can almost see Lucy still in this room. The way she moves, tidying everything up around her, like a smooth machine, attacking all the chaos, leveling it out into order. You can imagine her as a mother, weaving that intimate dance of habit and routine. Children's crayoned drawings on the walls. Messages posted on the refrigerator. But after supervising my eating and exercise, scrupulously recording the results on her iPad, Lucy always leaves me alone. During the day. All of the night. Visiting only in the morning and

early evening with tiny portions of unsatisfying
food. What she calls real food, or good food.

I'm so hungry and tired and lonely! What I want
now is bakery goods: cakes, scones, croissants,
bread, but also eggs, bacon, hash browns, waffles,
steak, burgers, tacos . . .

— I'M HUNGRY, LUCY! A high screech from the front room.
Fat fucking asshole.

My bad eating habits probably began when I was
around ten years old. Back in Potters Prairie, Otter
County, Minnesota. The Midwest is an expanse of
dreariness, punctuated by the odd sparkling jewel. We
were at the beating heart of its blandness: too far
from Minneapolis-St. Paul to be classed as a suburb,
but close enough to preclude anything that might
excite the imagination.

At ten years old my life started to go bad. It hadn't
been that way before. I was the miracle baby, the
one who'd come along just when Mom and Dad
had almost accepted that they would never
conceive. Mom actually thought I was a cyst for the
first seven months of her pregnancy. She was too
scared to go to the doctor. She would repeat to
anybody who listened, and, no doubt, to many who
didn't, "I just prayed, and those prayers were

answered." She never specified if she was praying for me to be a baby, or simply not to be a cyst.

Oh shit, we gone struck gold! Thank you, Michelle Parish! Thank you, Julia Cameron!

We lived in a small, comfortable home with a large yard, which sat right on the shore of Lake Adley. The beautiful lake and the surrounding forest ensured my childhood memories had a decidedly idyllic flavor. I recall long, warm summers, where the heavy air crackled with the hum of crickets and grasshoppers. I'd ride my bike to the Kruz's corner store with my friend Jenny. Buy a bottle of Coke or Sprite and some candy. Then I discovered the Couch Tomato Diner on Galvin, near my old elementary school, that place where could you buy over thirty kinds of ice cream. And wash it down with more Coke or Sprite.

The winters were vivid and white. The snow like a shroud of silence placed over the house; other than the big clock, the only sounds came from the kitchen, the odd muffled pot rattling or tray shunted into the oven, testifying to Mom's cooking and baking labors. Even if he was at home on Sunday (he worked at least six days a week at the hardware store), Dad remained an almost silent presence. If I was playing or reading in the living room, I'd hear him breathing deeply or perhaps turning a page of *his book or rustling a newspaper. But the main noises came from the kitchen and involved the preparation of food. There was always more food.*

Yet, by the time I was sixteen, I was still stick-thin. 118 lbs. Then, at around my eighteenth birthday, as I was ready to go to Chicago to prepare for art school, I was 182 lbs.

What happened in those two years?

— LUCY! Sorenson shouts. I snatch the papers from the countertop and head through.

— WHAT?!

— Where's breakfast?

— I'm trying to read your papers.

— But I'm starving!

— What do you want me to tell ya? Fight through that shit!

— No, I won't, I need to eat something—

— You know what I'm gonna do? I'm gonna go out to a local diner, have *my* breakfast, and relax and read those fucking pages.

— No, you have to—

— And before you start shouting again, it's your own fault, I wave the papers in her face, — for writing fucking *War and Peace*.

— Please, Lucy! Sorenson is up on her feet, jumping on the spot, chain clanking, as I split, getting the fuck outta the apartment.

I head down in the elevator and get back in the Caddy. There's a scarcity of any social facilities in Miami's dead downtown, and that includes decent places to get breakfast. After passing a few shitholes, I find somewhere palatable in a mall, and have a green tea and a wholegrain bagel with salmon and low-fat cream cheese, getting another of the same for Fatty Sorenson. She can't eat oatmeal and blueberries every morning. A TV in the corner distracts me from her journal, as it's running a feature on the twins. I can't make out what's going on but it doesn't look good as they've turned pointedly away from each other. Amy is crying, which makes her seem human, so different from the scowling, parasite self she normally presents to the world.

But back to Sorenson's shit:

You saw things, felt things, as you grew up. The human hurt behind all that apparent tranquility. A town where public lives intersected and connected through sheer custom, as well as a denying, studied civility and convention, blinding us to the poverty, meth labs, and large swathes of shit-blanketed, corn-stuffed nothingness. The silences that buried so much pain within the walls of those old family homes.

Mom.

Oh, snap!

When I was around fifteen, our happy house became less jovial. Mom and Dad started to behave differently toward each other. And she was growing very, very big. I once saw her weigh in at 270 lbs. What I didn't realize was that she wanted a partner in crime. In the crime of lovelessness, of becoming unlovable to justify that lovelessness. So we ordered ice cream from the Couch Tomato Diner and pizza from You Betcha Pie. "Uff da! You can eat anything at your age," she would say. I liked that I could eat anything.

My father, Todd Sorenson, was a short guy, about half a head smaller than Mom, with a habitually ulcerated expression and an air of piety. He said little. If anything contentious ever arose in discussion, or from the news, he'd dismiss it as "something or nothing." Dad did little else but work, and take Mom to the occasional dance. Every month he'd go hunting with some friends: dreary guys in the hardware business who were full of dull platitudes. Dad took me a few times, showed me how to load, shoot, and clean a rifle. I treasured the one he gave me, the same type he used, a Remington 870 Express Super Magnum. "Works just fine on everything from doves to deer," he said. I liked shooting, at tin cans and bottles, but the thought of taking the life of a living thing for sport disgusted me. Then I saw them shoot a young deer. It just looked inquisitively and started moving toward us. I thought, surely they have to let it go. I saw them look at each other for a second, as if deciding, then my father shot it. The small animal jerked back about five feet, coming to rest, its legs kicking into stillness. "Right in the kill zone, Todd," one of his friends yelped.

I knew from Dad's lectures that the zone included the shoulder area, and behind it the heart and lungs. Viewed broadside, it was roughly centered on the rear of the shoulder. It gave the hunter the best chance at hitting vital organs. From that range, he could hardly have missed. It wasn't "hunting" at all.

I was sickened to my core. To see something so alive, innocent, and trusting, callously exterminated by stupid old men, gaining nothing but a short-term buzz and buying into a deluded fantasy of how that defined them in the eyes of the world, just seemed so crass and pathetic on every level. I kept quiet, but they could see my anger and sense the contempt I had for them.

I obviously decided that I wouldn't be going with Dad on any more trips. He said nothing, and while on some level he seemed relieved, I could also feel his disappointment. And I'm sure he and Mom could feel mine. As I grew, I became less at ease in the home I was born into: developing more of an awareness that I was a misfit in this household, in this town, and that while I didn't measure up in its eyes, the feeling was mutual.

I was getting ready for school one morning; it was about 7:45. The phone rang and Mom switched on the TV. We saw one of the towers in the World Trade Center smoking. They said a plane had crashed into it, and showed the replay. I looked at Mom and Dad; we all thought it was a terrible accident. Around fifteen minutes later, another plane smashed into the second tower. I was scared, and so was Mom, and we held each other on the couch.

"New York," Dad scoffed, as if it were happening somewhere across the world. "Something or nothing."

I don't know to this day if he really believed that or if he was putting on a brave face, perhaps in the belief that Mom and I might become hysterical. I stayed home with her, sitting on the couch watching the events unfold, nervously eating candy, until it got too much and we had to switch off. Dad went to work as normal, in his hardware business in Minneapolis. It would never have occurred to him to do anything else. He smelled of the store: paint, turps, oil, sawn wood, glue, and metal particles that seemed to cling to his hands in particular. No amount of washing or aftershave could disguise that odor.

Sometimes Dad spoke so slowly I could feel myself perishing inside, desperate for him to finish his sentence so that I could resume my life. On a few occasions he would halt his speech in a pained pause, where he seemed to be evaluating whether or not it was worthwhile continuing.

As he worked increasingly longer hours, Mom and I did everything together and that "everything" involved food. Or what Lucy would describe as crap: sugary, salty crud. We ate whole pies, pizzas, and cheesecakes till we were sick. We would lie on the couch, immobilized, barely able to draw breath. We were almost drunk, almost drowned by food. Tormented by stomach cramps and acid reflux; beyond satisfied, in real physical pain, sitting in abject self-hate which throbbed inside us like the garbage we'd just eaten, yet just wanting this mountain we'd tipped into our guts to subside, to be broken up and processed by our bodies, the pounds of fat sticking onto what was already there. Just wanting that to happen so that we could start again. Because when it happened, we just felt so empty. We needed, craved, the same again.

Poor me! Daddy was a coldhearted NRA stumpy dick, who shot furry little animals with his subsitute prick! Momma was a big fat pig who stuffed herself, cause she wasn't getting enough schlong. BIG FUCKING DEAL, SORENSON! Doesn't will-power factor in here? Doesn't self-respect? Is there a fucking core? A person in there?

Then I saw myself in the large, ornate mahogany-framed mirror in our hallway, just after my exams. A blimp. I could no longer eat what I wanted. So I dressed in black, became a goth, a fat goth. I could draw, and I could paint. Always. But I could no longer eat what I wanted, because I wanted more than anybody could eat.

It caused problems at high school. Before my weight gain I had been not exactly popular, but, although quiet, thoughtful, and a little small for my age, I'd been able to go along with the usual games and schoolyard antics. Now I was sticking out from the crowd. It was strange the way the other girls looked at you: first a discomfort, then a cruelty would seep into their eyes. It was like a slowly dawning nightmare, where the people seemed like themselves on the outside, but were possessed by a demonic force. I had—quite literally—outgrown Jenny. I knew she was embarrassed hanging around with me. Then one day, in gym class, when a group of girls started tormenting me, she joined in. I couldn't even hate her. Like my mom, I had convinced myself that I was unlovable, and was suffering some sort of just retribution.

Even in art class there was no respite. I was working on a portrait of an old man. When I came in one morning, it was defaced, the figure rendered fat with black paint, the face altered to a crude, cartoonish approximation of my own. BLUBBER-ASSED BITCH was scrawled underneath it in big letters. I was mortified, saw the others in class laughing, but I couldn't show it to my teacher. I disposed of it discreetly in the trash and started another, my hand trembling as I sketched.

Other people could see that I was becoming more detached and withdrawn. A teacher, Mrs. Phipps, recommended to Mom that I should see a doctor, as I was possibly depressed. We went to our family physician, Dr. Walters, who had been feeding me antibiotics and antihistamines since I was a kid. He told my mother I was suffering from "lethargy." "I want to avoid pejorative terms like depression," he said to us.

Even I knew there was no such designated medical condition. But I could barely bring myself to shower or brush my teeth. Even the three minutes of the buzzing electric toothbrush was excruciating, and I'd pray for it to end, counting down the seconds as I poked it around my mouth.

But Mom still loved me. She showed it by treating me. Treats. Our life was one long round of treats. The dictionary describes that noun as "an event or item that is out of the ordinary and gives great pleasure." There was nothing out of the ordinary about our "treating" regime. And every pleasure it afforded was short-lived compared to the slow, throbbing pulses of pain it constantly left us in.

Um, hello! Wise the fuck up! And the doctor, in *Potters Prairie, Otter County*, was a fucking quack? Now who would have thunk that?

A nerdy kid called Barry King was my only friend at high school. He was as skinny as I was fat, a shy and awkward boy with Harry Potter glasses. As is often the irony in such situations, in retrospect I now clearly see that Barry, with his slender, athletic frame and dark, haunting eyes, needed only a minor change in attitude to be rebranded a conventionally good-looking kid. Sadly he was unable to take that small but giant step. Like me, he jailed himself with his self-consciousness: his movements, walk, glances, nervous, inappropriate pronouncements, they all invited persecution. In response, we created our own world, one which both sustained and shamed us. Our refuge was science fiction—we were particulary obsessed with Ron Thoroughgood, a British sci-fi writer—and Marvel comics. We'd bring in comic books and first draw the superheroes and villains in them, then create our own characters.

The world we constructed from those materials not only defined our present, but would also be our future. We made plans; he was going to write sci-fi adventures, and I was going to illustrate them.

We hung around the Cup of Good Hope Cafe and Johnny's One Stop, eating candy and potato chips, and drinking soda, always soda: Coke, Pepsi, Sprite, Dr. Pepper. Hiding, always hiding. Him behind those unflattering frames, me in my fat suit, peering out from the thick, black curtain I'd allowed to grow over my eyes, which made my father squirm in silent rage. "It's my style," I'd shrug, when he confronted me about it.

All the while I craved that comforting spike of sugar, awaiting, in choking anticipation, its future promise. One time Barry and I were heading to the Cup of Good Hope, when a group of kids from high school stopped us and started being abusive. They called Barry a retarded geek and me a beached whale. They said we were having sex. That he was a skinny pervert for fucking a really fat chick. One of the boys punched his face, knocking his glasses to the ground but not breaking them. They laughed as he picked them up. We walked for a bit, then went to the Cup of Good Hope. He sucked soda through a straw which sat on his fat lip. I remember him saying, "Nobody understands us here, Lena. You've got to get out."

His words chilled me, even then. It was the way he said "you," and not "we." It was as if he knew then that he himself would never make it.

And he didn't.

I hated Sundays more than any other day, as the promise of high school and a week of bullying lay ahead. The fearful anticipation of this was actually more crippling than the reality. Sunday was also the dreary, soul-destroying ritual of church, which seemed to foreshadow the slaughter. My mom's folks, Grandma and Grandpa Olsen, would come to the house early for breakast, then we would walk to church together. It was a horrible trek, boring yet full of dreadful anticipation, and it meant walking awkwardly with my family, along an exposed road, but we would never, ever drive. Even if it was raining or cold, we'd huddle underneath umbrellas. If I protested Dad would explain that it was "family tradition." Grandma would chat to Mom, while Grandpa Olsen was silent, only ever talking to Dad, and always about their respective work. I was made to dress in bright clothes by Mom.

I felt retarded, it was like they drew the world's eyes to me, much more than my preferred black ever could. Before we left the house, I'd force myself to stare at the image in the mirror. I was just like Mom, fat and stupid. A younger version, but dressed in the same ridiculous clothes. Dad barely looking at us. Shamed by us. Even though I was a teenager—a small, fat, zitty teenager who hid behind bangs—I was dragged along.

During vacations, I would go into Minneapolis with Dad, to work in the hardware store. I hated the silent drive, the flat nothingness ahead, the big hollow skies above us. The store itself was full of hokey old guys, both staff and the customers, some of whom I recognized as Dad's hunting cronies, who came in to talk about shit. They were usually bored, ancient retired men who had DIY projects that would take years, if they ever got done at all.

Grandpa Olsen was like one of them. He died suddenly; a huge heart attack at the wheel of one of his flatbed trucks, in the parking lot behind his business. Fortunately, the vehicle was stationary at the time.

At his funeral, on a cold, windswept day by an open grave, Mom cried, comforting Grandma, who kept repeating over and over again, "He was a good man . . ." Noting my boredom and discomfort, Dad gruffly told me, in a very adultlike way, as if he were talking to a friend, he believed that Grandpa Olsen knew he was going to die, and that was why he'd climbed into the cabin of his rig.

Grandpa and Dad had shared some sort of joyless bond, as both were successful in business. Then Dad's luck changed when Menards opened a new store in a mall barely a mile away. Dad grew very bitter. It was symptomatic of America's decline, he said. He started to voice his support for various right-wing politicians, going across the spectrum from the authoritarian to the libertarian, eventually settling for Ron Paul. He even became active in one of Paul's numerous doomed presidential campaigns.

We fought about this. We fought all the time on politics and social issues. Dad would debate up to a point, but whenever I was getting the better of him (which was more and more often as I was reading voraciously), he would raise his voice in threat, "I'm your father, and you will respect that," he'd command, and the discussion would be over.

Dad told me to keep away from Cherie, a clerk at the hardware store, who was a few years older than me, but who seemed a normal, cheerful girl. "She's not the sort of person you should be talking to."

"Why?"

"You can never be friends with staff. It undermines me."

"But they're co-workers, I'm only working in the store."

"Don't sass me. You're my daughter, and someday you'll be running this place!"

The thought filled me with dread. But I knew it would never happen. Instead I grew to love Menards. Every grumble from him about their progress, and disclosure that his store was struggling, ignited sheer glee in my heart. If I saw a huge ad for the chain in the newspaper, I'd rejoice at their corporate firepower, envisioning it crushing that horrible Twin City Hardware store in its bleak strip mall, literally razing it to the ground. I'd rather live a destitute life than manage his store.

Then something terrible happened. It was the following spring, when things were just coming strongly to life after another brutal winter. I was sitting in the garden, reading <u>They Perish In Ecstasy</u>, the new Ron Thoroughgood novel. Mom was weeding, tilling the soil, preparing to do some planting. Alana Russinger, a neighbor of ours, came by and told Mom that Barry was dead.

I froze, lowered my book. Mom looked at me, then back at Alana. "That's terrible . . . what happened?"

"I don't know the details, but they just found his body in his bedroom this morning."

"What do you mean?" I yelped, getting out my chair.

Alana looked at me with a pained expression, then turned to Mom. She dropped her voice and said, "They're saying he hanged himself."

I ran indoors and went to my room. Sat on my bed. Tried to find tears through my numbness. Nothing came. Mom walked in. Sat on the bed beside me. Said some words, about how Barry was in a better place, with God, and how he would never be unhappy again.

"How do you know he's with God?" I turned on her. "If he hanged himself that's suicide, and isn't that meant to be a sin that stops you going to heaven?"

"God is merciful," Mom said, squeezing my hand.

I looked at her, and we hugged, and then I asked her to leave me, which she did. I got out some of Barry's sci-fi stories in the ringed notebooks, the ones he'd had bound at Kinko's. But I still couldn't cry. I felt dead inside.

Later I found out that Barry had left a note which simply said: I CAN'T DO THIS ANYMORE. THERE IS NO PLACE FOR ME HERE. I would subsequently find out that he also wrote that his entire comic-book collection should be left to me. His family withheld that information. They agreed with my parents, that we were "a bad influence on each other" and were "fixated on death." I even caught my mom and dad in my room, going through my CDs and the music downloads on my computer, which they'd previously shown no interest in: Nirvana, Sisters of Mercy, Macbeth, Secret Discovery, Theatre of Tragedy, PJ Harvey, This Mortal Coil, Puressence, Depeche Mode, Crematory, Tool, looking for evidence, perhaps, of something that fuelled a suicidal folie à deux in the sleeve notes, lyrics, or cover artwork. It was almost as if I was being blamed for Barry's demise: the bullies who beat, taxed, and tormented him every day were, of course, exonerated.

I practically stayed in my room for the best part of a year, other than attend high school. Yet it got easier there. While I was still regarded as a weird loser, the overt bullying stopped. I don't know if Barry's suicide had induced a collective guilt, or they felt that if they also pushed me over the edge, they'd have more blood on their hands, but I was left alone. And I didn't eat, which worried Mom.

Then came Mom and Dad's 25th anniversary party at the Event Center. I was forced to attend. I was almost seventeen. Mom yet again told everyone her "miracle baby" story, looking at me as I blushed and wished I were anywhere else. I can't believe there was a single adult in Otter County who hadn't heard that tale.

I was surprised to see Tanya Cresswell, from high school, at the party. She was there with her family, who knew Mom from some church group she attended. Tanya was a weird kid too, but not like me. She was cool, but also aloof and disdainful of the bullying in-crowd, who seemed a little spooked by her. Tanya spoke with me for the first time. We talked mainly about music. I sneaked out some alcohol, a bottle of white wine, which we drank in the alley at the side of the center, and smoked a cigarette. We were excited and drunk. We kind of kissed, like on the lips. We looked at each other in surprise and fear. Neither of us knowing what had happened, or what to do next. Then we heard voices, and saw an older guy and girl coming outside, and dry-humping each other up against the center's entrance pillars.

A few days later, I saw Tanya in class. We glanced at each other in mutual embarrassment then looked away. We both knew we'd done something wrong. Like something that we would do again if we stayed close to each other, but which would really mess us up if people found out. So we avoided each other. But I never gave up on sex; I masturbated constantly. I thought about girls sometimes, kissing them, making out, but usually I thought about boys. I really wished for a boy, a dark-haired skinny boy, to come to my room in the night, and feel me up, touch the nipples on my small breasts.

Without Barry and his sci-fi distractions, I was more focused on my schoolwork, "starting to fulfill my potential" as Dad put it. But there was one class in particular that obsessed me. Miss Blake, the art teacher, repeatedly informed me that I was the most gifted student she'd come across in Otter County. She told me about a forthcoming presentation by staff from the School of the Art Institute of Chicago, for prospective students from our state, which was taking place at a community college in Minneapolis.

Grandma Olsen died the summer after her husband passed. Broken-hearted and lost, she never recovered from his death. This helped our perilous Menards-decimated finances. The Olsens had also left money in my college fund, described by Mom as a "considerable amount." I was excited at this news, but strived to contain myself, expressing a sorrow at my grandma's death that I didn't really feel. It sounds callous, but all I could think about was the money: I knew exactly what I wanted to do with it. I stupidly told Mom and Dad about my aspirations to study art. They closed ranks for the first time in a long while: art college was a waste of money. You couldn't get a job. Art college was full of weirdos and perverts on drugs. I should concentrate on math.

The only good thing about this depressing conversation was Dad's failure to raise the issue of me managing the Twin City Hardware store. It wasn't so much an acknowledgment of my patent unsuitability for this role, more the recognition that Menards' long-term victory was inevitable. As young and unworldly as I was, I immediately sensed the futility of arguing. I simply agreed with them: business studies made more sense.

Of course, I went along to the Minneapolis presentation of the Art Institute without telling my parents, taking my portfolio with me. There were about twenty kids in a college classroom, all with the eager, excited kind of engagement I never found from others in my art class at high school. The guy from the Art Institute had a shaved head and was dressed in black. He was introduced by the community college staff member as a professor. He immediately corrected the guy, with an emphatic shake of his head. "I'm not a professor," he said, "I'm an artist."

As soon as I heard this, I knew exactly where I wanted to be. These simple words were the most impressive I'd ever heard anyone speak. How galvanizing, how heady they were, to somebody who had been ground down by the steady accumulation of small defeats! A burden was lifted from my back, and I could _feel_ my spine straighten.

I knew _who_ I wanted to be.

I switch on the treadmill. I've gone in too high, as I begin sweating and panting immediately. Each thundering step is a trial . . . but I adjust the device to maximum climb gradient, heralding a new hell, shifting the burden to other muscles, which throb in pitiless intensity. Within ten *minutes a voice in my head is screaming: what in the name of hell are you doing? I try to ignore it. Soon all sense of my legs has gone, it's like nothing is keeping me up, and I'm beset by a shuddering panic that I will fall. I attempt to concentrate on the pounding rhythm my feet make on the rubber belt, trying to force my rasping, attenuated lungs to breathe in concert with it. I try to look at anything other than those digital display monitors that measure time, speed, distance covered, and calories burned. All of a sudden, the belt starts to slow down of its own accord. I realize, to my elation, that I've been running at this speed and gradient for thirty unbroken minutes!*

I stagger off the machine, so spaghetti-legged I'd probably have toppled over without the chain fastening my wrist to the pillar. I reel myself in toward it like a fish, and slump onto the mattress, wrapping my arms around my legs, pressing my face into the tops of my bare knees and closing my eyes, huddling into the ball of myself.

Well, thank you, Miss Sorenson. Fat geek, thin geek, both misfits, fat geek didn't fuck thin geek, but instead made out with nonevent church bitch. Thin geek had killed himself anyway, and fat geek goes to college on a trust fund. Well, I suppose it's a start. But that's all it is. Excuse me for being underwhelmed! I'm also less than convinced of Sorenson's reliability as a narrator. People like her—artsy types—they make shit up. That's what they do.

By the time I get back with her breakfast bagel, an hour has elapsed and Sorenson isn't happy but is silent, and her eyes never leave the food in my hand. I press it into her dirty, grateful paws.

As she eats, I pick up her bucket and flush her shit away, then her piss, then there's the pain-in-the-ass draining of the pervert-bear pool, which involves hauling it to the bathroom and tipping it deftly over the lip of the shower tray, letting the Sorenson grime fill the drains of Miami. Then the dull, mundane refilling of all the vessels.

When I've completed these horrible fucking tasks, I get back to Sorenson, who is remarkably still chewing on her food. Yes, she's forcing herself to eat slower, looking up at me between mouthfuls. So I sit on the chair opposite her, the Morning Pages in my hand. — This is a lot to take in. You've been very candid. Well done.

She looks hopefully at me. — I've really tried to be as honest as I can—

— On the downside, these are *not* Morning Pages.

— What do you mean? I wrote them first thing this morning, I did, I—

I raise my hand to silence her. — Morning Pages are three pages. There are over twenty here!

— The more the better, right? That's two weeks' worth!

— They are done three pages at a time, so we can bring up issues and deal with them in small, digestible chunks. This . . . all this stuff, I shake the papers, — is just overwhelming.

— The Morning Pages are my property, Lucy. Read Julia Cameron if you don't believe me, she says calmly. — They're not for you to do anything with. You're not a trained psychologist, or psychotherapist, or counselor—

— But *you're* not an adult. Don't you see that? Don't you see what you're doing right now? You're trying to manipulate me, the way the weak always try to, by trickery, seduction, subterfuge . . .

Sorenson sweeps her greasy bangs aside with her chained hand. — Lucy, this is stupid. It's twisted. Look, I know I have issues and I appreciate that you're trying to help, but kidnapping me, criminalizing yourself, it just isn't the answer!

— Kidnapping. Now there's an interesting term. Where is the ransom note? Who does it go to? What are my demands? Kidnapping? You wish! This is an intervention. This is tough love, I tell her.

— Love? What? Why? Why do you care!

— Figure of speech, I bark, unnerved by her assertion. — I'm doing my fucking job. You're a challenge. I'm going to get you in shape if it kills me. And it won't kill me, I emphasize, as fear clicks into her eyes. — You won't fucking win, I tell her, then add, — Cause *I* won't let you lose.

— This is because of the video clip from my phone. Sorenson shakes her head. — You're punishing me cause I gave it to the TV station—

— Shut the fuck up about that phone video, I snap, — although now that you mention it, it did considerably louse things up for me. But this has zero to do with that. This is about your obesity and your lies and denial that maintain it.

— No! Sorenson shouts, then winces, rubbing at her temples. — Damn . . . this headache is splitting my skull!

I head into the kitchen, returning with towels and soap. Sorenson begs for some aspirin.

— No. No pain, no gain. I *want* you to feel shit, and to remember this moment, exactly how awful it feels. This is all due to withdrawal from Coca-Cola and Pepsi, I tell her, chucking some more Volvic bottles in the cooler.

Her face scrunches up in horror. — Water seems to be your answer to everything!

— Coca-Cola was yours, and it was no fucking answer!

Those sunken, haunted eyes look up at me from under those bangs. — I need tampons.

I dig into my purse, retrieve a few, and chuck them to Sorenson.

She fingers her sullied sports bra and looks at her stinking panties, — I need a proper shower! I gotta wash my hair! I'm gross!

You fucking said it, fat girl. — You have the pool, I point to the smirking bear. What kind of a parent would let their kid sit on that face? Asking for trouble.

— I can't clean myself properly with . . . that. She waves it away and runs a hand through her greasy locks. — I really need to wash my hair!

I shake my head. — Sweat isn't gross. Blood isn't gross. Fat *is* gross. Lose that then we'll see. You earn the fucking right!

And once again, I leave the apartment serenaded by screams that dissolve into heavy, catching, self-loathing sobs.

28

CONTACT 11

To: lenadiannesorenson@thebluegallery.com
From: mollyrennesorenson@gmail.com
Subject: Please Get In Touch

Lena,

This isn't funny anymore. When I ring you it keeps going straight to voicemail. Please call me. Is everything okay? Did you lose your phone?

Mom x

Oh groan. Fuck off, Sorenson senior.

To: lucypattybrennan@hardass.com
From: michelleparish@lifeparishioners.com
Subject: ?!?

Gay woman? What do you mean? For your information I'm a mother and plan to marry my boyfriend next year. You're crazy. Please, no more correspondence between us.

To: michelleparish@lifeparishioners.com
From: lucypattybrennan@hardass.com
Subject: Come On!

You're an unreconstructed rug-muncher and it sticks out a goddamn mile. I get it: letting some faggot knock you up is good for TV deals. After all, bitch gotta eat. But jeeze, lady, when did the good ship self-respect sail the fuck out of your harbor? You really do have some serious issues concerning your sexuality, which you urgently need to resolve!

Stand up. Come forward. Don't moan it, own it!

Yours in sisterhood,

Lucy

Part Two
Hostages
Four weeks later

29

CONTACT 12

To: lucypattybrennan@hardass.com
From: kimsangyung@gmail.com
Subject: Worried About Our Mutual Friend

Hi Lucy,

You don't know me but Lena Sorenson copied you into an email I got from her, and she speaks very highly of you as a motivating trainer and a friend. I'm a good friend of hers, we were college roommates. I'm concerned that I haven't heard from Lena in ages, she hasn't responded to my emails, or returned my calls. This is really unusual, as we are in regular contact with each other.

I'm sure you know that she's had emotional issues, like guy problems, and her head isn't in a great place right now.

I was wondering if you knew anything?

I wish I was in Miami right now—Chicago winters aren't so good.

Yours sincerely,

Kim Sang Yung

This is the fucker who has been littering Sorenson's inboxes on her email and voicemail.

Subject: Worried About Our Mutual Friend

Hi Kim,

Yes, Lena has been training with me and we've become good friends. The guy problems issue has more or less resolved itself, and she's been seeing this hunky firefighter named Miles. It's not a challenging relationship, but it's just what she needs, and I think that's the main reason she's been off the radar!

But it's also motivated her to get back to work. She's currently renting a pretty isolated shack in the Everglades, where she's taking loads of photographs of the swamp in order to construct a landscape for her "future humans" in this new art project she's doing. The reception is bad out there but she called the other day to say it was going well, and that she would be back in Miami Beach in two weeks' time.

So all good.

If she calls again I'll certainly tell her you were worried and to get in touch, but you know how single-minded she is with a project when she gets the bit between her teeth! I'd like more regular contact as I worry about her out there alone in the Glades, but I'm so delighted that she's back "in the zone" as I was SERIOUSLY concerned about her state of mind a few weeks back. But now that she's out of that, I don't want to mess with her energy.

Never been to Chicago, but I hear it's a BIG sports town!

Best,

Lucy Brennan

To: lucypattybrennan@hardass.com
From: valeriemercando@mercandoprinc.com
Subject: This Is Becoming Pointless

Lucy,

I don't see how you can expect me to continue to represent you if you don't respond to my emails or return my calls. To reiterate, Thelma at VH1 is now confident that Congressman-elect Quist has lost interest in us. Thelma and Waleena want to talk seriously about *Shape Up or Ship Out*.

Please get back to me.

Best,

Valerie

Fake ass. Fuck your show. I've my *own* show, and this one is off-camera.

To: lenadiannesorenson@thebluegallery.com
From: mollyrennesorenson@gmail.com
Subject: Flying To Miami

Lena,

This has gone on for weeks! We're out of our minds with worry!

I'm going to call the local police and book a flight down to Miami unless I hear back from you straightaway. I don't know what sort of game you're trying to play, young lady, but your father and I are worried sick and going through hell! CALL ME! EMAIL ME! TEXT ME!

Mom

FUCK! FUCKING NEEDY CONTROLLING RETARD!!!

To: mollyrennesorenson@gmail.com
From: lenadiannesorenson@thebluegallery.com
Subject: I'm Done.

Mom,

I lost my phone and have yet to replace it. But that isn't the reason I haven't been in touch. I haven't been in touch because I've had enough of your FUCKING BULLSHIT.

DO NOT SEND ME THE CRAP YOU CALL "FOOD" THROUGH THE POST—IT GOES STRAIGHT INTO THE TRASH. I DO NOT WANT IT. YOU CHOOSE TO EAT YOURSELF TO DEATH BECAUSE YOU ARE DEPRESSED AS YOUR LIFE AND MARRIAGE ARE SHIT.

FINE.

BUT DO NOT FUCKING INTERFERE WITH ME!

IF YOU GET BACK TO ME STOP ALL THE CLOYING, MANIPULATIVE PASSIVE-AGGRESSIVE SHIT. I'M FED UP BEING YOUR FUCKING PARENT. GROW THE FUCK UP!

Please note that I am very well—in fact, I'm better than I've ever been. I regularly attend a gym, have a FABULOUS new trainer, am losing weight, and looking forward to getting back to work. And I feel better than ever because I've finally said what I've wanted to say to you for all these years.

L

30

THE BARRACUDA MAN

As if one fat Sorenson isn't enough, a second blimp has harassed her way into my life from Potters fucking Prairie! Stalked out by losers! And Michelle has run out on me; uptight bitch threatening me with cops and lawyers and finally changing her email address. All she's left me with is Sorenson's fucking Morning Pages!

It's warm outside, but the streets are wet after a heavy shower. I'm wearing brushed denim jeans with a studded belt and a black tank top. My hair's down and I've accessorized with a gold heart necklace and matching bracelet. And I wear this shit because he bought it for me.

He's the reason I've started hanging out at this dire spot, a one-celled backstreet dive between Washington and Collins. The joint is devoid of customers, except for two dudes playing pool, and him, in his usual spot. Yeah, Jon Pallota's perched against the bar, talking to the tattooed bartender chick. He's unshaven, bleary-eyed, and even has a distinct beer gut. Hideous to think that, only last year, he was one of the hottest dudes you'd ever meet. That smile's still there, deep, insinuating, now even more haunting than ever, hitting me like a ton of bricks, making me pathetically, reflexively, fix my hair. He briefly glances at my jewelry, then back to me, and I hold eye contact for a second as an entire universe of fatigue, pain, and pride boomerangs between us. I'm not prepared for that expression. It isn't the kind you generally share with another human being in South Beach. Fazed, I order a vodka and soda.

After some small talk, the conversation goes back, as it always does, to Jon's misfortune. We've rebonded recently, in that we have a mutual enemy in Quist, who trounced Thorpe in the election. — This compensation case is going nowhere, Jon shakes his head, a lot more salt than pepper now present in his spiky hair. — Big business, they got that shit sewn up. The company got that Quist motherfucker as some kind of special adviser. He toys with his neat double Jack, trying to resist it a few seconds longer. To fathom its pull over him.

— You survived though, Jon. I let my hand fall on his. — You're still in there.

As usual, it's like he's just shot a million miles into space. Or maybe just a few, up the Atlantic coast to Delray Beach. — You know, I still hear the screams of the swimmers and sunbathers. Still feel myself struggling in the shallows, thinking through the pain—*what is this?*—as that mushroom cloud of my own blood plumes up in front of me in the ocean. Then looking down to see the horrible eyes of this fucking barracuda between my legs. He shivers and emits a bitter cackle. The bartender chick shrinks back a little and pretends to watch the TV.

The Wilks twins have agreed to be operated on by a specialist team of surgeons, who believe they can successfully separate their bodies. — When I was expecting them, we got told that terminating the pregnancy was an option, explains Joyce Wilks, — but it wasn't for us. The Lord chose Annabel and Amy to be this way, and what He wanted was good enough for us. Then we was given the option of tryin to separate them as small babies, but we refused to do this. The risk was too high.

They keep the camera on Joyce for an unnecessary beat until she's compelled to take a nervous drag on her cigarette. Then they pull out to show that the interview is taking place on a porch, thus indelibly designating her in the seaboard psyche as Southern white trash.

However, the girls have pleaded with the courts and their parents to consent to the operation, despite the fact that Amy's chances of survival are not rated any higher than one in five. Annabel has an estimated 82 percent shot of leading a normal life following the procedure. Now they're showing the twins walking together in long shot, strangely harmonious, even graceful, in their synchronized movement, before cutting to Amy in close-up. — I know the risks, she says, — but I wanna to do this for my sister. If one of us can live a normal life, then that's a chance worth taking.

Man, I kind of want to listen to this, but Jon isn't playing ball. — Forty pounds of deadeyed fish attached to my junk, he laments, raising the Jack to his mouth, taking a sip. — I was swimming nude, Catriona and me had been fooling around, he says cheerlessly. — She had yanked my shorts down and hung them on a floating buoy, along with her bikini top. It was the ring that probably drew its attention, you remember that ring I got?

I can see the bartender tuning out the Wilks girls and taking an interest in our conversation. I give her a stare, and she hunkers down and starts loading bottles into the refrigerator. — Let it go, Jon. I lift my hand on his shoulder, rubbing the back of his neck.

He looks right at me again, and I see that those teeth, formerly even and white, are now chipped and yellow. — How can I let it go? I can't even tell you the number of hits it's had on YouTube. You're a hero on YouTube, you kicked ass, he almost accuses. — It never worked that way for my fifteen minutes. My humiliation is required viewing for every fuckin douchebag college student across the whole wide world, he sneers, with that rancid chuckle. — You see Catriona coming into the shot once she's struggled into her swimsuit top, then just standing there as the medics arrived. You know she wouldn't even get in the ambulance when they took me to the hospital, he snorts, sipping at his Jack.

— Oh, Jon. I rub his back harder.

It's all true, and I confess I've viewed that horror vid myself. It's very well shot, by a Sorensonesque bather, another watcher rather than a doer, and on a camera in preference to a phone. Most of all, you can hear people gasp in horror as Jon screams, then hobbles out the ocean with the giant fish attached to his genitals. Blood streaking his thighs as he collapses onto the sand. The barracuda gently twisted, Jon's hands on its head, his face in profile, eyes shut, mouth open. It's as if he's forcing the fish to fellate him.

Jon's dick was quite huge and handsome, but he was probably fortunate that he was a grower rather than a shower, and a good portion of it was retracted in the cold water, hidden from the fish's view when it took that bite. Then he's supporting the barracuda as he painfully eases them both down on the sand, and just repeating, — Oh my God . . . over and over again. A woman's voice in the background screaming, — Help him! Another guy instructively informing the crowd, — A big fish got him.

Then the barracuda starts bucking and twisting, like a gator with its prey, tearing off part of Jon's dick and one testicle. More screams, a beach towel passed to Jon, who never blacks out, just holds the blood-saturating yellow towel tightly to him, face lined in pain, eyes full of fear. A close-up on the exhausted fish, half of Jon's severed, bleeding cock in its mouth (the ball was probably swallowed), as its tail flops slowly, its gills flapping and its eyes assassin-cold.

Of course the video went viral. Much more so than mine.

— You know what half a dick, one ball, and 163 stitches to that part of your body looks like? How even the most hard-bitten hookers recoil when they set eyes on that goddamned mess? Catriona didn't stick around. Then he focuses sad, hopeful eyes on me. — I wish I'd, I wish we . . . He shakes his head, unable to finish the sentence, swiveling on his stool, back to face his drink.

I cringe and lower my hand to my side. Jon and I would casually fuck, over the years. At times it was on the cusp of a whole lot more than that, and he glances at me almost hopefully, but I *really am* so over mercy fucking. Especially when half the goods are missing. Besides, I don't wanna grind on the poor fucker's scar tissue. Cause I never have a man sweating on top of me; I like to be right on a guy, enclosing his prick, fucking it, fucking him. Jon always got that. Even Miles, admittedly only due to his bad back, dug that I needed to be on top. But Jon . . . man, I did love it when we fucked. I lustily recall making him lower that high and tight sack of fruit into my mouth, but now's there's just half of that sweet bounty left, all because some poisoned whore of a fish got fucking greedy. So I make my excuses and leave him looking back into his glass, and follow a familiar path down Washington.

I enter Club Uranus to a bass line loud enough to shake the fillings from your teeth. The freak factor, which increases exponentially as the clock ticks on, seems to have hit new highs tonight. The Liposuction Fuck immediately spies me and starts ranting stuff in my ear, totally wasted. I look into her fogbound eyes. — Not now, sweetie, and I spin off into the crowd, onto the dance floor, losing her. Then I'm gyrating with a musclebound black guy, but he pirouettes into the arms of a white faggot who pins me with that unnerving stare.

I feel that coming here was a mistake and it's already time to get the fuck out of this joint. Valerie told me to always go out the front door of a nightclub. Any paparazzi and wannabe star worth their salt would choose the rear exit, as the latter staggered out wasted and stupid. Both knew where the money shot was.

At that time of the pitch-black night they call morning, when there's nowhere to go that isn't full of toxic, wild-eyed people deranged on alcohol and drugs and screaming shit into each other's ears, I do what I always do and just drive.

I love to drive, listening to music. Always Joan Jett: when I found her as a teenager my life suddenly snapped into reality, like *somebody* fucking gets me. But also Motörhead, AC/DC, and INXS. Recently I've become like *totally* obsessed with Pink.

I suppose I should go up and see Sorenson. There isn't much time left for us; Mom and Lieb are due back in ten days. It's been four weeks and she's lost 41 pounds, just 9 short of her 50 target. Week one—8, week two—15, week three—11, week four—7. More important: the bitch finally got game. *She* ditched the Morning Pages, telling *me* that she was "done with frivolous, self-regarding, head-fucking shit and ready to bust my ass." I wished I had Michelle Parish's new email address to send her that info! Yes, Sorenson sobbed with disappointment so much at those last figures, I had to console her, telling her the numbers would be lower as her body adjusts and there's less of her to slim down. The downside is that it sure makes life harder for me; the way her brain is sharpening up in concert with her body makes her a more volatile prospect. Such a Herculean effort to shave and save that ass. Bitch might be on the mend but it's been a ton of work and it's fucked everything else up. At first the hoe even refused food for a couple of days. I said to her, — You? A hunger strike? Like that's gonna last!

Fat hoe defied me and threw her grub on the floor.

Sure enough, when I got back the next evening, the varnish was practically licked off that hardwood. I looked at her and said, — I think we're both starting to understand who the fuck you are.

She only looked up at me and said, — Don't you mean who *we* are?

— Don't fucking flatter yourself, I told her, but she'd gotten right under my skin and we both knew it.

There was another incident last night, so right now, I'm not going to talk with her. I sneak into the apartment and tiptoe into the bedroom. Exhausted, I fall asleep on the floor.

31

IMMEDIATE DECISIONS

No matter what she tells you, or what you tell yourself, every lonely night when you look at your reflection in that big window, and examine that shrinking you, it all just sucks.

The pain and frustration of confinement gnaws at you. It drips acid into your core. Every time I feel the handcuff and chain clinking against the steel pillar, I die a little. I can never escape them; even when I rest on the mattress watching the portable TV Lucy brought me, a constant awareness, both vestibular and visceral, is insinuated into my consciousness.

I hadn't understood how small one corner of a room could be. And how vast a prairie the rest of it constituted, the door representing something that could have been a mile away, thanks to this inhibiting, frustrating chain. Before, I could run. Minnesota. Chicago. Miami. New York. I could hide. Doritos, KFC, Boston Market, Taco Bell. Now I have no work, except what Lucy gives me. No food, other than that which *she* brings.

And my only releases are the treadmill and the Total Gym. Yes, I've so bought into Lucy's program. My body is losing fat, toughening up. So is my mind. I've started thinking about my work in a less abstract and more practical way. Speculative projects I was considering have fallen aside, peeling from me, exposed as frivolous, superfluous. Real goers harden like rock in my consciousness, gaining sharper definition. I quit the Morning Pages. They were doing me good, but they were also giving Lucy more power over me. And I don't want *anybody* having more power over me. I feel strong. But just let me sleep in my own bed and work in my studio!

FUCKING CRAZY BITCH!

I'm still constantly hungry, but my food fantasies have completely turned. I'm not thinking of eggs over easy and crispy bacon, they now seem so greasy, toxic, and repulsive. Now I envision coarse, grainy oats, the prescribed amount of honey drizzling onto their surface, courtesy of the small plastic bear in Lucy's hand, and the blueberries, which will explode with juice in my mouth. It's the sun-saturated, natural Florida staples of fruit—the incendiary oranges, the exquisite nectar of the peaches—that now excite my imagination. Lucy's wholegrain bagel breakfast is another treat, usually served with peanut butter and banana.

And then there is my work: the work Lucy gave me.

I'm on the cusp of what promises to be a heavy period; several pimples throb prominently on my face, my hair is lank and greasy and an elephantine bloat around my stomach seems to signal a horrible weight regression. I have to keep reminding myself: it's only fluid retention. It'll go when I start to menstruate. So I get on the treadmill. I do forty-five minutes.

But when I'm finished I don't rest, I go onto the Total Gym and work till my body and spirit can give me no more. Then I clean myself with the baby wipes Lucy's left. She's given me a huge test, but now she has to be tested too. And that's my job. Of course, with nothing to do but think, you have one of two options: either you go completely insane or you come to conclusions. Conclusion one: I was already going mad, so that wasn't working. Conclusion two: I've been a pushover for too long. I habitually acquiesced to people, thinking it would make my life easier, when it's done the reverse, as it always does. And those people weren't strong. They didn't deserve such subordination. They were weak, vain, and scared. So thank you, Lucy, but now I'm going to make *you* work, you Boston psycho-fucker. Because if I can break a hardass like you, nothing and nobody will ever stand in my way again.

And she comes through from the bedroom, where she's obviously spent last night. She thinks I didn't hear her, crawling around like a sneaky rat. Thinks that only one of us is the prisoner here.

In this crazy dance we've gotten to know each other so well. Our periods synchronized, I don't even need to ask if she's also feeling puffed up with fluid or curmudgeonly with menstrual cramping or a stinging UTI. The tone of our voices, the movement of our bodies, has become so easily discerned by the other. I don't know what she is or, for that matter, I am capable of. One of us ostensibly has the power (but how much power, in those circumstances, can the other really have?) though we're both making it up as we go along. So I challenge her. — Oh, you spent the night here again.

Lucy pauses like she's going to lie, but instead makes the pathetic excuse that she got here late and wanted to fix me my breakfast early. All because she had a busy day.

— Forgive me if I don't empathize, I snap back.

She looks like she's going to say something, but doesn't. She's guarded; although I sense she's becoming more isolated, the only time we talk about anything that isn't to do with my weight is our discussion on the conjoined Wilks twins from Arkansas. But I can't be too confrontational right now, not as she's heading into the kitchen to do her stuff, then emerging with my scrambled egg whites, smoked salmon, and wholemeal toast, which I love.

— I really do appreciate what you've done here, I tell her in between mouthfuls of our food. She dispenses a kindly smile as she sits on the chair, eating off her own plate, balanced on her lap. Her eyes are circled and tired-looking. — Now you couldn't keep me out of this place if you tried. It's saved . . . it's saving my life.

— I'm glad you feel that way. She puts her fork on the plate and pushes her hair back, — You really are making progress, and you're looking so much better. Forty-one pounds is good. She chomps on a slice of toast.

— Yes, but now I feel that I need to start taking responsibility, I tell her, watching her eyebrows raise. — I need to get a balance. If you gave me my phone I could record my own exercise, food, and weight on Lifemap—

Lucy scoffs, — Don't insult the both of us.

— I need to be out of here. I need to get back to work.

That bladed glint in Lucy's eye returns, the one that negotiates against reason, as she shakes her head, lowering her plate to the floor. — You're not ready.

I feel something perish inside. I try to remain composed. — Lucy, what gives you the right to make that call?

— I earned the freakin right, and she springs up, stepping toward me. Standing over me, she lifts up her top, displaying that ripped abdominal wall. I almost feel like I could grab it, like the rungs of a ladder, and climb my way to freedom. — This gives me the right! Eat your breakfast, she barks.

I hear the girlish trill of my voice in pathetic retort. — Bring me some books!

But she's turned on her heel with a flourish, heading off and leaving me with my food and my thoughts.

I had to get out of Potters Prairie. The town was like an open prison. The wide streets, the big lots surrounded by pine and fir trees, the endless gray skies. People were quick to tell you how much they were shopping and praying—spreading stupidity, passing it like a baton to the next generation. It was the currency of Middle America. An hour and a half away sat the twin cities of Minneapolis and St. Paul. Prince came from Minneapolis. Nobody came from Potters Prairie. I had to go somewhere else, a place that would let me see things differently, would let me become the kind of woman I desperately wanted to be.

In downtown Minneapolis, in a Chase Bank not far from Dad's store, sat my college fund of Grandma Olsen's $65,000 dollars, gathering dust. My spoiled, entitled kid's share of Grandpa Olsen's trucking business, that wheezy, bony-fisted old man I barely knew and had zero connection with. Yet through him buying a truck in another age, another world, driving it all over the Midwest, then buying another and employing somebody to drive it and so on, his granddaughter—a small, lazy, fat girl in a suburb who struggled to do minimal chores—would be able to sculpt and paint. Since I've been here, I've been thinking about him, that frugal man of few words. When he stoically traversed all those road miles, could he ever have imagined he was doing it for this?

It would certainly be anathema to Mom and Dad. I had to be sneaky with this one. So I researched business studies options online, settling for the Driehaus College of Business at DePaul University. It had the advantage of being located in downtown Chicago, close to the Institute of Art. I told my parents I was planning to enroll there. — What's wrong with a school in the Twin Cities, cherub? Surely a state college would be less expensive? Mom asked. She called me "cherub" a lot, because cherubs are small and fat.

I told my folks DePaul had one of the best records in the Midwest for placing graduating business students in employment. Dad applauded my enterprise and gave me his blessing. — There's a head on those shoulders after all.

— But I'll miss you so much, Mom cried.

I was off for sure, but I wasn't going to any business college. My destination was art school. I caught a bus to Chicago, and checked into a cheap B&B in Uptown. I was scared; the place, and the surrounding streets, seemed full of disturbed and outright crazy people. I kept my room door locked at all times. Fortunately, I quickly found a basement room on Craigslist, in an apartment near Western Avenue. I got a job in a local video rental store and lived on coffee and cigarettes. Soon I was down to 120 lbs, shedding with the speed of somebody suffering a terminal illness.

I was way too young to get into bars, and didn't have

the courage to attempt using a fake ID, so my social life was limited to coffee with my co-workers. I started hanging out with a guy called Mikey who worked part-time at the store. He was two years older than me, a creative-writing major at Columbia College. With his rash of spots and an Adam's apple that bobbed like a pig in the belly of a snake, Mikey looked nothing like Barry, but somehow reminded me of him. He was a sincere, sweet guy: perhaps a little full of himself, but essentially harmless. (I would later realize that this is possibly the most offensive thing you can say about anyone.) We talked a lot about movies and went to see a ton of them at the Gene Siskel and Facets. He insisted on reading me his stories, which I thought were pretty lame, but we made out and soon he was clumsily helping me free of my virginity like it was a heavy old greatcoat.

The weather was so brutal; I wanted to cry whenever I stepped out the door. Potters Prairie was cold, but that first Chicago winter—the icy snowdrifts exacerbated by the wind blasting off the Lake—relentlessly hunted me down. I could literally feel my eyeballs freezing and jaw cracking as soon as I stepped outside. I could see why the electric and gas companies were forbidden to switch off power to any households during January, February, and the first two weeks in March. It would have been tantamount to committing murder. Getting to that bus stop and taking the short ride to work and back home was a fearful, punishing twice-daily ordeal. Growing up in Minnesota, you knew snow. You'd dived into it, squashed it to the form of a grenade to chuck, shoveled it from driveways, and driven tentatively in it. You'd watched it from behind glass in your heated tank of a home, as it fell for days into thick layers that stayed frozen for months on the bleak earth. City snow was different: after a benign arrival, it offered nothing but bleakness and grime. Yet when spring came on, it was like a switch being pulled. The city seemed to thaw instantly, with blossoms opening on the tree-lined streets, almost before your eyes.

As per the late Grandma Olsen's instructions, I got the college money released into my own bank account on my nineteenth birthday. Before that, I'd been operating on my video-store paycheck and an allowance Mom and Dad sent from home, in the mistaken belief I was at DePaul Business School. I insisted that I was paying the first year myself from my savings, a "gesture" that had Dad looking at me in genuine awe, like I was a budding entrepreneur.

I went to all sorts of lengths to maintain my deception, even going to DePaul campus and buying branded stationery from the college store and obtaining copies of the various semester programs. But all I was waiting for were those two vital spring days which I knew, even in the depths of that bone-shaking winter, would determine my destiny. The week leading up to them I barely slept, I was so shattered.

Then it was time; I went to the Art Institute to apply for what they referred to as "immediate decision."

This process happened over forty-eight hours: an educational-opportunities version of the Black Friday post-Thanksgiving sales. I took my portfolio to the Institute's ballroom, and was issued with a number: 146. Then I joined the other applicants; there were 250 of us, all sitting at several round tables. When their number was eventually called, the candidate took their portfolio upstairs and presented it to a member of staff. The professor then went away and got someone else to agree, or disagree, and you were in, or not, as the case may be. The decision really was made right then and there.

So I went through the terrible procedure, sitting nervously, sometimes looking around at all the other hopefuls. Some struck up conversations; the cool, the entitled, the anxious, and the deferential. But mostly I kept my head buried in *Spores of Destiny*, the latest Ron Thoroughgood novel.

Then, number 146 was called, and my skeleton seemed to step outside my flesh, pick up my portfolio, and walk to a station. When the rest of me caught it up, I saw that I was sat in front of a lazy-eyed guy of about thirty-five, who wore a leather jacket. He looked very like (but wasn't) the "artist" who came to talk at the college in Minneapolis. I was so nervous at first, I just couldn't speak, merely look into his wearily compassionate eyes. Then, when I started, I thought I'd never stop. I talked about my comic-book drawings of superheroes. About how I loved to draw and paint everything I saw, replicating it. Then how that wasn't enough, how I needed to transform it, and how all my paintings, drawings and models had to have not just an idea behind them, but a story. I was lost in my tale, exhilarated, but then grew self-conscious again, and ran out of steam. The leather-jacketed guy went impassively through my portfolio. I felt gravity pushing my head down, trying to screw it into the table. I could almost feel the tendons in my neck snap with the effort of keeping it upright. Then he looked up and I heard him say, — Interesting. Could I ask you to wait here a while?

Then he left and he didn't come back. The clock on the wall ticked by. My self-sabotage tendency was in overdrive; I was thinking I'd made an irredeemable fool of myself, by just blabbering on like that. I grew edgy. I wanted to go, to just get out of there. My period was heavy and I needed to change my tampon. So I went to the bathroom. Then, for some reason, no, not "for some reason" but because I was hamstrung with anxiety, I picked up my portfolio and walked out into the sun. I immediately saw the leather-jacketed guy outside on the big front steps of the building, smoking a cigarette and talking to a pretty girl. They were laughing. I obviously thought that I was the target of their humor, that he was telling her about this silly little fat kid from Otter County, Minnesota (although I wasn't fat anymore), who drew comic characters and had the arrogance to think that she was an artist. I was about to sneak past them and just run away, thoroughly defeated, when he saw me and called out my name. — Lena!

I wasn't even going to stop. He shouted again, more formally this time. — Miss Sorenson!

I had no option but to turn around to face him. I could see him, through my bangs, but I couldn't lift my chin, felt the point of it pushing hard against my chest. I had never in my life been as painfully aware of the crippling passivity of that reflex.

— Where did you get to? I thought you'd run out on us. I'm afraid it's not that easy. I glanced up to see his face crinkled in a sardonic smile. — We're offering you a place here.

— Really? I gasped, looking up again.

— Yes, really.

I couldn't believe it. This had been a pervasive, all-consuming fantasy of mine ever since that talk at the college. And now my life was going to change on the basis of a casual assessment and a couple of perfunctory sentences from a complete stranger. Then I surprised him, this artist, whom I would later learn was called Ross Singleton, by bursting into tears. — Thank you, I sobbed, — thank you for this opportunity. I won't let anybody down.

— No, Ross Singleton said with a wry grin, — I don't think you will. Anything else I can help you with?

— Can I have a cigarette? I asked, daring to smile at the other girl. Her hair was blond and cut into an asymmetrical bob. In her expensive clothes she was the epitome of cool, and I instantly saw my old high-school cheerleaders, to whom I'd previously afforded that designation, as unsophisticated hick girls. And instead of a sneer, or a look of cold embarrassment, a warm, open smile and an outstretched hand came back my way. — I'm Amanda. I got in here too!

— Lena, I said, as Ross proffered and lit the best cigarette I'd ever had. My head spun as I looked across the street, to the sign indicating the start of Route 66. I giddily watched the tourists and prospective students milling around in the sun. Endless possibilities were dancing ahead of me. Ross Singleton left me and the other girl, Amanda Breslin, from New York, to go back to his interviewees. We went for a coffee and talked excitedly about art school. Then Amanda raised her hands to the side of her face, and manically

301

stamped her feet against the floor. — Oh my God! This *totally* calls for a celebration!

She took me to the bar at the Drake Hotel, ordering a bottle of champagne and two glasses. Astonishingly, they never asked us for ID. As the champagne bubbled and fizzed in my skull, and we talked about our respective plans, I had never been so happy in my life, and I wanted the moment to go on and on. I felt a hollow thud when Amanda had to get the El out to O'Hare to catch her flight back to New York. We swapped email addresses. She went home to a life I imagined as wealthy, cosmopolitan, and sophisticated; I returned to my basement and the video store. I couldn't wait for the term to begin.

In the run-up, Mikey grew more clingy, regularly showing up at my place on Western and talking about "plans." He was obviously sensing that my art-school objectives were going to form a glacier-sized wedge between us. — We'll both be downtown. We can meet at lunchtimes!

I nodded with contrived enthusiasm, as Columbia College was close to the Art Institute, but in my heart I knew I wouldn't be seeing much of him. Everything I did would be about art school. Mikey was like the boyfriend I should have had in Potters Prairie, the one to leave behind. It seems trite and cruel to say that he was the Barry King who survived, but being locked up here has taught me to be honest with myself, and that's exactly what he was.

I quit the video store, deciding that most of my time before becoming a student would be spent reading, sketching, and painting. I was anxious to get away from my Western Avenue neighborhood. While it was cheap and technically in the Ukrainian Village, it was by Humboldt Park, on the fringes of a Latino neighborhood, which was no stranger to gang activity and shootings. So I would take the Blue Line El downtown, where I hung out in the Harold Washington Library, in coffee shops, and, most of all, at the Art Institute itself. I'd see all those important-looking people examining the pictures, sculptures, multimedia installations, ancient artifacts, and I wanted to tell them as they browsed over the art, or discussed it in the coffee bars or bookstore: I AM LENA SORENSON AND I HAVE A PLACE HERE. I WILL STUDY TO BECOME AN ARTIST.

But most importantly, I saw two things there, which I was constantly drawn to, and that would inspire my own art and thus change my life. The first was Francis Bacon's *Figure with Meat* (1954), where I was initially pulled in by the juxtaposition of his name and the theme of his painting. With my morbid obsessions, I was drawn to Bacon's view of us all as potential carcasses. The second work that really moved me was the sculpture of a batlike man, by the French artist Germaine Richier. I read all about those artists and others, studied every school, period, and great work. I went to see all the new exhibitions that came to town, explored all the galleries. By the weak lamplight in my basement room, I would read, draw, and paint, until I fell into my bed, exhausted. Then get up, full of excitement, and gratefully do it all over again.

I went back to Potters Prairie for a spell, ostensibly to see my folks before starting my second year at DePaul Business School. My real motivation, though, was to photograph and sketch my hometown.

My mom looked at the slimmed-down me in a kind of perplexed terror. It was as if she was just about to start a sentence but didn't know what to say. Dad just asked me about my classes, only half joked that I'd soon be running his hardware business; things seemed to have had a minor spike. The thought made my blood run cold. I cursed Menards' incompetence; they had long had Twin City Hardware on the ropes, as Lucy might say, but couldn't seem to land that knockout blow. But Dad was manifestly pleased with me; the solitary occasion he yelled was when he saw me watching an old Pee-Wee Herman show on TV. — This is just stupid! And strange! Turn it off!

The only strangeness that struck me was that of these small-town people. They could talk about something utterly mundane; how their kids were doing, what was going on with their car, or the everyday humdrum items they'd bought from the store, and easily waste half an hour on each subject. I wanted to scream: leave me the fuck alone, I can't listen to you waste your life! Then successive waves of guilt would flood me, as I knew that most of them were decent people and I had no right to feel superior.

Returning to Chicago, I started to paint the town scenes from the pictures I'd taken and the sketches I'd done. Then I populated it with zombie-like figures whose decomposing, peeling skin exposed the angry flesh underneath.

And here, locked in this absolutely mundane but also so utterly outlandish tower prison, I can feel my own flesh, not slackening and hanging off, but tightening and toning.

32

CONTACT 13

To: lucypattybrennan@hardass.com
From: kimsangyung@gmail.com
Subject: Thank You!

Lucy,

Many thanks for your email: that puts my mind at rest! So relieved that Lena's turned the corner (in no small part due to your encouragement, I'll bet) and is happy in her life and her work.

Yes, I know what that girl is like when she puts her mind to something, so I'm going to quit playing mother hen and let her get on with her project. But if Ms. Sorenson deigns to surface and grace us all with her presence, do let me know!

Best,

Kim

PS Perhaps a girls' night out in Miami Beach in spring?

To: kimsangyung@gmail.com
From: lucypattybrennan@hardass.com
Subject: Sounds Good!

Kim,

You got it!

Best,

Lucy

Jesus Heroin Christ!

To: lenadiannesorenson@thebluegallery.com
From: mollyrennesorenson@gmail.com
Subject: I'm Done

I couldn't believe those cruel words you wrote I showed them to daddy and he was as hurt as I am what has happened to our baby girl we hardly recognized you I have just been sitting indoors crying all day

Be-fucking-lieve!

To: mollyrennesorenson@gmail.com
From: lenadiannesorenson@thebluegallery.com
Subject: I'm Done

Oh, how terribly sad for tragic little you! Write me back when u r done with all the fat, crybaby, poor me bullshit. And, like, learn to use a period and comma, dude.

L

Asshole!

33

APARTMENT

I'm under the shower when this brown, rusty stuff gushes out over me. I stand back, in disgust and loathing, shivering, running the water till it turns clear again. I rinse the gunk off my body, nervously waiting for another volley of crap, which thankfully fails to materialize. As I step out and dry off, I'm looking at the mold growing up the bathroom walls in clustered black spores; my apartment is falling apart. I can't stay here. Fucking Sorenson, *whom I am waiting on*, is living in new-build luxury! I get out into the car—no paparazzi on the street these days—and switch on the radio, looking for something that doesn't make me too nauseous and finding jack.

After her constant pestering, I've agreed to meet Valerie Mercando at Soho Beach House. I find her sitting in the patio bar, drinking coffee. I take a stiff peck on the side of my face without returning the favor. After the usual small talk, she gets down to business. — I can't understand it, Lucy, you're no longer on the radar of Quist's team. So why not just do this?

— I can live without the fucking harassment.

Valerie looks sadly at me, shaking her head. — I guess I never pegged you for a quitter.

I feel a rage searing my insides. — I'm not fucking quitting. Don't try and fucking manipulate me.

— I wasn't—

— Yes, you were, and I watch the bitch fry under my gaze. — Don't dress up your personal fucking greed as a phony motivational speech to me. I wrote the fucking book!

Her head wobbles side to side as the bitch squeaks, — I'm sorry if it came across that way, she says, that shameful look of the bastard agent who knows their client has rumbled that they'll barbecue them in a salivating feast if they're hot, and discard them like an old Tampax if they ain't. — Look, she continues, — you're obviously under stress.

— Yes, I am. And you want to add to that.

— You look tired, she suddenly purrs in fake concern. — Are you getting enough sleep?

— No, and it's because of a fat bitch, I tell her. — They're the ones who mess things up for you. Two chicks; one will get gangbanged, but the fat bitch, she gets off scot-free, cause who'd wanna fuck a fat bitch?

She's blinking uncomprehendingly at my broadside. — I really don't think being offensive to me is—

— Ha! I wasn't taking about *you*. Everything isn't about you—

— You're confusing me, Lucy—

— But on that note, you do seem to have put on a bit of weight—

— What?!

— Around your face, midsection, thighs, I persist.

— I suppose I've been busy—

— Exactly what I thought, and that's what concerns me.

You're looking after a lot of people, I drop my voice, — but who's looking after Valerie Mercando? Kids, partners, clients, they all make demands. Have you got time to be *you*?

— Look, Lucy—

— I must go. I rise. — I got a client to see. I'll be in touch.

I dismiss the Botoxed media sleazebucket; she and her ilk are just toilets, superficially smooth and pristine but ultimately tawdry and full of piss and shit. I head downstairs to the valet, who brings up the Caddy DeVille. I drive back down to Bodysculpt. It's very slow these days. A lot of clients are cutting back; instead of renewing their memberships, they're buying new running shoes and Total Gyms. False economy: these home gyms always just gather dust. Most people in life aren't self-starters. They need to be told what to do. That's where people like me come in.

In the fitness club, the bank of TV screens still blasts out shit. It turns out that Balbosa, the fleeing pedophile who killed the kid, was an illegal. — Hayzoos J. Christo, Lester jokes.

I'm not laughing. Quist is on the TV again and he's going crazy. I can't look at his big red face. Then I glance at another screen, where the channel features a crappy magazine program. I can scarcely believe it: the fucking wannabe celeb Miles is sitting on that gross leopard-skinned couch in his apartment. — She was into chicks, and I wasn't complaining. We had three-ways all the time. Life was pretty damn good.

I look over to see Lester's eye whites glaring at me. I run out of Bodysculpt, pushing past two incoming clients, scrolling my iPhone and hitting Miles's digits. He picks up straightaway. I'm tugging at my hair, screaming into the phone, — You fucking asshole! I never did a three-way with you!

— Poetic license, babe, these newshounds need a little juice. Dunno why the hell you're so sore, I portrayed you as a goddamn sex bomb, I oughta be charging publicist's fees! Did you a big favor; dudes and chicks'll be lining up around the block for some action from you now!

— Yeah, fucking sleazeballs like you! Like I need your help to get dates!

— Look, I'm sorry, babe, but I needed the money. I already told you about my financial circumstances.

— Fuck you and your financial circumstances. I silence the cell. Look around to see if any nosy asshole has witnessed my distress. No. A couple of Latin guys are unloading a beer truck, sliding kegs into the basement of the bar across the street. Then another buzz on my ringtone, playing Joan Jett's "Bad Reputation" as a call from Dad comes up. I let it ring till the phone's blanded-out tinging of a favorite tune becomes excruciating, before hitting green. I tell him how I am, and to be fair, he commiserates, before inevitably slipping things back to him. — I'm in South Bend, Indiana, at the Notre Dame University campus, but I'll be in Miami next weekend for the Books & Books event at the Biltmore.

— What's happening in South Bend?

— Not a whole heap, but the reading was good last night. Went out for a few beers with Charlie Reagan, the Notre Dame quarterback. He was giving me all that "biggest fan" B.S., but he's a good kid. A football scholarship and bound for the NFL draft, and he wants to write. Go figure. Anyway, we had a fair old drink.

— You can't play football forever. It shows he's got a head on his shoulders.

— Yeah, for sure. The kid's from good stock: Boston old money and Galway and Clare before that. Now he's stuck in Buttfuck, Indiana.

— Did you know that apart from Ohio, Indiana—at 29.1 percent obesity—is the only northern state in the top fifteen fattest states in the union?

— Still got it with the numbers, kiddo. Love it. Yeah, the town is dullsville, but the campus seems vibrant enough. But I still dunno why they call them "The Fightin Irish" with a name like that. I guess "Le Pussy French" don't quite have the same ring to it.

— For sure. . . . So how's the rest of the book tour been going?

— It's okay, but I keep meeting that dyke tennis player, Veronica Lubartski; she's on the circuit promoting her biography.

In spite of everything, I'm interested. Always had a thing for Lubartski. I remember sneaking home from school to watch the US Open at Flushing Meadow and enjoy some of the best clandestine frigs I ever had. — I read *Game, Set, and Snatch,* and it's pretty damn good, I tell him. It was too. There was a great story of how she totally fucked this Dutch chick on the court, *then* did her in the locker room afterward. I sure as hell got all wet and wide reading that bastard!

— I wouldn't know about that. But she's made impossible

demands on the literary escorts and she's usually only one city ahead of me on the circuit. So I tend to get them in a grouchy mood.

— Sucks to be you. Call me when you're in town. Love you, I shout dismissively, then hang up. I've got more to worry about than his bullshit. Mom and Lieb are due back in nine days and I've got to get Sorenson to her target weight before then.

When I get back into the club, Toby lisps something about people looking for me.

— *Nobody* is looking for *you*, I tell him. — Nobody ever will.

Toby bitches back but all I'm picking up is some vague, impotent hiss, as I'm now focused on Lena Sorenson.

When I get to the downtown apartment, I can hear her footsteps on the treadmill, sounding lighter than I recall, and her chain scratching a clanking rhythm against the side of the machine. I get inside and see her moving well, working up a proper sweat. — Three . . . seven . . . five . . . cal, she wheezes. — And two hundred this morning . . .

— Lookin good, Lena S, I hear my own words slipping out cheerlessly.

Sorenson immediately picks up on my mood. She puts the machine onto cool-down mode, moving from run to jog to walk within thirty seconds. Sweeps the hair out of her eyes with her free hand. — What is it, honey? What's wrong?

I tell her the story of Miles's betrayal.

—Assholes are assholes. Sorenson upturns her cuffed palm, walking on. — They'll always be there. You said it yourself.

I'm not stoked on this bitch's offhand attitude. — Do you know what it's like to be betrayed, to be violated like that?

— Yes, I do. Sorenson, still walking on the mill, turns her head and rounds on me. — What the fuck do you think this shit is? She waves her bracelet, shaking the chain against the steel pillar.

— I do it with your best interests at heart, not my own. Try it when somebody does it with *their* best interests at heart. When you know something about that, then come back to me! And as I'm talking, I realize I want her to tell the story of her own betrayal, by this Jerry asshole. I'm thinking of that package she got sent, which I couldn't help opening. But to reveal its contents to her now would bring her down and set her back. And I'm still her trainer. — That Jerry guy, he sure messed you up, didn't he?

— Yes, but we've been through that. She turns to the control panel.

— I know there's more, Lena.

— I've told you everything, she says, then lets out a tired exhalation of breath, and she kills the belt, stepping off the machine. She sucks in her lower lip, unaware that when she does this she's so visibly adjusting the gears in her brain. No wonder that Jerry creep ran rings around her. — Look, Lucy, I can help you, she says. — Let's stop all this. She shakes her shackled hand, starting her old shit again. — Let me get rid of this, and we'll spend proper time together. We should be supporting each other. I'm on the right track now. She pats her slimmed stomach. — And I'm certainly not going back. There's no need for all this anymore, and she shakes the chain once more. — I want to work in my studio again!

And for a split second I'm almost ready to oblige. But I see that duplicitous spark in her eyes. — I see what you're doing. Get back on that treadmill!

— I wasn't—

— Not acceptable! The fucking treadmill!

— This is just torture for torture's sake! You're a sadist!

— TREADMILL!

— I wanna do Chuck Norris, she says petulantly, looking at the Total Gym. — I've done enough cardio!

— Get the fuck outta here. How many times do I have to tell you? We keep our cardio and our weights days separate. A twenty-minute warm-up or warm-down is acceptable cardio if you're doing weights, but no more. One builds up the lactic acids, the other depletes them.

Lena looks at me and nods reluctantly, but climbs back onto the treadmill.

— Good, I nod at her, and head off.

Fucking scheming bitch.

34

CONTACT 14

To: lucypattybrennan@hardass.com
From: valeriemercando@mercandoprinc.com
Subject: A Parting of the Ways

Dear Lucy,

It's with great regret that I have to take cognisance of what you said at our meeting in Soho House yesterday, and accept that your heart is no longer in this project. So I'm sorry that I officially end our business relationship.

I wish you every success in the future.

Yours sincerely,

Valerie Mercando

To: lenadiannesorenson@thebluegallery.com
From: mollyrennesorenson@gmail.com
Subject: God Can See What You Are Doing

Lena,

Daddy and I are brokenhearted. We sat down last night and prayed for you. Then we had a heart-to-heart about where we'd gone wrong. I look back, and

I can see that we were mistaken to try and stop you moving to Chicago, and yes, also to follow your vocation as an artist. But we were worried for you, going to that city, with its drugs and gangsters and ghettos, full of people who will try and take advantage of a young girl on her own. We wanted you to study in Minnesota, but accepted Chicago because the business crowd would keep you out of trouble. Is caring for your child such a crime? Is wanting to protect her such a sin? If you are ever blessed with a child of your own—and you are still, in spite of everything, our blessing—then hopefully you'll be spared from feeling what we are now!

May God be with you.

Yours in love,

Mom

To: mollyrennesorenson@gmail.com
From: lenadiannesorenson@thebluegallery.com
Subject: God Can See What You Are Doing

Blah fucking blah fucking blah

35

AN INSTITUTE OF ART

The sculptor and personal trainer are both in the molding business. I'm Lucy's very own piece of clay. Why, then, does she need to see the fat burn from under my skin, replacing it with the definition of toned muscle and sinew? Can I understand her motivations through my own? One thing I certainly know: enduring this shit has made my previous trials seem less hard and any future ones less daunting.

Fortunately, I've grown unconcerned about whether I feel infinitesimally thinner than I had the day before. This is because my journey seems fraught with paradox; while I can feel my muscles growing stronger by the day, at the same time I'm aware of my tendons and joints breaking down. My calves and knees ache, while my knotted shoulder, back, and arm muscles burn hard and hot. Most torturous of all, my inflamed, itching feet: covered in blisters, rashes, and darkly scabbed where my skin has broken open from being chafed by my sneakers. Thank God for that bear kiddie pool! To doctor my blistered, tired feet and rest them on that happy, grinning face!

The second run on the treadmill, an hour at 7.5 mph, has scorched me to my core. I sit back on the mattress, stretching out legs too sore to lock into the lotus position, and I'm too exhausted to concentrate on anything other than regulating my heaving breaths. I realize I've probably let myself get dehydrated; so easy to do indoors under the air conditioning. I take a bottle of water from the cooler by the mattress. Why am I here? You look at causation, but nothing in life is linear. We pretend on our psychotic social networks that we can be reduced to a timeline, but we are a stew, a constantly cooking, bubbling casserole. And I'm thinking about one of my main ingredients.

The sculptures of Germaine Richier (1902–1959) evoke the destruction and atmosphere of violence in Europe following World War II. The pitted and scarred surfaces of her figures, as well as their mutilated facial features, speak eloquently of human suffering. At the same time, the solidity of these personages and their strong expressive presence asserts the ultimate survival of humanity despite the legacy of war. A model for her sculpture was an old man who, fifty years before, had posed for Rodin's representation of Balzac—an archetypal figure of male potency and creativity that Richier now represented as scarred and decaying. When I saw the exhibition of Richier's work at the Institute, I was taken right back to that day in Potters Prairie, watching the terrible images of the attack on the World Trade Center.

Germaine Richier, born in Grans, southern France, was a true original. She was neither academic nor modernist but followed her own unique path, heading for Paris, working with Bourdelle in his last years. The devastating impact of the war had a profound effect on her imaginative landscape. Her previously large female figures became increasingly insectlike, yet determinedly remaining women, while other large, intimidating forms (both male and female) such as *The Storm* and *The Hurricane* seemed to represent the brutal, indifferent forces of nature.

One might speculate that the unequivocal artistic choices of this vibrant, strong-willed woman, who bore no children other than her sculptures, were a means of expressing her own femininity. Indeed, Richier's personal silhouette evokes the robust figures she chose to limn.

Esthetically, Richier shuns the baroque mannerism of the surrealists. While clearly grasping their idiom, she deploys it bluntly, without an excess of affectation or ritual circumlocution. The paradox of Richier's work is that it is both extensively acclaimed yet generally overlooked, principally due to its lack of congruence with any established conservative or progressive artistic movement. In both form and subject matter, the work of Richier displays an unaffected authenticity, which merits value above all else.

Authenticity.

What a strange fucking word for an artist to use.

What was "authentic" about my life?

Merits value above all else; I wrote that. I said that. I remember Nick Vassiliev, my tutor, flushing almost sexually when he read back that sentence. Lena Sorenson, pompous and arrogant, a soon-to-be art-world superstar. They smelled it off me. Nobody on this entire planet was more designed for the School of the Art Institute. And the Art Institute was made for me to shine.

Authenticity.

I wanted a social life. I wanted a sex life, as much as any freshman student at the Art Institute. But I wasn't there to hang out, party, get laid, and be cool. I was there to learn as much as I could and to become an artist. I was driven by a hunger for success more voracious than any business-school student could have displayed. And I was far, *far* more determined than any other student at the Institute. I felt I had greatness in me. I wanted to learn how to be good enough to be great.

There were two principal requirements of being a freshman student at the School of the Art Institute. You needed to buy an Apple Mac and you were required to live in the residencies on State Street. They were housed in an interesting building by the Borders bookstore, and near the Gene Siskel film center, which made it wonderful for me, in spite of the possible embarrassment of running into Mikey.

The white, bright rooms, with large windows and track lighting, were shared with another student, and I was fortunate to split the space with a lovely Korean girl called Kim. Along with Amanda, she became my closest friend. But I had to pay for the dorm rental upfront: almost $20,000. That shared box turned out to be the most expensive rental I and a lot of other people would ever have in Chicago. The huge turnover of students meant big money for the school. Each of the rooms had a bathroom and kitchen. Students had their own drafting table, chair, and closet, but the beds were in loft areas, offering minimal privacy. There was a communal laundry room, and recreational facilities, like a TV lounge and gym, and we all had safety deposit boxes. The best feature of the rooms was that they were a short walk from the school.

I loved all the tutorials and workshops—most obviously 2D (painting), but 3D (sculpture) was a revelation to me. Even 4D (performance art/video) though I had no empathy for it whatsoever, I studied without resentment. And then there was the history of art, which I adored. Other students couldn't wait to get away after a full day's work. I always felt a hollow thud in my chest when a tutor insisted that I had to go home, or even get lunch.

While I was far from the worldliest of art students, I knew what was going on. All staff had to be working artists, and most had a Marxist esthetic, which frowned on elite distinctions between high and low art. This often produced strange results; when I arrived at the Institute, a childlike art movement was ascendant. Prevalent in its oeuvre were effete depictions of unicorns and the like. Art now considered rather ridiculous and lame, such as the copious representations of cartoon characters like Garfield, were assigned a pseudo-Warholian credibility. I knew I wanted none of that, but I strangely benefited from it, as my images of wasted, future humans would soon be lumped into that populist school.

I also learned that socializing with staff members, and fucking them, was rife, indeed considered almost de rigueur for the more ambitious students. If there was such a thing as gross moral turpitude in art schools, it was certainly applied less rigidly than across other strands of academia.

What else did I learn from art school? Certainly, there was the cruelty of critique. Classes often seemed to be a competition to determine who could be the most subtly cold-blooded and pitiless, who could best justify their vitriol intellectually, and it was all about alliances. I soon realized that while we didn't produce many great artists, the place was a factory for people who could deploy verbal sadism with aplomb.

But the most important lessons I quickly grasped—how extremely important curation is, and how crucial it was to meet the right people.

And then I met Jerry.

And when all these things fell into place, I thought I had everything. I *did* have everything. Now what do I have?

An airplane roaring above, coming in from the ocean, ready to head out to the Glades, before circling back into the city to touch down at Miami International Airport. Sometimes, as they soar, I think again about those images of the World Trade Center going down, imagining myself being crushed in rubble or seared with fire, until I'm sick and dizzy with palpitations.

I move cautiously toward the cool glass window, now cruddy with the marks of my forehead, fingerprints, and breath. Look out onto the emerging grid of street and car lights as the day fades away. This is the only window within reach; I've learned instinctively to know the limits of my freedom, before that unforgiving metal bracelet twists and wrenches my arm. The way the tempered steel of that cuff works through the soft fur, giving me a reprimanding slash if I struggle too much. I think of what Lucy might have done with those shackles; how she might have used them on others, prior to me. Attached to that terrible length of chain, with no weak links. So unnegotiable.

I look out the window across to an adjacent block of apartments. On one floor a light clicks on at 8:15 and goes off again at 12:30. It's on a timer, like the ones in here, servicing a ghost apartment. Once I saw two men over in that unit, engaged in quite animated discussion. I waved (screaming is pointless but irresistible) but I knew it was hopeless; even if they did look my way, all they would see is another cold, black window.

Lucy usually comes back in the early evenings, hopefully bearing the luxury of hot food. If it's cold I detest her to my core. Otherwise, my feelings are more complex. The small TV she brought after my opening week of double-digit weight loss is an absolute godsend. It gives me the time, and lets me know what's going on in the world outside. It means I can speak about the Siamese twins with her.

Stephen's role as lead guy in this drama has been usurped by Troy Baxter, a handsome, youngish media-friendly surgeon. He is to lead the team of thirty medical staff who will separate the girls. He's on Channel 8 again, upping his contention of Amy's life chances after the separation procedure to as high as 40 percent, with Annabel's around 90 percent. — The girls share a liver, but have separate hearts and, crucially, they do not share a biliary tract, one of the most vital aspects in the separation of conjoined twins.

They cut to the Wilks mother, who once again robotically advocates prayer as the sole coping strategy. I used to loathe this willful mindlessness, but now I know how she feels. But I also know that it's driven so much by desperation and fear, because that's been my life here. The most chilling aspect is that I still don't know what Lucy's plans for me are, after I hit that target weight loss. I keep telling myself: *she isn't a killer.*

She leaves my phone back in the kitchen, on vibrate. I can hear it purr and beep from the countertop. She keeps it charged, but won't tell me who is trying to call or email me. I make up scenarios about who those calls could be from, long poignant narratives involving Mom, Dad, Kim, and Amanda. But mostly I think about Jerry; so stupid and pathetic, but I can't shake the bittersweet fantasy that he'll kick in the door and rescue me and hold me and be somebody else: the person his words always promised.

I'm running my hand along the bottom windowsill, and there it is, an indented handle! My pulse races as I pull it out and start winding, as the window opens to about two inches. Cool air from the ocean rushes in; its welcome contrast from the recycled gunk that blows through the vents makes me instantly giddy. This slight gap is useless to me; but even if it were wide enough to get through, at forty floors up I'd still be as much of a prisoner as ever. Then I turn to my comforter and my buckets, and my spirits soar euphorically.

36

DOGS

Mona: I swear to fucking God that someday I will sledge-hammer in that bitch's fake, plastic cunt! I'm driving over the Julia Tuttle Causeway toward Midtown as her text pops into my phone, gleefully telling me that Carmel Addison, a Botoxed, vinyl-faced troll, but a good payer, is the latest client of mine who came in to terminate her membership.

Fuck you fake ass fuck you fake ass fuck you fake ass.

I'm running around so much, I realize in despair, I haven't even recorded my data on Lifemap for a couple of days. I feverishly try to recall what I've eaten and done, but I'm passing the spot where the incident happened, and through the muggy heat, a shiver spreads across my back. As I arrive at Miles's place, he's leaving the apartment building and getting into his Jeep, wearing wraparound Ray-Bans, a bomber jacket, which looks like calfskin, and baggy blue brushed-denim pants. In tow is a washed-out Eurotrash blonde, frizzed locks falling out a freakin beret. She looks like she's just come off the plane and a gangster boyfriend has given her a grand to splash on clothes, but only on the proviso that she spends it in his shabbily stocked money-laundering Russian boutique.

She sees me stealing across the road toward them, and nudges Miles. As he turns, I shout, — You fucking asshole!

He's panicked as he starts pushing the green-card-sniffing whore into his vehicle. It still has that irritating sticker on the windshield: IT'S A JEEP THING, YOU WOULDN'T GET IT.

The bitch looks at me and says in a Commie accent, — Eet ees hore! Eet ees thee crazy kung-fu cheek!

— Get in, baby, Miles says. — I'll handle this.

Chico the dog is pissing up against a tree. Miles, who has him on that fucking extension leash, advances toward me, his arms outstretched and his palms upturned. — Lucy . . . we gotta talk . . .

It's a bad stance for him to adopt as I kick out straight for his balls, but he swerves and I only catch his thigh. He jumps back. — You crazy fuck!

— FUCKING LIAR!

He runs to the Jeep, getting in, slamming the door shut, and groping for the ignition as I kick at the body of the vehicle, denting a panel. — FUCKING BITCH!! he screams, pulling off quickly, forgetting Chico and not noticing his leash is caught in the door, as the line unspools. As he tears away I shout at him to stop but there's no way, and, as the line reaches the limit, the pissing dog is yanked from the tree, shooting like a missile, still attached to the leash. Miles hears the yelps and screeches, as Chico rockets past the passenger window, smashing onto the road and bouncing along it like a rubber ball before being snapped back by the leash. Miles gets out the Jeep. — Chico . . . buddy . . .

Chico is miraculously still alive, the poor little guy pulling himself on his front paws, dragging two broken back legs

326

behind him, onto the sidewalk and under a bush. Miles is in tears, begging the animal to come out, every tug on the leash eliciting a sickening snarl. — WHAT HAVE YOU DONE?! He turns to me, face etched in agony.

— What have *you* done?!

— Zee poleece . . . we must call zee poleece, demands the Russki, who has gotten out the car.

Miles gets a hold of the lowly growling dog and carries it to the Jeep. The Commie gets in the driver's seat and they speed off, vet-bound. My nerves are shredded as I jump into the Caddy DeVille and drive. I pull up into a service station and buy an aerosol can of black spray paint from the store. Then, doubling back to Miles's apartment, I gain entry to the building after pushing every buzzer. On his white door I write in capitals: ***IT'S A CREEP THING AND I TOTALLY FUCKING GET IT.***

Heading for downtown, my head is wrecked: I never meant for his dog to get hurt, but it was his own miserable fault for being such a fucking cowardly douchebag. I punch in that egg salad I'd forgotten about yesterday, also recollecting a stress-relieving triple set of pull-ups, and as I control the Caddy with one hand, a lane-changing asshole in a truck pulls in front of me, not even indicating—

FUCK.

As I slow down and hit my brakes, I look up at the apartment block from the Interstate 95, and feel myself sink in dread into the Caddy's ungiving seat. There's a banner drapped out the top floor . . . of our block. Of our apartment!

Two words on a white comforter, thickly scrawled in what looks like . . . surely fucking not . . .

HELP ME

FUCKING SORENSON!

I turn off into Bayshore Drive and park outside the block, running in and pulverizing the elevator call button. *C'MON!* It slams and slaps down through the empty floors and the door springs open. I hit the top-floor button and my heart races as the door snaps shut and the elevator ascends, picking up speed. I'm hoping passing motorists on the Interstate 95 who might have seen the banner figured it represented some sort of urban chic humor; the empty block screaming for help in the real-estate desert. Surely nobody would have stopped and investigated. But the cops . . . how fucking long has it been there?

I get into the apartment and steal down the hall, assailed by a foul stench as I step inside the front room. Sorenson's sitting on the floor on her mattress, but the upturned buckets sit in a lake of stagnant piss and grotesque melting turds spilling across Mom's hardwood floors. — OH MY GOD, YOU FUCKING GROSS WHORE!

— FUCK YOU! Sorenson looks like a malevolent little leprechaun, a real fat person, twisted and hateful as they always are, beyond that sickening jolly-fool facade. *Bitch might shed pounds but bitch's soul's still corpulent.*

I run straight to the window, yanking handfuls of the comforter inside. It's covered in shit; bitch has scrawled in her own fucking mess! I'm shouting, — You fucking foul— then there's a metal swish in the air, as something wraps tightly around my throat. My hands go to my neck, fingers groping at a cold, uneven metal. Fat bitch has whipped her chain around it and she's throttling me . . . I reach behind to grab her wrists, pulling them toward me, as I lever my feet against the plate glass, pushing off back into Sorenson, then reverse headbutting her, hearing her nose crack. The animal shrillness of her scream tells me she's in pain and shock will follow, and, sure enough, I can sense her grip weakening. I ram my elbow into her gut and feel her letting go, and I'm pivoting to watch her crumble to the floor in jagged installments. The chain against my neck, gravity, and her bulk are pulling me toward her and I use the momentum to land on top of her, my palm on her chest, forcing her down. I tear the slackened chain from me with my free hand. — You wanna play rough, fat girl?

To my surprise, Sorenson's recovered her rage. Blood and snot jet from her nostrils, but her eyes blaze in defiance as her hands go round my wrist. — Fuck you!

I pound her fat chops, get in a left hook, and, as she relinquishes her grip on my arm, I follow with a sharp right to the nose. The blood gushes out and tears blind her eyes. I can feel the fight ebbing out of her. — You want me to fuck you up good? Huh?

— No . . . I'm sorry . . . she whimpers.

I get off her, and pull her by the hair, dragging her like a dog over to a pile of her disgusting, sloppy shit. — NOOO! FUCKING LET ME GO!

She's at full-stretch on her cuffs and chain, kicking out as I force her face right into it, screwing her head deeper down into the mess, as she chokes and retches. — I'VE HAD A BAD FUCKING DAY, SORENSON! I'VE HAD A BAD FUCKING LIFE SINCE I MET YOU! YOU AND YOUR FUCKING VIDEO CLIP!

Choking and gagging, Sorenson throws up into the excrement, forcing me to relax my grip. She tears out of it and looks at me, face covered in blood, snot, shit, and puke, eyes bulging. — WELCOME TO MY FUCKING WORLD! *I'VE HAD A BAD FUCKING LIFE!* MY MOM . . . She takes tight, rapid breaths, fixing me in a demented stare through her shit-puke face mask, — . . . she and Dad disapproved of everything I did, my art, when everybody told them I was good . . . she stuffed me to try and make me as fat and miserable as she was . . . Jerry . . . and now . . . her eyes glare, — FUCKING YOU!

Then she forces air into her lungs and springs forward like a sumo, grabbing my shoulders. I swear the bitch would have decked me, but for the chain snapping her back like a cartoon bulldog. We're thrashing around on the floor, wrestling in the stinking, vile mess, before I put her in ju-jitsu armlock and I'm ready to rip that fucking side of ham from her wobbly frame till she screams for mercy and once again comes to rest in a declining cacophony of sobs and retches.

I'm covered in her pungent shit and I'm saying to her, — I'm trying to make your life better, Lena, I really am.

She shakes her filth-caked head, her sobs heavy and angry. — You're fucking ridiculous . . . *this* is fucking ridiculous . . .

— Yes, I am, and so are you!

I go into the bathroom, taking my clothes off and jumping

under the tepid shower, cleaning the rancid shit and mess off me, struggling to control the gagging reflex in the face of the toxic stink. I dry myself off, wrapping a big bath towel around myself. The thermostat is set high, but I'm shivering after the confrontation. I go to the kitchen and put my clothes into the washer, then I pick up a large pair of scissors from a drawer and go back to Sorenson.

She's sitting there, in her own mess, in a trance; silent, save for the sound of heavy bull-like breathing through her nose. She looks up at me, her shit-caked face set in a mocking sneer. Then she sees the sharp implement in my hand and recoils, pleading, — What are you going to do? . . . Please, I don't want to die!

— What the fuck are you talking about, Lena? I snap. — I want your dirty things, I'll put them in the wash. I was going to cut them off you cause they're covered in your fucking shit. I stretch my hand out, keeping my distance in case the filthy whore tries another lunge.

She complies, pulling off her filthy bra, cringing fearfully as I wave the scissors, indicating that she sticks it on the end of them. I then lower it into a plastic bag. God, the fucking stench! Then she yanks down her panties, stepping out of them, placing them in the plastic bag, eyes not moving from my scissors. — I thought you were going to . . .

— Stab you? I hold up the scissors. — With these? Jesus fucking Christ, gimme a break! You started the violence. I rub my neck and turn, heading for the kitchen, musing as I go, — You try and help a fat bitch and as soon as she gets stronger, she attacks you! Not acceptable!

The place is a mess. I'm so relieved that the bear pool happened to be empty, that could have seriously fucked things up.

I get her fresh underwear from the bag and put her filthy clothes into the washer with my own things and the shit-defaced comforter cover, starting up the cycle. After composing myself through a series of deep-breathing exercises and a stretch routine, I return to Sorenson, filling the bear pool with soapy water, then handing her some paper towels. — Do the best you can, I tell her.

Sorenson gets into the pool and starts to clean herself, sponging the feces and vomit off her face. She's like a child. She catches me looking at her and her weird gaze electrifies me and I turn away. I grab up her turds in kitchen roll, flushing them down the toilet, then mop the rest of the gross shit off the hardwood floors. Mom and Lieb would go fucking crazy if they knew they were getting so messed up. I'm doing a circular mopping motion, then screwing out the pukey shitwater into the grid on the bucket. The next thing I hear is a gasping sound, and I turn around to see Sorenson, on the mattress, doing a set of frenzied sit-ups and ab crunches.

I lean against the mop, like a tired sentry. — Don't do those. All you'll do is hurt your back, and the only muscles you'll develop will be buried under layers of fat!

No response, Sorenson still puffing through the set. Then she rolls over and starts doing push-ups. I'm quietly impressed that she's now taking her whole body off the floor, instead of that girlie from-the-knees shit.

— It's the quads, Lena. The squats. I lower myself in

crunch position in front of her to demonstrate, satisfyingly grappling my own steel-cable thighs. — They are your weapons. They burn 115 percent more cal than any other muscle group, I lie, making up a stat on the spot.

— Thirty-one, Sorenson puffs, — thirty-two . . .

— Do you think the skinny bitches in the magazines do push-ups and ab crunches? Leave it till you look like one of them, then we can start thinking about grating some cheese!

— THIRTY-FIVE, she roars, — THIRTY-SIX . . .

— Well, fuck you! Wreck your back and play the martyr, I swing the mop and go back to work on that floor, — that time-honored game of the Sorenson women—I start, quickly checking myself.

Lena catches my reaction, gapes up in horror, springing to her feet and lunging forward before being spun back by the chain. — What the fuck are you talking about? Have you . . . have you been looking at my emails? She rips again at the chain in frustration, using both hands. — MY SHIT WITH MY MOM?!

— You've been told, and I head back to the kitchen.

— WHAT DID YOU MEAN?! WHAT DID YOU MEAN WHEN YOU SAID THAT?!

I'm ignoring her fucking garbage. I note that in her trashing extravaganza, she put the portable TV in the corner, out of harm's way. There's calculation in that bitch's soul; everything is contrived and fucking fake. I feel like taking it from the double-crossing rube, but I'm not going to descend to her level. I check the phone messages: yep, there's another hysterical set of them from her mom. No wonder Sorenson's the way she is with that nutty bitch busting her ass. At least that Kim asshole in Chicago knew when to back the fuck off.

— TELL ME! What did you mean? . . . Tell me . . . As I listen to Sorenson's squeals dying down, I check my own emails on my iPhone. Dad has sent a pic from some town he's in on his tour; an obscure dumbassed-looking cousin stands with him, getting a book signed. Mom has sent me one of her and Lieb, on the deck of the boat, in staged, classical, creepy love pose. She's tucked into his side, looking up at him, as he stares off toward the horizon, the archetypal man-of-destiny look. I swear that pair produce more cheese than Wisconsin. Yet it always strikes me how synchronized they are, Mom and Dad, even after all those years; I get an email, or a call from one, and something similar invariably follows from the other. Long-term association must do something to your biorhythms that you can't shake off. It's just a pity for Sorenson and *her* mom that this connection seems solely to involve stuffing crud into their bodies.

I get the clothes out the machine and stick them in the dryer. As I watch them spin round, I hear more noises outside from Sorenson, and go to investigate. Astonishingly, she's back on the mill running, sweating slowly toward sweet freedom. I give an approving nod, but she refuses to make eye contact, and just carries on pounding. Fuck that ungrateful bitch; I return to the kitchen and send some more emails.

The clothes are still a little dampish when I take them out, but it's stifling outside so I put mine on and drop Sorenson's beside her mattress. — I'm going now, Lena.

— Like I care? Get the fuck out of my face, she pants, not looking at me. — You waste my time.

— Fuck you! I give her the finger and exit. Who the fuck does that bitch think she's talking to, *me* wasting *her* miserable time?! Wouldn't have any fucking time left if it wasn't for me!

When I get home I take another shower, and change into a short leather skirt and red tank top, tying my hair back in a ponytail and sticking a rose clip in it. That bastard Quist is on the TV again. At least he's not talking about me, but defending a beleaguered former business associate, Miami real-estate developer Bill Philipson, accused of trying to bribe several local officials. — Without the Bill Philipsons of this world, this state, now a sun-drenched paradise and haven of opportunity for millions of hardworking Americans, would still be a mosquito-infested swamp!

Anger rattles my frame: some motherfucker is going to suffer. I change channels to Channel 8 and another feature on the twins, as I stuff my cock into my purse, opting not to pack plastic, which would be too visible in this short skirt. Let those butch-bitches think I'm a meat magnet before I whip my American Excess on their stiff, bossy flaps.

An older surgeon is on, a tetchy, arrogant-looking rummy, and he's gunning for golden boy Troy Baxter, rubbishing claims that Amy's chances of survival and leading a normal life are anything like as high as 40 percent. The bar at the bottom of the screen announces him as Professor Rex Convey of Northwestern University School of Medicine. — To play the numbers game is dangerous, but the most wildly optimistic estimates of 40 percent survival for Amy Wilks are arrant nonsense and, frankly, heartbreaking in their stupidity, he growls. — The overwhelming odds are that this girl is sacrificing her life in order that her sister can live a so-called normal one.

Yeah, it's tough shit, but if both bitches have signed up to be sawn in two, it's gotta be their fuckin call, Doctor Country Club.

I click off the TV and consider my options. Tonight I have enough for some empty alcohol calories. Red wine: high in antioxidants, 640 cal per bottle, or four large glasses at 180 each or six small at 116-ish apiece. I decide I'll drink three small glasses, 350. They might be empty calories, but they keep me on track as I need to go 200 over the line today to keep this week in equilibrium.

The heels aren't that high, but they'll be more than sufficient to push my snake-swallows-football calves up into the world's face. Sure enough, whistles from a passing car just as I'm outside on 9th in the warm air. An annoyance, yes, but one, when all is said and done, it would be totally shitty to live without, as silence would be the seal of unviability. Then it would be time to get the fuck out of South Beach and into some Central Florida walled-and-gated waiting room for God.

A coy but vampish nod to the doormen and I'm moving through the crowded bar in Club Uranus, eliciting a pointed moan from a simpering faggot I elbow past. — Excuse me!

I'm about to say something, when this coppery-haired chick sneers at the guy in those stretched Massachusetts vowels I know so well. — Man the fuck up, dude. The bar's crowded!

The fag looks like he's going to respond, but merely pouts and slithers impotently off into the crush.

— Fuckin asshole, the chick mutters.

— I know, right, I affirm with a smile, liking this bitch's style, and rewarding her with a vodka soda. In the usual war of attrition, we push our asses onto two stools at the bar and start talking. Despite the buckshot of Paddy freckles peppered on her pale, luminous skin, I sense that the trailer-park garbage-mouthed shit is an affectation, and that this chick could quote Henry James at will. The collar-length hair gives it away, parted in the center and pinned on the side by some plastic butterfly clip. My mom's more of a butch than this U-Haul-scented ingénue. This chick dressed like she knew she might be called back to a family function and they'd shit housebricks if she turned up with black dye in her hair, never mind some bulldyke crop.

Henrietta James, you are gonna feel my big plastic dick. So I suggest we get out, and she's swift to join me shoving through the sweating bodies. It's so tightly packed near the door area, that being expelled into the night air feels like a rebirth. We walk up Washington, our steps clicking in rhythm on the sidewalk. A bum, sitting outside Walgreens, looks up and shouts at me, — Any change?

— Let the bathroom scale be the judge of that, and I drop a card in his lap.

Henrietta looks at me in some surprise. — Wow, what was with the card?

— I'm a personal trainer.

— Surely a guy like that won't give you much business!

— It's not about business, I shake my head, — it's about confrontation. Hopefully you might just sow a seed if he turns his life around. A human life is worth the price of one card.

— Wow . . . guess I never thought of it like that, Ms. James says, looking back at the bum.

We talk about hitting the Blenheim Hotel but I can't face that stinking carpet or the stiff-assed, closet-case of a desk clerk, in the morning walk of shame downstairs. Henrietta has a place on Meridian, not too far from my own apartment, so we go back there. Despite the fact she's obviously no dummy, Ms. James is a chick of few words, which I like, but as I'm looking at her film posters, Lang's *Metropolis*, Hitchcock's *Rear Window*, the bitch fucking jumps me! Her hand twists up my skirt and inside my panties, diving like a stricken sub for my snatch, her forefinger cattle-prod-zapping my fucking boatman! Before I can think about the plastic dick in my purse, my thighs have opened up like a bag of potato chips. Ms. James gets a rhythm going quickly, boxer-pulverizing my speedbag clitty. Her eyes are ablaze, and there's a raspy insistence in her voice. — You packin heat?

— Yeah . . . I groan, — but it's in my purse . . .

Either she's a real novice, or crucial shit has been mislaid on the move from Boston, but one thing's sure, she fucking well wants it. But now she isn't the only one crying out for dick. I twist and grab my purse, careful to let her keep working on me, now in long, delicious power-frigs, and pull out my cock and tell her to strap it on. — Give it to me. Give me my own fucking cock right up my cunt, I command her.

Ms. James is more than happy to oblige, deftly attaching the device to her, sliding it round, her hand on its shaft, grinding the base of it onto her pubic bone like a pepper mill. — You really want this, don'tcha?

— Fill my fucking snatch *right now*, bitch, or I'll take it from you and give you it right up your lilywhite Paddy ass!

She don't need to be told again.

37

CONTACT 15

To: lenadiannesorenson@thebluegallery.com
From: mollyrennesorenson@gmail.com
Subject: Please Talk To Me

I'm trying to talk with you, here, Lena. You won't pick up the phone or respond to my texts or emails! I'm trying to speak with my own daughter about something that greatly affects us both, but you won't answer anything!

To: lenadiannesorenson@thebluegallery.com
From: toddpaulsorenson15@twincityhardware.org
Subject: This Has Gone Far Enough!

Lena,

I'll have you know that you've not only upset Mommy, you've torn her heart out. I hope that makes you feel good, and is a source of amusement for you and your worldly artsy friends down in Miami. We tried to give you everything. Is this how you repay us?

We want you home. I don't know what sort of crowd you've fallen in with down in that pseudo-Caribbean voodoo-infested hellhole, but it's obvious to me that you're on drugs. Those emails are hateful and vindictive. You were never brought up that way!

Talk to your mother!

Dad

38

THE PACKAGE

I still haven't told Sorenson about the package. I keep it in the walk-in closet, on the top shelf. It contains a letter, a small notebook, and thirty-six high-contrast black-and-white photographs.

The letter is from a woman called Melanie Clement.

Dear Lena,

Your ex-boyfriend—also, now, my ex-boyfriend—is a twisted, evil, manipulative psychopath: a serial menace to women who belongs in jail. He's wasted, stolen, and extorted a good chunk of my money. He's more (or less) than just an utterly worthless leech, or a talentless, self-obsessed delusional bore, he's also a con artist and a thief. If you have any lingering doubts about that fact, the contents of this package should convince you otherwise.

Don't take him back if you have any basic intelligence and/or a shred of self-respect. You and I both know he'll try.

I'm sorry that he left you for me. Sorry for me, delighted for you.

Best,

Melanie Clement

PS The pictures and the negatives are for you—do what you want with them.

The photographs all show Sorenson, naked, in three different poses: front, back, and left-side profile. There are twelve sets of those three prints, all taken in the same spot, under an identical lighting set-up. What they show is her in different stages of transition, from a slim, petite woman to an obese bloater, in the space of a year. Underneath each print is the month, starting at March, and a number, the pounds Lena weighed, going from 129 to 226.

The most arresting and scary transition is not in Lena's ballooning body, but in the expression on her face. In the first series of pictures, though she's obviously been instructed to keep a neutral gaze, there's a phantom grin, like some sort of collusive, sexy game is being played out with a partner. This expression dominates from months 1–3. Then, in month 4, an overwhelming look of embarrassment insinuates itself, followed by the onset of anger, then frustration and despair (months 5–8), before the light goes out in her eyes and she's beaten (month 9 onward). Lena, thanks to this Melanie, now has all of this creep's work on his "project." Or, rather, I do.

I decide to read some entries from the notebook.

THE LENA SORENSON PROJECT
by Jerry C. Whittendean

I first met Lena at the Art Institute. She was just starting out in her freshman year, while I was about to graduate at the end of that year. It was the traditional "fuck a fresher" week, where the would-be studs scoured the parties and events for fresh prospects.

Lena wasn't the type of girl I normally went for. Pretty enough, but chronically shy, with one eye occasionally peeking out from behind those long, black bangs. Those functioned as her shield, but then, when she did look at you, it could be with a steady, challenging ferocity.

We always think that we can change people, mold them. Sometimes I think she was always my project, even back then, as I walked toward her, while she stood trembling like a mouse at the edge of the kitchen. But maybe that's a little too fanciful.

I knew who she was. I was attracted to her work; other students and professors talked about it, I had to check it out. I would go into her classrooms during breaks and contemplate it. For such a timid girl, she was so fucking ballsy in her art: huge canvases, radiant colors, and stark, apocalyptic landscapes. Then I was attracted to her, the mystery of her talent, her fearless, unquestioning, swaggering brio. Seducing her was a means to try and solve this puzzle. But nothing she said or did could answer the question that burned in me: why her? Why did this tiny, dark-haired girl from some Midwest, God-fearing hick shithole, have the talent and drive to gain such unprecedented recognition?

The conversations I had with Lena interested me at first. Then they grew samey, and I sensed we were getting into a rut. I quickly started to resent her, those silly, hayseed affectations, which had, at first, a certain novelty. Eventually, the plethora of "gotchas" and "allrightys" and the "whole heap" of "gosh," "darned," and "hey you's" started to nauseate. She was an airhead, a square suburban housewife, without a bohemian bone in her body but blessed with the talent, drive, and belief of a Warhol.

When you resent somebody you are in such close proximity to, they very soon start to reciprocate. Being Lena, hers was nice, understated resentment, shrouded in an all-too-apparent guilt. But she started to take over. I've learned in life that people flock to charisma in the short-term, but on a deeper level, they always love and admire talent. Friends began to whisper that I was holding her back. That cut me to fucking pieces. I believe in myself as an artist. Without self-belief any artist is nothing. Without me Lena would never have promoted herself, never got the most out of her talent.

Miami was my idea. Lena would have suffered the Midwest winters forever, with her stoical, nauseating, folksy Minnesotan cheer. But it wasn't just me wanting light for my photography. I wanted Lena away from Chicago. She was doing too well. Every time I walked into a Logan Square or Pilsen bar, the cognoscenti would call as one: "Where's Lena?" I grew to almost puke at that question. We hate it when our friends become successful, observed Wilde, Vidal, and Morrissey; but our lovers, by God, how we utterly loathe that!

Nobody knew how humiliating it was to be constantly in her shadow. Lena fucking shone, and I hated both her and myself for it. The only way I could get rid of that feeling was to get the upper hand. I'd render her fat, repulsive. I'd encourage her to overeat: Pizza Hut, McDonald's, Taco Bell, and Gyros. "Let's stop off at Starbucks for a latte and muffin. You worked hard in the gym. Burned off about 150 calories. You deserve a 600-calorie treat," all that sort of shit. I was pushing at an open door: her mother had done her duty.

And so I photographed her. I had her weigh herself the first Friday morning of every week. She didn't realize that she was a project: The Transformation of Lena Sorenson. Short of killing her and leaving a camera on her corpse, watching the maggots devour it (and I had considered this, before coming to the conclusion that murder is a loser's pastime), this was the best thing I could do. I took pictures of her naked, from the front, back, and side, turning to the left. I did this once every month for a year, each one yielding three high-definition black-and-white exposures in identical lighting. A completed project of thirty-six prints: with the date and her weight written on attached cards.

The issue is Lena's consent. No gallery will stage the exhibition unless she gives me written permission to use the images. So while she lies bloating in a darkened corner of the house in Miami, I stew in New York, thinking of how I can get her to just sign that fucking contract.

In the meantime, I try to convince Melanie about the exhibition potential of

the downtown Chicago homeless. Women
of talent, women of wealth, what can I do
to make

Now this is one seriously damaged fucking creep. You can
tell by the conniving content of the emails he's sending her
to get her to sign this fucking contract. These emails also tell
me that he seems to have worked out that Sorenson might
have been the recipient of his missing photographs. It shows
how weak, pathetic, and fundamentally incapable Sorenson
is, if she let a loser like that manipulate and dominate her.
That bitch is fucking blessed to have come into my orbit.
I will empower that flabby ass! But, like the team of surgeons
with the Arkansas girls, you gotta rip out a lot of shit as you
do the renovation, and if the patient dies on the table, well,
at least you gave it your best fucking shot.

39

CONTACT 16

To: mollyrennesorenson@gmail.com; toddpaulsorenson15@twincityhardware.org
From: lenadiannesorenson@thebluegallery.com
Subject: 85 Degrees This Winter

I'm sending you a joint email, as my previous ones have apparently got you two talking to each other. (No need to thank me.) I'm also copying you both into any emails I send the other, so you're not able to play the stupid, manipulative, and self-deceiving games you've both become so adroit at.

First Dad:

Thanks for the first email from you in, like, FOUR YEARS and THREE MONTHS. Glad to know you still care.

1. Sorry Mom's upset, but surely you must be able to see that she is morbidly obese. Anybody as fat and isolated as she is obviously has mental health/depression and extreme denial issues. You and I are partly to blame; we've enabled that depression. In my case it was through collusion. In your case it's been emotional neglect. Well, I'm done. So how about you manning the fuck up and giving the woman you profess to love a little attention? Even—whisper it—a little affection?

2. Yes, speaking the truth does make me feel good, though it's a topic of discussion for us alone, and NOT anyone else, including my so-called "worldly artsy friends" who exist solely in your imagination. I should be so lucky. If I had the sort of social network you imagine, I wouldn't have spent most of my life so utterly fucking miserable.

3. I'm not on drugs—they've never been my thing, either when growing up in Potters Prairie or as an art student in Chicago. If you want to find evidence of drug abuse, check out your own medicine cabinet: Mom has been seriously abusing prescription drugs for years.

What I guess I'm trying to say is: FUCK YOU.

Now Mom:

You want to know where you went wrong?

1. Stuffing me full of junk food, making me as fat, depressed, and unhealthy as you are. I was heading for type 2 diabetes, and I'm assuming that you are well into that zone and experiencing the associated health issues. You can still fix it: CHECK YOURSELF BEFORE YOU WRECK YOURSELF!

2. Disapproving of every single friend I had growing up. Even the squeaky-clean "friends" you handpicked for me from the church groups eventually weren't good enough. Way to make a girl feel as bad as you, bitch!

3. Trying to stop me doing what I was put here to do. Every expert, from that teacher at elementary school to the Art Institute, told you I was a prodigious talent and excelled at art. What was so wrong about letting me paint and draw? Are you fucking kidding me?

4. Trying to stop me leaving PP, MN. It might be your place, but it was never mine. GROW THE FUCK UP AND RESPECT THAT.

5. Trying to guilt-trip me with God. I don't know if there is a God. I actually hope that for your sake there ISN'T, as He's going to be really pissed at you come Judgment Day for BUGGING HIM ABOUT EVERY FUCKING TRIVIAL THING IN YOUR LIFE and putting words in His mouth. I'm delighted you have faith—now fuck off and enjoy it (quietly) and don't use it as an excuse to control/manipulate/feel superior to/bug the living shit out of everybody else.

Miami Beach is lovely and warm at 85 degrees. How the fuck is Otter County?

L x

40

WEST LOOP LENA

Sitting in a Miami high-rise, lying in my own shit. Feeling my nose and cheekbone throb in pain as I sit naked in this bear pool, washing almost every possible bodily fluid from my face. Movements perfunctory. Oddly not nauseated. Blowing my sore nose softly on a paper towel: still some feces, vomit, and dried blood mixed in with my mucus. The colors, texture, and mess of what I see in these towels creating a pulse of morbid excitement. Strangely wallowing in this ludicrous predicament: the wild, mixed-up, oscillating feelings it produces. Wanting to cry and squeal in pain, and then just laughing at it all. Looking at the contents of my face drip into the pool's shit-brown lukewarm water. The TV, which I couldn't bring myself to wreck, playing soundlessly in the corner. My sole stimulus, my only company.

And as an artist, you have to face up to unflattering things about yourself. The shit. At first Barry King's death shattered me, but all the time there was a phantom exhilaration to it. It put me at the center of a compelling drama.

I'm like an exhibition. A show. A human exhibit: future human, past human. Past Lena, future Lena. The one emerging relentlessly in that glass reflection in the window. But that's one thing I could always do: I knew how to put on a show.

Like back in Chicago. I got in with the supposedly cool crowd, mainly through Jerry. Olivia and Alex were his acolytes (a very Jerry word), though I brought Amanda and Kim into the scene. We partied a lot but were always on time for our classes, largely at my instigation, even if we often took it to the wire. We would charge through the Art Institute, past the medieval artifacts and exhibits of armor, pushing aside members of the public, to get to our workshops and lectures at the rear of the building.

Then Jerry. Where to begin?

I was at a party in Wicker Park, clutching a bottle of cheap Chilean red in the kitchen, trying to decide whether or not to get drunk. Hoping it would give me the confidence to interact with the normal people there. Now I see how foolish I was to think in that way. It's more likely that we're all aliens—at least those worth bothering about are. And each of us is making the mistake of trying to disguise ourselves as human beings.

Of course I'd noticed him earlier, but I was far from alone there. Jerry was in his final year and elevated by many freshmen, as well as the most popular tutors. All those reverential mutterings that whistled through the college grapevine: "Is Jerry coming tonight?" "What's Jerry working on?" "Does Jerry have any decent shit?" It all seems so ludicrous now.

And then he was staring at me, really staring, as if I were an exotic object of curiosity. Framed in the doorway. Handsome: a strong, lithe figure with a shock of black, bushy hair. His eyes dark pools; I couldn't look at them. I could feel his bristling confidence and power radiate from across the island counter and I felt myself wilting inside when he came over to me.

Jerry then did something strange. He introduced himself, and as I mumbled "Lena" in reply, he removed my beret, brushed the bangs from my face, and then replaced the hat, securing back my hair. I noticed then that his eyelashes were inordinately long, like a girl's false ones. — I like to see who I'm talking to, Lena. And these are not the kind of eyes that should be covered, he said with a big smile that disarmed my rage at his presumption. Pathetically, I smiled—that little-girl smile. I was too intoxicated by his presence to even detest myself for it. (Self-loathing would come later.)

We chatted for ages, sipping wine; more and more wine. Then, by intoxication's strange social alchemy, we were trudging through the white-and-black threadbare streets, past the snow-covered cars that lined the road like giant teeth, back to his place, which was thankfully close by. He lived in the top part of an old house that had been split into two apartments. It was spacious, even luxurious. I thought we'd have sex then, I really wanted to, but instead we just talked and made out and drank coffee. The morning light came up, showing Jerry's pores and the tight angles of his jawline and cheekbones, and he suggested that we took the El downtown back to my student dorm. He wanted to see my work. I remember the warmth of his body next to mine on that crowded train, and just wanting that journey to last forever.

The train spilled us back onto the frozen, empty, downtown streets. When we got to my student residency, Kim was fortuitously up and dressed. Jerry greeted her politely, and then looked over my series of sketches and drawings, and the couple of pieces I'd got mounted and hung in the meager wall space in the dormitory. — You're good, he acknowledged, — and, even better, you're prolific. We have to get people to see this stuff.

He confessed that he'd heard about my talent, and had been checking me out for a while. I was suitably flattered. No, I was totally enraptured. A few nights later, we were back in his apartment, the kitchen, and started making out again. I sensed this was our time, so I slipped down the wall, and we sat with our backs against the cold refrigerator, kissing with an intensity alternating between teasing control and wild abandonment. I broke the spell of rapture to advance the deal, and unzipped his fly, reached in and felt his hardness. He started making a soft whistling sound, like blowing compressed air through his front teeth. It was strange, but then he got me to stand up and step out of my pants. I didn't need any encouragement. But when I did, he just looked at me, as if locked in some weird stasis. I took charge again, gently pushing him onto the kitchen floor, conscious only fleetingly of the dirt that he seemed to register in faint distaste. — Can we—he started, but I silenced him with another kiss, and unbuckled him, yanking his boxers aside, watching his veiny dick spring free. It thumped flat onto my stomach, so I straddled him with one hand pressed against the old, chunky, cream-colored Kenmore refrigerator.

His wide hand cupped the back of my head and neck, and then we were moving sluggishly, uncomfortably, my knees pressed into the floor, until he shimmied up, leaning against the Kenmore, caressing my ass (still through my panties) with his other hand, and also kissing, then biting, my neck. I kissed his mouth, deeply. His hands were fastened onto my hips, pulling me down onto him, me yanking my panties to the side, and then I felt myself enclose him all at once, and a fire burning somewhere near the base of my spine. Almost immediately, I was contracting hard, fucking him faster, and with force, till his grasp on my hips tightened as he tried to push me up and off him, gasping, but I shouted, — Wait, and felt myself shunting into another space and dimension as Jerry groaned, me pushing with final, determined strength right to where I wanted to be, then, afterward, slowly peeling my spent body from his. As we slumped to the floor I saw that he'd spilled onto the hardwood, over my panties (which were still half on), my thighs, and his own crumpled pants. I watched him slowly bang the back of his head twice against the refrigerator. Then he drew in a deep breath and exhaled in a gurgling, euphoric laugh that warmed me as I curled into his side and fell into a slumber.

I was woken by the biting cold, with no idea whether I'd been out for seconds or an hour, feeling myself bobbing into consciousness from being deeply submerged, a sensation I'd always associate with satisfying sex. Jerry had disentangled from me, and tucked a cushion under my head. He was gone and a window was wide open. Although it was his place, a bolt of panic and shame still gripped me; I recalled my mom's one attempt at sex education: — Don't. They're only after one thing and once they get it they're off. God made fingers for rings!

These words must have burned deep, as, in mounting dismay, I squinted in the moonlight to find my pants, pulling myself into them. As I straightened out, I realized with great relief that Jerry was still there; I saw him through the kitchen window above the sink, standing out on the fire escape, smoking a cigarette. It was dark but he was dimly lit from the spotlights. His arm was resting on the window ledge, and he was looking out at something in profile. His hair was wrecked, his lips were parted, and his breath billowed out almost as densely in the cold as the blue tobacco smoke. I joined him and noted he was wearing a T-shirt; he hadn't even put on his sweater or coat. It was as if he were oblivious to the bone-tapping cold. His eyes were shut, those long cow-lashes resting on his cheeks. They opened when I stepped outside. — Hi, he said, drawing me close, then making a motor sound in my ear, — Brrrrrr!

I laughed and looked at him. Snowflakes disintegrated in his hair. I wanted to reach up and touch them but instead we stood face-to-face, me pulling myself closer to him, my hands gripping his T-shirt. I stepped further into his warmth. My chin spiked his chest. I could feel the dumb brutality of the redbrick building, the sticklike winter trees, gray sky, and white streets below us, pressing in on our drama.

Anything seemed possible with Jerry. He bristled and crackled with an intoxicating power. He had the confidence and sense of entitlement I lacked but desperately wanted to access. Over the weeks, I felt some of it starting to rub off on me. I soon stopped thinking of myself as tubby little Lena from Potters Prairie. I was an artist. I was Jerry Whittendean's girlfriend.

But what was I bringing to the table? I didn't see it then, because, like almost everyone else, I was so in awe of him. But what I brought was the talent. Jerry's tragedy was that, to paraphrase him, he was neither good nor prolific. He had passion and ambition, but little skill to back it up. Nor did he possess what all successful artists require more than anything: an engine. That had never been developed, perhaps due to his background of relative privilege: a father in the oil industry, a large house in Connecticut, and a private education. For me there was no such thing as a blank canvas. I couldn't wait to defile it with my strokes. And I couldn't wait for Jerry to defile me with his. I couldn't take my hands off him. And I discovered, to my surprise, that, in love as in art, I was by far the hungrier of the two of us. Although I didn't realize it at the time, it seemed that with Jerry everything was poured into the initial seduction. After that, he grew bored and complacent quicker than I could imagine any other man ever doing.

But my warning bells ought to have started ringing when he announced he was moving his focus from multimedia and concentrating solely on photography. Even his most sycophantic *acolytes*, like Alex, balked at this. Art school operates on a hierarchy. Painters are number one in terms of prestige and credibility, closely followed by those who choose to pursue sculpture. The multimedia people are harder to classify, as the discipline was then too new and too amorphous to get a proper handle on. But those specializing in photography tended to be a very confused breed. Apart from the central question as to whether photography could be considered art at all, it was the poor relation at the Art Institute of Chicago. Frankly, my high-school facilities back in Potters Prairie, MN, were superior. For half the price of the Art Institute's fees, you could go to Columbia College, or even rent a photography studio. However, the snappers weren't quite at the bottom of the pile—that honor went to the viscom students (why would anybody pay so much money to get a degree in graphic design?) — but they were pretty damn close. And Jerry wasn't a bottom-of-the-pile sort of guy.

While my social life was on the up, his visits to my dorm, where we made love in my single bed, poor Kim often pretending to be asleep, or leaving to shuffle out to Dunkin' Donuts in the cold, were its undoubted highlight.

There wasn't an enviable leisure scene in the student accommodation back then. We were isolated from the city, trapped in a downtown, which, at the time, was near dead and occasionally hostile. Considering the number of students there were at various colleges, there was precious little in the way of social facilities catering for us. Basically, you had to make your own entertainment. A lot of my first-year downtime was comprised of standing or sitting around, usually smoking cigarettes outside the residencies, on the steps of the Art Institute, or hanging out in Dunkin's, where we competed with local bums for free donuts. There was practically nowhere else to go for food, and it meant that the weekly red line L trip out of downtown to a Jewel-Osco was a welcome adventure.

Yet the spartan tedium of student life in some way facilitated its creativity. Artists (professors) and students socialized together a lot, and Jerry introduced me to the big hanging-out culture. It made sense as the tutors had the status and the apartments outside of Chicago's then ghostly downtown, with six-packs of PBR and bottles of vodka in their refrigerators. And it proved useful. You were supposed to take twelve credits per year, and I took twenty-one, probably around eight of them accrued just through hanging out with teachers. And I didn't have to fuck a single one: I was fucking Jerry, and it was tacitly understood by even the biggest predators that I was his girl.

I glance at the soundless TV. Stephen, the suitor of the twins, is on. I reach for the remote, with an urgency that shames me, and turn it up. He has become a celebrity, this poor boy from Arkansas; he has the status that the East Coast, educated, bohemian Jerry Whittendean sought so desperately. I would once have disdained the crassness of our sick, sensationalizing reality-TV-dominated society. Now I find myself giving thanks for the crass, leveling, bizzaro democracy it confers.

Stephen looks harsher across the eyes, his gestures and tone have a cocky defiance about them. He's embraced the narrative of his fame with a sense of entitlement, wearing the mantle of arrogance well. — I told Annabel, don't y'all be separatin' on account of me.

— But you say you love her, says the disembodied voice.

The camera closes in, as Stephen goes faux shy at this question, but there's a tight slyness to his features, followed by an acknowledging shrug. It's actually a great, but chilling, TV moment: he knows he's been outed, but he's now too full of his own sense of power to actually care.

— Will you carry on your relationship with Annabel once she's separated from Amy?

— I guess.

We cut to the studio, and after a banal summary by the anchor, the story switches to a corrupt local real-estate deal and I drown the volume. I wonder how much Stephen is getting paid. I muse bitterly that it's too much for this imbecile, then turn the full circle, fearing for the boy, concerned that he's being exploited. Angry that his story will be torn from him and broadcast to the world, and that he'll have no reward bar his fifteen minutes of fame. I can see him in five years, a semilush on a bar stool, pulling up his YouTube clips on his smartphone, sticking them in the face of anybody who will listen.

Was Jerry's need for recognition really any different?

At the end of my first year we moved into an apartment together. Or not quite together: a bunch of us, Kim, Alex, Olivia, and Amanda, rented a huge industrial space. There was a burgeoning gallery scene emerging in the West Loop district to rival the more established one at Near North, and we decided it was the place for us. We painted the beige walls a brilliant white and used display boards to partition the space into "rooms."

The West Loop was a postindustrial area of old factories

and meat markets, retail suppliers and warehouses. It felt so desolate across from the foreboding triple barriers of the Chicago River, the railtracks, and the concrete freeway overpass, all of which seemed to cry "keep away."

But the homesteaders weren't hearing anybody. High-end restaurants opened on Randolph, and reputable galleries like the McCormick set up on Washington. Our second-floor loft was close to Washington and Halstead, and a rash of new exhibition spaces.

Jerry and Alex had a blue neon sign made for the window, which simply said, *Blue*. And so we curated and exhibited our work. I was the most prolific, but Alex, Amanda, and Kim also produced stuff. Jerry would mostly drink, and talk. We leafleted the crowds who came into the area for the gallery walk on the first Thursday of the month. Word of mouth operated and our first three shows were packed, though largely with friends and those drawn to the free beer that bobbed in big plastic buckets of icy water. We knew how to throw a party. We were the student in-crowd, privileged and exalted. Although we were secretly hated by the many, they were also desperate to be in our circle. I was possibly the only one of our group who fully understood this dynamic. A willowy blond girl, Andrea Colegrave, was particularly pushy. She tried to befriend me, then Kim, Amanda, and Olivia, eventually sleeping with Alex. Her neediness was pathetic, and it repulsed me. But what was even more threatening was that smug private look she gave me, a look that said "I know who you are." And that "who" was the fat nerd I thought I'd left behind in Potters Prairie.

Then, for our fourth show, one of our professors, Gavin Entwhistle, brought a visitor along. Up until then I had little idea what an art collector looked like. Jason Mitford was nothing like the old moneyed, wavy-haired, blazered, and cravat-wearing crust of my imagination. He was dressed all in black, with a contrasting shock of electric white hair. He looked like a rock star, or, rather, what he was, a failed rich-kid artist.

As he looked over my canvases, I couldn't help but pick up on the way people, even professional cynics like Jerry, were watching him scrutinizing the paintings. Jason's body language was intense and amazing. He would never screw up his eyes or indulge in chin-stroking. He would face the canvas, go totally still, and let his arms fall by his side. He looked like a boxer ready to fight. Then he'd take a backward step, followed by a forward one, shuffling on the balls of his feet, then suddenly dance back, or move to the side. I was producing huge canvases, influenced by Damien Shore, the illustrator of the covers of the Ron Thoroughgood sci-fi novels. I hadn't realized at first that Shore, like so many people working in that genre, was inspired by the English painter John Martin and his gigantic apocalyptic paintings. Jason did his swagger around the gallery, then took me aside and said in a matter-of-fact way, — You know, I'm going to come back here next week, and if you add a zero to your numbers, I'll buy a painting. But I can't do that right now. I would just look foolish.

My mouth hung open by way of a response.

— You have to put a more ambitious valuation on those

363

works. You can't sell them as junk; that's worse than giving them away.

I thought Jason was joking, that I was once again the object of ridicule, that the high-school culture of Potters Prairie had followed me out here with my Ron Thoroughgood novels. So I kept quiet about the conversation we had.

But then, when he did show up again the following week, I hadn't officially changed the numbers, but had taken the tags off just in case, keeping the prices on a list. This practice produced some negative comments from Alex and Gavin Entwhistle, but Jerry was very supportive. So Jason came up to me, accompanied this time by a stick-thin but good-looking magnesium-blond woman. He introduced her as Melanie Clement. — I'll take this one, he said, looking at *Void*, my biggest piece. — How much?

I steeled myself and quoted the price, with an extra nothing on the end. Jason nodded, sucking in his bottom lip. Then he asked me about my second Martin-via-Shore homage canvas, *The Fall of New Babylon*. Though he was casual, I was still astonished when he wrote me a check right on the spot. (And I never quite believed it until it cleared the following Wednesday!) So two paintings I had on offer for $700 and $900 the previous week were sold for $7,000 and $9,000. I should have been elated. Everybody around me was. I was a second-year student and this was absolutely unprecedented.

Instead I was scared out of my darned wits. I could barely look at Jerry, Alex, Kim, Amanda, Olivia, or any of the others in the room, especially the sneaky Andrea, who seemed to perennially hover close by. And I certainly couldn't tell them what Jason had whispered to me afterward, as we stood in the corner, sipping cheap white wine, with an almost postcoital vibe humming between us. — These friends of yours, you can never exhibit with them again. He shook his head, in regret, like an enlightened Roman emperor who was personally opposed to blood sports but ruefully forced to concede that the masses needed it. — They don't have it. Any association with their stuff only drags you down.

I wanted, for about two seconds, to protest, to scream, "How dare you! Those are my friends!" But I didn't. I couldn't, not just because I was validated and intoxicated by his words, but because I knew in my heart that they were absolutely true. The others were good: quirky, interesting, maybe, in patches, even great. But there was no compelling voice, no overriding thematic concern, nothing whatsoever that attested to their unique brilliance as artists. And when they did one piece that was decent, they sat back and emotionally dined off it, as childishly grateful as the kids at my school in Potters Prairie. And while I was thinking this, I was looking at Andrea, all thin, angular frame, and gleaming teeth, holding a wine glass, flirtatiously hanging around Jerry. There was no desire. No engine.

One cold but sunny late November, just a few weeks after this, Jerry and I woke up on our mattress in the morning light, to the sound of stage coughing. Alex stuck his head round the side of our partition. — Call for you, Lena.

It was another collector from New York, called Donovan Summerly. He told me he'd heard about Jason's purchases

365

and wondered if he could arrange a private viewing? I said "sure" as casually as I could, and a couple of days later he came into town and I sold three more paintings, at $8,000, $5,000, and $9,000.

At this point I allowed myself to show my excitement to the world. This gave Jerry, who had hitherto been enthusiastic, the cue to sound a note of caution. — We're underselling. That guy probably flew first class here from New York and checked in at one of the best rooms at the Drake.

And with these comments he had, de facto, taken over the management of my affairs.

— Now we cool it, no more sales. Let things settle.

But they weren't going to do that. I was invited to exhibit at the prestigious Cooper-Mayes gallery in the Near North Side. Then Melanie Clement, the girl who had been at the show with Jason Mitford, invited me to show at her GoTolt gallery in New York. She explained that both Donovan Summerly and Jason had kindly agreed to lend their purchased works to the show, so I would have a complete viewing of my pictures. I would call the exhibition Void, after the largest canvas. In passing, I mentioned that I admired the sci-fi writer Ron Thoroughgood. To my shock Melanie's gallery immediately commissioned him to write the catalog copy for Void.

If I was excited, Jerry went crazy. He'd now graduated, and was spending his nondrinking time taking pictures of the downtown bums who hung out around the liquor stores and halfway houses, panhandling the tourists and office workers. I quickly realized he felt that my New York exhibition was as much his calling card as mine.

At the New York show, as legitimate collectors would be present, we decided it was time to try and sell the rest of the work, with prices revised northward. I was initially shocked and delighted to find that Ron Thoroughgood was present. He looked nothing like the mustachioed wizardlike character of his dust jackets. He was older, a sleazy and lecherous drunk, who made lewd proposals to me, then several other young women present. Jerry befriended him, as despite his highbrow affectations, he had a taste for genre fiction, particularly crime and thrillers. Increasingly inebriated on the free booze and after copious complaints, Thoroughgood was eventually escorted outside by gallery security. It was a considerable disappointment, but nothing could ruin a great night. Jerry's schizoid intensity was useful; he could work a room. His warm smile drew in the right people. He sniffed out and flattered the buyers, not in an obvious way, yet still rounding them up like a sheepdog; friendly, enthusiastic, and oddly compelling. Conversely, his frozen psycho look made people disinclined to remain in the vicinity. He repelled the wrong interlopers—the bums and hustlers—whom he could scent out like a bloodhound. And now I know why: he was one of them.

We, no, I, made a fortune. Next summer, when the lease ran out on the loft, we decided to renew it, but not ask Alex, Olivia, Amanda, and Kim to join us. Blue was, after all, as Jerry explained, the Sorenson brand, and I needed more room to work. Amanda and I had become firm friends but she didn't like Jerry. She was seeing an architect guy back in New York. She spent a lot of weekends there, or he was here, and our friendship cooled. Jerry convinced me that she was a "straight rich girl, jealous of your talent" and no great loss. Kim stayed friends with me, as did Alex and Olivia with us both.

So we got some drywall partitioning done. The space was divided into a proper bedroom, then an office and a workshop for me, with a photography studio for Jerry, replete with new equipment. But most of all, we retained a large, bright exhibition area with bare white walls. Blue was a proper gallery.

Jerry and I were busy socially, still partying a lot. Bars. Gigs. Shows. Buckets of beer. Shots. Good wine. Jerry was still popular, but he got stuck, while I was thriving. I kept studying for my degree and continued to work hard: I wasn't stupid enough to think I wasn't learning technique anymore. But as I bloomed, there were more shows, sales, and features on me as a rising star. The *Tribune*. The *Reader*. The *Sun Times*. *Chicago Magazine*. Chicago is very kind to its sons and daughters, even its adopted ones, who don't jump ship to New York or LA at the first sign of success.

So I had a thriving art career while still a student, which was unheard of. I learned that it was impossible to enjoy that kind of success and not excite jealousy, particularly in people from wealthier homes, whose sense of prerogative outstripped their talent. It was just the source that surprised me.

Jerry seemed to get more edgy. One time at a party in Pilsen, at Alex's new place, he was really drunk and high on coke. A group of us were huddled in the kitchen, talking about our future plans, when he burst into a bitter rant, which culminated in him fixing me with that unnerving stare of his and proclaiming, — I was the one who was supposed to exhibit! Me!

But he didn't. Because he didn't have anything worth exhibiting. His photographs, high-contrast black-and-whites, were a rich white liberal's clichéd and largely patronising view of disenfranchised African Americans. So good at selling my work, Jerry found would-be suitors massively under-whelmed when trying to attract any interest in his own. It got to the stage where he couldn't even bother disguising his pain when a painting of mine sold.

I came in one day to find a pretty freshman girl naked in his studio. This was his new project, he brusquely informed me, studies of the female nude. I wanted to tell him how pathetic and creepy, but worse, how *artistically mediocre* this was making him appear. Even Alex was losing faith. But Jerry was lost in the self-righteous world of the cokehead. He brought more girls along. As I painted, sculpted, and made my figurines, I could hear them joke and giggle and smoke pot and drink as he snapped them in his studio area. Yes, I was chokingly jealous of all the girls he photographed. But I loved him. So I kept my mouth shut. After all, I was meant to be a liberated artist, sophisticated and worldly, not a frumpy girl from Potters Prairie, MN.

With regard to my mother and father, I could no longer live the DePaul Business School lie. I gathered up a load of my press cuttings, photographs, and copies of bills of sale, and wrote them a letter, explaining that the business college I'd never gone to hadn't worked for me and that I had transferred to art, and that I was astonishingly successful. They

369

didn't take it so well at first. Then they drove down to Chicago, and saw the operation—the school and the gallery. I told them that I no longer required their financial support and that I would pay back Grandma Olsen's college money. Although Mom fussed and fretted, I could tell Dad was quietly impressed. When they were leaving, he just looked at me and uttered one word, — Enterprise, then climbed into the car. I'd never felt so good around him.

It was a mundane fall evening, not that long after, when I heard Jerry making excited noises. He had found some old pictures of me, from when I was a fat teenager. He couldn't believe that I had ever looked like that. He said I had an amazing ability to lose and gain weight quickly.

And he convinced me to pose nude. At first I was flattered. I loved him so much, and he immediately seemed to lose interest in the other girls. — I was just learning about the process with them, the light, the shade, the angles. It was all just preparation for you, he told me. And those words were so sweet—fool that I was, I couldn't sense the treachery in them. Like everybody looking out at life through the veil of love, I saw what I wanted to see.

On the first Friday of every month, for one year, Jerry took three pictures of me in black and white: back, front, and left-side poses. All in one identical spot and with the same lighting. But he also encouraged me to eat. He said he wanted to see my body change. It was real art. He was right. I was De Niro in *Raging Bull*. I could gain weight, yes, but I would lose it, easily. I would have done anything for him.

And I was still working hard, still studying. Not only was I taking additional classes at the Insitutute, I was also learning taxidermy. I found this guy, Russ Birchinall, a hale-and-hearty outdoor type, as I realized the breed always was, who specialized in small mammals, and who had a workshop near Western Avenue. Russ guided me thoroughly through all the stages of the process, from the grading of the specimen, to skinning, tanning, coding, mounting, finishing and placing it on a custom-made habitat base. I learned how to inspect an animal's condition, skin, measure the hide—or *cape* as he called it—the volume of flesh; turn the lips, eyes, and ears; split the nose; code, salt, and tan the cape. I learned custom-form alteration, as well as mounting practices and finishing and airbrushing techniques. I thought I'd be squeamish, but I wasn't. Once an animal was dead, it was dead, and I loved the idea of restoring it to some sort of flawed approximation of what it was.

Jerry scoffed at me with his now customary derision. Why was I wasting time on this? What was the point? He sounded like my father. The patriarchal voice, the controller's voice, is always the same. When it's filtered through the haze of love, though, you don't hear it properly, and you make allowances. I still ate, still grew, and kept posing for the pictures, but began to dread those Fridays, circled by Jerry in a red pen on the wall calendar.

A lot of the money I had made—big money, from selling my paintings—seemed to be vanishing fast. Disappearing into the dive bars, or the pockets of cocaine dealers. Shrinking, as I grew. And Jerry just kept on encouraging me.

Encouraging me to eat. He cajoled and begged, then, ultimately, rewarded me, with food.

And when I changed too much, shortly after the twelfth set of monthly pictures was completed, Jerry told me that it was time for us to leave Chicago.

41

STOCKHOLM SYNDROME

I'm in such a fucking hurry cause Marge was late again. Three twenty-three and she jabbers on with bullshit *I do not wanna hear* about her fucking cat and the vet's. My margins are tight: a bitch rolls with me or she don't fucking roll. There are 24 hours, 1440 minutes, and 86,400 seconds in a day, too much of which I squander on losers. (I devoured all Lieb's time-management literature when I first came to FLA.) I've Dad's book presentation in a couple of hours. So I put Marge through her paces and split with maximum haste.

When I get to the Caddy, my gut is knotted with anxiety. Traffic will be building up on the MacArthur and I need to feed Sorenson. The only fast-food place handy is this pizza joint, so I order a couple of slices. The line is busy with just one fat chick sweating behind the counter, trying to keep up with the orders. — Sorry about the wait, she says.

— Well, that's a start. But don't beat yourself up, take action, and I hand her my card.

She looks at me like she's going to burst into tears. — I meant . . . I meant the *wait*! The wait you've had in this line!

— I beg your pardon, I misunderstood you, and I look into her haunted eyes. — Gimme two slices of pepperoni.

She bends down, cheerlessly scooping the gloopy mess into a clear plastic box. I throw her the olive branch. — I know what a bitch working in fast-food retail can be. You have my number: use it and you'll lose it.

As I leave I can see that I've hurt her. Good: I've brought it home. The first step. Act two is all down to this bloated sister.

I get back into the Caddy and drive over the MacArthur, beating the worst of the crazy rush. When I reach the apartment, Lena's sitting on the mattress in the lotus position, watching the news on TV. — I did number twos twice today, she says nodding to the gross bucket.

I put the pizza box down on the floor in front of her.

Sorenson gets up, puts her hands on her slimmer hips. Stares at the pizza slice. Then me. — What the fuck is this, Lucy?

I'd come here to tear strips off her, but Sorenson looks like she couldn't give a rat's ass. She doesn't even seem like herself, and it isn't just the lost weight. Her jaw has a hard set to it and her eyes are like slits. The skin on her neck and chest has a ruddy, blotchy flush but her face has gone wraith-white.

I feel myself backpedaling. — I'm sorry . . . I was in a hurry. Things have been hectic . . .

Sorenson pushes the box aside with her foot. — You know what this is? This is fucking shit! And she grabs the box and tips its contents into her toilet bucket. — That's where that crap belongs! You fucking *kidnap me* to *force me to lose weight* and then you feed me THAT FUCKING

SHIT! How am I gonna lose weight eating that fucking shit?

— But there was nothing else open—

— You could have gone to Lime and got me a low-carb burrito with Baja fish, or something from Whole Foods! If you're going to be a twisted kidnapping bitch, at least do it right and get me some fucking *food*, cause I'd rather starve than eat that fucking crap!

And there's nothing I can do but concede. — You're right. I'm sorry.

So I dump the bucketful of crap down the toilet, then get back out and into the car. When I return half an hour later with the low-carb Baja-fish burritos, Lena is doing push-ups. — . . . eighteen . . . nineteen . . . twenty, she gasps, catching her breath.

— This food is getting cold!

— One more freakin set . . . she puffs, and goes through another twenty reps. She finishes and sits up, peels the foil back from the fish burrito, holding it in her cuffed hand, eating it slowly and deliberately. I didn't get lunch thanks to my fucking unreliable clients, so I'm ravenous and can't hold out till dinner with Dad later, so I'm packing my own one back. Sorenson looks up at me with a startling glare. — Slowly! she ticks.

— I'm in a hurry!

— Where are you going?

— Over to the Gables, to my dad's book presentation at the Biltmore.

— Oh yeah, the crime writer, Lena laughs, throwing back

her head, exposing capped teeth, — he should know plenty about that, having produced a psychotic criminal bitch of a daughter!

— Look, Sorenson—

— No, you fucking look, Brennan! Don't kid yourself this is about me. She rattles a cuff again. — This is about *your* fucked-up shit!

— You were dying! You were eating yourself to death—

— And you have the nerve to go on about my issues with my mother, she spits. — Sort out your own fucking shit! Does somebody without issues behave like this?

— Fuck you!

— Just fucking go, and she leans back on the mattress, clicking on the TV at the remote.

I let go a ton of breath I never realized I was holding back. I keep telling myself that her behavior is normal; she's gone from dependent child to rebellious, acting-up teenager. She's testing boundaries, and it's all just part of her journey back into functioning adulthood. I feel like taking the remote from her, telling the dwarf bitch that she's lost privileges. But all that would do is relegate me to her level. I can take her shit. But boy, am I glad to get out of there and away from the crazy hoe! I don't like taking backward steps, and Sorenson, *a chained Sorenson*, is pushing me around! Jeeze, it's true what they say: fat people, even ones *in recovery* like Sorenson, really *are* hard to kidnap!

* * *

It took me ages to get a decent parking spot at the Biltmore, the lot was crammed with gas-guzzling behemoths. I walked toward the uplit Spanish cathedral-like tower, a golden palace against the blue-bruised sky. There's quite a crowd and it seems that they're all heading to Dad's event. I get inside the hotel lobby, and although I've been here a couple of times for presentations and seminars, I never fail to be awed by this building: its huge marble pillars and arches, expensive floor tiles, mahogany fittings, antique furniture, and towering palm trees housed in giant pots. I walk straight through, out onto the terrace looking over lush, lamplit gardens to a massive pool and, beyond that, a golf course.

I was supposed to meet Dad in his suite but I'm running late so I text him and go straight to the hall, which is filling up with a mix of old white-haired suburbanites, walled-and-gated retirees, and several autistic-looking crime-fiction geeks. And most of all, a shitload of the spry, superannuated Irish-American Massachusetts transplants who make up Dad's core readership. The place stinks of the entitled reek of expensive cologne and cigar smoke.

I head up to the bar. I've probably drunk more in the last month that I have in the previous ten years, but I need a glass of red to calm me. A saggy old soak, who looks like JFK or Bobby might have done had they managed to duck WASP-funded shrapnel, fixes me with a gaze of lecherous cheer. And fuck me, as I pick up my comp ticket and drink, and take my seat, I see Mona stage-waving at me then coming over and plonking herself down by my side. — Hey, you!

— Nice of you to come, I spit through my clenched teeth.

— I've always been too embarrassed to tell you that I really love your dad's books. I can just *hear* those voices in my head, like how you talk when you get mad. *I paak my caww in a Bawwwston street.*

I try to smile but feel my face crushing like a discarded bag of potato chips, as Dad emerges through a curtain to polite applause. He's being led by a middle-aged academic type, who's dressed like he's just left the adjoining golf course. Dad's studiously casual, sporting a gray New England Patriots sweatshirt, and he's lost about thirty pounds since I last saw him. Not only has he grown his hair longer, he's run some dye through it, retaining some strategic gray at the temples. He sees me close to the front and gives a mock salute.

— Your dad looks so well, Mona says. — How old is he?

— Fifty-eight, I tell her.

— Wow! He looks sooo much younger! Is it wrong of me to say that he looks quite hunky?

— If by wrong you mean inappropriate and gross, yes, it fucking is, I snap, watching her head shrink into her shoulders. Bitch had to eat that one up like a one-thou-cal slice of Key lime pie.

I vaguely hear a mumbled qualifiction, but it isn't hitting home. All I'm aware of is the feeling of my hair standing up on my body and my skin breaking out in goosebumps. Because I see *Mom* and *Lieb* in the audience! They're settling down a couple of rows in front of us. I can't fucking believe it! They're supposed to be away for eight more days!

I don't know what to do, and my overwhelming impulse is to run out of there right now, and I actually go to rise, with

378

Mona still jabbering in my ear. But Mom turns at that moment, registering me, smiling and slightly taken aback by my undisguised horror. I'm panicking, my skin's frozen, as an image of a chained Sorenson floods my brain. No time to run the fuck out, as Mom and Lieb come over to us, another couple grudgingly sliding down the row to let them in. I make a clumsy intro to Mona, trying to get a hold of my breathing. Now it's so fucking hot in here, and I'm aware of the smell of those surrounding clammy old bodies as Mom and Lieb greet me amicably. To my monumental relief, they obviously haven't been up to the apartment and found Lena. Yet.

The academic approaches the microphone and clears his throat, the static crumbling the rest of the room into silence. — Welcome to the Biltmore Hotel. I'm Kenneth Gary, from the department of English Literature, University of Miami.

As I'm thinking: *I didn't even know the University of Miami had a department of English Literature*, Lieb leans over to me. — This was not my idea, Lucy, he emphatically states. I've forgotten what a nice guy he is. He tried to be a stepdad, but I guess I never gave him that much of a chance.

— I know, Lieb, enough already. Mom shakes her head and playfully pushes him back into position, then slides closer to me. — Morbid curiosity got the better of me, pickle, she grins. Then her face takes on a serious hue. — How are you?

— I'm . . . I'm good, but when did you get back? What are you doing here? The reconciliation trip—

— Went better than expected, picks, and she extends her hand showing me a sparkler. — Meet the future Mrs. Benjamin Lieberman. And I'm turning a.s.a.p.

— Congratulations . . .

Mona gasps, — It's sooo beautiful . . .

— But what about the cruise? I hear myself urgently gulp.

— We got back yesterday. Cut the trip short by jumping ship in Jamaica, skipping the South American coast, flying across via Miami, she says, narrowing her brows and peering over her glasses. — Is my apartment okay?

— Yes, of course it is, I tell her, in abject relief, as we focus back on the event interviewer.

— Tom Brennan has emerged from almost nowhere to become not just one of the bestselling crime novelists in America, but also one of the finest literary voices we have, in any genre, and he looks into the crowd, almost challenging dissent, as Mom rolls her eyes. — Looking at the quality of what is called crime writing these days, he continues, — I'd say the real crime is that those works do not get considered for top literary awards like the Pulitzer Prize . . .

Mom drops her voice and bends in close to me. — Good, cause we need you to look after the place for another month. We decided the Caribbean had worked its magic, and there was no point in hanging around, it was time to close the deal, she says, Lieb giving her hand an affectionate squeeze. — We fly to Tel Aviv tomorrow, she gasps, again displaying the ring, — to tie the knot.

— Congratulations, I whisper.

— That is great, Mona squeaks at that irritating high frequency of hers, causing the people in front of us to turn around.

— My idea, says Lieb. — I've never been to Israel before. I wanted us to get married there.

— Jerusalem, picks, everybody should have that place on their *must-see* list. I say must-see as opposed to bucket, as Debra Wilson advises us edit out morbidity from our language, Mom says, then sits back in her chair, examining Dad on the stage. It must be the best part of two decades since they were in the same room together.

Dad's trying not to look too smug as the academic continues to sing his praises, — . . . a remarkable man who made the transition from fighting crime to writing crime. And his Boston, and that of his complex protagonist, Matt Flynn, is rendered so vividly by a fluid but spare, scalpel-precise prose style . . .

— Won't that asshole stop already? This is feeling like one big mistake, Mom moans, as a man in front turns around again.

Lieb shoots her an I-told-you-so look.

— Dad looks well, I tell her.

— Well, yes, she says grudgingly, squeezing Lieb's paw, — but I got the real goods on my arm here. She drops her voice another octave, and I can smell the drink on her breath. — A Jew versus a Paddy in the sack? If ever there was a no-contest, honey!

As the sycophantic intro closes and Dad gets up to the podium, Mom starts again, only to be shushed by a battleax sitting behind us. Mom abruptly stands up and turns on her. — That man couldn't silence me in nearly seventeen years of marriage. He ain't gonna start now! And she grabs

Lieb's hand and drags him to his feet behind her, as they take a ceremonial walk toward the door.

The academic remains unfazed. — So I invite you all to join in the wit and wisdom of Matt Flynn, and, above all, Mr. Tom Brennan!

The audience erupts into cheers, a few of them following Dad's eyes as he tracks Mom and Lieb. She yanks open the door and departs without looking back.

—Another satisfied customer, Dad remarks into the microphone, to middle-class laughter, barely breaking his stride. I'm wondering if he even recognised her. — Anyway, this passage I'm going to read is from the new Matt Flynn novel, entitled *The Doomsday Scenario*.

42

MATT FLYNN

Mick Doherty knew how this one would play out. Every time his daughter Lindy returned home to Boston from her current haunt in Miami it meant trouble. Big trouble. Mick rose in the filtering sunlight, wrapping a robe around himself, feeling that familiar mild sting of dismay as the ever-tightening cord slipped under his solid ball of a gut. He could hear the bland sounds of early-morning TV seeping through the house from the living room. Lindy was already up, crouched in a lotus position on the recliner, watching infomercials and eating a power bar. She was dressed in running gear: a tank top and shorts, with her Nikes kicked off onto the rug. Thin runnels of sweat on her forehead attested to recent physical exertion.

He looked at his daughter, taking in that noble, slightly long face, inherited from him, and those flowing brown locks, tinted with streaks of gold. Then there were those eyes, blazing lamps which could narrow into focused slits of hate; they came straight from her mother's arsenal. It was always so hard not to see Jenny in the girl. Right now those eyes were set on neutral, which suited Mick; he generally avoided asking Lindy about her personal life.

But she wouldn't have changed. She would be the same hardcore, demented, dyed-in-the-wool slut of old. That was such a terrible thing for a man to admit about his daughter. But the stone-cold truth was that since puberty Lindy had seemed unable to resist the attention of just about any suitor; male or female, she wasn't picky. Worse, she actively pursued the bulk of them in the most wanton, predatory manner.

He recalled with his customary shudder the trauma of that horrific day, now so long ago but burned into his psyche so as to cast it up as vivid and stark as if it were yesterday. Taking a run through the parking lot behind the strip mall, he turned the corner, coming across a crowd of youths tightly gathered round at the mouth of a narrow L-shaped alley. This was a popular spot for kids to hang out, and Mick reckoned by the jeers and the charge in the air, it would be two boys having a fight. As a conscientious Boston Police Department Officer, he went over to break it up. But it had been Lindy, just in ninth grade, lying there, getting fucked by a kid who barely looked old enough to have a set of balls in his sack! Mick had stood for a second, uttering a disbelieving curse as the kids around them scattered, then his next shout echoed across the park, as he pulled the copulating pair apart like two dogs. The terrified boy fled, yanking his pants up, while Lindy did the same with her underwear, then tugged down her skirt, Mick turning away till his daughter had completed this mortifying task. Then he dragged her to her feet and out of the park. The thing that struck him on his tense, shameful walk home was that Lindy seemed totally unrepentant, unconcerned, and barely even embarrassed once she'd gotten over the first flush of shock. — We were just making out at first and things kinda got outta hand, she said with that shrug that seemed only slightly affected.

Mick Doherty had been about to react, when he'd looked at his daughter's profile. It was the same one she was displaying to him now; glassy and vacant, her arms folded across her chest. Back then it was still the chest of a child, he considered, now swamped by a vision of Lindy in her communion dress. How could this be his little girl? How could this have happened?

Now she was sitting there, watching the infomercial, and Mick felt as shut out from her life, her thoughts, as ever. Her behavior was rendered all the more incomprehensible, given the parental framework he and Jenny—for all her faults had provided their offspring. And her sister, his younger daughter Joanne, was now working in the war and famine zone of Darfur, trying to help imperiled children.

One kid attempting to save the world, the other seemingly determined to fuck it to death.

Mick had long faced up to the disturbing facts. Despite the discipline of the sporting background he'd provided for her, Lindy was a demanding, insatiable borderline nymphomanic with psychopathic tendencies. And Mick sometimes blamed himself for instilling that competitive drive, that will-to-win-at-all-costs attitude within her.

But was she also a killer? Arthur Rose was as dead as he was ever going to be, his back weeping with multiple wounds, in the very alley where he'd discovered his daughter's grim copulations all those years ago. Lindy had gotten into town a couple of days before the body was discovered. She had publicly threatened Rose once, over another dark chapter in her troubled life. And she would be in the frame; the Boston homicide tecs hadn't come calling yet, but that would happen as sure as night followed day.

Lindy looked up, only cursorily acknowledging Mick's presence, her face set in that expression of mild disdain she hadn't been able to shake off since those teen years. His casual overture, when he asked if she'd had a good run, produced little more than a brief, contemptuous raising of her shoulders. Yet, for all their estrangement,

Michael Patrick Doherty couldn't believe that his older daughter was capable of cold-blooded murder. But he knew one person who could find out for sure, an old colleague of his in the BPD.

It was time to call Matt Flynn.

43

THE MIAMI BEACH TRUTH AND RECONCILIATION COMMITTEE

I'm seething in silent rage at that fucking rancid old pig, feeling his words hit me like shattering blows. I see Mona glance at me in my peripheral vision, as I grip the hard edge of the seat. *FUCKING ASSHOLE!* I need to get him alone and ask him what that fucking public humiliation was all about, and in front of a bitch I work beside! The gig ends in polite ovation, the old bastard smugly declaring during the audience questions, — I think every writer uses their own experience. That's inevitable.

What is inevitable is that I'm going to give this asshole a piece of my mind. He has no fucking business using me like that! He doesn't even know the real story! But as he finishes up, Mona follows me to the side of the signing table where a huge line has formed. — He was *sooo* good!

My prick of a father sees me, flashing a grinning apology at a woman in the front of the line, before turning back to me. — Honey! Great to see you! Then he fixes Mona with a wolfish gaze. — And who is this treasure?

I'm sucking down my blazing anger, trying to remember

that revenge really is a dish best served cold. — This is Mona, she works with me.

— Another trainer! I thought as much. You kinda radiate it, that health and vitality.

— Thank you. Mona pseudo-blushes and touches her hair, as my guts flip over.

— The restaurant options here in the hotel are very good, but I booked us into a place over in Miami Beach, he lowers his voice and cups a hand over his mouth, — so I can get away from my adoring public. So please excuse me for a while, ladies, but, Mona, I do hope you'll be joining us for dinner?

Before I can react, she says, — I'd love to!

So there we are, sitting at the bar, waiting on that reptilian old bastard getting through the signing line. It's as crass as you can imagine as the bartender asks Mona for her ID. — Always happens to me, she says, her smile lupine, caused by a new Botox strain stronger than liquid nitrogen. She produces a state driver's license, the image stamped on it less laminated than her actual face.

The bartender raises his brows. — Well, you had me fooled, he smiles, turning away.

Mona touches her hair again but it's because she thinks she sees a guy on the Miami Heat roster. I follow her line of vision but as it isn't LeBron, Dwyane Wade, or Bosh, there's no point whatsoever in even checking them out. My brain is in a riot, and I'm thinking, in spite of what she said, what if Mom and Lieb stop off at the apartment and discover Sorenson? I'm besieged by the memory of that horrible time in the park

. . . I'm fucking over that now . . . can't let the weak and sick rule your life . . . and that old bastard knows fucking nothing! And Mona is chattering some more fucking nonsense in my ear, — . . . I'm not sleeping with Trent again. He thinks he can just call me like that, she snaps her fingers, — and I'll come running. It's okay saying "it's just sex," and she makes the quotation marks sign, — but it gnaws away at your self-esteem when you constantly find yourself going back to a thirty-year-old child, who can't commit to anything . . .

It takes about the longest fucking hour of my life for my father to finish and dispense with the hangers-on. Then we're outside and Dad, shaking off a stalking, dotty housewife who is asking him all sorts of jackass shit about Matt Flynn, says to me, — Let's just get into your car, he points at the Cadillac DeVille in the lot, it looks like a sorry drunk who's gatecrashed a society bash, — or we'll never get out of here.

So the three of us pile into the Caddy, heading over to SoBe. It's a silent drive for me and a chatty one for them: Dad craning around to Mona in the back seat, full of cheerful tittle-tattle about the tour. As the inanity spills from their mouths, ricocheting around the car, my wrath incubates. I pick up speed and think of ripping off his seat belt and shoving the treacherous old fuck out onto the asphalt. I'm relieved when we're back over in SoBe and into this French joint on Collins. As the waiter seats us and brings cocktails, Mona is looking so intensely at Dad that her bulging eyes suggest a rabbit being fucked by a fox. — I just love the way that Matt Flynn is never vulnerable. He's always in control. A real man. I mean, one who'd just like, *take* a woman.

— I think they call that rape, I hear my words hissing out from between my tight jaws as if they were being spoken by somebody else. A low buzz plays in my head and the lights in this restaurant seem suddenly overpowering. I can't stop my jaw clicking. *Sort yourself out.*

— Are you okay, Lucy? The words emerge thinly from Mona's paralyzed face as if from the grille of a car stereo speaker.

I sit back in my seat, forcing some air into my lungs. — I'm good, I spit out, feeling like some teenage goth chick who's been taken out to meet her dad's girlfriend—no, her future fucking *mother-in-law*—this tanned strip of beef jerky, pumped strategically with silicone, who is *eight years* younger than me.

— Mona's right, pickle, there's a crisis of masculinity in contemporary America, and us guys, instead of blaming society and the economy for this emasculation, should just man up, pansy down, and have the balls to admit we've done it to ourselves. He raises his cocktail to his lips.

— That is *sooo* on the money, Tom, she says, with a big smile, as I realize I'm pretty much invisible here.

I wait for the irritating waiter to get out of our faces, then turn on Dad. — What the fuck was all that shit about? The nympho daughter!

— What?

— It was about me! That time in the park!

As Mona's eyes widen further and she edges forward in her seat, Dad protests, — It was nothing to do with that!

Those are fictional characters! This happened in a parking lot, not in a public park—

— Every other detail is pretty much the same! Except, I — I wasn't — it was . . . I try to clamp my mouth shut cause only shit is coming out. Why can't I say RAPE, why can't I look him in the eye and say the fucking word?

— You know what it was, Dad says, and he's angry, the liver spots flaring on his neck, now making me feel like a kid again, — don't act like it was just making out, you know what it was, and you were just a damned child—

— Yes, I do know, because it was—

— Let's not go there, he shouts, and raises his palms to the side of his head, as Mona looks on intently. He takes a long, deep breath and twists his features into a puppet smile. His voice is low and measured. — Anyway, it's beside the point. It's fiction, honey, and you're being *waaay* too sensitive. Writers make shit up, that's what we do.

I also take a deep breath and a slug of my martini. My hand is shaking, as I lower it to the table. I focus on that glass—anything other than his grave, sandpaper-skinned face, or that frozen Botoxed ornament.

— You do it so well, Tom, Mona purrs, and she drops her hand onto his wrist, as his teeth flash in a crocodile grin.

— I've been lucky, I guess.

— I don't think luck comes into it, Tom . . .

The hovering waiter returns to take our order as I get control of myself. I can't be weak and allow a frightened little prick like Austin a seat at this table. I go for a nearly raw steak, with a mixed salad, and order a bottle of red wine. Mona preens and fusses, finally opting for linguine with scallops, shrimps, and clams. Dad, surprisingly, bypasses the steak; he goes instead for some sea bass. — Too much goddamn red meat on this tour, he says, in response to my arched brow. — You see, I do listen to you!

I decide to take the tendered peace offering. I tersely clear my throat. — So how is the Biltmore?

Dad hesitantly turns a weather-beaten smile my way. — The absolute last word in luxury, pickle. I got me one of them poolside cabana suites. It's surrounded by palms, bougainvillea, and hibiscus. Don't get me wrong, he swivels back to Mona with a deep grin, — the hotel's rooms are unbeatable, but when I'm in the tropics I like to *feel* as if I'm in the tropics, if you catch my drift.

— Oh, totally, Mona almost pants. — Is there a spa?

— Not just *a* spa, *the* spa, he says, his eyes twinkling. — You should check it out. If you're a spa aficionado, it's pretty much essential.

I've had enough. It suddenly dawns on me how easily that bitch left her fucking wheels over at the Biltmore parking. Could she make any more of a play if she tried? I slam back my martini and pull myself to my feet. — This is *waaay* too gross for me, and it's fucking well creeping me out. You, thanks for the drink, I say to Dad, pointing at the empty glass, — and you, I turn to Mona, — thanks for nothing! Fucking fake!

I spin on my heel and head to the exit, announcing to

the other diners as I point back at her, — Bitch is fucking fake! Ain't never seen a fuckin faker bitch!

As the waiter approaches with the wine, I can hear Mona pleading in a sorry little voice, — What did I do?

— Nothing whatsoever, the lying pig says. — She's been under a little pressure . . . let's just let her go and blow off some steam . . .

I stop and take a step back toward the table. — Bitch is fake, I again announce to the crowd, — fake ass, fake tits, fake lips, fake hair, fake eyes, fake teeth, fake nose, fake voice . . . she's a fuckin impostor! My Barbie dolls bled more than that bitch!

— Lucy! Please! Dad snaps, on his feet, as diners gasp in horror, and cluck in outrage.

A maître d' surges forward: — Miss! You really have to leave!

— Don't worry, I'm going! Bitch's fake, and I again jab a finger at the crying Mona. — You fake, bitch. You fuckin fake!

Bitch had to take that to the back of her throat like it was a barbed-wire dildo.

And I'm walking out, pushing through the door, into the warm night air. Standing outside in the street, I shout at the faggot valet to get my car. I'm pacing up and down, waiting for the Caddy to appear, as I anxiously check my phone. No calls but five new emails and I realize I'm on Sorenson's account. One that makes my fucking blood stew:

I am your father!

Asshole! I write back:

I AM YOUR FUCKING DAUGHTER!!!

As soon as I press send, a psychic rock immediately thuds down in my gut. Fuck. I had myself signed in as Sorenson on my fucking iPhone! I've gotten so used to corresponding with those assholes.

I'm waiting for what feels like hours until my Cadillac arrives, watching the dramas of street drunks as they stagger along the sidewalk to the beat of hip hop and EDM from cruising convertibles. I glance back inside through the restaurant window to see Mona spilling fake-bitch tears as Dad's hairy, withered tree branch of an arm coils around her bony shoulders. I can't think which one of the two is the more oily, manipulative scumbag.

I jump in the car, leaving the valet without a tip. — Thank *you*, he minces bitterly.

— Fuck you, I snarl, giving him the finger and speeding off, taking 14th toward Alton. Asshole should have shown some fucking urgency, then I'd have been spared the sight of that fake-assed bitch hitting on my dad. On Alton I'm passing the liquor store when I notice a sloping, shuffling figure emerge, carrying a bottle in a brown paper bag. Timothy Winter. He heads across the parking lot and I do a sharp right turn into it, eliciting a toot from some asshole behind me. I look back to make sure he hasn't stopped, as I see Winter's thin, Hawaiian-shirt-clad back appearing in my dipped headlights. I pull up close to him and stop the Caddy. Even though it's dark, I put my shades on.

As I jump out the car, he turns to me, looking malevolently curious.

— Listen, buddy, I *really* need a drink. Gimme a slug of that and I'll buy another when we're done and then we can party!

His eyes squint in the mottled darkness. Looks to me, then to my beat-up wheels. Then he smiles, exposing those yellow teeth. — Best offer I had all day!

I'll make you a fucking offer, pedophile trash. I take the proferred bottle from his extended greasy hand, then pivot, smashing it with force across the side of his head. It shatters, leaving me with the jagged base in my hand. I jab it at him, turning my wrist boxer-style, as the twisting spikes and shards of glass rip into his waxy puppet face.

Winter doesn't make a sound, just rocks back on his heels. Things seem to freeze, then a deluge of blood falls from his face, splashing onto the asphalt. Then his head jerks up and he seems ready to scream, filling his chest with air, but I spring forward and punch the motherfucker hard with a larnyx-crushing blow to his throat, which produces a muffled, gargling noise. Winter's blinded by the blood and disoriented by the choking as he staggers off, gasping, making for Alton and safety. *No dice, short-eyes.* I'm right into the car, starting it up, accelerating at his swaying figure, smashing into him, as he spills over the hood and crumples to the ground in a series of staccato thumps. I wind down my window and shout out at the broken mass on the deck, — JUST FOR OLD TIMES, YOU CHILD-BENDING FUCK!

Then I'm tearing out the lot and heading north up Alton.

After the charge of excitement has dissipated, I find myself shaking and sobbing outside Lena's house on 46th Street. I was so fucking stupid. I could go to prison. For a fucking *pedophile.* I'm trying to get a grip of myself, to sort out my short, jagged breathing. Suddenly, there's a tap on the window. Fear is searing my skin; I'm expecting a uniform to be on the end of the knuckles, but instead two sharp black eyes peer at me from in between a mop of dark hair, and an ironic hipster mustache.

He's garbed in a black T-shirt and jeans; I instinctively know who he is, even though I've never met him before. It's the would-be artist turned photographer. Sorenson's squeeze. What the fuck did she call the prick? Jeffrey?

— Hey. You okay?

I roll down the window and switch off the ignition. I quickly decide I'm gonna play the dumbass here. — Sorry . . . it's been one of those days.

— I know those days, this guy says with a glum smile and empathetic nod. His face is cute and bright. God, this guy is fucking good.

— A friend of mine vanished recently, I say. — She's not answering her calls so I keep coming round here, to her house, just to see if she's shown up.

— That friend wouldn't be Lena Sorenson, by any chance?

I'm nodding, as I climb out the car. — Yeah . . . do you know her?

— Well, he smiles and shrugs, — we're . . . well, I guess we were kind of married, then he fixes me in a fervent, brooding gaze. — I'm Jerry Whittendean. And who might you be?

Jerry: that was it. — I'm a friend of Lena's.

He looks at me in this searching way, but that's all he's getting. I can stare. I can do this shit all fucking night. He concedes, and nods slowly. — Listen, I need to get inside to pick up some stuff of mine. Did Lena leave you a key?

I'm not thinking straight, still partly fixating on the mess I left Winter in, back at that parking lot, wondering if anybody saw me or called it in. So I lamely fucking hand this Jerry the key, instantly regretting it as his strong but manicured fingers close around it.

— I'm glad I met you, he smiles in smug triumph. — I was getting so desperate I was gonna break in. As you say, she isn't picking up the phone, or replying to her emails, and nobody's seen her around. I thought I'd figure out where she was if I managed to get inside.

— Right, good thinking . . . I'm saying blankly as I'm

following him through the gate, down the path and into the house, — . . . why don't you have a key?

— We've been going through a rough patch, he says, with a charmless smile. — I've been up in New York, giving her some space.

By that he means banging that other sorry-headed bitch. This is one smooth asshole. That Melanie chick called it right in her letter: he's dangerous to women. But *I'm* fucking dangerous to men like him. So we're hunting around in the house, me knowing that he'll draw a blank as I've made sure there's nothing incriminating lying about, like his fucking notebook.

His frustration soon starts to show. — Do you swing by this place often? Only there's no sign of any mail, and I know she got sent a package that has my property in it.

— No, I quickly tell him, — a friend of ours, Mona, she picks up the mail.

— Where does she hang out?

— She lives in SoBe or somewhere, but she's in Atlanta, I lie. — Her boyfriend's a writer. They're doing a book tour.

— Yeah? Anybody famous?

— Some asshole who writes crappy crime novels.

— What's his name?

— Tom Brennan.

Jerry smiles, and points a digit at me in recognition. — The Matt Flynn guy? Man, I love those damn books!

— Yeah, that's him.

Jerry nods but he's lost interest and starts going through the bureau in Lena's office. — Nothing . . . he moans, then his face ignites. — Wait . . . He pulls open another drawer and produces a key. — Jackpot! I think this opens the studio. I've a hunch that what I need might just be in there.

I've a hunch you're fucking wrong, asshole. — I don't feel so good about us going through her shit, especially in her studio.

Jerry seems not to hear and heads off, compelling me to follow him out into the dark backyard. A motion-sensor light shines in his face, and he blinks in annoyance as he thrusts the key into the studio lock and turns it. — Eureka, he says, as he opens the door and I follow him in. He clicks on a light. The big sculpture, still a work-in-progress, dominates the space. This prick barely registers it. Instead he starts going heavily through Lena's cupboards, pulling shit onto the floor.

— Hey, take it easy! I protest, as he hisses "fuck" every time another drawer or cupboard produces no bounty, but it's soon evident that there's nothing there, or nothing this motherfucker wants; the notebook and pictures are at my apartment.

We go back to the house and Jerry takes a bottle of wine from a rack in the kitchen and opens it. He pours himself a glass and offers me one. I can take the odd glass of red wine as it's high in antioxidants, but I've had more than enough of that shit at the reading and the restaurant and I'm fucked if I'm drinking alcohol with this prick. I open a San Pellegrino. This asshole sure loves himself; he seems less concerned with Lena's disappearance than his own career, such as it is.

— I was getting stuff together for an exhibition; I got people in New York and London lined up, but it all takes money and I kinda ran out of bread. I'd been hoping that Lena . . . well, that's another story, he shrugs, lifting the glass up to the light then taking a sip. — Any idea where she could've gone?

— She was banging on about some big art project and wanting to go out to the Glades to shoot film, I lie again, then adding, — She wanted a filmed landscape as background for her little green men.

Jerry looks intently at me, like he's trying to work out if I'm bullshitting. — Her future humans, he laughs, sitting down in one of the leather chairs.

— Yeah. I force a smile, annoyed at myself for colluding with this prick against Lena. I sit down on the couch opposite him.

— Cool . . . he says, then nods. — I tried to get her into multimedia, so I guess I gotta take some of the credit for that, and he flashes a self-satisfied smile. — So how do you know her? Are you an artist?

An aggressive snap of the air conditioning clicking to life makes me shudder. He catches the weakness and acknowledges it with a smile. It chills the room as much as the cold air pumping out of the ducts. — No, I'm a personal trainer. She works out with me.

— Wow, I thought you looked kind of, well, fit. He raises an eyebrow. — But that doesn't seem like Lena's thing.

— No, she's been — I check myself, — well, *had been* working very hard.

— Good. Well, um . . . He raises his brows, settling his drink down on the glass table.

— Lucy.

— Well, Lucy, his eyes narrow, — if you're feeling better, you should get off and I'll carry on with my bad Sherlock Holmes impression.

— No, I'm going to have to ask *you* to leave, and to give me that key back. It was entrusted to me, and I can't let you keep it.

Jerry suddenly switches on that cutthroat gaze again. It unnerves me and I detest myself for it. — Why would Lena entrust a key to you, Ms. Fitness? I'm not getting this.

— I dunno, she just did. Look, I know who you are, and I know that Lena doesn't want you here!

— Oh yeah? He smiles, pulling himself out the chair and standing tall. He must be 6', 6'1". There's nothing but cruelty in his eyes and his tight mouth. That utter certainty of his own power. I feel fear rippling through me, weakening me. — Well, I don't know who *you* are. You got some fucking nerve. You gonna take the key back? You gonna throw me out?

Oh my God. The last thing I want now is another fight. But the adrenaline is starting to rise in me, to burn off the anxiety. — If I have to. I stand up from the sofa. In addition to his height, he has a swagger, like he's maybe done a bit of boxing or karate.

— Well, he smiles, patting his pocket, indicating the key, — come ahead, little lady.

Fucking patronizing creep; I just want to get close enough to do to his balls what that fish did to poor Jon's. I open my palms in a conciliatory gesture. — Look, it doesn't need to be like this . . .

Then he suddenly lunges toward me, his hand reaching out and grabbing my chin. *I didn't react.* I feel his alcohol breath in my face and I didn't react. — Know what I reckon? I think you're the one who's been up to no good. I can smell it off you!

I have to stand strong. Thank God that the fury is rising, melting fear's paralysis, and I break his half-grip with a sweep of my forearm, then smack him with a left jab, which rocks him back. It's not a killer blow, but I'm relieved to be in the zone, reacting like I was trained to do. — I'm warning you, back the fuck off!

He touches some blood around his lip. Looks at it, then me. — Too late for that now, bitch!

Then he leaps at me and, once again, I'm found wanting in my response, trying to bring up my knee, but missing, as we crash to the floor, him on top of me, his weight squeezing my breath out. I'm struggling to get traction, as he's punching at my face. I'm blocking, but I'm pinned, and if he connects properly and I see stars it'll be ground-and-pound and it's all over. My sacred numbers aren't stacking up. The stats never lie. They predict the outcome of the tennis game before a single ball has crossed the net. The election result before a single vote is counted. And as he connects again, a hook around my guard, I can feel it, feel *him*, pressing against me, hard against me, and I shout, — STOP! . . . and he halts for a second, and I tell him in an urgent, desperate gasp, — . . . we should fuck . . .

— What?! His fist is clenched above my face, ready to pound down again. — What did you say . . .?

— Don't pretend this isn't where this is going, that you don't want to either . . . you get off on this as much as I do . . .

He looks flabbergasted for a second, then an abhorrent smile rips his face. — Looks like I've finally found a bitch who fucking gets me . . .

— And some, I pant, as he rocks onto his knees and starts to unbuckle his belt and unzip himself. I'm groping behind me with my left hand, and feel something solid in my grip, I'm thinking it's a fireside implement, like the brass tongs or a poker. I see his expression change in recognition, but as I lift it and bring it down on him, with everything I've got left, I realize it's the ax, and it's swinging toward his head: wedging into his skull, almost perfectly splitting his parting.

I immediately feel not just the strength, but the life flooding out of his body, as he collapses, his dead-weight on top of me, half rolling off as I crawl out from underneath him, the ax still embedded in his head. There's no blood at first. Then it starts to gush out, like a gurgling Miami Beach drain, almost fountainous, soaking into the antique rug. I sit back on the couch, my arms wrapped around myself, unable to move.

I'm there for a very long time, cold in the air conditioning, immobilized as the lifeless body's blood seeps through the rug, pooling on the wooden floor and flowing slowly toward my feet. Luck, skill, deceit: you can upset the odds. You can force the hand of chance. Fuck the numbers; life is about exceptions. The exceptional make the exceptions, Dad used to say to me.

But to what end?

I don't care about him. Some people can do nothing except exploit others. They see themselves as lions or tigers, high-end predators, but in reality they're more like rats or cockroaches, just dirty fucking time-wasting pests. They are there to teach us to be guarded, cautious, and circumspect in our dealings with others. But they are vermin and they need to be crushed. There can certainly be no remorse at their passing.

I look through to Lena's small office where the big Apple Mac sits on the desk. I've really messed things up, and it strikes me that there's only one thing I can do to try and make it all a little better. And as I get into the computer and Lena's email account, I can see my perfect opening.

44

CONTACT 17

To: lenadiannesorenson@thebluegallery.com
From: mollyrennesorenson@gmail.com
Subject: Please Can We Just Talk?

Lena,

I've been doing a lot of thinking about what you said. I just wish you would try and be less hurtful in your tone and more like the daughter I know. And whom I love more than anything, whatever you might think.

Yes, we do fear for you. Maybe it's stupid. We're small-town, God-fearing people, and perhaps we're wrong to feel that way, but the world sometimes seems such a horrible and dangerous place, and perhaps when you become a mom, you'll realize the overwhelming need to protect your children.

But I do realize that I have made mistakes, and I want to put it right. I want this because I really love you so much.

I've actually lost some weight myself, as I've been following a Weight Watchers' program.

I noticed you have a new iPhone. Can you please answer it when I call?

Love,

Mom xxx

To: mollyrennesorenson@gmail.com
From: lenadiannesorenson@thebluegallery.com
Subject: Yes We Can

Mom,

I'm sorry if I've seemed hurtful. I had to get things off my chest. I hope we can now have a more measured correspondence without recourse to manipulative behavior (you) or nasty, coldhearted abuse (me).

First things first: I want to express how proud you've made me, taking the first steps with this Weight Watchers' program. We can argue the effectiveness of different programs, but mine is working very well (I'm at 132 lbs) and we should be encouraging each other. I'm enclosing an exercise plan and a diet sheet, which my trainer, Lucy, feels is appropriate for someone of your weight and age and general health. Follow this and you will see rapid and sustainable improvement.

The iPhone number isn't mine, but belongs to Lucy. I only borrowed it to check some texts. My own phone isn't up and running yet, as, to be quite frank, I'm enjoying the freedom from interruptions as I'm working flat out on my new art project and have a deadline of two months from now. After this I'll get a new phone number sorted out.

I've been renting a space in a high-rise in downtown Miami, and working from there rather than the dark old studio. It has great views over the bay, the light floods in, and it's working wonders with my mood.

Love,

L xxxx

PS Lose the weight for YOU. Dad's affection/attention shouldn't be related to how much you come in at on the scale, but if you respect yourself and realize that YOU are worth the effort, then other people will respect you more too.

45

FLA VERSUS NYC

When you suffer from depression, you just have to hang in there. I read every darn self-help book on the subject. Unbelievably, following the advice of one, I even wrote stupid letters to and from my ten-year-old self. "Lena, you are such a brave and beautiful person . . ." All silly, hollow, useless stuff from snake-oil salesmen, profiteering from the misery of the weak, desperate, and insecure. There are plenty of miserable people in America. I know, because I was one.

It took me a while to realize that Jerry was having an affair with Melanie Clement from the GoToIt gallery in New York. Or not so much to realize it, but to *admit* to myself that I realized it. I sat and ate and painted and sculpted. Or tried to paint and sculpt. The more I ate, the less I worked. I usually watched movies or shows on cable, pretending, as many artists do, that it was all research, all about the images. How many episodes of *CSI Miami* do you need to watch?

It was a sunny Chicago afternoon, where spring had just kicked in and the city was visibly coming back to life. Jerry had returned from a "business trip" to New York, (or perhaps it was a "visit" to his parents in nearby Connecticut, in whom he'd hitherto shown zero interest) and he looked at me as if seeing me for the first time. There was something in his scrutiny which went beyond embarrassment and concern. Culpability? Guilt? Whatever, his tone was softer than it had been of late. — You're depressed. So am I. We're in a rut here. We need new inspiration. We have to get out of Chicago.

— I'm not moving to New York!

— Who said anything about New York? Baby, this stuff with Melanie is all in your head, he preemptively attempted to assure me. — No, fuck New York. Miami is the place. Every photographer worth their salt, he began, then corrected himself, — every *artist* worth their salt goes there, for the light.

I had no interest in leaving Chicago, I loved the city and had come to regard it as home, but Jerry persisted. And I knew we couldn't carry on like this; at least by leaving town it seemed as if we were doing *something*. So we drove south, a U-Haul truck towing Jerry's car. We mixed it up between luxury hotels and seedy drive-through motels, where every room looked like it had a horrible story to tell. We pulled into Miami Beach just as the sun dipped over the back of the downtown skyscrapers. When we reached Ocean Drive, an angry rasp of neon assailed us, screaming *party time* in our faces.

We headed for an art deco hotel on Collins, pulling into a parking lot, which was a field of tiny white pebbles, cemented into place. Inside, the hotel lacked the promise of its facade: a stack of functional rooms with floors covered in linoleum and windows darkened by shabby curtains. Ours faced onto an alley and another parking lot. Not that we

409

were around much; we immediately hit the bars, nightclubs, and galleries of South Beach. Initially, it was wonderful, it seemed like the big adventure we needed to restore our relationship. We decided it was for us and went house-hunting. I took out a mortgage on the place on 46th, which had a big self-contained workshop space at the back. I instantly decided to convert it into my studio. This took a long time and consumed a lot of my energy. My weight started to drop.

I had planned to work with metal in addition to plastic, so I needed welding equipment as well as a kiln, drying racks, tool storage, and workbenches. Good fireproofing was also essential due to the proximity of inflammable materials, as was a proper extractive ventilation system because of the chemicals and resins I'd be using.

My biggest purchase, though, was a large stainless steel Phoenix incinerator, designed for animal carcass disposal. This model was both highly efficient and simple to operate. Unlike other incinerators, it had one chamber only, as it functioned at extremely high temperatures. You just loaded in the carcass, switched it on, and walked away, without needing to monitor the heat levels. It even had an inspection door so you could see when the animal carcass was reduced to ash. And you could get a medium-sized dog in there.

Inspired by Germaine Richier, I was enjoying my move into sculpting, and loved my new space. The workshop became my refuge. It seemed like the transplant was working out for me, at least creatively. Jerry was out all the time, drinking ("networking," as he put it) and, for all I knew, fucking.

But by that point I scarcely cared. My work was my real passion. I had my first exhibition in a gallery in Wynwood. Although many of the critics were still sniffy, the smaller 3D pieces I was producing were even more popular with collectors than the paintings. I was doing well: working hard, and losing weight, having gotten out of the habit of rewarding myself with eating.

Jerry told me he was desperate to exhibit his pictures of me. Before, I might have acquiesced, but my confidence had grown due to the success of the sculptures and the validation it gave me as an artist. I also knew his so-called project was a shallow, pitiable attempt to cash in on my fame, and would humiliate me in the process. I point-blank refused and told him he was crazy. He kept on at me, growing more enraged with each rejection, to the point I grew fearful at what he might do. Jerry was strong, physically intimidating; he'd wrestled and fenced, and he regularly worked out with heavy weights. We argued, and he slapped me hard across the face. Time froze. All I could feel was the steady throb on my cheek. That and my heartbeat. Jerry didn't even try to apologize. Then he packed up his stuff, and the strangest thing was that I begged him to stay, even though I knew, with that slap, it was over. He said he had to go to New York as he needed "time to think and to get his exhibition together." In his sulky, disappointed tones, he acted like I was the abusive party.

I watched him load up his car and drive away. It was a stormy night and the hot air tasted like dust, the dry wind whipping my hair into my eyes. I was both terrified and relieved that he was going. I had grown scared of him, of what he might do to me. Yet I couldn't see what my life would be like without him. Everything I had ever imagined about myself had disappeared into the last slam of his car door and that engine starting up.

So he stayed up in New York, with her—Melanie—trying to get his stuff exhibited in her GoToIt gallery. Still flogging the dead horse of his clichéd pictures of Chicago's downtown homeless. He called me most weekends, usually from a bar when he was drunk. In between trying to harass me into signing a "contract" he had sent down, allowing him to exhibit those horrible pictures, he would make everything out to be my fault. — You never want to come out and enjoy life. You've reverted back to being the no-fun fat girl from Potters Prairie you were when I first met you. I tried my best. But I guess we are what we are, he'd muse: pretending to be sad, but sneering and dismissive.

His words ate away at me. I kept trying to work through it, but they resonated in my head. It was like a switch I couldn't turn off.

And Mom kept sending me food. She always had. Her brownies, cakes, and pies, wrapped in those vacuum-sealed packs, arrived in a box each week, sometimes twice a week. Back in Chicago, in the loft, I just put them out where the other occupants or our constant traffic could gratefully munch through them. Here, alone in the house on 46th Street, they were all mine. Previously, I had just guiltily trashed them or let them go stale, but now I started to reward myself with them again. When I was rushing with the sugar or feeling that comforted, satiated way, I couldn't hear Jerry's voice. *The voice of disapproval.*

The weight came back on, and as for the art, I got stuck. I could put a lump of clay on a wheel, but I couldn't form it. The welding I kept messing up. My touch and eye were out of sync. The molds wouldn't set right. I took out my frustration on the suppliers, criticizing the quality of the materials they sent me. Inevitably, they stopped supplying.

Then Jerry told me that he was opting to stay in New York for a while, as it was more "vital" and "real" than Miami. In reality, he'd left me for Melanie Clement, that immensely privileged daughter of a wealthy financier and his fashion-designer wife. Melanie's trendy GoTolt gallery ran one space in TriBeCa and another out in the Hamptons. I heard she was opening a third in Brooklyn, which promised to be "a new cutting-edge environment for more challenging artists." I assumed this was the niche Jerry was desperately trying to wedge himself into.

Yes, and he still had the audacity to keep hassling me to sign a release form to exhibit the photographs of me at Melanie's gallery.

I kept refusing.

He stopped calling.

I got fatter and more depressed. I couldn't understand how I'd gotten from Chicago—fulfilled, successful, and in a relationship—to this lonely, humiliating existence in Miami. I was so desperate that I went back to Potters Prairie for a break, weighing in at over two hundred pounds. Dad didn't seem to notice. He only really spoke about his work, usually to complain about Menards driving him out of business. Mom was actually pleased. — I thought you were anorexic before, and she'd shovel another slice of pie toward me. — I was so worried!

It wasn't all a waste, though. I'd enrolled to do another taxidermy course with an experienced instructor who gave one-on-one tuition. Kenny Saunderson was a manic guy who existed on coffee and chain-smoked. He was an amazing taxidermist, specializing in waterfowl, and had once been world champion in this category. I admired his skill at gutting, cleaning, stuffing, and reconstructing dead swans, ducks, geese, and restoring them to some sort of former beauty. I wasn't afraid to get my hands dirty. It was the only time I felt like myself.

But most of the time I was slumped with Mom and a jumbo bag of Doritos in front of daytime TV. My depressive descent was even more rapid than back in Miami. How could people live like this? I wanted to go, but couldn't face Miami right away; I drove back to where I now regarded as home, Chicago.

I returned to the West Loop. The building that housed the Blue Gallery was now being remodeled as condos. All that was left of Blue was the website. Although most of my friends had gone, Kim was still there, working for a downtown advertising agency, and I stayed with her in her Wicker Park apartment for a while. It was great to just hang out, to see the towers of downtown, hit the old neighborhood bars like Quenchers and the Mutiny, hear the El train rattling above me in its baritone of turbulent metal. But I couldn't stay, as I had to try and get reengaged with my work. Although I had done nothing in it for a while, I missed my studio and headed back down to Miami.

Seeking to continue my taxidermy education, I found another tutor there. I wasn't exactly revitalized by my break, but I was at least trying to work, on both smaller and larger mammals. Davis Reiner was a tall man with a hangdog expression and a smoker's cough. His lean body, and his tanned, sagging jowls, drooping down the sides of his wrinkled face, reminded me of a friendly Great Dane. Although he was much older than me, I was lonely and warmed by his kindness, and I slept with him. Like many taxidermists, he had the rough, heavy hands of a man who worked for a living but which were so deft when it came to more intricate measures. I scarcely minded the slack flesh of his wattled turkey neck swinging down on my chest, and his flinty but glazed eyes, fierce with purpose. Aged and a little gross he might have been, but this guy *wanted* to fuck me.

But Davis's attentions didn't stop my eating. I ate and I ate and I ate. Jerry started calling me again. Telling me I was worthless in one breath, begging me to let him show the pictures in the next. I was ashamed and humiliated by his hold over me. Broken, I told him to send down the contract. That I would sign. I was confused and depressed. I stopped sleeping with Davis, stopped going to class. I sat in my house, unable to work: eating, watching TV, watching the walls close in on me.

It reached its zenith that night, when I was driving around, thinking that I would stop the car on the Julia Tuttle Causeway, get out, push through the jagged undergrowth, climb the balustrade, and drop off into the dark, cold waters of the

415

bay. It seemed the only way out. There could be no other salvation. I wasn't just driving around aimlessly. I had put a small note inside a Ziploc bag, placing it in the pocket of the ridiculous pink sweatsuit I was wearing to make myself appear "breezy." It had the words scrawled in capitals:

THIS IS NOT GOOD ENOUGH.

The embarrassing thing was that I had snagged myself on some thorns and it took a while to work free from them. Then I was too small and fat to scale the barrier with ease. Instead, I was soon crying in frustrated rage as I tried to haul myself over, screaming hatefully through the lashing rain that I was useless, even to the last. Then I heard the screeching of the brakes from the highway and lights spilled everywhere. I grabbed my phone and called the police. Then came the shots. I saw Lucy get out the car, and the terrified look of the man who had been banging on her window. Then the gunman came into view. He walked right past her. Then she kicked him and he went down. I moved closer, filming her straddling him. When he peed I stopped recording.

Lucy.

In my mind's eye I see her jogging in Lummus Park, hair pushed severely back in a ponytail, magnificent breasts bouncing (although in reality they never did, secured as they were by an unyielding sports bra), her face set in that mode of cool, vicious determination.

Who is she? Why does she care about me? What is the pathology that drives her, in the way my subconscious pushes me—with its need to be dominated, bossed, and manipulated? My low self-esteem—treating every compliment and accolade like it was a booby trap. But that's me; what is going on with *her*?

Do I try to understand me or her? Are we opposites, or twins—like the Arkansas girls?

We're entrenched in our positions over the operation for the conjoined Wilks sisters. Lucy is for the surgical separation, while I'm against. She says that the odds of 40 percent are worth the gamble for Amy, and that it's her choice. But I know that Amy has been bullied into this by Annabel. I also know that the odds are nothing like 40 percent. I believe the other experts, not the glamour boy who wants the kudos of performing the operation live on television.

What about *my* aberrant "sister," my "twin"? What does that magnificent, hardassed bitch want with me? Lucy, Lucy, Lucy. The cracks are showing. I have to keep you strong. To keep encouraging you. Because this is all going to be so worthwhile. We really need to find out exactly who we are. It's time.

I take that sliver of soap, the one I used to wash my feces- and blood-stained face, from its secreted location in my sweatpants pocket. Also in there is the fur material from the cuff, which I've been slyly tearing away at. I apply the soap to my wrist and pull and push and pull again. My hand goes a little white, but I'm amazed at how easily it slips off. A bolt of fear strikes me in the chest. I slip my hand back in, look at it, and wave the shackle like a bracelet, as my pulse slows back to normal. Then I start to laugh.

On–off. On–off.

My body hurts with pleasure then trembles in a sick fear as I cross the room, moving carefully, stealthily, over that formidable space, as if each step might detonate a land mine. I feel my free arm, liberated from the weight of that shackle, almost rising ceilingward of its own volition. I look back at the chain, lying sprawled on the wooden floor like a slain snake. Move over to the support pillar. Kick it. Kiss it. Swing gleefully around it like a kid in a park.

I go to the bathroom. How good to do a supported piss and shit! Stepping into the shower, a *hot* shower, I can feel the water jets blasting layers of my sweat and grime away, as if actual fat is vanishing down the drain. When I'm done I gaze at myself naked in the mirror: my body is so lean and toned, I almost expect a fat girl to come lumbering into the reflection and elbow this strange elf out of the picture. My ridges of muscle, which have replaced the soft fat, leave me awe-struck. Most of all, I can't believe my neck. It is swanlike; I've *never* had a neck like that!

In the kitchen, on the countertop, sits my purse with my cellphone and my credit cards. I deftly slide a card from the wallet, leaving everything else as it was. I go back into the room Lucy's been using, and find some sweat pants and a top. I get dressed and ride the elevator down and head out to the warm, deserted street, moving nervously along the sidewalk. Outside is so strange. At first I fear my own shadow, overwhelmed by a sense of danger lurking on every corner. But then I see that my shadow is so much thinner and I'm loving the glimpses of my reflection. I squint up at the green, glassy tower, trying to count the floors up to my prison. Forty.

Walking a while, I pass a bar full of people I can see through the big plate-glass window. They all wear fancy-dress costumes and are drinking beer and shots. A man inside meets my eye and points drunkenly at me to two girls in sequined masks, his face breaking into silent laughter.

I cross over to Bayside, watching the people in the bars and restaurants, all eating and drinking garbage that holds absolutely no interest for me. I stop a taxi and ask the chatty driver to take me to the nearest mall, to go shopping for some important items. He looks at me as if I'm another of Miami's transients. — Looking good for the Heat, he says. — LeBron on fire last night.

I don't know what he's talking about but I reply in the affirmative, shocked at how my voice sounds—strange, higher and faster than I recall, as if every word is a butterfly fluttering just out of my reach.

At the mall, I make my purchases, then, anxious to get back before Lucy, I return to the apartment.

Back to my comforting prison.

419

46

EMPTY CUFFS

The first dead body I've seen. Already waxy, already something other than human. A small kidney-shaped lake of blood leaking from it. I start to cry, my throat swollen in an unstable mix of emotions. I'm thinking about what Jerry must have been like as a kid. I see a small boy, full of astonishment at the world, and wonder how he grew into such an asshole. And where did it get him? A hated, loathed pile of flesh and bone on the floor, still a young man, dead before his time, and only the air conditioning stopping him from putrefying.

In my paralysis, the only move that suggests itself is to drive back to the apartment. Freeing Lena and telling her everything about Jerry, showing her the notebook, the pictures and the negatives. It chills me to think of it that way, but Dad's bullshit story was a prophecy. Yes, I'm a killer. Okay, it was self-defense, but I need Lena's backup or I'm on a diet of pussy minus plastic for the next twenty. I'm a killer; possibly a double killer; fuck knows what shape I left Winter in. And what it all means is that I'm now at the mercy of my hostage.

Self-defense. I keep saying it over and over again as I walk outside into the dappled light, climbing into the Caddy, my movements like an automaton. Noises—faint but keen and insistent—leak from a source that can only be me, but are like the sound of someone whispering in my ear.

Self-defense. Though on another level, I know I'm lying to myself; wasting that Jerry asshole was something I was destined to do for years. I knew that prick before, or at least versions of him. That bastard was fucking toast as soon as he crossed me, and now I have to pay for that.

Rubbing my eyes. A dense night sky, lit by two brilliant stars. The lights of the cars around me muted in the patchy dark. I stop by my apartment, to pick up something, then I'm back across downtown. I'm a fucking mess, my hands shaking on the wheel. Trying to turn at the last minute, I almost collide with a convertible at a crossroads. A driver honks me, a dapper guy dressed in a suit and a Panama hat. — Cheese and crackers! he shouts, tapping the side of his head, — Eyes on the road, please, lady! Thank you! Hello!

When I get into the apartment Sorenson's fucking gone! The empty cuffs lie there, attached to the end of the chain. Then suddenly I can hear her, rustling about in the kitchen. I expect her to have a knife, and come at me with it. I'm not even scared; if that's my fate I'm resigned to it, too broken now to assume a defensive stance. She can do what she wants. Or perhaps the cops are already on their way, summoned by my former prisoner. Either way, I'm totally fucking screwed. But as Lena comes through, she just waves at me and steps onto the treadmill.

— Don't mind me, Lucy, I got another fifty cal to shed today.

— You . . . you got out, I say in disbelief, as she switches on the machine and goes for it. — How . . . when . . .?

— I first slipped out of the cuffs the day before last. My wrists . . . I'm 131 pounds, Lucy. She gawps in delight, pushing up the speed controls. — I haven't been that since sophomore year at the Art Institute!

— You look great, I tell her and I feel myself tearing up. I'm seeing her for the first time as she really is. She *isn't* fat anymore. — You . . . you could have escaped before now . . .

— Why would I, though? I can see the results, she beams. — Of course, I *really* wanted to kill you as well, she giggles, then gasps, keeping her breath and holding her stride, — but instead I went out and got some champagne! It was weird and scary just going outside at first . . . you crazy fucking beautiful bitch you, she grins, pulling up her tank top to show a gut so drastically reduced as to be almost gone, — but the means really do justify the ends!

I can't fucking believe this. — Wow . . . I dunno what to say, I thought you'd hate me! I thought you'd go straight to the cops!

— How could I? She shakes her head. — You saved my life! I must admit, there were times I wanted you dead, but I was in cold turkey. Now I see what you've done, what you've given me . . .

— What YOU'VE given you, I gasp, — . . . but, Lena, listen, there's something I gotta tell you—

— What you *enabled* me to do, she cuts in. — To bring back *me*, and I thank you from the bottom of my heart

422

. . . she looks at the monitor on the treadmill, — . . . and fiff-tay . . .

She shuts the machine down and steps off, heading to the kitchen. I'm following her in stupefaction, all those thoughts and images cascading through my brain. I find her pouring two glasses of champagne. — Lena, we need to talk, something's happened—

— No, we drink first. She turns to me and says forcibly, — After what I've been through, give me *one fucking moment* before you hit me with any more of *your* shit. Jesus!

There's nothing I can say. She really does deserve this moment and a lot more besides. Certainly more than I do, and so I'm trailing behind her again, following her to the living room. — Cheers, I say grimly, raising the glass of Cuvée to my lips, and thinking of Jerry on the rug, in his puddle of blood. I take a long drink.

— You've made me what I am, Lena says, — by making me confront who I was. What the others took away . . . but I can barely hear her as this shit is going straight to my head, and I feel so slack-jawed and heavy-limbed, — . . . you gave back . . .

— Gave back . . . I repeat numb and dumb, aware of Lena Sorenson looking at me with a shit-eating grin.

— But you're an evil fuck and you need to be punished, she smiles, as I sit down on the mattress, sinking back into it. And I'm powerless to do anything as she clips the cuffs onto my wrist.

* * *

I'm back at junior high and I'm running in the track event against Sally Ford, the fastest competitor. I was always number two. I could see my dad's red face, willing me on, and I almost beat her. Almost. It was the closest I'd ever gotten to the bitch.

Dad was silent on the drive home. — I nearly won, I pleaded.

— Nearly's no good. You let that stuck-up little thing beat you again. He shook his head. — But you can't help it. You're just a girl.

And then it comes back to Clint Austin smiling at me in class, asking me if we're gonna make out. Me saying maybe. But then when he and his friends surrounded me in the park, I just froze. Then he kissed me, put his tongue in my mouth. They started cheering. Then he took me into the bushes beside the tree, a big make-out spot, an almost concealed cave of overhanging branches and thick shrubs, but then he shouted for his friends to come in. — We wanna see your pussy, he said, and then I was on my back and they were grabbing me, holding me, and pulling at my clothes, and Clint was on top of me, and in me. I didn't struggle, I didn't protest. I was determined not to be a girl, like Dad said, not to cry and be weak and beg. I just lay there, in a trance and let him do it. I shut my eyes. Dug my nails and fingers into the ground beneath me as I felt a burning sensation sear me between my legs. Then the rest of them were scattering like flies, and Clint was out of me and off me and I saw Dad's face looking down. I forgot the pain between my legs, and stood up and pulled up my panties and smoothed my skirt down. I didn't want to tell him that I was raped, that I was bullied by a psycho and his gang, and that I couldn't or didn't fight back, like a real

Brennan would have done. That I would have been probably been gangbanged by the rest, had he not found me then. No, I'd rather he thought me a slut than a weak coward, or even a girl: that would have been the biggest shame.

After that I went to tae kwon do, kickboxing, and karate. I wanted to show them all that I would never be scared, would never freeze like that, ever again. That I could do any fucking thing they could do. That I could damage those motherfuckers, that I could break them . . .

. . . I blink into sludgy consciousness with a team of miniature construction workers laying the foundations of another Walgreens inside my head. Lena Sorenson is standing over me. There's an assortment of McDonald's and Taco Bell fast food in bags on the floor, beside the two buckets. — Similar game, slightly different rules, I hear her explain, my throat too dry for me to speak out in protest. — You'll be in here until you weigh two hundred pounds. That's doable: thirty-five hundred cals per day equals an extra pound of fat. If you cram you should be out of here in no time. I've got Coke and potato chips for you to snack on, and cans of beer and wine boxes . . .

I look at the bags she's placing before me. My mouth is so dry. There's no water so I pick up a can of Coca-Cola. It tastes like battery acid in my mouth and throat, and even more corrosive when it hits my gut, but it helps me find my voice. — Lena, I can see why you might feel that you want to do this, but you have to listen to me . . . back at your place—

425

— Shut your mouth, you fascist psycho bitch! I'm fucking through listening to you! This is the part where *you* fucking well listen to *me*, she screams. — I'm gonna stuff you like a frigging French goose! Two hundred pounds! You get outta here when you hit that mark on that goddamned scale!

In panic I pull myself up to a seated position. — My mom's back! She's gonna be round here soon!

— You said we had another two weeks, you fucking lying bit— she stops herself, — you fucking liar!

We actually have more; they are heading for Tel Aviv tomorrow morning. I sit down and look at the shit in front of me. I glance over and I can see my iPhone on the table, with the Lifemap app.

— It's . . . there's something I have to tell you—

— I said you're through telling me—

— IT'S JERRY! I FUCKING KILLED HIM!

She looks at me in disbelief. — Don't be stupid, how could you kill Jerry? He's in New York—

— He's on your rug with his head caved in.

— You really are fucking crazy! Lena roars, but there's a look in her eyes that tells me she knows I'm not shitting her.

— No, no . . . listen, I urge, convulsing, struggling for breath.

Lena's mouth hangs open. Her eyes burn.

— I was over at your place to check your mail and he was waiting outside. I was confused, I'd had an argument with my dad, and I wasn't thinking straight—

—As opposed to your normal, rational . . . Lena interrupts, halfheartedly.

— He tricked me into letting him into the house. He was turning the place over, looking for some shit I had, I confess, a guilty shake of my head. — There's a letter and notebook and some pictures in my purse, I nod over to the chair.

She goes to the purse and pulls out the package. Looks at the photographs, reads the letter, and starts to scour the notebook. Her eyes expand, then go glassy, then narrow. She's struggling to keep her breathing under control as her nostrils flare.

— Like I said, I let him inside. I wasn't thinking straight. Then I realized what he was doing and tried to get him out. He went crazy and we fought and I thought that he would kill me! He had me pinned down and I reached behind me and hit him with that ax, the ornamental one that you keep sharp, cause you sometimes use it to chop your animal carcasses . . . it was an accident Lena, I swear it! I was trying to protect myself, but I didn't mean to kill him!

Sorenson continues looking at the photographs. Then she turns on her heel and heads out of the apartment.

— LEEENAHH!!

But I hear the door slam shut and she's gone. I'm left to contemplate my last meal on this planet that isn't jail food. I pick up one of the Big Macs (540) and large fries (540) and start to take bites, chewing and swallowing, letting the sugar, salt, and chemical toxins rush through me. Rendering me giddy. Making me want more . . . then I feel something rising in me as my body rejects the poisonous shit . . .

I look at the pile of vomit on the floor in front of me, through watery eyes. I need to do this. It's my penance. I go to the bag and try again, this time small nibbles, feeling the rush of sugar and salt flooding every part of my body. So I'm eating and drinking factory-made chemical excrement, waiting for the sound of far-off police sirens to draw closer and the cops to come and take me away, to share the same fate as McCandless and Balbosa. Then, as the time drags on, I realize that it'll maybe play out even worse; perhaps an unhinged Sorenson will be at a Home Depot, stocking up on power tools to torture and mutilate me, the way I did with Winter, or even destroy me, like I did Jerry.

I'm scared, and I'm pulling, pushing at this bracelet, at the obstinate pillar, screaming in anger and fear and frustration for I don't know how long. She's gone for ages and it's pitch black outside. I'm on the mattress, all cried out, staring at the ceiling, floating between horrific thought and terrifying dream. I feel weighed down by a grief so old it could have grown in the Garden of Eden. Then the dread snap of the bolt in the front door as I wait for the end of my life, or at least this phase of it. The morning light is almost up when Lena reappears, looking frazzled and exhausted, heavy bag slung over her shoulder. — Lena . . . what happened . . . what did you do? Where did you go?

— Home. I had to stop off at the Home Depot to buy some new tools.

Oh my God, it's going to happen . . .

— Lena, please . . . I back toward the steel support pillar.

She shakes her head at me as she lowers the bag. — I'm not gonna hurt you, she says contemptuously, making me feel like a pathetic fool. — I fixed everything.

— What . . .?

— I cleaned up your fucking mess.

— But . . .

— That's all you need to know. We won't mention this, or his name, ever again. You got that?

— But—

— I asked you if you got that.

—Yes, of course! But God, Lena . . . I . . . I really owe you—

— Big fucking time, she snaps, reaching into the bag, pulling out a carton full of warm, early-morning bakery goods and dropping them in my lap. — Now eat!

47

CONTACT 18

To: lenadiannesorenson@thebluegallery.com
From: mollyrennesorenson@gmail.com
Subject: Things I Need To Say

Lena honey,

We never told you just how proud you made us when you got into the Art Institute, then had your first exhibition while you were still an undergrad. Your father more than anyone. He tells everybody at the hardware store, and church, about how famous and talented his daughter is. As do I. I know he still keeps that article from the *Star Tribune* as I see him take it out his wallet and glance at it from time to time.

Why are we always so quiet and guilty in our pride?

Why can we tell other people those things, but not each other?

You're so right, Lena, all those things you said were harsh, even cruel, but they needed to be said. All we really have in this life is each other, and we really should give those close to us our appreciation and support.

So I'm trying to follow your plan, although the fruit and vegetables thing is harder than you think—this is Minnesota, not Florida! Most of all is the news that I've stopped baking! I've been reading online about flour, and how it has bad qualities.

I've always wanted to learn a language and I thought, it's never too late, so I've started beginner's Spanish at the community college. So when I come visit you in Miami, I'll be hablo española!

Whatever we go through, you are our wonder girl and we love you.

Much love,

Mom xxxx

48

ONE WAY OR ANOTHER

I feel tiredness in every nerve and bone. But there's a wave of exhilaration, pulling me up. My work, which is my destiny: it's all going so well. This is what I was put here to do. I walk into the apartment and go straight to the bedroom. I can hear Lucy's cries coming from the living room. — Lena! Why are you doing this?! It makes no sense!

I've stopped talking to her as it disquiets me. I don't like to hear the gloating Hollywood villain coming out in my voice. Who can have such power over another person and not descend into showboating arrogance? As for her: after what we've been through, I wonder why she even bothers to try and work on me!

This bedroom she would sneak into at night; the inflatable mattress, the thin comforter. Her books; mostly sports science and obnoxious performance-management stuff. The few personal items: purse, makeup, clothes. Yes, she really was almost as much a prisoner here as me. The most amazing thing, apart from that horrible mess she left me to clean up back at my home, was the string of emails from "me" to my mother. The mail I always wanted to send, but never could. And they have changed my relationship with the woman, possibly forever.

As I'm putting on my new purchases, I realize that I'm wearing a matching bra and panties for the first time in, months, many months. What a sin for a single woman! My major item from my shopping trip feels strange. I start to walk; it's so awkward and uncomfortable at first, then I relax, and I move down the hallway and push open the door.

Lucy stands there, yanking helplessly at the chain. — Why? she softly asks, those huge, manipulative eyes, almost batting. — Why are you doing this?

I move toward her. She seems not to notice my uncomfortable gait. I look at her. — Well, the question is why the fuck did you care about me, to the extent of wanting to do this shit to me? To the extent of ending up killing my fucking ex-boyfriend?

Lucy starts to blink rapidly, like she's got a shiver in her eye. — I do care! And now you're trying to punish me! Look at you! She points at my torso with her cuffed hand. — I gave you that!

— So now I want you to tell me why. I'm assuming that kidnapping your clients and keeping them captive is not the way you habitually deal with them, so why me? Either that explanation, or two hundred pounds. The choice is yours, I tell her. — Either path to freedom will do.

— I'll go to two hundred, she sneers, — and be ripped again at 125 in two months!

I move closer to her. — Just tell me: what was in the kidnapping for you?

She actually steps back, but her blazing eyes are locked into mine. — What are you going to do to me?

I reach out and push her hair back from her face. She looks curiously at me, like she's affronted, but she doesn't stop me. So I step in closer to her and wrap my arms around her. — Something I wanted to do for a long, long time, I whisper in her ear, — but I didn't feel worthy, and then my mouth is on hers and as I feel her respond, a slow yawning tremble spreads through my body.

— I wanna touch you, I tell her.

— Yeah, she rasps, like a drunk.

So I'm undoing the knotted cord on Lucy's sweat pants, then tugging them over her hips, letting them slide down her thighs to her ankles. She's breathing heavily as I fall down onto my knees, getting between her legs. She doesn't ask to be uncuffed, as I slip her panties down and spread her outer lips, entranced by those soft, brown pubic curls, resplendent above her clit, glistening with her juices and sweat. I pull on her hips, guiding her to a recumbent position on the floor. Then I move onto her, darting my tongue into her entry, licking north like a Chicago snowplow from her soaking cunt to her clit. Lucy's body involuntarily jerks and a moan explodes from her. I can't believe how wet she is as my finger glides inside her and I start to softly lick the hard knot of her clitoris. I slide my finger in and out of her, increasing the velocity of both clit-licking and finger-fucking until she emits a sound like a long squeak. I feel her hand resting on top of my head, gently but firmly securing me to my task. Her cunt tastes so sweet, and I really want to tease that hateful bitch, to make her beg, but that option is unavailable as her grip tightens on my hair and she comes in the spasms of a heaving epilepsy victim, spraying my face with her juices.

For a few seconds I think that I've made a terrible mistake, that I'm hers again, as her grip is so strong and that sinewy, muscular arm radiates power, but then her hips buck in a startling reprise, as another moan bursts from her lungs and her legs kick out and twitch like somebody dying, before she slumps into peace and her fingers open to the relief of my burning scalp. I rest my head on her rippled abdomen (she could never be described as having a belly), as she strokes my hair, and I almost absent-mindedly push two fingers back deep inside her, a couple of light strokes forcing another orgasm to rip through her. — Oh, Lena, baby . . .

49

EAT OR BE EATEN

And after a stunned, prostrate few minutes I'm calling out to Lena Sorenson to finger-fuck me again, to make me come, telling her how good it feels, and she says, — You've been such a bad girl, and she pulls back and I see her heat: that dildo she's wearing that I hadn't even noticed. — I'm going to stick my cock into your cunt and fuck you hard. Would you like that?

— Yes, I nod, thrusting my hips forward in anticipation. I could put her in a boa-constrictor hold with my legs now, choke her into unconsciousness with my free hand. Just the thought of it is exciting me, but I won't do it, cause this, a good fucking, is what I crave more than anything.

Lena does exactly as promised, inserting the dildo head into my wet cunt, thrusting slowly forward. When it's all in me she rotates her hips to batter the cock against the perimeter of my cunt. Her initial thrusts are slow and easy, building my excitement as she feels out my insides. The cock pistons in and out of me, Lena's strokes increasing in speed and power until she's gripping my ass and pounding me, biting frantically at my neck saying, — That was it, why you wanted me here, so we could play like this . . . wasn't it? Wasn't it?!

What the fuck . . .

— Oh my God, Lena, keep fucking me . . . I'm begging, as it feels so good. Really good. Fuck knows how she learned to use that dildo! My surfeited cunt is electrified, as my whole body tingles. — Make me . . . make me fucking come!

She stops, buried deep inside me. For one second all movement ceases; I can hear her breathing, ponderous and straining, then a popping as she suddenly pulls out, tearing part of my soul away with her.

— No . . . don't stop . . .

She looks at me with a cruel expression and tells me, — You are such a sexy fucking bitch, I knew you wanted it, then she suddenly lunges at me again, throwing herself back on me, pushing that plastic power cock back into my starving pussy. But there's no hip movement this time as she yanks up my T-shirt and bra, exposing my breasts. Her hands grope my tits hard, mangling them like a clumsy high-school boy desperate to shake off his virginity. Then she cups my breasts, pushing them together, her eyes wide in fascination. — Do you want me to *really* fuck you?

— Yes! I want to come! Make me fucking come, Lena. I squirm under her leg to try and get her to start fucking me hard again.

Lena just pinches my nipples tightly, provoking a pained yelp from me. — I think that's what you want. But I wanna hear you fucking beg for it like the bitch you are! Beg!

— Lena . . . please . . . fuck me, it's no joke . . . I need to come, I *really* need it more than anything . . . please fuck me!

She flashes the victor's smile, then goes back to pounding me with her dildo, while stroking my clit in hard tight circles. As I grab handfuls of her ass with my free and shackled hands, the shock waves of orgasm tear through me. My hips shunt forward as my nails sink into her flesh. She lets out a gurgling sound as she's climaxed too, as she stops fucking but stays inside me. Our faces are cheek to cheek, our rapid breathing subsiding into a gentler rhythm.

I could wrap either arm around her now, but I can't move; I don't want to move. Even some groggy minutes (hours? days?) later, when she's getting up, and pulling her clothes on, I'm still immobilized. I hear her move over to a big brown paper bag full of polystyrene cartons. — Now you eat, Lena says.

I can't even begin to move. I'm fucked and stuffed with sex. I manage to say, almost dreamily, — What purpose . . . what purpose does all this serve?

— I had to learn a lesson. And I did. But now you have to learn one too.

And I look up at Lena, and feel this tearful veil mist over my eyes. I get it. And I sit up and munch on this sugar- and fat-filled, carb- and calorie-laden shit, and I do it in gratitude and love.

— Good girl, Lena coos.

As I'm forcing it down, Lena suddenly takes the burger from my hand. Lays it down. Then she's holding me in her arms. I don't know why. Then I realize that it's because

I'm shaking and crying. — Let it go, she whispers. — Let it all go.

I look up at her. — She's gonna die, that Amy chick, the twin, yeah?

— It looks that way, she says, and clicks on the TV. Professor Rex Convey is condemning the forthcoming operation as barbaric. — It is nothing more or less than murder. The plans to film this procedure on television as some kind of reality show are sick and depraved. Is this what we've become? Televising the medical execution of one young young woman, while we sing in triumph that the other gets to lead a normal life?

Lena shakes her head, switching over to a news program. Several pundits are discussing Guantánamo Bay. Suddenly, a breaking news bar appears, flashing at the bottom of the screen.

CONJOINED TWINS OPERATION CANCELLED
. . . ANNABEL WILKS PULLS OUT . . .

Lena and I look at each other in bemusement. The Botoxed TV anchor cuts off a speaker who's talking about terrorism, and says, — Obviously important ramifications for civil liberties in this country. But we have to stop there, in order to give you a sensational update on the development of the Arkansas conjoined twins story. Annabel and Amy Wilks are sixteen-year-old conjoined twins, and after differences between them, they agreed to a risky separation procedure, where

439

Amy's chances of survival were estimated at a high of 40 percent and a low of 10 percent by differing experts. Now Annabel, the dominant twin, expected to recover fully and live a normal life, has pulled out of the operation, scheduled to take place in a few weeks' time. Antoinette Mellis reports from Yellowtree County, Arkansas.

They cut to this leafy glade and the Wilks house. The cloying voice-over: — Amy and Annabel Wilks are normal teenagers, but with a difference. They are literally tied to each other. Like all teenagers, they quarrel and fight some-times, and decided, after a falling-out over a boy, that they would go their separate ways. Now Annabel, the twin who stands to have a normal life, has called time on the dangerous separation procedure.

We cut to the girls, rocking on their swing seat on the porch. Annabel looks at Amy. — I'd rather have Amy with me every day of my life, than never see her again and be so-called normal. God made us this way, and we was meant to live together, not to die apart.

Amy looks back at Annabel. — I love her more than I can say.

— She showed me she was ready to die so that I could have a normal life, Annabel tears up, as the camera moves toward her in close-up, — but there ain't no such thing as a normal life for me without her in it.

— I guess we had to remember that we are different, Amy says. — That it can't be just about one of us and some-body else.

— It has to be about the two of us, Annabel says, a serene

440

glow in her eyes. — I need her and she needs me. It ain't easy, and life is a big mystery, but one thing's for sure, it's gonna take us both to work it out together.

I look back at Lena. — I really do need to stay here a while, don't I? I ask her.

— Yes, I think you do, she says.

Part Three

Transfers

Twenty-two months later

50

A DREAM TO SHARE (WITH THOSE WHO REALLY CARE)

Thanksgiving yesterday was so stiflingly hot—even after the sun had gone down—that a cooling downpour would have been greeted with hallelujahs, despite our atheist–agnostic household. Even through the air conditioning, you could feel the dense gravity pulling your bones into the couch. The sky had threateningly rumbled and drummed, without delivering on its loud promise, but, finally, the heavens opened in the night. The lightning flashes, X-raying the bedroom, and the thunderous sound of the air crumpling didn't bother me, at least not directly, but I could feel Lucy writhing in the clammy sheets, almost in time with nature's brutal music.

Time to get up and steal a few hours before Mom and Dad rise. Dammit, why do old people never sleep?! When I think of them it's always with such intense guilt: how can you love somebody on a deep level with every fiber of your being, yet be so desperate not to become them?

Thankfully, Lucy is now soundly in dreamland, her stiff mouth half open, nostrils flaring with every breath. As I rise, she turns into the space I've vacated in the bed with a slightly truculent murmur. I put on my sports bra, silky sleeveless shirt, shorts, sneakers, and tie my hair back, threading my ponytail through a Twins baseball cap.

Slipping outside, I'm pounding the dawn pavements, heading south by the bay, enjoying the cool breeze on my arms and shoulders before that oppressive sun comes up. The air has the scent of wet pavement, as vines of mist weave up from the sidewalk.

It's nice having my parents down, but they're totally lost here in Miami. I practically had to buy them both a new wardrobe when they arrived. I don't think my dad has ever owned a pair of shorts in his life. Mom looks a lot better having shed that darned weight, though there's still plenty of work to do. It's not always easy being around them, although we have a better relationship than ever, and it's all thanks to Lucy and her emails! The irony!

That's what all that weird business a couple of years back has taught me: don't avoid a problem, meet it head-on. But while Mom and Dad can be very demanding time-wise, I'm delighted that Thanksgiving at Tom and Mona's passed without incident, especially after last year's trauma. With the added factor of my own parents being present, I'd been concerned, but it was Lucy who told *me* to chill, said I was trying too hard. I swear, we become more like each other every day!

God, how I *love* to run. There are practically no cars on the road, so I'm finding a nice rhythm in both pace and breathing, as I skip over another set of lights. When you get into this sort of stride, you feel the tension leaving your body, which is so invaluable at this time of year, Thanksgiving being

446

so complicated. After last year's debacle (Mona and Lucy fought), I felt like suggesting to Lucy that we should just blow it out and head over to the Bahamas, leaving Nelson with Tom and Mona for a few days. She'd never have agreed, though: that kid was such a game-changer. I have to tread warily on that issue, but it's true, as his birth mother Lucy is much more protective of him. I'm like the fun dad. Also, she's been on a big downer since Marge Falconetti's funeral last month. That poor woman ate herself to death after she stopped going to the gym. As Marge was her client, Lucy's taken it really hard.

The finest darned thing about having a kid, though, is that you're so busy cleaning up after them, you don't have time to dwell on all the other bullshit life throws your way!

The sun is coming up over the bay and I can see the Wynwood art and design district across the bridge. It was big fun over there a few weeks ago, Lucy and I partying (the first time for her since Nelson came along) at a function after my exhibition at the new Miami branch of the GoTolt gallery. My exhibition was a huge hit in New York, and now it's pulling in the crowds down here. I really do owe Jerry tons.

I turn back up West Street toward home, cutting over Alton, getting into the 30s, skipping past the scalped saw-grass verges, already turning a darker green after last night's rain.

Bliss, the house is still quiet! I mix a banana-and-peanut-butter protein shake and think of Lucy, the morning's ruminations crystalizing into a nagging desire to speak with her.

I hear her laughing from another part of the house, and

find her still in our room, sitting in the lotus position on the bed, watching that new weight-loss show, the hybrid of *The Bachelor* and *The Biggest Loser*. It's called *There's a Date in There Somewhere*. Simon Andrews, a wealthy young Connecticut stockbroker, has worked with their training and fitness expert Michelle Parish, to take, as the host says, "four morbidly obese women and turn them into the highly datable, and extremely *marriable* lovelies you see before you today."

Simon arches a brow, and looks painfully sincere as he faces the four girls. "I should have been flattered, Patti, when you said that my love would stop you gaining back the weight. But that comment set off alarm bells. I'm sorry, Patti, but you do it for *you*. You're missing the point of the program. It says to me that, despite the slim, hot body, you are still a fat girl inside. I'm going to have to let you go."

As Patti breaks down in tears, Lucy pulls on a Bruins ice hockey shirt. — Check this shit! That Michelle Parish is such a bitch!

I kiss her and she playfully grabs my ass, without diverting her attention from the screen. I head to the office to check my emails. There are quite a few but one grabs my attention: the bill of sale has gone through on *The New Man* sculpture. A surge of elation hits me as I realize that we're rich again! Stinking fucking rich! I open the attachment, print off a copy of the contract, sign it, scan it, and email it right back to the agents. It's done!

Euphoria is quickly displaced by a pang of loss. *The New Man* is my best and most personal work and he's leaving me. I suddenly have the urge to spend as much time with him as possible, before he's shipped off to his new resting place. So I go outside to the studio.

I find him as I always do, crouching down, looking up, almost doglike in his posture. I walk around him, studying, from different angles, his frozen, stupefied expression, like he's trying to figure it all out. Yes, by far my finest creation. I draw the blinds, shutting out the stream of light, and put on the video presentation of the Everglades, creating that swampy environment around him. That was Lucy's idea, and it really works. The speakers rumble with the squawks of birds and the wind brushing through the mangrove bushes. I sit there in the blacked-out darkness, suddenly full of fear for my invention, wanting to put the lights back on, or open the blinds. *The New Man* suddenly looks angry, resentful, like he might pounce on me and tear me to pieces. I rise and yank the dark drapes apart, blinking as the cascading light floods through the workshop and bathes my exhibit, lulling him back to serenity.

51

THANKSGIVING

Lena's been for a run and I'm watching repeats of crap on TV. Now she's off again, presumably to steal some working time at the studio. She never stops. I can remember when I had that kind of juice.

My weight's gone down again, though it's hard to get motivated. I'm 147, which is far from ideal, but better than the 200 she made me go up to in order to learn my lesson. Well, it was more like 199.5 and I drank a lot of fluid for the weigh-in on the scale that day, but we didn't split hairs. Lena had begged me to stop and had actually unchained me a few days earlier (some people are just not cut out for hostage-taking), but I insisted on staying to the end.

I get off the bed, and pick up my laptop. I turn it on and look back at my blog, reliving the craziness and the pain.

Ate the last of the candies, then instantly craved a burger and fries to obliterate the sickly sweetness. But once I had that, I knew I would want more candy. So I glugged back the last bottle of Bud, lining them up like soldiers, feeling its lush kick augment the dim, fuddled charge the others had built up. I thrashed at my chain. "IS THIS WHAT

YOU WANT?! MOTHERFUCKERS! COME TO ME, COME ON TO ME AND I'LL TEAR YOUR FUCKING SLIMY EYES OUTTA YOUR PUSSY HEADS!"

Then Lena comes in with more chips, cookies, and beer. "We don't need to do this."

"Don't unchain me, or I'll rip your fucking throat out! Bring me more fucking fries!"

"I can't . . ."

"Show some fucking balls, Lena! I kept you here for six fucking weeks! FOOD PLEASE!"

"Tell me, Lucy. Just tell me!"

"I can't. Now be a fucking woman and feed me."

But all that shit she gave me, it really was addictive. I never realized how much before: it took the best part of a year to get clean. I secretly binged for over six months, unable to pass a fast-food joint or avoid sneaking a candy bar. It wasn't easy, and now I can see how hard I was on her, and some of my other clients. I guess I bullied them, and trying to drive the weakness out their systems was a twisted way of trying to drive the doubt from my own.

I don't like looking at the last entry. At what we call *the conversation*, the one I could have had with Lena to avoid all this weight gain, junk food, captive shit, but which I couldn't indulge in until I'd popped the target on that scale. It was my perverse kind of penance.

But I scroll ahead to it: the final blog in the journal, *the conversation*.

451

I'm already craving starch and stodge; it had been more than an hour since I'd devoured the two large orders of fries Lena brought back from a Burger King drive-through. I washed them down with a sugary chocolate milkshake. It made me want more fries. Salt, sugar, fat, carbs. There really was no end to this.

I sent her back out twenty minutes ago. Where the fuck is she?

The welcome distant snap of the elevator door, and Lena comes with my shit. It isn't food. I can barely look at the swell of my gut over the waistband of my pants. She's sitting with a carton of salad and couscous as the Big Mac sweats on my lap like a carcinogenic turd in a bun, looking up at me. I'm on the cusp of 200 lbs. It suddenly dawns on me that I can't eat this. And I realize it's time. "I'm ready to have the conversation," I tell her.

Lena sits down beside me, and then tries to pull me to her, but I'm rigid as I hear a hollow voice coming from deep inside me, so she backs away, giving me space. "It was a Sunday back in Weymouth, and I had been at my friend Lizzie's house, listening to some music and hanging out. I was walking home up North Street. As I was getting under the bridge, I became aware of some boys walking behind me, whispering, occasionally laughing. The way their voices dropped in conspiracy, I knew they were planning something. But I didn't look back. I quickened my step, and carried on up the street."

"Oh, Lucy . . ." Lena soothes, squeezing my shoulder.

"At that point I made a big mistake. Turned right and cut through Abigail Adams Green, a small space full of trees and shrubs, which was a shortcut to my house in Altura Road. A second group of them were waiting there for me. Clint Austin, the leader, approached and glowered at me. He said he wanted that kiss he'd asked me for earlier in class. His friends surrounded me. I didn't know what to say. What do you say?"

A tighter squeeze from Lena.

"Then suddenly I was on my back; somebody crouched behind me and a solid push from Austin sent me tumbling onto the grass. Before I knew it, two boys were pulling me by my arms, dragging me along the ground, into the shrubs. There was a hand clamped over my mouth as my skirt was pulled up, my panties yanked down, and Austin, measle-faced, green eyes circled black, was violently spitting on me then forcing himself into me, in a horrible, sharp, tearing motion. I bled for days afterward. I turned my head to the side and felt little, other than a numbness. I heard cheering, yes yes yes, then I opened my eyes and saw Austin looking at me in rage and fear, as if he'd been trapped, coerced into this too. Then the cruel smile reappeared and he started saying things I couldn't quite understand. But he hated girls. I knew and understood that he hated girls."

"Oh my God, Lucy . . . that's so horrible . . ."

"I wasn't going to cry or plead. I was a Brennan. I sneered back at him, and I saw his fear reappear. Then another voice cannoning across the park, dispersing the kids like a starter pistol at the track. Dad's face towering above me, Clint Austin off me, terrified, running away. Austin's anger now supplanted by the deeper rage of him, my fucking father."

"Didn't you ever try to talk to Tom? Why didn't he realize?"

"Cause I fucking faked it!" I scream in her stiff face, squeezing her hand by way of apology, as she recoils. "I couldn't come up short again. I had to dig in, to suck it up, I couldn't be the victim. I'd rather be the slut than the victim. So we walked as I waited for his blow, the one that never came. But I was fake. Fake. Fake. Fake."

"No, Lucy," Lena says, "not you. Never you."

"When I got home I showered and washed and scrubbed myself. I said nothing. I had to face him in class the next day. At first he had a scared, sheepish expression, and avoided me, perhaps fearing retribution from my father. When he realized that wouldn't be forthcoming, the arrogance returned. I was routinely called a slut, a whore, a nympho, by the members of his gang, who put it around that I had consented to sex with a multitude of the boys."

"That's awful . . ."

"I got no fucking respite at home. I had a lecture from Mom. When Dad looked at me, all I could see was the bitter disappointment in his eyes."

"A few months later the same gang, led by Austin, attacked and raped another girl, Crystal Summersby. This was in Beals Park, not far from the same spot. They ambushed her and her friend on their way home from the Coffee Express in Bridge Street and dragged them off the path that went through the green, into the trees. They threatened her terrified friend with the same if she said anything. At the trial, Crystal said she could see the white spire of the church she went to with her family. And they did this, because *I* said nothing. Me, the Julia

Tuttle Causeway hero, stood by, fucking mute, ensuring this vile prick was free to do what he did to the other girls. I was a fucking fake!"

"No, you were just a scared kid!"

"The real hero was Crystal Summersby, and her friend, who came forward and had the sick bastard sent to juvie."

"You were a child, Lucy! You should have had someone there for you!"

"There was nobody." I feel Lena's hand moving slowly up and down my back. "So I learned to fend for myself. I immersed myself in the tae kwon do, karate, and kickboxing, planning a reception for this asshole on his release, but his family had moved away and I never heard of him again."

"But . . . but . . ."

"I didn't come forward because I could never be cast as a victim. But that's what I was. But I resolved: never, ever again. You have to stand up. You have to come forward."

"Yes. You taught me that. *You*." She points at me. "Lucy Brennan."

My hand grips her smaller one and she presses back. "I now need to tell Dad this real story. You're the only person I've properly explained it to. When I . . . you know, with Jerry . . ." I lower my voice and instinctively look around the empty apartment, and Lena does too, ". . . that was me done. It was like exorcising a ghost. I was ready to be wrapped in chains, to let anybody do what they wanted. I was ready to voluntarily surrender . . ." and I squeeze her in a hug, drinking in her beautiful, reassuring scent, ". . . and I'm just so glad it's been to you and not the police . . ."

455

I look into Lena's jade-green eyes, feel her cool lips on mine. I can't resist as I feel her slipping off my cuffs.

It's done.

We kiss for a bit, and a mountain of passion starts to bubble in me. My fingers are pushing aside cloth and working Lena, showing her where the fuck I'm coming from. As she starts to get aroused, I stick my other fist into my own pants, knuckles grinding my clit like a fighter trying to open up an opponent's scar. I come straightaway as Lena gasps, but I keep working my wrists at maximum force against my pubic bone and hers. I only briefly see Lena's eyes roll heavenward as she growls like a savage and kicks her legs out like a swimmer, before I feel my own eyeballs curving toward the sky. "Fuck . . ."

I spread my legs to better enjoy the delicious throb, a sensation so gorgeous that I feel my teeth nipping my bottom lip in appreciation. "Fuck . . . fuck . . . fuck . . ."

"Fuck . . ." Lena gasps, as I unravel my limbs, pushing my damp hair from my face. "That was so goooooood . . ."

"I know, right?"

God, I get myself so goddamn horny reading that last part. But I had to reward myself after that confession, by reliving that *post-conversation* moment in the blog. The crux of it all, though, was that I was finally the most free I had ever been, *and* I had Lena. Then all I had to do was lose the blubber. And I did. Then came the pregnancy, and back on it went, though I'm getting it off again.

Once Lena and I decided we wanted a kid, there was

never any doubt as to who would be inseminated and carry it for the term. Lena's art career was taking off again, with a massive renewal of interest in her sculpture, especially *The New Man*, and, of course, the photography exhibition, so she really had to work. — It took me so long to get to this point, she'd argued, — whereas you're an expert, you'll be able to get back in shape in no time.

It sounded plausible, but it hasn't quite worked out that way. But I'm not complaining—well, not much. I guess we're all great self-justifiers. I know I'd have been just as fulfilled in a career, though in a different fashion. But as a mom, in many ways, I'm at my happiest now. It isn't all roses, though, nothing is, and I do get a little tired out with Nelson. He needs a lot of attention, and sometimes Lena can't help that much, as she's working most days in her studio.

I shut my laptop and I'm watching that Michelle bitch in her crappy weight-and-date show. Lena comes in with a big frown on her face. — What's up?

— Nothing . . . in fact, it's pretty damn good news, she says, forcing some cheer into her expression, as she hands me a copy of a bill of sale.

I look at the bottom-line figure and hear my own gasp of disbelief. Then I throw my arms around her. — Jesus fuck almighty!

— They'll be coming to take him away next week, she says glumly, like she's talking about Nelson.

— Oh, right . . . I try to inject concern into my voice. I never get this crazy artist thing about selling their work. I'd just think about the money and get on with knocking out the next piece of shit.

She reads my mind. — I know, she smiles, kissing me, giving me a scent of her fresh sweat, — I gotta let go. Mom and Dad up yet?

— Haven't seen them, I drop my voice, — but I've heard grumblings from the guest suite. I feel my mouth tighten, as I cup my ear. — And gurgling noises tell me Nelson's awake.

Lena goes to shower and change and I start to get myself and Nelson ready for the short drive to the airport. The Sorensons join us for breakfast bagels and orange juice. It's strange how different they are from how I pictured them during that clandestine email correspondence (which they still believe was with their daughter). I'd envisioned Todd as a tall, thin man, but he's short and squat, with a gray-blond crew cut and a deep-lined face. He says very little. Molly talks for them both: wasteful, inconsequential chatter. She has a steel-wool permed mop, and hawkish features, with a double chin, fleshy arms, and a ton of cellulite. We eat while discussing mundane stuff, Molly going on about some kind of dream she had about yesterday's Thanksgiving. — I think it came from being in a house surrounded by water . . .

I never, ever thought that my father would move down here, but he bought the house from a fading basketball star Miami Heat traded to Cleveland, or some other Rust Belt franchise on its last legs. I confess to sometimes feeling aggrieved that Mona's living in that level of luxury and she's almost certain to be Dad's main or even sole beneficiary, especially when their kid arrives. I can't exactly complain though; I like living up here with Lena, and she's let me put my own touches to the house, like splashing a little color on those walls.

We get into the 4X4 which we bought when Nelson came along. Lena is driving, and I'm sitting with Nelson and Molly in the back, the Sorensons' considerable, largely redundant luggage behind us. Molly's gamely trying to distract Nelson from the squealing pig toy he loves. Todd is looking uncomfortable in the front; I see his creased face in the mirror as he blinks in the unaccustomed sunlight like a black bear disturbed in its hibernation. The day is described, as always, as "unseasonably hot" on a local radio station. It's the high or mid-eighties, depending on which phone app you open, with an angled golden light blinding me at the intersections, even through my Ray-Bans.

— Oh, for cute, Molly says to Nelson, as the pig wheezes breathlessly again.

It's bad manners, but when an email from my mom pops onto my iPhone, I'm happy to open it, and escape from the Sorenson banalities into the more familiar Brennan ones.

52

CONTACT 19

To: lucypattybrennan@hardass.com
From: jackielieberman-pride@realrealestate.com
Subject: Happy Thanksgiving

Lucy,

Didn't want to phone you as I knew you were at you-know-who's, and I've made my feelings plain enough about that lunatic and his controlling ways. If you and Lena ever consider having a second child: DO NOT LET THAT IDIOT HAVE ANY INVOLVEMENT WITH IT!

It's beyond me that you think you owe that old fool some control in your life because he caught you fooling with some boys in the bushes of Abbie Adams Green. Yes, we were both worried about you back then. But you never disappointed us, honey—the promiscuity was all about you as a young girl acting up, because our marriage and our family was crumbling and breaking up. But do not let him pull that Catholic guilt-trip shit on you! Your mistakes are your own (and we all make those—hell, I married the asshole), so don't allow him to dictate your life!

Enough. I'm ranting.

I'm still loving Toronto. The Canadians would never have a national holiday that celebrates land theft and genocide. I was saying to Lieb the other day, this is the future for you and Lena—not to be treated like second-class citizens as in the US. And to think I was a Republican for years—though that was mainly to annoy your father. The real-estate market is booming, and we have a great standard of living and free universal health care. All I miss is the Miami weather. It's so *cold* outside! Even Boston is temperate in comparison.

Come see us soon, and bring that adorable child of yours.

Much love,

Mom

53

THE RAID

Jesus, that woman is a fucking fruitcake. But her shit tells me that I'll never really be free until I've had *the conversation* with both her and Dad—separately of course. We've dropped the Sorensons off at Miami International Airport, and are heading down the 95, toward the Beach. We're traveling in total silence, relieved that it's just the three of us, but drained from the stress of enforced, extended family contact. Even Nelson is uncharacteristically dozy, strapped into his seat.

Just as we turn into SoBe on 5th, I see the big movie poster above us:

THE SEX LIVES OF SIAMESE TWINS

It shows the actors Kristen Stewart and Megan Fox attached from the hip up, sitting on a park bench, snootily turned away from each other. Ryan Reynolds stands behind them, looking on in hapless appeal.

It has the split logline:

TWO FEISTY GIRLS
ONE SMOKIN' HOT BODY
BIG TROUBLE

The real twins, not the movie variety, have settled down and found religion. I saw them recently on one of those kooky daytime programs. The movie has brought them back into the spotlight, with Amy disowning it, and Annabel, apparently, refusing to comment.

Good luck to them with that circus. I like the quiet life and I certainly don't miss the TV people or the paparazzi up my ass. I love that there isn't anything about me in the media. Jillian left *The Biggest Loser*, and it hasn't been the same since. They gave the gig to some Russian tennis chick who wanted out after six months. *Shape Up or Ship Out* is due to start its first season this summer, with another ex-tennis player, Veronica Lubartski, of *Game, Set, and Snatch* fame, as one of the presenters. Good luck to them all.

The really fucking great news is that Congressman Quist is set to resign after some financial scandal. There hasn't been a politician in Florida who has refused some type of kickback, and it was inevitable that Quist would fall, like so many others, on the sword of a shady real-estate deal. I watched his red face on TV in a soundless interview a few months back, while I was cooking lunch. In the background, behind him, the head of a panther on his wall. Assholes like him are the reason panthers don't exist in Florida anymore, except on sports jerseys. But Quist soon won't be existing in Florida politics, which is good news, if a little late for my benefit.

But I did learn a lesson through being incarcerated by Lena and pumped up with crud; I'm more tolerant to other people now. Yes, I'll have to check my name-calling shit. Lena has told me to quit referring to other women as bitches and hoes. She knew that those were Clint Austin's words, rasping menacingly in my ear in that park, and coming out my mouth in the same way since then. Now that I've acknowledged that as a truth, I should be able to stop. Except in the case of Mona, of course. If the cap fits, as they say, and no other names are more accurate in her case.

Yes, family life is good, and it's improving dramatically, with the Sorensons now bound for Potters Prairie, Otter County, Minnesota. The very thought of such a place existing causes a chill to spread over my bones. There might be more rabid, religious dumbass fuckers in America than ever, but the response to that has just been more irony. Now terms like "America," "Democracy," "Freedom," and "God" are used in a mocking, derisive way, usually by people who realize that those deploying them *without* irony only want to control you, or sell you shit. The Sorensons weren't that ambitious, they only wanted to dominate one daughter. Lena takes the words out of my mouth as we leave the 95 from Miami International: — It'll be so good to have the place to ourselves, love them as I do-oo!

But our peace is short-lived. We aren't long back home, and I'm in the garden watering some plants. The sun's starting to go down and a musty darkness is insinuating itself. My sweat is trickling and dripping, as insects whir round me. The pool attracts mosquitoes at this time of night and I feel one fat bloodsucker injecting my ankle. I slap at it, making contact with nothing but my own flesh. As I curse, I look at the light from the office window, and see Lena with Nelson on her lap, printing stuff from the computer and coloring it in for him.

I'm suddenly aware of a vehicle pulling up outside the front of the house, and somebody, more than one set of footsteps, exiting and marching down the driveway. Then a forceful knock at the door. I go back inside, as tense as a guitar string, following Lena down the hallway, Nelson in her arms, as she opens the door.

It's the police. One of the officers present is Grace Carillo, whom I haven't seen in a couple of years. As our eyes meet, she dispenses a curt nod, but one which lets me know that this isn't going to be about catching up. She's put on weight; the promotion I heard she'd been given must mean longer hours and less gym time.

I know what it's about. I've been waiting for this day. I kept my word to Lena (barring the night of *the conversation*, when she set me free), the promise that I'd made to her when she first imprisoned me, about never mentioning Jerry's name. But I can't help thinking about him, given that it's a strong possibility that I see bits of him every day. Lena's finished the construction of *The New Man*, but I know through previous cop visits that at least one senior Miami police officer believes that parts of Jerry have been incorporated into the piece—the skull and pelvis in particular. And they do look like human dimensions and shaping, just about visible through the glaucous, translucent skin.

Now I feel the heat draining out of my body as Grace Carillo tells Lena that the installation is to be removed, where it will be broken open, so that a DNA sample can be taken from the bones. She points outside, where two blue jumpsuited men start pushing a large cart down the driveway.

Lena shakes her head. — I'm afraid I can't authorize that.

— It's no longer in your hands, Ms. Sorenson.

As the shock waves bombard me, my heartbeat races. I look to Lena, who remains totally unfazed. There's a playful smile enlivening her face as she casually shrugs, — That is exactly what I'm trying to say to you, Detective Sergeant Carillo. I'm not in a position to authorize it, as the sculpture is no longer my property. The gallery sold it to a private collector on Tuesday morning, and she moves, swiftly but with poise, into her office and returns brandishing an email, which she hands to Grace. — The individual in question, who now owns the work, is estimated by *Forbes Magazine* to be the third richest man in the world. Once the sculpture has been breached, even by the thinnest needle, the resin cracks and it will be ruined. You'll note that the buyer has paid 16.25 million dollars for it. If the bones inside are the bones of Jerry Whittendean, then I obviously have a big problem. If, however, these are my moldings rather than human bones, then the big problem becomes yours. The new owner will almost certainly sue Miami-Dade Police Department. And he will almost certainly be successful. So the question is, Detective Sergeant Carillo: just how darned lucky do you feel?

Grace glares at her. Lena's cloying soccer-mom-from-Minnesota expression never changes. Grace then turns to me, in some sort of desperate appeal. I shrug, and look toward the other plain-clothes cop, who has taken the email from her and whose neck is flaring in red liver spots as he reads it.

Lena points at the email in his hand. — You now have to take this up with the individual in question.

Grace flushes, glancing at her fellow officer. Trying to claw back some power, she barks, — Rest assured: we will do just that!

But she's like a cocker spaniel trying to impersonate a pit bull. Lena reads it as such. — Good luck with that one, she smiles as Grace and her colleague exit, grimly. We watch them instruct the two guys to wheel the empty cart away and load it back into the truck.

When did she get those balls? Lena played those suckers and they backed the fuck down! Mind you, I had always suspected that Grace (the pussy formerly known as hot) was a little gun-shy.

And the big bones sit in there, the pelvis and the skull, suspended in Lena's translucent sculpture like big chunks of fruit in Molly Sorenson's Jell-O. I dunno if they are Jerry's bones. They could just as easily have come out of one of her molds that the police took away. All I know is that the wealthy buyer intends to donate the piece to the Art Institute in Chicago, in the new modern art wing. I never asked Lena, although I know I will someday, but I really do hope that it is the vestiges of Jerry in there. I kind of like the idea of him being on permanent display in his alma mater. I think, in a strange way, that he might be at peace with such an arrangement.

Of course, if it is Jerry in there, life would have been so much simpler had we stuck to a version of the truth. Lena was working on an art project, I was looking after her house. Jerry came by, tricked his way in, and ransacked the place. I asked him to leave, he refused, he attacked me, and I accidentally killed him in self-defense.

But I think Lena tore off and intervened in the way she did probably not out of revenge over Jerry, but simply because she was an artist, and the authentic materials to finish her compelling project were suddenly at her disposal. Like Dad with his crappy novels, the world and the people in it are all just potential resources to those ruthless scavengers!

So once again Lena is making a big splash in the art world. She's still basking in the success of her recent photography exhibition, the one that shows her getting fat, retitled *A Year of Boy Trouble.* Melanie Clement exhibited the photos at her GoToIt gallery to considerable acclaim. We had a great night at the subsequent Miami show a few weeks back. It was like old times; Chef Dominic, Emilio, Jon Pallota, Lester, Angie Forrest (whom I used to know as Henrietta James, and who occasionally babysits for Nelson), and even Mindy Tuck (the Liposuction Fuck) were all present to show support and, of course, to party. At the launch of the exhibition, Lena graciously repeated her acknowledgment from the catalog. — I couldn't have done it without the assistance of both Lucy Brennan and Jerry Whittendean, who, in their different ways, really did enable my art career.

So I guess it's true, as all those crappy books tell us, that great art is made out of a meeting of opposites. And this also might be true about great sex. Right now I can hear Lena putting Nelson to bed, and I'm hoping that the little guy gets down to sleep real soon. *Real* fucking soon.

ACKNOWLEDGMENTS

Thank you to Chris Andreko, Sarah Kahn, Emer Martin, Amy Cherry, Don De Grazia, Jon Baird, Trevor Engleson, Alex Mebed, Robin Robertson, Gerry Howard, Katherine Fry and, most of all, Elizabeth Quinn.

To various trainers, artists and friends in Chicago, Miami, London and Edinburgh, for not being Lucy and Lena.

To everybody who has bought the books and watched the films and thus saved me from having to get a proper job for years.

Irvine Welsh